other books by ROBERT DALEY

Year of the Dragon

a novel by
ROBERT DALEY

Simon and Schuster
New York

This novel is a work of fiction. Names, characters, places and incidents are either the product of the author's imagination or are used fictitiously. Any resemblance to actual events or locales or persons, living or dead, is entirely coincidental.

Copyright © 1981 by Riviera Productions
All rights reserved
including the right of reproduction
in whole or in part in any form
Published by Simon and Schuster
A Division of Gulf & Western Corporation
Simon & Schuster Building
Rockefeller Center
1230 Avenue of the Americas
New York, New York 10020
SIMON AND SCHUSTER and colophon are trademarks of
Simon & Schuster
Designed by Irving Perkins Associates

Manufactured in the United States of America

1 2 3 4 5 6 7 8 9 10

Library of Congress Cataloging in Publication Data

Daley, Robert.
Year of the dragon.

I. Title.
PS3554.A43Y4   813'.54   81-8963
AACR2

ISBN 0-671-41045-8

FOR S.L.

Part One

1

OUTSIDE THE Golden Palace on the night of the massacre a hard rain was falling.

The building had been constructed in rococo style as a movie house and had served as one for decades, coping more or less with each change in the neighborhood. The one change it had at last failed to cope with, the one that put it out of business, had resulted from the decision by Congress to rewrite immigration law; the new law admitted Asians, mostly Chinese, for the first time in proportions equal to Europeans. Chinatown, only three blocks south, had responded by expanding in all directions, at first slowly and then fast, engulfing many bastions of old New York, one of them the Golden Palace, until at last the movie house gave up its struggle to survive and became what it had so much resembled from the first, a Chinese restaurant.

The new owners, principally a man named Ting, had seen no need to change the name, much less the decor. Everything was still painted red and black, or else gilded, and the theater's florid ornamentation suited the restaurant perfectly. Dragons in bronze or imitation jade, whether balanced on balustrades or brooding in niches, were as much at home as they had ever been. Symbolically at least, the Golden Palace seemed proof that the two cultures, East and West, had come together at last.

Captain Arthur Powers, waiting that night in the former movie lobby, stared out at the rain. The glass doors kept opening to admit umbrellas, none of them hers, umbrellas that folded as they moved past him and up the rather grand staircase, for the lobby was at street level and the restaurant was above. From time to time Powers caught a glimpse of Mr. Ting up there, coming forth to greet someone, menus in his arms. Powers was dressed in brown: a brown tweed sports jacket and sturdy brown wing-tipped shoes such as policemen favored. His .38 in its clip-on holster was jammed inside the waistband of his brown slacks. He was not really aware it was there. It hung slightly to the right of his navel, its two-inch barrel pointed toward his testicles, which in some way was perhaps symbolic also.

He kept glancing at his watch. She was fifteen minutes late. He was not sure he should be here at all and he was becoming irritated. He was worried about being seen with her, worried about what she might ask him; and worried also about the check—when it came should he insist on paying? And as he glanced at his watch still again he was worried about his reservation. This place was popular. Should he wait for her upstairs at their table? Should he at least go up and tell Ting he was here? If Ting gave their table to someone else, they would have to wait for another, standing up for half an hour making small talk—a very long half hour. Or else they would have to go out into the street and hunt down something else. But most restaurants in Chinatown were seedy and some were none too clean. He knew this place was good. Elsewhere he would be guessing, and he might guess wrong.

Life was not going well for him and lately he worried about nearly everything. In a sense he waited in this lobby —as he waited everywhere—not for a woman but for the call. But he did not expect it to come tonight. Indeed so many years had now gone by that he no longer expected it to come at all.

"Hello."

She had somehow materialized beside him. A transparent plastic rain hood covered with water droplets was tied like a kerchief under her chin.

"You look nice," she said. She was smiling warmly, looking as if she meant it. For a moment he felt as disconcerted as a boy, though why? Because compliments from females were rare, and therefore absurdly gratifying? Or because she had somehow usurped his role? Powers was a traditionalist, the new values were not for him. It was the man's job to compliment the woman, not the other way around.

They were standing under a crystal chandelier of grotesque size and taste, but the lighting it gave was kind to her. She was a year or two past her prime—so was he—but in this light, and to his surprise, he found her stunning. But he could not tell her so now. To utter her own words back to her would have seemed to him imbecilic.

She was heavily made up, and he supposed she had come here straight from the set of the Seven O'clock News. He had always hated makeup on women in the past, but at this moment did not hate it on her. It made her look younger, almost new. She must have been a really beautiful girl when she got out of college—how long ago? Fifteen years? Twenty maybe? The network makeup man seemed to have pointed up contradictory elements in her face that most probably existed also in her life, and Powers, even as he shook hands with her, found himself studying her for the first time. Her eyes were blue, beautifully delineated, and drawn with such eloquence that they seemed to suggest not only youth and innocence, but also suffering, a quality Powers could respond to. She had been married once, he believed, but was not married now, and divorce did not come without trauma. She had a teenage daughter somewhere whom she was trying to raise by herself and that guaranteed more trauma. Her eyes nonetheless seemed soft, kindly; suffering had not made her hard. Her lips were faintly outlined in pencil. They were nicely shaped and rather fleshy, and to Powers they looked sensual, a notion that clashed with the accentuated line of her jaw. Her jaw looked aggressive, and certainly she must be an aggressive woman, for she had fought her way to the top in a man's world. According to a newspaper article he'd seen, she received a salary of over $200,000 a year, to Powers a sum as out of proportion and as incomprehensible as the nation's defense budget. It was about five times what he got. He had always imagined that success on such a scale would change any man's outlook upon life. There was no reason to suppose it had not changed this woman's.

She had shaken off her rain hood and was putting it in her pocket. She was so theatrically beautiful and so unknown to him, such a presence beside him, that he became thoroughly ill at ease. However, he was old enough to conceal this, and in addition he had been a policeman a long time—a cop was used to pretending an assertiveness he did not always feel. So he spoke her name, Carol Cone, murmured something about being so glad to see her, and led her up to the landing where Mr. Ting and his menus waited.

Ting was about five feet tall. Skin as dry and taut as a Chinese scroll. Hair still jet black. It was impossible to guess his age. He was beaming.

"I not see you velly long time, Captain," Ting said. "Sad for me."

Did he really remember Powers? Ting was a political presence in Chinatown, had been since before Powers ever set foot there. Remembering people was Ting's business.

"How are you, Mr. Ting?"

"This way, Captain and lady."

They followed him into the restaurant. Carol was immediately recognized. Heads turned. A few heads, Powers noted; not everyone by any means, but enough to irk him. A society that valued police captains less than a woman who read the news on television, that turned such a woman into a celebrity, was to Powers a sick society.

He led her through tables by the arm, as if she were under arrest.

"The reason I was late," said Carol over her shoulder, "was that I signed my new deal with the network tonight." She was grinning up at him, and looked exceedingly pleased with herself.

Did this mean a $100,000 raise? Was he supposed to congratulate her? He didn't. He said, "Mr. Ting is mayor of Chinatown."

"Mayor of Chinatown?"

"He's president of the Chinatown Fraternal Organization and also of the biggest tong. It's a ceremonial title really."

Ting, several paces ahead, had reached their table and was holding a chair for her. "Since you're not," said Powers, "a native New Yorker, I thought you probably wouldn't know that."

They sat down.

"I was born in Boston," said Carol.

Powers gave a wave of his hand. "Wherever."

Carol's eyes dropped. Did she feel insulted? Wounded? Possibly she was merely noting how beautifully the table was set: white tablecloth, flowers, lacquered cups and bowls. With women you never knew. Women could conceal anything: emotion, the age lines on their faces, sexual arousal. It was part artifice, part the way they were constructed, and its sole purpose seemed to be to disorient men.

Powers surveyed the restaurant. Not quite full. About half the patrons were Chinese—Oriental, anyway. The other half were tourists. That's the way the Chinese would see it. In a Chinatown restaurant every white face was a tourist.

"You want nice dlink please maybe?" said Mr. Ting.

"Do you have champagne?" inquired Carol.

"Oh, is celeblation? You like Chinese champagne, maybe?"

Carol turned to seek Powers' opinion. "Chinese champagne?"

"Is flom Shanghai. Is velly nice."

"Sure, why not," said Powers, thinking, if she wants to pay for champagne, let her. But it made his thoughts turn inward. Red China had opened up, even to the extent of exporting a so-called champagne. Meanwhile, he was still a captain. He had once been the youngest captain in the job. Now he was one of the oldest.

"Tonight I became the second-highest-paid woman in television," said Carol, and she mentioned the name of the newswoman who was first.

Instead of complimenting her, Powers said carefully: "What do you make of Ting's accent? Is it real, or a put-on?"

Carol picked up her chopsticks and studied them.

She seems easy to hurt, observed Powers. It made him like her more, and also it made him ashamed. To resent her triumph demeaned him.

"I'm sorry," he said. "You deserve every congratulation. I know how hard you must have worked to get where you are today."

This seemed to mollify her. Her eyes rose.

"And next year you'll go into first place, because you're a hell of a lot better-looking than that other broad."

"Looks," said Carol, "have nothing to do with it."

Of course they do, thought Powers with renewed irritation. With their made-up faces and outrageous contracts these people were show-business stars, not journalists— whatever they pretended—and he stared into her hard blue eyes.

Ting and the waiter had appeared with the Chinese champagne. The bottle was shown to both of them. The cork went pop.

"Sounds like champagne, anyway," murmured Powers, and he gave her a smile. Truce. The evening had a long way to go, and unless somebody smiled it would be a long one. But he wondered again why she had asked him here.

Into his glass spilled the champagne. He saw that she waited anxiously for him to taste it.

"Well?"

Powers decided to have fun tonight if he could, starting with this terrible champagne, and he smacked his lips as if with delight.

The waiter filled Carol's glass. "Let's have a toast."

Powers, grinning, said, "Better taste it first."

After swallowing she set the glass down and sat there thoughtfully.

When their eyes met, both burst out laughing.

"Add ice, lemons, a little Triple Sec and two or three bottles of orange juice and that would make a pretty good punch," said Powers.

"It does have bubbles. You can't deny that."

"The French champagne producers must be gnashing their teeth," said Powers. "As soon as this stuff gets widespread, their whole business goes down the drain."

He had her laughing, and was pleased. To cause someone to laugh is a triumph of sorts, and he hadn't had many lately.

"A country always exports its best," he said. "If the Chinese exported this, I wonder what they kept for themselves."

She had small perfect teeth.

Powers felt a visceral lurch inside him. It occurred not in the region of his heart, but just below the place where he carried his gun. In his present depressed state, he would have been vulnerable to almost any responsive woman, much less one as glamorous as Carol. Antipathy vanished, and from one second to the next was replaced by desire. He wanted to go to bed with her, an emotion that astonished him.

"A toast," said Carol, raising her glass.

The confused Powers, though smiling as broadly as she, was surprised even further when she twined her arm inside his, so that their faces were separated by little more than the diameters of their glasses.

She said, "A toast to—"

"A toast to tonight," interrupted Powers. He didn't want to hear any more about her money.

"Yes."

Though their glasses merely clicked together, their glances had collided. He saw that she was grinning inanely too, and he imagined that, from across the room, they must look like lovers.

Carol said "At this stage of my life, there's hardly anything I haven't done with a man before. But this is the first time I ever drank a toast with one with Chinese champagne." She made it sound like some new, mutually gratifying sexual act, and he was pleased.

"You mean I'm the first?"

"You're my very first."

She set her glass down. "Artie—" she began shyly. She had never before addressed him as anything but Captain Powers. Calling him Artie was a deliberate act, and it warmed him. She caressed him with his own name.

The basis of their relationship had shifted entirely. He did not know how this had happened, nor where it would lead. He was a faithful husband, and he was past the restless age. He was not a man to have casual affairs with women.

"Artie," Carol continued, "tell me how you feel about the police department, and about your own career."

Powers' first reaction was terrific disappointment. An interview. She only wanted to interview him and this was the start of it. She had provoked in him these inchoate romantic desires only to make him as complacent a subject as possible.

He felt his hackles rise. "My career? I'm executive officer of the seven-nine precinct in Brooklyn. As for the department, I love the department."

"I've read up on you," Carol persisted. "You're one of the most famous cops in the city. We have a clip file on you this thick. But you've been a captain eleven years and never had a precinct of your own."

"So?"

"So why is that?" Her eyes came up, appraising him as coolly as if he lay naked on a table. He had never had a woman look at him like that before, and he did not like it.

BELOW THEM in the street in the rain a car pulled to the curb. Behind the wheel sat Nikki Han, twenty-five, American-born leader of the Flying Dragons, a prominent Chinatown youth gang. In the back rode the Hsu brothers, aged seventeen and eighteen, street hoodlums and murderers from Hong Kong. Neither spoke English. They weighed ninety pounds each. They had been brought to New York three months previously for just such a job as tonight's.

Water ran down the windshield and was swept aside. Han looked over the slick, empty streets. He kept the engine running. Chinatown streets normally were crowded with tourists at this hour. Though it had been under consideration for weeks, tonight's job had been hurriedly laid on an hour ago because the heavy rain would ensure a minimum of witnesses.

"Do it," ordered Nikki Han in Chinese. He spoke the dialect common to Canton, Hong Kong and New York.

He watched the Hsu brothers tug ski masks over their heads, grab weapons up out of the darkness at their feet, and throw open the car door. In an instant they were across the pavement, had pushed open the glass doors, and had begun their sprint up the ornate staircase.

Nikki Han, left behind, wore dark glasses and a snap brim hat pulled well down. Very little of his face could be seen. The engine was purring. The back door hung open. Rain drummed on the roof. He waited.

UPSTAIRS CAROL was describing the police documentary she hoped to produce and narrate. It would focus not on corruption or police brutality as in the past, but on waste, mismanagement, archaic techniques—failures that were all the more insidious because they were not against the law and were therefore resistant to change.

Powers set down his glass. "This wine really tastes sour."

She wanted Powers to help her, Carol explained, to point her in all the right directions.

"Why me?"

"After eleven years without a promotion you don't owe this administration anything. Do you want to know the journalist's first rule for getting information? Seek out people who are dissatisfied."

"Detectives have the same rule. The two professions are really quite close, by the way. Good detectives and good journalists are the same even to the bravery." Then he added purely out of hostility: "Some of them."

"Will you help me?"

"Why? To guarantee myself eleven more years as a captain?" He had no intention of helping her. Why should he help her when he didn't even like her? But he never told her any of this, his concentration being fixed by then on the Hsu brothers who had just appeared in the doorway. He identified their weapons before entertaining any other conscious thought: a .45-caliber M–3 submachine gun and a semi-automatic 12-gauge shotgun of a type he had seen and handled somewhere at an earlier date, possibly when he was a rookie, an instrument said to be powerful enough to turn over cars.

He saw that the youth with the shotgun was having difficulty cocking it, whereas the one with the submachine gun had coolly chosen his target—Powers himself, apparently. Powers saw the weapon swing around until he was staring down its muzzle. The terror that came over him was instantaneous, for he had been in gunfights before—these were the news clips Carol had studied—and recognized this one before it started. Adrenaline surged. Blood rushed to his head. His perceptions became acute. He was aware not only of the decibel level of the room but even, from two tables away, of certain individual words, and when he glanced momentarily at Carol he perceived the depth of the crow's feet beside her eyes, clues to her exact age if only he had a moment to study them. As for the two boys, they were obviously Chinese, despite the idiotic ski masks. And they were tiny. They were far less muscular and therefore less substantial than any jockey. The weapons in their hands looked as heavy as jackhammers. One expected them to be knocked over backwards when they pulled the triggers, if that's what they planned to do. The incongruity—small boys carrying big guns—was almost comical. Though immobilized by terror, Powers almost wanted to laugh.

Mr. Ting stepped forward to intervene.

The youth with the submachine gun swung it sideways. The jackhammer clubbed Ting to the floor, then began to break up walls. Carol had her back to all this. Powers observed it only over her shoulder while she prattled on about her stupid documentary, putting her smile into it, and her eyes, and her body, seeming to promise him the untold wonders of her person if only he would cooperate.

She had no suspicion of what was about to happen, what was already happening. No one did except Ting on the floor and Powers at last rising out of his chair, certainly not that waiter there, carrying a tray burdened with silver tureens, who was about to step between the doorway and himself, thus saving Powers' life, if he lived that long. He saw the weapon begin to spit, and saw what came out—not bullets, which are invisible, but smoke and flame, followed immediately by incredible crashing noise. He saw that the shooter was leaning into his job, trying to hold the barrel down.

Powers dove across the table onto Carol, a skidding belly flop that cleared the table even of its cloth. His shoulder caught her above the breasts. Her chair went over, and she went down beneath him. He heard all the air go out of her, noted the grimace that contorted her face. Lying on top of her he tried to get to his gun, but she was writhing, whether in pain or surprise he could not tell, so that his hands became entangled in the tablecloth and in her dress, and he could find no way to get the revolver out of his pants.

The waiter crossing in front of the submachine gun was thirty-eight years old and the father of seven children. He was an illegal immigrant who had been in New York almost a year. He carried a counterfeit green card for which he had paid $20,000 in Hong Kong, this sum representing the life savings of himself, his brothers, his parents and other members of his family. He worked fourteen hours a day, and spent virtually nothing, so as to pay off the loans, plus 30 percent per year interest, as fast as he could. Once this was done he planned to bring his oldest sons over at the rate of one a year, after which they would pool their combined savings and be able to save faster. He hoped to be reunited with his wife and youngest children within nine years.

The submachine gun's first bullet caught the edge of his tray and spun it like a Frisbee against the back wall. The silver tureens, unsupported, crashed to the floor. The second bullet, as the barrel climbed, took off the top of the waiter's head. His family would not now be reunited with him. Since the green card in his pocket was in another name, they would never even learn what had happened to him.

The rest of the bullets from that burst went into the ceiling. The boy—the older of the Hsu brothers—had never fired such a weapon before and could not control it. In Hong Kong one killed with knives. He began firing in longer bursts, yanking the barrel downwards as he did so, indiscriminately hitting the floor, the ceiling, people.

When at last he got the weapon level its kick drove the butt back into his belly, folding him in the middle, and he sat down heavily on the floor, from which position, still firing, he shot off the toes of his right foot. This too was almost comical. Once again, no one laughed. For a moment the boy only stared stupidly at his ragged shoe, then resumed firing.

The younger Hsu, having solved the mysteries of the shotgun, had begun firing also. Its kick was, if possible, even more tremendous. Its first round took a tourist in the nape of the neck and decapitated him, and its second brought down the chandelier, which was the same size as the table and which hung directly over it. The third round tore the gun out of the younger Hsu's hands, breaking his thumb, forefinger and wrist in the process. He went to his knees scrabbling for it, sprang up again and, like his brother, resumed firing.

The noise was deafening. It was like an anesthetic. It numbed all sensation. The Hsu brothers were conscious of no pain. They stood shoe to shoe absolutely single-minded, guns bucking, creating a racket so thunderous that it submerged all other reality, it appeared even to impose some dreadful sense of order. In all that tumultuous scene only their noise was important. All other noise—of crockery smashing, of tables going over, of people screaming—was not.

Five seconds had passed, perhaps less. Magazines empty, the Hsu brothers turned and ran.

Powers had observed almost none of this. Seeking to extricate himself he was impeded by cloth, crockery, upended chairs, and also by the thrashing Carol. His face was buried in her left armpit, and the table itself lay across the back of his knees. He was still trying to free his gun. His hand, searching for it, searched Carol—himself too—in intimate places, without gaining the access he needed. Afterwards he would remember these frantic seconds in erotic detail, like his earliest sexual gropings in the back seats of cars: the feel of her body through silk, or whatever her dress was made of, of her belly that was soft and pelvic bone that was not.

His gun at last came free. He watched Carol's eyes widen as she spied it. Tablecloth and table still had him by the legs. Gun outstretched, off balance, he had almost gained his knees when she grabbed him, yanking him down again as if to continue their furtive love-making. Crying, "No, Artie, no. They'll kill you," she half rolled on top of him, pinning him down.

He tried to push her off, but she fought him like a wife, and several seconds more passed before he had got free of her, had sprung to his feet, and had begun his headlong pursuit of the Hsu brothers.

Too much time had gone by. The getaway car was waiting at the curb, engine turning. Powers should have been too late. But the Hsus had been delayed also. The older brother, though not really aware of it, was now missing nearly a third of his right shoe and foot, and although this did not very much hinder him when running across the landing, the same was not true when he came to the stairs, which he attempted to take two at a time. He started down left foot first—so far so good—but as he sought the next step the distance was wrong. The toes that might have sensed its whereabouts no longer existed. The boy negotiated the rest of the staircase in a swan dive. After only two bounces, he reached the bottom where he lay in a stupor. His submachine gun, meanwhile, now bounding down the stairs on its own, had caught between the legs of his younger brother. It not only sent him flying, it also continued downstairs itself at virtually his speed, so that at the bottom it fetched him a terrific clout in the side of the head. He too lay stunned, though only for a moment, before jumping up and heading once more for the door. The sight of his brother struggling to rise slowed him. He offered a hand—the broken one as it turned out. When the older Hsu grasped it, the younger one screamed.

The noise of other screams could be heard upstairs, as well as stampeding feet, which the Hsus took to indicate pursuit. This was America, the posse was forming or formed, and if caught they expected to be lynched. Grabbing up their guns they stumbled out onto the sidewalk just as Powers reached the landing above.

The stampede they had heard was real, but not pursuit. It represented unwounded patrons surging towards Ting's kitchen looking for a back door. The carnage was over except for whatever might happen on the street, but no one yet believed it, and all sought some other exit than the one favored by the Hsus.

Powers dashed out the door just as the brothers were piling into the car. It was raining and he had nothing to aim at but a pair of vanishing legs, at which he pegged three shots. There was no other practical target. One cannot stop a four-door sedan with bullets from a .38 special short-barreled revolver, whatever the movie heroes do, especially with only two shots left. The car's tires were not visible, the engine was forward, the gas tank was protected by the sheet steel bumper, and to send bullets through the back window at the driver was to risk wounding or killing motorists and pedestrians the length of the street. So Powers ran toward the car, waving his puny gun, a foolhardy decision if they should choose to fire back at him with any gun at all, much less with the devastating weapons they had employed in the restaurant. But the car merely surged away from him. A second later it had turned the corner and was gone.

Powers stood in the rain. He could hear the first siren coming, though it was still a long way off. Breathing hard, he turned and rushed back into the Golden Palace. Except for Carol, standing open-mouthed halfway down the staircase, the former movie lobby was empty.

As he jammed his revolver back into his trousers, Carol, her face drained of blood, came the rest of the way down, and into his arms.

He was furious with her. "I might have stopped them."

"Might have got yourself killed, you mean."

"Don't you ever do that again."

"You saved my life, I saved yours." She giggled, whether from relief or hysteria he did not know. "One good turn deserves another, I always say."

He held her, and she clung to him.

"There's a human head up there on the floor."

He found he liked her in his arms, and so let her stay.

But a moment later she had disengaged and was peering about for a phone.

"I've got to get a crew here right away." She was not thinking of him any more, he saw. She recognized this as the biggest news story of the day. So did he, and the realization appalled him. Bulletins would interrupt TV programming the rest of tonight, trumpeting his name. Tomorrow's headlines would proclaim him a hero once again, though he wasn't. He was in for another bout of sustained publicity, and his career at this point couldn't stand it. The reporters would make him sound like a western gunslinger. Worse, they would most likely turn tonight's dinner meeting with Carol—an interview was all it was—into a secret love tryst in "out-of-the-way" Chinatown, and this he had to prevent at all costs.

As he took both Carol's hands, he imagined her an hour from now, standing in front of cameras giving an eye-witness account of the massacre. He imagined her describing her precious life saved by her date, the fearless gunslinging hero of the action, Captain Powers. And so he began to plead with her.

"Call your story in, then disappear," he begged. "Let some other reporter handle it. I'm a married man. If the media finds out we were together—"

"There's nothing between us."

"They'll turn it into a scandal anyway." Outside the sirens were closer. There wasn't much time. "You know they will."

"You're asking too much. This is an important story. It's one of the biggest stories of my life. You can't ask me to give it up." Her eyes, still roaming, had located phones, and she strode toward them.

Ting staggered out onto the landing above. Blood from his scalp leaked down the side of his face, and he grasped the balustrade for support.

Powers took the steps two at a time.

"The police are on their way, Captain," said Ting.

In a few minutes this place would swarm with uniformed cops, and in his head Powers began to apportion jobs. A crime scene needed to be established. Witnesses had to be prevented from leaving and statements taken. Detectives had to be summoned. Ambulances too, of course. Commands had to be notified: precinct, division, borough, the chief of detectives' office, the police commissioner's office, the medical examiner's office, the district attorney's office, even, for something this big, the mayor's office. Until the top brass arrived he was in charge. He would use Ting's office as his command post.

He would have to phone his wife before she heard whatever news bulletins went out on the air, and became terrified.

He glanced down at Carol, now turning away from the phone. The press would turn up in droves. He would have to station cops at the door to keep them out. Carol too. She was on the outside now, and would remain there.

"It's bad, Captain," said Mr. Ting.

Powers strode past him into the slaughterhouse inside.

2

THE RAIN started again. It fell straight down. Carol waited under an overhang while the street, already full, swelled fuller. People running. Sirens. Shouts. Cars. Slamming doors. Despite cordons at both ends, vehicles kept entering the street: detectives' cars, commanders' cars. She didn't know what all of them were, but she saw they were official, for they double- and triple-parked, they parked on sidewalks. Cops in dripping black slickers worked to keep the crowd back, and to keep one lane open. Forensic vans inched through. Ambulances backed up to the restaurant entrance. Their back doors were flung apart and men in white coats jumped out.

Carol had found her crew and done her standup. Her face intruded into a million houses, a living presence in living color. Uninvited, she interrupted a sitcom for sixty seconds, the span of four weak jokes and their canned accompanying laughter. The jokes became like the corpses upstairs. Not even a machine would laugh at them now. Her grim report turned the next jokes unfunny also, a thought that occurred to her as she spoke. Well, that's television.

She told what she knew, or thought she knew, which wasn't much. An attack on a Chinatown restaurant with automatic weapons by unknown assailants for unknown reasons. Casualties unknown. Assailants escaped after a gun battle in the street with the well-known hero cop Captain

Powers. She could not as a conscientious journalist keep him out completely. She would have lost her fat contract had she tried. But after much thought she had decided not to present herself as an eyewitness, nor even to place herself inside the restaurant. She didn't do it for his sake. But she had, after all, witnessed nothing. She had spent the entire action on her back under a man, a position that was familiar to her, though the circumstances were not. There seemed no way to describe her part in this without making it sound like kinky sex. For her the experience had a distinct flavor of kinky sex anyway, as if birth and death had been present at the same time. She had never before lain under a man while people died around her, and her remembered sensations were acute. She could feel Powers' weight on her still—he was heavier than he looked—while his hands learned all about her. She could feel his hands on her also, and this disturbed her.

As she did her report she was wearing her plastic rain hood, but not her coat, which was upstairs checked. She considered it lost and planned to replace it, billing the network. Her blond-streaked, lacquered hair, being protected, was still neat, but her dress was soaked through. This was spring rain, and she was cold. Microphone at her lips, she stood in the sudden blinding glare, sunlight without warmth, which illuminated her face and upper body, the facade of the Golden Palace behind her, and that segment of sidewalk that had become her stage. As she spoke she was aware as always of spectators. She felt them pressing forward to hear her secrets.

The illumination was cut off. She handed back her microphone. A sound man threw his coat over her shoulders and was rewarded by two seconds' worth of her famous smile.

She watched rival correspondents, also using the Golden Palace as background, perform similar rites. Projectors came on. Fragments of rainy night were transformed into hallucinatory fragments of day. In an earlier age the same thing would have happened, Carol reflected. A generation ago press photographers had used strobe lights, and a generation before that, with press cards stuck in their hatbands, they had exploded the flash bulbs attached to the sides of their speed grafflexes. The tradition extended backwards through the flash pans of daguerreotypers to the upthrust flaming torches of cavemen. Disaster was and had always been a riddle that had to have light thrown on it. Present-day illumination seemed brighter and longer-lasting only by comparison; it conquered no greater darkness, revealed the essential riddle no better than anything in the past.

The Golden Palace seemed to her like a bastion under siege. Its defenders could not be seen. She and her colleagues had it surrounded. Network vans waited on the perimeter, as watchful as tanks. Cameramen moved into position, their instruments primed and aimed. Light men carried projectors forward, their job to throw up flares for the gunners to sight by. Television was the besieging army, no question about it, and if you did not believe this, ask the police. The police knew who the enemy was, and hid.

At last the bastion's doors were flung open. The crowd became agitated and pressed forward: mixed tourists and Orientals crowding the barricades, crowded Oriental faces in windows and doorways, individual crowds of wet, uncomfortable newsmen in the street. The first stretchers came out. It was as if the building had dined too copiously and had begun now to vomit. More stretchers. Shouts. Projectors blazed. Cameramen ran. Stretcherbearers ran. Doors slammed. Engines came on. Headlights came on. Vehicles lurched into motion. Sirens wailed. The building was expelling all it could not hold down.

It was a scene of wild disorder, and Carol watched it enthralled. High tragedy and low comedy had become the same, funeral and carnival were the same. Disorder had become beautiful, as seductive as illicit sex, as seductive as vice. She felt giddy with excitement, and at the same time felt that her excitement was somehow lewd. She was taking pleasure in a perversion. Violent crime, she saw, created disorder and disorder created more disorder. And she wondered if it was not the disorder that men—beginning with the police—found so dangerous, rather than the crime itself. If disorder of such magnitude was allowed to prevail, then no one was safe. Perhaps it was to this intellectual concept, and to no other, that the police responded. They had rushed into the Golden Palace to restore order. On a room littered with corpses they rushed to impose routine. They closed off the room and would let no one in until they had done it. Without being able to see them, Carol saw what they were still doing in there, filling out forms, drawing diagrams, signing their names.

First the room, then the street itself. When the last ambulance had squealed away a squad of patrolmen came out. These cops, she saw, had their orders: they had been ordered to order the crowd to disperse. Their uniforms were buttoned. The buttons shone. Their caps were straight. They moved forward blunt as truncheons.

"Go on home now."

"It's all over here."

She heard the lines they spoke, and foresaw the result. Their lines were poorly acted and had been poorly written in the first place. As they moved into it, the crowd became amorphous. The cops sank in like blows into dough. They intimidated no one. Tonight's play had at least one more act to run, and the crowd was eager to see how it ended. The crowd was single-minded. Recognizing this quickly—that the crowd was more disciplined than they were—the cops recognized also their own failure, and since there were no commanders urging them into the breach against such hopeless odds, their bullying ceased. They pretended to become nonchalant. They attempted to make jokes, and even friends. They accepted the status quo, and so did the crowd.

The doors to the Golden Palace sprang back once more, and Chief of Detectives Cirillo strode forth accompanied by Chief of Patrol Duncan. Cirillo was short and fat. Gray hair. Gray suit. He was chewing on a cigar. Carol did not know him. Duncan, who wore braid on his cap and three stars on each epaulet, was a man of commanding presence and ramrod-straight posture. When in civilian clothes he was often taken not for a policeman but for a general. Carol did not know Duncan either.

But the news crews, recognizing both officers, grasped immediately what their appearance meant.

Press Conference.

The outlying citizens only pressed more firmly against the barricades, leaned more perilously out of windows, but the crowds of news crews converged. Truth was to be dispensed, and they wanted some. They sprinted for position, fought for it. Encountering resistance they shouldered forward. Elbows flailed. Gear flailed. Women's handbags flailed. It was as rough as a cavalry charge. It was punctuated not by bugles but by curses. Like many searches after the truth, this one was not pretty.

Cirillo and Duncan, one step up on the stoop, were responsible for what was happening. They had willed it to happen for they wanted to shine, and this was their moment. Yet they pretended indifference. They were superior to the moment and to the scuffling news crews as well, and wore half-repressed half-smiles to prove it. They were as smug as film stars. While microphones were lashed into place in front of them, they made whispered sardonic comments to each other. They made each other chuckle. Many among the newsmen recognized this for the arrogance it was, and hated the two men for it. As they set up their gear hatred and need vied for the upper hand. Need, as always, won. Hatred was a luxury, and would have to wait.

The press conference began.

Chief of Detectives Cirillo read from notes in his hand: "At approximately 2100 hours this date, two as yet unidentified Asians—"

Cirillo and Duncan were the same age, and had moved upwards in rank concurrently, one in the detective division and the other in patrol. These were parallel rather than competitive courses. For more than twenty years, principally because they had not been rivals, they had imagined themselves friends. At the next stage of their careers, if there was a next stage, they would collide, for there was only one four-star chief on top of them, and on top of him only one police commissioner. Lately, because the chief of detectives had by far the more dramatic and therefore more visible job, Duncan had been reluctant to let Cirillo out of his sight. The chief of detectives could get press attention any time he wished to announce that a major crime had been committed or solved. In the first instance Cirillo would be showing off his deep concern and in the second he would reap his detectives' glory. In both cases he would reap the publicity. Duncan, who had no such access to the press, was like a runner who risked being lapped. He could not afford to let it happen. Therefore on nights like this when the mayor remained in his mansion and the police commissioner chose not to appear (both fearing no doubt to be identified in the public mind as messengers of bad tidings) Duncan had taken to standing always at Cirillo's side. Duncan could not worry about bad tidings. To him bad tidings meant not to be there at all. As for the sardonic Cirillo, he was an expert in black humor and when microphones were present knew how to present catastrophe in an amusing manner.

In other words, both men had resolved to exploit press conferences, the only terrain available to them, as much as possible. If there was tension between them it did not yet show. When they looked at each other, both still smiled.

Tonight's plan was for Cirillo to describe the crime and for Duncan in his turn to identify the casualties. It was a reasonable, workable plan but it was foiled by Captain Powers, who came out the door behind them and attempted to sneak away unnoticed. Since Powers, though only a captain, was better known than the two chiefs, and was the hero of the evening as well, the news crews abandoned Cirillo in mid-sentence, and the still mute Duncan as well, and surged off to the side to surround Powers. They pinned him to the wall.

"Captain Powers, can you give us a statement?"

"Captain Powers, can we ask you a few questions?"

Powers, blinking from the glare, threw a glance back at Cirillo and Duncan. They were watching him, and they did not look friendly. "Chief Cirillo and Chief Duncan have all the facts," said Powers.

Hand microphones were being thrust into his face. He kept glancing from the microphones to the two chiefs and back again.

Reporters continued to clamor.

"We understand you were in a gun battle with them out here in the street."

"We have a report that you shot one of the gunmen."

"You'll have to see Chief Duncan—"

"Did you hit him?" asked Carol.

"Yes."

"Did you get the make and license number of the car?" asked Carol.

For a moment Powers eyed her. "Yes. Chief Duncan will—"

Though Carol lapsed into silence, the clamor continued.

"Duncan only got here an hour ago."

"Be reasonable, Captain Powers. You were an eyewitness. You were in the shootout."

"There was no shootout," said Powers.

"You're the one we want to talk to."

Powers again glanced over at Duncan and Cirillo. It was so dark over there—in contrast to the lights he had been staring into—that he could barely see them. But he could tell they were glaring at him. After a moment he moved in their direction, stepped up onto the stoop beside them, and then, when voices below insisted on it, stepped between them. He took center stage. The two three-star chiefs flanked him.

"Your public awaits you, Powers," muttered Duncan.

"Mustn't disappoint your public, must we, Powers," said Cirillo.

Powers was aware of Duncan beside him grimly folding his notes, and he was aware of Carol in the crowd holding her microphone outstretched as close to his mouth as she could reach. He was more aware of Carol than of the chiefs. He was aware of her raincoat which he carried in his clenched fist, having first folded it over several times so that it might pass for his own; and he saw her eyes go to the raincoat also. Since he could not give it to her in front of all these people, he was forced to keep it, which transformed it from a raincoat into a hostage. It would be tomorrow at the earliest before she could ransom it back. She would have to phone him to open negotiations.

"All right," said Powers to the newsmen, "what did you want to know?"

3

THE PHONE rang louder than the sirens outside. Though the proprietor of the Flowering Virtue Funeral Parlor had been half expecting it, it made him jump. He had been checking over ledgers at his desk, the safe open behind him. He had ignored the sirens but could not ignore this. He took the call. After listening a moment, he spoke only two words into the mouthpiece, then hung up, and stood up.

He was big for a Chinese, almost six feet tall; in the villages of Kwangtung Province where he was born he would have seemed a giant. His name was Koi Tse-ven but he went by the name Jimmy Koy. It was difficult to guess his exact age because he affected smoked glasses even at night. He was wearing them now and they turned his normally impassive face into something totally inscrutable. But his hair was still black, as was his mustache, so he was probably in his mid-forties. He had very white teeth but rarely showed them. He rarely smiled, and when he did it was usually, in the manner of the Chinese, behind his hand.

Moving without haste, he put the ledgers into one side of the safe, and withdrew a small package from the other, then swung the door shut, spun the dial, and rang for Chang in the basement mortuary. But Chang did not respond, and Koy found him, as he had expected, on the outside stoop peering up the street at the commotion in front of the Golden Palace.

"Something's happened," said Chang. "I heard the sirens."

"What else did you hear?" asked Koy. "Did you hear shots?"

"I heard no shots. Why, did you hear shots?"

"No," said Koy. "There's a package on my desk. Put it in your bag. We'll take the hearse. We have work to do."

"What do you think happened?" Chang was still peering up the street.

"Every day there are seven Chinese newspapers published in Chinatown," said Koy. "Tomorrow morning you buy one and read about it. Get your bag."

Koy, waiting, stood under the canopy. The rain was coming down. People were hurrying past him along both sidewalks. Every restaurant and curio shop in Chinatown must be emptying out as the news spread. In front of the Golden Palace, three blocks ahead, the entire street was choked with traffic. He saw that a number of police cars had been abandoned on sidewalks up there, red dome lights still turning. From this distance, seen through the rain, the lights looked orange, and they stained the walls of the buildings orange all around.

"That's auspicious," said Chang, who had come back out. He stood beside Koy, clutching his medical bag. Chang spoke in Cantonese dialect, his only language. If you wanted to converse with Chang, that's what you spoke.

"What's auspicious?"

"Orange means good luck. Orange is always a good omen. With an omen like that nothing bad can happen to us tonight."

"I see," said Koy.

"Of course real oranges are best."

They got into the hearse, Chang driving, the medical bag on the seat between them, Chang prattling about omens, demons, evil spirits. Good omens, as everybody knew, protected only Chinese people, Chang said. He gestured toward the tourists flocking toward the Golden Palace. These white demons and demonesses, would not be protected, he said.

Koy, preoccupied, scarcely listened. Many Chinese still believed such nonsense. Half the businessmen in Chinatown bought and sold according to omens. Women consulted horoscopes before setting a date to wash their hair. Major decisions were made only on auspicious days and astrologers were consulted first—a number of these charlatans still did a brisk business in Chinatown. Superstition, when dealing with the Chinese, was not a variable but a predictable, Koy knew. One factored it in.

They crossed the bridge into Brooklyn, and on the Expressway headed north toward Queens. Presently they were driving down dark residential streets. There were trees on both sides, no oncoming traffic, and Chang began weaving from one side to the other.

"Stop that," ordered Koy sharply.

"Just a precaution," explained Chang. Possibly they had picked up evil spirits before leaving Chinatown. If so, Chang had just shaken them off. "Evil spirits can move only in straight lines," he said.

"I didn't know that," said Koy. Chang was a distant cousin who came from the same ancestral village as Koy. Chinese loyalties were rigidly prescribed; family first and then co-villagers, and family alone was usually a burden and often an albatross. The Chinese albatross, Koy thought: family.

Two blocks from the house Koy ordered Chang to pull over and park, and they walked the rest of the way. The risk began now, and Koy watched carefully for activity in lighted windows or for men seated in parked cars—anything that could constitute police surveillance. But he noted nothing. He was not worried about being conspicuous on the street. This neighborhood in the Flushing section of Queens was about twenty-five percent Oriental—Koreans and Japanese mostly. Koy had placed his safe house there as a means of hiding it. Americans could not differentiate one Asian from another, and fellow Asians, who could, were not likely to consider the arrival in their community of one or several Chinese to be in any way significant.

The apartment was in the basement of a six-story building. Koy and Chang entered through the lobby. No one saw them. They went down the service stairs, being met by a blast of rock music as soon as they opened the service door. To Koy the music was loud enough to attract attention, and therefore in itself it was dangerous, but behind it, overriding it, more dangerous still, rose what sounded like the sustained bleating of farm animals being tortured, goats or sheep perhaps, animals in terrible pain. Outright screams might have attained a more penetrating noise level, but not much. Such bleating would be audible to anyone who happened down into this cellar—a housewife doing her laundry would hear it, and her instinctive reaction would be to call the police.

The police could be en route even now, and would find Koy inside the apartment.

As Koy rang the bell, he felt the hair raise on the back of his hands, felt the rush of blood, and the sudden shortness of breath, sensations every gambler felt, sensations that he found, despite himself, intensely pleasurable. The risk quotient had just risen amazingly high. Well, he told himself, it was already high. Men of wealth and power were involved and depended on him. They had waited a long time, and Koy himself had come under increasing pressure. They would not be pleased to fail now. It would be unwise to frustrate them further. He was obliged to accept this crazy risk because, although the first part of tonight's activities had evidently succeeded, the second part was deteriorating fast. This needed to be reversed, and decisions made, something only he could do. And so he told himself he was glad he stood where he did. Heady triumphs came only after risks such as this. The risk was often more fun than the triumph. Man had to risk his life constantly in order to enjoy it.

Nikki Han opened the door, closing it quickly behind them. The apartment, which served as dormitory for that part of the Flying Dragons youth gang controlled by Koy, was small, airless, cluttered. Koy glanced into the empty front room. Chinese comic books. Unmade beds—they looked like terrain that had been fought over. The cheap suitcases of boys without homes. Transistor radios, plates of half-eaten food.

The back room was similar, though not empty. The back room was where the noise was coming from. Nikki Han, who looked to Koy to be on the edge of panic, stepped into it, and Koy and Chang followed.

The Hsu brothers lay on cots, thrashing and bleating. Han or someone had wedged towels into their mouths and this was all that kept their agony from being audible in the street. The older brother's ravaged foot was what Koy noted first. The gruesome shoe, dripping with gore, was still attached. It looked like something that had got caught in a lawn mower. But there was no lawn mower at the Golden Palace, and Koy looked to Han for an explanation.

"I don't know," said Han in English. His panic, Koy noted, was very close to the surface.

The brothers looked out at the world through dumb animal eyes. They were conscious only of their pain. Repeatedly they tangled and untangled themselves in bed sheets unwashed for months and newly soaked with their blood—though neither seemed to be bleeding now. This was understandable considering the tourniquets—clothesline rope twisted tight by wooden hangers. They had been stripped of trousers and just below their underpants on the right thighs the tourniquets girdled them, biting into bare flesh. Their thighs were as hairless as bamboo, as thin almost as arms, and the ropes cinched them in, making waists scarcely thicker than the bone itself. Han or someone had wound those ropes up tight as trolley wires, and both legs had turned blue. The younger brother's hand and wrist had turned blue also, though there was no wound there that Koy could see.

Nikki Han had moved to the nearest cot. "The Cho Kun is here," he said in Cantonese dialect. "The doctor is with him. You'll be all right now."

The literal translation of Cho Kun is "the person seated within the lodge." It is a rank not subject to precise English translation. Leader, boss, big brother, chairman, executive secretary—Cho Kun, when applied to Koy by his partners and associates and by the men and boys who worked for him, meant all of these things.

The Cho Kun, having caught Chang's eye, pointed to the older brother. He pointed not with his finger but, in the Chinese manner, with his chin.

Chang moved to the bedside and opened his medical bag.

"The doctor will take care of you," said Nikki Han, and it was clear that the word doctor had brought hope to both boys.

Chang was not a doctor but an embalmer. Reaching into his bag he held up the package he had found on Koy's desk. "This?" he asked.

"Yes," said Koy.

Chang took the package into the kitchen, nicked one corner of it, and brought out a quarter-spoonful of white powder to which he added a few drops of water collected from the faucet. He then turned on the stove and held the spoon over the flames. The white powder dissolved almost instantly. Setting down the spoon, Chang drew the fluid up into a hypodermic syringe. All this time the agonized bleating in the other room never ceased.

Back at the bedside the embalmer raised his needle to the light. "Are either of them users?" he asked Nikki Han.

"No," said Nikki Han.

"This may kill him," Chang said to Koy.

Koy again pointed with his chin, this time impatiently.

After injecting half his solution into the arm of the older brother, the embalmer stepped back to wait for a reaction.

"Now the other one," ordered Koy.

"I should wait to see—"

The younger brother having partially spit out his towel, had begun screaming.

"Give him the whole dose," said Koy. "Hurry."

The reaction was not long coming. Within sixty seconds the two contorted faces began to relax, and the room became silent. For a brief moment both boys smiled almost beatifically. Then they were unconscious.

Chang had used the strongest painkiller known to man. He had injected almost pure heroin.

He withdrew the spittle-soaked towels, wiped off their faces, and loosened both tourniquets. The younger brother's wound was in the calf, a puncture. The bullet must have struck bone. In any case it had not exited. Seeing that the younger brother no longer bled at all, Chang released his tourniquet completely. Clearly the younger brother could wait, and the embalmer began to work on the older one. When he had unlaced and removed the gory shoe, and then what was left of the sock, he saw that part of the boy's big toe remained, and he got out scissors and clipped it off, leaving the skin. The other four toes already were gone. With tweezers he probed for pieces of loose bone, removing several, being sure to leave himself additional skin to work with. Next he threaded a big curved needle such as embalmers use on cadavers, and with it began to sew up the foot, keeping up a stream of chatter in Cantonese dialect as he worked. He would have preferred a smaller needle and thinner thread, he said, but didn't have any. This thread was as thick as fish line, he said, you could land a ts'ang fish with it, he could barely push it through the eye of the needle—the needle's nose in the Chinese idiom.

Koy watched in silence. In the morning a ship would leave New York harbor bound for Hong Kong. The Hsu brothers were supposed to be on it as crewmen. They would miss their ship. Perhaps there would be another ship for them later, but Koy did not think so. Recovery would take too long. He knew he should decide about them tonight, but forbore doing so. The Hsu brothers were from his ancestral village also, and deserved to be accorded whatever small chance was left them. He would give them a week or two. He would decide then.

The embalmer moved to the younger brother. "He's got a bullet in there," he noted. "If I cut it out he'll bleed."

"Leave it in there," Koy ordered.

The embalmer began to sew the wound shut over the bullet. When he had finished he made splints out of wooden coat hangers and bound the boy's broken wrist. The fingers looked broken also, but would heal by themselves, he decided. He stood up.

"They'll wake up in an hour or two," he said.

The Cho Kun had been talking quietly to Nikki Han, who at last looked calmer. "The package is in the kitchen," Koy said now. "Your job is to keep them quiet." No doubt the other gang members had been driven out of the apartment by the noise and suffering of the Hsu brothers. Presently they would begin to drift in again. This was where they slept. They could not stay out forever.

"Set up a schedule of watches," said Koy to Nikki Han. "I want someone on watch at all times. Have the needle ready. Every time they come to the surface, put them under again."

Together with the embalmer Koy left the apartment, being careful no one saw them come out. But outside in the night under the trees, his manner became almost jaunty. If the Hsus died, whether from an overdose or from shock, they could be disposed of. If they lived, then in a week or two Koy would make his decision. But basically he was pleased with them, because they had done their jobs well. They had made the future extremely attractive to Koy. When he got back to his office, though it was late, he would begin making calls, setting up the meeting for tomorrow during which, he believed, Ting would be deposed and Koy elected mayor of Chinatown in his place. To the rest of the city this might seem only a ceremonial title, but in Chinatown, if properly exploited, it carried real power and guaranteed immense wealth. A number of people had died tonight so that Koy should become mayor and be able, together with his partners and associates, to implement certain plans and investments, some of them worldwide in scope.

The embalmer noted Koy's change of mood but forbore mentioning it. Partly this was normal Chinese reticence. One did not invade that part of a man's being where his spirit sunned itself. Mostly it was because Koy was Cho Kun. Lowly individuals did not question such exalted personages on any subject at all.

"It's a nice night," said Koy in Cantonese. "The rain has stopped."

The embalmer agreed.

The two Chinese gentlemen, one wearing smoked glasses, the other carrying a medical bag, walked two blocks to the parked hearse, got in and drove away.

4

THE SILENT alarm clock awakened Powers, slants of sunlight that fell across the covers as heavy as lumber, as loud as noise. Gathering his clothes, keys and money, his shield and his gun, he slipped downstairs without awakening his wife and dressed in the kitchen. After measuring out coffee and plugging in the percolator, he put on a leather jacket, and went out to the corner for the papers. His shield in its leather wallet was in his back pocket. If he sat down he would sit on it. He sat on it every day of his life, noticing it only if it was not there. His gun was in his right-hand jacket pocket. He could not have gone out without it. He was not comfortable without his gun, would sooner have gone out wearing no underpants or no socks. Without it, even now at seven o'clock in the morning, he would have felt as awkward and off-balance as a man walking the streets wearing only one shoe. The gun's weight was partly counterbalanced by the weight of his keys. He carried, usually dangling from a clip on his belt, a lot of keys: house, car, garage, desk, locker, handcuffs. He carried as many keys as a night watchman. He was a man used to a certain weight of metal around his middle.

The newsstand was two blocks away outside a candy store. The dread with which he approached it proved justified. The papers were laid out on the stand and from ten feet away he could see his picture and the accompanying headline. He occupied the entire front page of the *Daily News*. On the front page of the *Times*, his picture was smaller. He put money down, tucked both papers under his arm, and walked thoughtfully home.

The coffee was perking. Hanging his jacket over a chair, he poured two cups and, with the papers again under his arm, carried them upstairs to the bedroom. His wife was still asleep but he woke her. Kicking off his shoes, he sat down against the headboard. His wife in her nightgown sat against the headboard too. They sipped coffee and read the papers.

"Let me see that one," said Eleanor at last.

He had finished it and was waiting his turn at the other. They exchanged papers.

"They make you sound pretty heroic," said Eleanor.

"It wasn't heroic." She needed a new nightgown, he noted. This one was old and part of her left breast jutted through the tattered lace.

"It sounds pretty dangerous too. You'll get yourself killed one day. Then where will I be?"

They had been over this ground before, and he had no desire to go over it again. "I'm not going to get killed."

"Oh no? You only chased them out onto the sidewalk. They had machine guns." She frowned. "If you keep doing things like that you'll get killed."

"Things like what?" In an attempt to lighten her mood he reached across and poked her breast back inside. "Like what?"

She caught his hand. "Dangerous things. You're forty-six years old."

"So are you."

"I don't get into shootouts."

She was, he saw, seriously concerned. "Honey," he said earnestly, "They weren't thinking about me. They were running for a car. I wouldn't have done it if it felt dangerous."

"The reporters thought differently, and I notice you didn't try to change their minds. Let me read you what you told the reporters."

"You can't change reporters' minds. So I tried to low-key this thing. You can't disclaim what other people take to be heroism. It only makes you sound more heroic."

She smiled. "Pompous too."

"Right. People hate you for doing an act they wouldn't dare try, but they hate you for the pompousness even more."

"Cirillo and Duncan, you mean."

Eleanor turned back to the front page of the *News* where her husband's face, life-size, stared up at her.

Powers pointed. "This ear here—you can just see it —is Cirillo's. This ear is Duncan's."

"They've been cut out of the photo completely."

"Yeah. The real danger was not last night, it's this morning. And it's not bullets." After a moment Powers added: "Last night's television was not so bad. Television is on the air one minute, and a minute later it's off. But news-papers hang around all day. They make people mad every time they look at them. This photo alone should guarantee me another ten years as a captain."

"You could always quit."

"Quit the department!" Powers' voice had anguish in it, and the anguish was real. "But I love the department. Quit a failure?"

Leaning over, Eleanor gave him a kiss on the cheek. "I know."

Her breast had popped out again. "Hey," he said, ogling it, "are you trying to seduce me, or would you prefer another cup of coffee?"

She gave him a fond smile. "Coffee."

"In bed?"

"I'll go down with you."

They got up, Powers stepping into his shoes. Eleanor put on a dressing gown. "I'm glad I wasn't there," Eleanor said conversationally.

"I'm glad you weren't there also," Powers said. But it made him remember Carol's raincoat in the trunk of his car.

At the stove Eleanor fixed her husband bacon and

eggs. Their two sons were at college and the house that morning felt unnaturally empty to both of them. They had been married twenty-three years.

She set the plate down in front of him. "It scares me, what you did last night. *You* scare me."

"Oh, honey."

As he spoke, the meeting that would change his life got under way at police headquarters.

THE POLICE commissioner had reached his desk at 7:00 A.M., two hours in advance of normal, and the uniformed deputy inspector who was his chief secretary, and who normally worked the same hours as the PC, had handed him a sheaf of reports on Chinatown crime.

"Chiefs Cirillo and Duncan are in the building as ordered," said the secretary, who had been up all night finding and collating these reports, and who looked it.

The PC had already started through the pile. He did not look up. "Have them wait outside. Is there coffee?"

The deputy inspector said there was, and left the office to get it.

The police commissioner was a careful, meticulous man. He had a full schedule of appointments today which this Chinatown business threatened to disrupt. His calendar might get backed up for the rest of the week. He intended to forestall this if he could by inventing and implementing a new Chinatown policy right now in the two hours left before the business day started. The mayor could be expected to call soon, and he was worried about that too—he had best have a plan ready to divulge to the mayor. But chiefly he was worried about his appointments calendar. To the PC a calendar that did not run smoothly was the mark of a sloppy executive.

The phone rang. It was the mayor already, and the PC had not yet reached the bottom of the Chinatown reports. He was not ready, and therefore was obliged to listen to a twenty-minute harangue. In the course of it the deputy inspector entered, and set down the cup and saucer. He had left the door ajar, through which the PC could see Cirillo and Duncan pacing and waiting.

"Yes sir," he said into the phone, and gave a curt nod of dismissal in the direction of the deputy inspector.

Outside, the deputy inspector sat down at his desk. He was like a sentry on guard. He was like a court eunuch —he guarded the throne room. He had gold oak leaves on each shoulder.

"He's still on the phone with the mayor," the secretary said apologetically.

From the sofa opposite, the two waiting chiefs began to watch the miniature traffic lights over the PC's door. The red light was lit, and remained lit, interminably it seemed. Finally it went out. After a moment the green light came on.

The deputy inspector glanced up at it: "The PC will see you now."

Duncan and Cirillo went past him into the office. The PC, in shirtsleeves, looking grim, was seated behind his desk. He did not offer to shake hands, nor invite them to sit down. He was still going through the reports.

Behind them the door opened again and the secretary showed in Deputy Commissioner Glazer, the department's chief public affairs officer. "Good morning, good morning," said Glazer cheerfully. "Sorry I'm late."

The PC at last looked up. "Anything to tell me?" he asked Cirillo.

The chief of detectives said: "We have the perpetrators tentatively identified as members of the Wee Ching. That's a Chinese youth gang. A new one, just starting up. That Golden Palace restaurant is supposedly a hangout for the Ghost Shadows. That's supposedly the biggest youth gang in Chinatown. Supposedly five or six Ghost Shadows were at a table in the back. That's the information we have at this time, Commissioner. We think that's who the shooters were aiming at.

"They didn't kill any Ghost Shadows," said the PC.

He came around his desk and began pacing. "They killed three white tourists and two waiters."

Cirillo opted for black humor. "It's a way of inducting five new Ghosts into their ranks."

"I don't think that's very funny."

Was this a reprimand of Cirillo? Duncan thought so and, though he kept his face blank, he was pleased. He said carefully, "Commissioner, you'll notice the use of the word supposedly. We don't really know." Most previous police commissioners had been career cops, but this one, until three months ago, had been a prosecutor. Duncan didn't really know him. He was a tall, skinny, baldish man, fifty-five years old. He was a lawyer, and to career cops lawyers were more dangerous than criminals. Duncan said carefully, "Even though we have a precinct and two hundred cops in Chinatown, we've never been able to penetrate even the legal side of Chinese society, much less the illegal side."

The PC was pacing up and down. "What's happened in this city?" he demanded. "The Chinese used to be the model minority. The commander of the Chinatown precinct had the softest job in the department. I go off to work for the Justice Department a few years, and I come back and there are Chinese corpses on every street corner."

"You're right, Commissioner," agreed Duncan.

"And not just the street corners," said Cirillo. "Say you find a parked car with bullet holes in the trunk and a stink coming out. You open it up. Nowadays it isn't a Mafia guy in there, it's a Chinaman. You can't rely on tradition any more."

Duncan waited for the PC's reaction. When the PC smiled, Duncan did too.

But the PC's smile vanished, and he resumed pacing.

"The Chinese are now the most trigger-happy citizens the city has ever known," he said. "Two weeks ago there was a gunfight on Confucius Square in broad daylight. Three Chinese dead. The week before that they started shooting in Madison Square Garden during a basketball game. One Chinese dead and two wounded."

"You forgot one, Commissioner," said Cirillo. He was grinning.

The PC stared at him.

"About a week before you took office, the head of the Chinese Merchants' Association goes to the Pagoda Theater for some light entertainment. Somebody shoves a bicycle spoke through the back of his chair into his heart. He didn't even pitch over. When the show ended they tried to wake him up. They thought he was asleep." Cirillo waited a beat, then added grinning: "Since then business has really fallen off at the Pagoda, I hear."

This time the PC did not smile. "I was just on the phone twenty minutes with the mayor. He wanted to know what the hell was going on in Chinatown. I want to know the same thing."

Duncan said carefully, "With the new immigration laws, the population of Chinatown has quadrupled. As you can imagine, I've had to beef up my uniformed patrol forces there. We've got Hong Kong money and people taking over the New York tongs, taking over the Mott Street gambling dens. The youth gangs are Hong Kong kids, and they're violent. Our intelligence is very poor. We can't understand their language or read their newspapers, and we've got nothing to infiltrate them with—we have only six Chinese cops in the entire department—all of them well known in Chinatown."

The PC rapped the desk with the back of his knuckles. "The mayor wants this Chinatown violence stopped. So do I."

Duncan, studying the PC carefully, said, "There's not much we can do beyond what we are already doing."

Deputy Commissioner Glazer gave an unctuous smile. "What we have here," he said, "is a public relations problem. Some cosmetic changes should do the trick."

There was a moment of heavy silence.

"I intended today to appoint a special Chinatown major case squad," said Cirillo. "We can say I will head the investigation personally. The newspapers usually go for that kind of thing. That might take some of the heat off."

"That's not enough," said the PC. "Not for the mayor, not for me. I want a new commander in the Chinatown precinct to start with."

"I brought along a list of five possibilities, sir," said Duncan. He had come to this conference better prepared than Cirillo, and was pleased with himself, though no expression showed on his face.

"Have you got a name on there that would make a headline?" asked Deputy Commissioner Glazer.

The PC, after looking over the list, grabbed the *Daily News* on his desk. He slapped the back of his hand against Powers' photo. "What about this guy?"

The question was addressed to Chief of Patrol Duncan, who did not immediately answer.

"The press would certainly be happy with him," said Glazer.

Duncan glanced at him. The deputy commissioner was another former prosecutor. Since technically he outranked Duncan, and since he had the PC's ear, he had to be dealt with almost as carefully as the PC himself.

Duncan, when he answered, spoke directly to the PC. "Not a good choice, Commissioner. Powers has been a captain I think ten or eleven years. A number of your predecessors have considered him for command of a precinct, but decided against it.

"Why was that?" demanded the PC.

Duncan had no intention of standing alone against the PC on this or any other subject, and he did not expect Cirillo to come to his aid. But his rival surprised him.

"Powers rubs people the wrong way," said the chief of detectives.

"For instance," added Duncan carefully, "when he was a lieutenant he had command of a midtown burglary squad. A sniper with a rifle got into a comfort station in Central Park and began killing people. Powers went in there and blasted the guy."

The PC stared hard at Duncan. "I may be missing the point here."

"He was a burglary lieutenant," explained the chief of patrol. "That was a job for the patrol forces or for Emergency Service."

"I see."

Duncan was trying to decide how far he dared push this. "When he had command of the Auto Squad, he managed to get an entire magazine article written about himself. In *The New York Times*. He promised to cut auto thefts by twenty-five percent."

"And did he?" inquired the PC.

Feeling the heat, Duncan waited for Cirillo to comment. The chief of detectives, Duncan considered, would always rather talk than keep his mouth shut, a flaw that could be useful.

"The then-PC transferred him," said Cirillo.

Duncan added carefully, "A series of police commissioners up to and including your predecessor decided that he had too many friends in the press."

"He wasn't above criticizing his superiors in print," added Cirillo helpfully.

The PC picked up the list Duncan had given him, and again studied it. "Captain Gibson is in command in Chinatown at present, I see," he said. "Who is Captain Gibson?"

"Gibson is a good man," said Duncan. "Used to have the Mounted Squadron. Very popular in Chinatown. Keeps his horse there, you know. Likes to ride it up and down the streets. Believes it helps establish the police presence in people's minds."

The PC walked to the window and stared out. When he turned back it was to announce his decision. "It's not Gibson's fault necessarily, but he's got to go. I don't know any of the names on your list. The mayor wants a name that will take the heat off the mayor. I want the same thing, is that clear? The mayor would be satisfied with Powers."

When Cirillo and Duncan walked out, their faces were expressionless. From his desk the deputy inspector smiled up at them, but they ignored him, and once outside in the hall they began muttering. Their own offices were one flight down. Both went into Duncan's.

"Is it worth trying to talk him out of it?" asked the chief of patrol.

Cirillo was making no jokes now. "I don't know that you could." After a moment he added, "There's a yellow curtain around Chinatown. If Powers wants the job, give it to him. When he falls on his ass, we're rid of him for good."

The two men stared briefly at each other. Then Duncan strode to the door and called out to his own chief secretary, a captain. "Reach out for Captain Powers for me," ordered Duncan. "Get him down here. Give him a 'forthwith.' "

Forthwith was the most urgent command in the police lexicon, and commanders enjoyed using it. It made subordinates hop.

About an hour later Powers, in uniform, arrived at headquarters, and asked Duncan's secretary, an acquaintance, what it was all about. But the secretary didn't know, and Powers began to wait.

Duncan might have received him at once, for he had nothing pressing to do. But partly out of spite after last night, and partly to impress upon this subordinate as on all subordinates his own rank and power, Duncan had decided to make the wait a long one.

And so thirty-two minutes passed before Powers, cap under his arm, stood in front of Duncan's desk, gazing into Duncan's flat stare.

"You are to take command of the Fifth Precinct forthwith," said the chief of patrol.

Duncan was not a stupid man. He saw the emotions pass across Powers' face: at first surprise, and then bitterness. Powers, Duncan saw, perceived exactly what was being done to him, and also why.

"Eleven years I've been waiting for a precinct," said Powers, "and now I get one forthwith. Suppose I refuse?"

"Then I think it unlikely you'll ever be offered another."

The two men stared at each other. Neither dropped his gaze. Stand-off.

"Who's in command there now?" asked Powers.

"Gibson," said the chief of patrol. "Do you know him?"

Powers walked to the window. "The Lone Ranger? Sure I know him. We went through Captains School together. You, me, the chief of detectives, Gibson. As I remember, he finished at the bottom of the class, and he's had two precincts already. Him and his horse. Can I think about your kind offer?"

"You have twenty-four hours."

"Don't threaten me."

Again their eyes locked. Another standoff.

"You have twenty-four hours," said the chief of patrol.

Part
Two

Part
Two

5

BEFORE THE arrival of the Chinese in Chinatown most of the buildings there already stood. That is, earlier waves of immigrants had used them first and they were of indeterminate architecture that could best be described as Lower East Side tenement. They were narrow four- and five-story buildings, as narrow proportionately as the chests of the consumptives who so often in the past had inhabited them, and they were pressed one against the other, rib to rib. Their roofs extended into beetle-browed eaves that protruded above the topmost windows like scar tissue above the eyes of boxers, like evidence of generations of pain. Extending out half the width of the sidewalks below, they served no purpose except to shut out sunlight, and perhaps dreams. They made the sky look small. From street level the sky, and by extension the horizons, appeared more limited even than the congested streets themselves, and the streets of Chinatown offered the Chinese very little hope. Nowhere else in New York were so many people crowded into so small a space, nowhere else was the mean income so low. Although New York was not China, most families lived in a single room, five or six families to each flat, to each kitchen, to each toilet. But then the Chinese were used to limited horizons. To the Chinese a sense of privacy was unknown. They were a realistic people, and their dreams were not large.

A few structures, however, did pretend to Chinese-style architecture. The new branch of the Manhattan Savings Bank was thought by those of its officers who had approved its design to resemble a Buddhist temple. This was expected to be good for business, because the industrious Chinese, if you could attract them, were great savers. Similarly, the Bell Telephone Company some years ago had removed all its standard street-corner phone booths. It had yanked them out like teeth, and had replaced them with booths in the shape of miniature Chinese pagodas—their peaks peeked above the hurrying throngs the way real pagodas peeked above the morning mists back in China. Or so the company liked to believe. The coin boxes inside were American.

And, finally, at the confluence of Mott and Pell streets there stood a single Chinese-type building that was as spurious architecturally as all the others but which, nonetheless, was the most important structure in Chinatown at the moment. The corner of Mott and Pell was where, even today, the heart of Chinatown was said to beat most loudly, because it was here around 1880, with the installation mostly in cellars of a handful of Chinese laundrymen and restaurateurs, hard-working men, not stupid men by any means, men without women, that the oldest of the world's civilizations had first taken root in New York. The early Chinese, in self-preservation, had formed themselves into numerous associations. Men with the same family name gouped together as did men from the same village back in China. Restaurateurs formed their own group, and merchants, laundrymen, and other tradesmen. In addition, there were the tongs. Chinatown had always had tongs, and the new building at the corner of Mott and Pell was today headquarters of the Nam Soong Tong, and the Nam Soongs ruled the New York Chinese.

Tongs, whether in New York or elsewhere, were never quite the benign, fraternal organizations—Oriental versions of the Rotary Club, or Kiwanis—that the Chinese pretended. But neither had they been, at least until now, the sinister criminal conspiracies that the police liked to believe, although certain of their activities, according to American law, had always been and were still criminal. Tongs were not charities, though they supported worthy causes, nor were they political parties, though they supported on occasion particular politicians. That the Chinese conducted tong business secretly was clear. That tongs were nationwide in scope, each chapter having its affiliate in every other American and Canadian Chinatown, was also clear. That these tongs exerted dominance over the Chinese in America was clearest of all, because they both imposed and collected taxes. From their subjects they exacted tribute—keeping no records of how much money they took in, or what they did with it. Or at least no records had ever come to light. That the tongs dominated the Chinese in America was never questioned, but whether or not this was solely due to fear was never clear. Violence, until now, had been rare. In San Francisco a hundred years ago two tongs went at each other with meat cleavers and the blood ran, but such unsavory deportment had not been repeated. Lately there had been, especially in Vancouver and Toronto, in San Francisco and New York, a spate of what appeared to be executions—numerous corpses had turned up—and there had been other acts of violence as well. To the police eye there seemed to be patterns emerging, though no common motivation, and the cops blamed the tongs, which were said to be acting for reasons obscure to the western mind. One other thing the police noted: the leaders of nearly all the tongs had grown extremely old. This was almost the only hard information about them that law enforcement possessed. The same men had been in power half a century more or less, meaning that there was perhaps a struggle for succession going on.

In New York there were two important tongs, plus a number of minor ones, but the Nam Soong was the most powerful by far. It had the largest membership and the fullest coffers, it controlled the most businesses both legal and illegal, on the most streets—it controlled the most territory.

The meeting of the Nam Soong hierarchy that Koy had called began at three o'clock in the afternoon in the pagoda-style building at Mott and Pell streets, in a second-floor conference room whose far wall was decorated with tablets commemorating past presidents of the tong—the ancestors, in effect, of those present. Beneath the tablets on a raised dais sat a statue of Tien Hau, queen of heaven and goddess of the sea, who was said to have power over the storms that beset men's lives. Smoldering joss sticks stood upright in an urn before her and their smoke imparted a cloying incense to the room.

The conference table was oblong, and when Koy entered the room six men were already seated around it. All were in their late sixties or seventies, or even older, and all were millionaires. Because there are only about a hundred Chinese surnames, all of one syllable, and because even fewer than that are current in New York's Chinatown, it happened that three of the six men, none of them related, were named Lee. Two of the others were named Hong, and the sixth was named Lau. Koy, entering, bowed to each of the men in turn—good manners demanded that he bow, not shake hands—and took his place halfway along the table. The head chair was vacant and remained so for some minutes. There was a porcelain, handleless teacup in front of Koy, and he picked this up and toyed with it, while the other men made small talk in Chinese—conversation in which Koy did not take part. All waited.

Presently the door opened and Mr. Ting entered, his head heavily bandaged, followed by a waiter carrying tea on a tray. There was more bowing and smiling, and the waiter poured tea into all the cups. Oolong tea, Koy noted, scented with jasmine. Oolong was tea from the area of Canton, southern tea to match the southern goddess on the dais, to match these southern gentlemen. Every man at the table was from Canton or one of the villages around it.

Ting's right eye was swollen nearly closed. He looked like a man winking at some colossal joke. But there was nothing funny about him or this meeting.

"We have come together," Ting said in English, "to consider last night's incident at my place of business."

His English, Koy noted, was as perfect as that of any other American, bearing no trace of the sing-song accent he offered to patrons of his restaurant.

The man named Lau, New York's largest importer of jade and ivory, spoke in his cracked old-man's voice. "The word in the street is that the attack was carried out by members of the Wee Ching gang, an offshoot of the Ghost Shadows. The Shadows, as you all know, are affiliated with our rival tong across the street."

"If the Shadows themselves had carried out the attack," said one of the men named Lee, "it would be clear that our rival tong was responsible." Lee owned textile factories employing Chinese immigrants under sweatshop conditions, and he was the oldest man in the room, eighty-one.

Another Lee, a landlord, owner of most of the buildings on Pell Street, murmured, "But we cannot be sure who ordered the attack, or even why. It is simply not clear."

Ting said, "It is difficult to see how to react appropriately. And in any case, to react directly against our rival tong would be bad for business. There has been too much violence in Chinatown lately. It has affected all of us. Tourists are afraid to come to Chinatown. Receipts have fallen in many of our businesses. We all hold shares in gambling places and whatnot, and receipts there have fallen too. Although our own people still frequent these places, Filipinos, Japanese, Koreans and others from uptown are becoming afraid to enter Chinatown. The violence must stop."

Setting down his teacup, Koy glanced at each of the old men around the table. "I think all of us are missing the point," he said. "Last night's attack must be seen as a serious loss of face for our tong, and also, I am sorry to add, for our leader, Mr. Ting. You other men are much older than I am. You have been here longer." Koy spoke with great deliberateness, manifesting, at least outwardly, the exquisite Chinese courtesy that was expected of a younger man when addressing his elders. "My respect for men of heaped-up years—men such as yourselves—is very great. But I must suggest that it is time for us to consider a more vigorous leadership."

The unspeakable had been spoken, and silence descended upon the room.

"There is considerable justification in the words of Mr. Koy," said Lau, the importer of jade and ivory, at last.

"Mr. Koy, you've been here how long, five years?" said one of the two men named Hong. He wore thick glasses, and was nearly blind. He had arthritis, and had had to be helped to his chair by his man, who waited outside. He owned ships that sailed from New York and San Francisco to Taiwan and Hong Kong; he was the richest man in the room apart, possibly, from Koy himself. "And formerly, in Hong Kong, you were a policeman. You came here, you observed the tradition of the red envelopes, and within a year became secretary of our tong. It is perhaps better now if you await additional seasoning and experience before advancing further."

A number of heads nodded agreement.

"I would of course observe the tradition of the red envelopes again," murmured Koy.

On both sides of the table, men began whispering to each other in Cantonese dialect. Only Ting at the head of the table sat stock-still. He had been staring at Koy for some minutes, and continued to do so.

Ah, thought Koy, noting this, the subtlety of my plan becomes clear to him. He knows but doesn't know. He is sure, but cannot be sure.

The whispering ended.

"Whoever heads our association becomes known to our people, and to the city at large, as the mayor of Chinatown," said the elder Hong. "It is a position accomplished with honor by Mr. Ting for the last twenty years."

"It is no loss of face for Mr. Ting," suggested Koy piously, "to step down after so many honorable years."

Ting rose to his feet, bowed toward each side of the table, and left the room. Since he was himself the subject under discussion, his presence, according to Chinese custom, had become discourteous. And partly also, his departure was dictated by face. If Ting should be deposed while present, this would constitute a loss of face from which he could never recover. During the time it took him to stride to the door and open it, and for the door to close behind him, no word was spoken. But as soon as he was gone all the businessmen except Koy leaned forward across the table. Koy himself sat bolt upright, like the goddess on the dais on her throne, manifesting the dignity and reserve of one already chosen.

"What steps would you take?" asked Lau presently.

"Of course the first job," said Koy piously, "would be to find and to chastise those youths who carried out the cowardly assault last night on the mayor of Chinatown, Mr. Ting."

The men around the table had lived a long time and had acquired the wisdom that comes with years. Also they were Chinese. That Koy had engineered the massacre himself seemed to them possible, even likely. But they did not pursue their suspicions. The subject held little interest for them. The dead were dead and Ting was about to be superseded. The Golden Palace was no longer their affair. Provided the proprieties were observed, they were prepared to overlook it.

And so the conversation continued in generalities. Business was not good. The world was changing too fast. Too few opportunities for investment existed. It would have been impossible for an outsider to understand what point exactly was being made. Too many street thugs from Hong Kong. But prosperity, they were sure, could not be far off.

Koy nodded agreement. The leaders of the youth gangs, he said, could be "talked to." Future violence might well take place outside of Chinatown. He knew of a number of interesting investments which he might propose at the next meeting. And they were right about the upturn, which he assured them was imminent.

He had just dealt these aged men in as partners, but then he had known from the first he would have to. Without their approval he could not operate in Chinatown at all. Though perhaps too old to start new ventures of their own, they were still powerful enough to stop his. A word to an underling would be enough. Henceforth they would share in his profits—his losses, if any, would be his own. In exchange he could ask them for advice or contacts or for important favors, such as rerouting a ship, or moving currency around the world. For as long as the profits lasted he would have their sanction. They would not want to know too much about where the profits came from.

Koy had many partners already—one could not run a worldwide organization without them—and Ting, when he returned to this room, would be another. But partnerships insured harmony, up to a point, and harmony was a quality greatly prized by the Chinese. Without harmony success in business was difficult to attain.

"The weight of responsibility is heavy on my shoulders," said Koy, inclining his head.

The elder Mr. Hong said, "In Little Italy, only two streets to the north, there is a candy store affiliated with one of the Italian families. The proprietor furnishes guns to Chinese youths." Removing his thick glasses, he rubbed his nearly blind eyes. "The Chinese community has lost much face."

"I will look into the matter," said Koy.

Hong's generalized statement, together with Koy's polite answer, seemed the last of the details to be settled. All heads except Koy's came together, and there was much whispering in Cantonese. When this ended the old men sat back and all turned to Mr. Lau who, as spokesman, would deliver the verdict.

Lau said, "Mr. Koy was perhaps sent here by the gods to return our community to the prosperity of the past."

"Yellow gold is plentiful compared to white-haired friends," said Mr. Koy.

ABOUT AN hour later Koy went through the glass doors, up the rococo staircase and into Ting's restaurant. The place was noisy, for plasterers, painters and electricians, about a dozen men in all, were at work. Mr. Ting, who had been watching from his cash desk, came forward. He and Koy gave each other perfunctory bows.

"Won't you sit down?" asked Ting. "Would you like a cup of tea?"

While a waiter went for tea, the two men sat at a table and stared at each other.

Ting said: "The two waiters who were killed last night—"

"They will be buried tomorrow from my establishment at no cost to you or to our tong. They will be given appropriate funerals."

The tea was served. Both men sipped from small porcelain bowls.

"When will you be able to reopen for business?" asked Koy politely.

"The workmen have promised to be finished tonight. But there is much to do."

"It was gracious of you to serve me tea," said Koy politely. He stood up. "I must go."

Ting also stood. The ceremony of the transition of power, which now took place, was extremely brief and extremely private. Koy handed over a red envelope—red envelopes were on sale in shops all over Chinatown—passing it with both hands. To the Chinese, the giving of a gift with one hand is discourteous. Ting did not open the envelope, which was as fat as a small pillow. To open a gift in the presence of the donor is discourteous also, and neither man wished to slight the other. To do so would be to court unacceptable risk for the future.

But this ceremony had been conducted with perfect manners on both sides. It was now over. If Ting felt pain at losing his prestige and his office after twenty years, it did not show. Nothing showed. When in the presence of your enemy, the Chinese say, hide your broken arms in your sleeves.

Ting waited until the door had closed behind Koy, then fingered open the red envelope and glanced inside. He saw that it was full of money, and he was satisfied. Form had been preserved, and therefore face. Indeed, Chinese delicacy in this matter—as in all such matters—had altered the nature of the entire transaction. No one now could go to war over it. No one could any longer be certain that Ting's office had been taken from him. Even he and Koy could not be sure. Perhaps he had merely sold it, and at a good price.

As for Koy, he was now the most important Chinese in America, but outside on the sidewalk he did not smirk or gloat, or contemplate his new domain, or stretch out his arms to embrace it. Instead he strode purposefully past the crowds and the hawkers, past the fruit and vegetable stalls pushed out almost to the curbs, toward his undertaking parlor. There Chang and Nikki Han awaited him, as did a number of other persons, some of them employees, some clients. His instructions to Chang could be given publicly; he ordered the embalmer to collect the two waiters from the city morgue and to prepare them as best he could for burial the next day. Then after brief bows to the other men, he took Nikki Han into his private office, where he outlined what he wanted done about the Italian candy store, a simple problem for which he proposed a simple solution.

6

THOUGH NOT expensive, the caskets would have pleased their inhabitants very much. The two waiters lying in state lay cushioned by more luxury than either, living, could ever have aspired to. For many years both had been sending small sums back to China for their eventual funerals—funerals were important to the Chinese—but what they had hoped for was nothing like this. This was beyond their imagining.

Most of the family associations, trade associations and even the tongs had sent floral pieces, and the crowds filed in off Mott Street four abreast. Chang had done a good job on the corpses. Both waiters wore open-necked shirts, and one had been furnished with the traditional skullcap of Chinese scholars, as a means of concealing the missing crown of his head.

The viewing room was extremely smoky, and not just from the joss sticks. To pay their expenses on the other side the waiters would need money, but money in its physical state could not accompany dead persons through the barrier; first it had to be reduced to insubstantiality through burning. But Chinese mourners, however traditional and superstitious about death, are by no means sentimental about it. Real money is not needed; play money will do, and Koy furnished stacks of it to be burned in urns in front of each casket. The queues therefore moved past slowly, each viewer bowing three times to each corpse, then pausing to light up money, and the smoke from the money rose to mingle with smoke from the joss and with perfume from the masses of flowers, and the nostrils of all present were assaulted by an abundance of powerful and conflicting odors.

At last Koy gave the signal for the caskets to be closed. The lids clapped shut, the corpses had seen their last of this world. The pallbearers hefted the boxes, and the procession went out the door and started past crowds that filled both sidewalks. Koy, who wore a white suit, was in the lead, followed by other businessmen in white, and he stepped forward with exaggerated slowness while Chinese instruments, particularly cymbals, played a tinny dirge behind him. Along the curbs stood policemen in blue uniforms, and far ahead the precinct commander, Captain Gibson, sat on his horse, the better to observe the curious burial customs of the heathen Chinese. As for the Chinese multitudes, many of whom fell in behind the coffins, they saw the scene as much more than a funeral. To them Koy was the equivalent of a general at the head of an advancing army. He was like an emperor leading a nation, and the nation was themselves. A new dynasty had come to power, and their fears were thousands of years old—that their sons would be conscripted for some dirty job or other, and that their taxes would be increased.

Ahead was Canal Street, the frontier between Chinatown and Little Italy, where Koy's hearses already waited.

Across Canal, a short distance inside alien country, stood a candy store belonging to a medium-level Mafioso named Carniglia. Although he actually did sell candy, comic books and such from time to time, Carniglia's real business was guns. The organization to which he belonged regularly hijacked trucks carrying arms shipments, often with the connivance of insiders at the factories, and after each successful hijacking Carniglia was allotted his share of goods to dispose of. He was well placed. In the gun business, a candy store counted as an ideal front, the best imaginable. Teenaged boys were always hanging around candy stores. The candy attracted them first and they stayed to buy guns. The cops didn't even notice. To them boys and candy went together. Because Carniglia was not in business to get arrested and do time, teenaged boys constituted by far the major part of his clientele—he never sold guns to adults he did not know, in case the adult turned out to be an undercover cop. By selling only to teenagers, such risks were eliminated entirely. His potential adult market, therefore, was small, whereas his teenage market was limitless. There were new teenage customers every year. Carniglia and a few others like him armed all the New York youth gangs. Carniglia did not care what happened to the guns he sold. He considered himself a businessman. It was simply none of his affair.

Lately a whole new market had opened up for him— the Chinese. All Carniglia's life the Chinamen had been there south of Canal Street. The Chinese youth had been passive. Suddenly they were not only buying guns but using them. Carniglia read the papers. He knew how to count corpses. Every time he read about a dead Chinaman, it made him laugh. He had no use for the Chinks. They talked garbage, and they ate garbage. Worse, they had now invaded Little Italy. They were flooding across Canal Street. Recently the stores to either side of Carniglia had both been taken over by Chinese. The yellow flood would submerge his entire neighborhood, Carniglia saw, and although he hated this, it was good for business. The Italians were beginning to move out and soon Little Italy would be no more, but before it happened, if business stayed this good, Carniglia would be rich. In tapping the Chinese youth market, Carniglia was not trying to cause the Chinese to lose face. The idea had not occurred to him. He was not trying to affront the tong or Koy or anyone else. He didn't know Koy existed. He knew nothing about Chinatown society and hadn't troubled to find out. He was simply making money.

Unaware of the funeral taking place across Canal Street, Carniglia was engaged in a transaction even now in the back room of his store. He had unlocked his safe and tossed several guns onto a table. Three Chinese boys were fingering them, talking to each other while Carniglia watched with shrewd sharp eyes, trying to judge how much they would be willing to pay.

"How much for this one?" one of the boys asked.

It always surprised Carniglia to hear a Chink speak English with a New York accent. To Carniglia, if a Chinese boy spoke perfect English he must be a genius. There was no other way he could have learned it that good.

"That's a Ruger Security-Six. Stainless. Nice piece, factory new. That gun will set you back $500."

There was more conversation in Chinese. It irritated Carniglia. He frowned.

"How much for three?"

"You want three, I could come down a little bit. You want a dozen, I can come down a lot."

Just then Carniglia became conscious of a customer out front. Leaving the three teenagers, he went out and stood behind the counter.

The customer was another Chinese youth, who seemed to be looking the place over. Carniglia had never seen him before. To his experienced eye this was a potential buyer of guns. He was making his first visit, feeling his way.

"You want something?" demanded Carniglia.

The boy held up a Hershey bar. "How much?"

He had a Chink accent, Carniglia noted.

"Thirty-five cents."

The boy put the money down and went out. Carniglia watched him stroll toward a car containing other Chink kids. He'll be back, Carniglia thought. He put the thirty-five cents in his pocket and went back to conclude the gun sale.

The boy, meanwhile, had got into the car. The driver was Nikki Han. A third Chinese boy was in the back seat. All three stared at the entrance to Carniglia's store, while the first boy gave his report in Cantonese. There was nobody in front of the store; in the back was Carniglia, with three members of a rival gang.

"Couldn't be better," said Nikki Han in Cantonese and he ordered the other two to check their pieces.

In the floorwell at their feet both boys had machine shotguns. Nikki listened to the loud clicks as the shells were chambered.

BY THIS time the funeral cortege had proceeded about one block, and Captain Powers, searching for Captain Gibson, had entered Mott Street on foot from the Canal Street end. Although there were dense crowds on both sidewalks, Powers, who was in uniform, spotted Gibson on his horse and went up to him.

"Hello, Willy," Powers said. "How's the view up there?"

They had known each other twenty years, and liked each other no better now than at the beginning. "You can see a long way from up here," said Gibson. He sat stolidly and answered stolidly, and he seemed to Powers as stolid as the horse itself. He did not offer to get down and talk man to man.

"Still believe in keeping a high police profile, I see," said Powers.

If Gibson saw the sarcasm, he gave no notice. "Police visibility is the strongest deterrent to crime," he said stolidly.

"You haven't been deterring too much of it around here lately."

Gibson looked straight out between his horse's ears.

As Powers considered what to say next he could hear the tin dirge, and from time to time he caught a glimpse of the oncoming men in white. "What's this," he asked, "a wedding?"

"A funeral. The Chinese wear white for funerals."

"I didn't know that."

"There's a lot you don't know."

Powers was getting a crick in his neck from looking up. "Who's the big guy out front?" he asked after a moment.

"That's Mr. Koy, the undertaker. He's also the new mayor of Chinatown."

Powers was surprised. "What happened to Mr. Ting?"

71

"Deposed."

Powers waited for details. None came.

"Willy, I want to ask you some questions."

"I have nothing to say to you," said Gibson.

"Yes you do."

"I'm busy."

"Would you get down off that goddamn horse and talk to me for a minute?"

"Why?"

"Because you're not in command here anymore, that's why. They just cut off your oats."

A stricken look came over Gibson's face. Powers recognized it at once and was moved to pity. "There's a fuel crisis on," he said, his voice softening, "haven't you heard?"

Gibson got heavily down off his horse. "Is it because of the Golden Palace?" he asked. "Does headquarters blame me for the Golden Palace? How was I supposed to prevent that? How am I supposed to prevent anything around here? I've been asking for additional men. I asked for all kinds of things. I wrote I don't know how many forty-nines. At headquarters they didn't take no action on any of them. Chinatown is a very low priority item, you'll find. What else did you want to know?"

"All of it," Powers said. "Tell me all of it. How bad is it here?"

LESS THAN two blocks away Nikki Han put the car in gear and inched forward. "Now," he said in Cantonese dialect. He had stopped directly in front of the candy store.

The two youths brought their shotguns up from the floor, stuck the barrels out the windows and pulled the triggers. Their explosive fanfare commenced. Their tune played. For the first time in their lives it seemed to them that they could actually see noise.

The plate glass front window shattered, and the glass front door. Inside the store the glass showcases exploded, and the counter stools spun wildly about. Plaster fell. Candy spattered the walls, and ceilings. It mixed with plaster and clung like glue. Only after the shooting stopped did all that smoke and dust begin to seep like incense out the door, out the window to hang in a small cloud above the sidewalk. By then, squealing as if with excitement, as if with delight, the assault car was gone.

Inside the store for almost a minute there was no movement at all. Then Carniglia peeped carefully out of the back room. As the smoke cleared, the wreckage of his store gradually became visible. He could see part of the empty street outside as well, and he knew instinctively that the shooting was over. Stepping over the broken plaster, the candy, the shards of glass, he reached the sidewalk and stared around. The three Chinese customers came running out past him. He watched them. They took off, running in three different directions.

Across Canal Street the assembled multitudes had heard the noise, and people had begun murmuring among themselves. Many of the men in the funeral cortege had glanced up startled, but they did not break ranks, and Koy in his white suit took no notice whatever.

The two police captains, Powers and Gibson, had reacted immediately, however. Neither needed to be told what they had heard. Gibson had vaulted up into the saddle, wheeled his horse around, and cantered up Mott Street to Canal, a busy eight-lane intersection at that point, the main cross-street linking the Holland Tunnel from New Jersey to the Manhattan Bridge over to Brooklyn. He cantered straight across through the cars and trucks, barely slowing his horse down. Powers, running hard, was not far behind, and he had been joined in his sprint by a number of foot patrolmen.

In front of the devastated candy store Gibson dismounted, and hung the reins over a parking meter. "What happened?" he demanded, but Carniglia only stood there, and the two men stared at each other. Powers and the foot patrolmen ran up.

"What happened?" asked Captain Gibson again.

"What do you mean, what happened," answered Carniglia. "Somebody shot up my fuckin' store, that's what happened."

"Why would anybody want to do that?" asked Gibson.

"You tell me, pal," replied Carniglia. "You tell me."

But Carniglia believed he knew why. He understood the message, and believed his superiors would also. The Chinese wanted in. They wanted their share of the business, or perhaps more than their share, and would not hesitate to back their demands with force. They had served notice. They were very strong. They had more men, more money and a far more widespread organization, and the Italians had best not try to stop them. Carniglia turned to study the Chinese-owned stores to either side of his own. They were untouched. We're going to lose more than real estate before this is over, Carniglia thought.

"The shooters," demanded Powers, "were they Chinese?"

"That's quite a question," said Carniglia. "You got any other good questions like that?"

Gibson turned to Powers. "Why should they be Chinese? This is not Chinatown here, Artie. This is Little Italy here."

"Were they Chinese?" repeated Powers.

Carniglia turned away. "I got nothing to say, pal. You got any questions, you put them in writing and send them to my lawyer."

"I'll handle the interrogation if you don't mind, Artie," said Gibson stiffly.

Powers, needing a place to sit down so that he could think, went back to the 79th Precinct in Brooklyn where he was second in command. Although technically not on duty at this hour, he went into his office and sat in his swivel chair and stared out the window. After a time his attention was caught by the messages on his desk. There had been two more calls from Carol Cone. That meant five in all, including yesterday's. He had not returned any of them. He was surprised at her persistence. The next thing he knew she would call him at home. Although his home number was not listed, nonetheless she was a reporter and could probably track it down if she tried. Either she would call him at home or she wouldn't. He did not care one way or the other. He was not interested in Carol Cone at the moment, but rather in whatever might be left of his career. His entire life seemed at stake in the next few hours, and he was trying to figure out what to do.

An idea came to him, and he mulled it over. After a few minutes he picked up the phone and dialed a number. The police commissioner's eunuch came on the line. Powers, who did not know him, said he had confidential information on Chinatown to give the PC. He asked to meet with him alone. The man said he would call Powers back, and hung up.

By Police Department standards, Powers had made an outrageous request, outrageous for two reasons. First, because the PC's time was precious. He met only with two-star chiefs and above. He met only with deputy commissioners. Even they never dared seek audiences, but were summoned. To communicate with the PC, captains like Powers were supposed to write out their grievance on a forty-nine and send it, unsealed, up through precinct, division and borough commanders, collecting endorsements and comments along the way, until maybe it reached headquarters a month later. Or it might get short-circuited by someone, either deliberately or accidentally, producing the police-department equivalent of total darkness. Or it might just get bucked right back down again. The PC might never see it.

So Powers' request might outrage the PC. Certainly it would outrage any intervening commanders who heard about it. Powers had just taken a terrible risk, and knew it, and for what? Even if granted ten or fifteen minutes with the PC, what could he hope to accomplish in so short a time?

And secondly, he had promised confidential information. "Confidential" to cops was a sacred word. To police ears it had a pure bell ring to it. Confidential information

came to cops from confidential informants, usually criminals, so that the word signaled each time the existence of a
human relationship that was wholly new, fragile, more rare
than love, as dangerous as life itself. "Confidential," in the
police world, signaled usually the first step in the triumph of
good over evil; the triumph of man's noblest ideal, justice,
over all of his other baser instincts. It signaled the onset of
emotions that were basically religious in nature. It was a
word to raise hopes sky high. It was almost another word for
God. Like certain other words, "fire" or "wolf" for instance,
it evoked unreasoning responses. For a cop to abuse it was
blasphemy, a sin against faith.

It was a word that unlocked doors. It was a word that
captains could use to get in to see police commissioners.
And yet, what could Powers tell the PC that was justifiably
"confidential"?

He spent the next twenty minutes seated at his desk
arranging and rearranging the five telephone messages from
Carol Cone. He laid them out vertically, and horizontally,
and in a circle. He pushed them around like playing cards
and wondered why he imagined that the PC would give him
an answer right away.

After a time he noted that Carol had given two different call-back numbers, so he got out his address book and
wrote in both. He entered the numbers, but not her name,
in the W section, under the call letters of her station.

His phone rang. The deputy inspector. He said
the PC would see Captain Powers at 8:45 the following
morning.

As Powers hung up he felt a smile come onto his face.
It was his first that day, and he went out into the muster
room, where the desk sergeant stopped him.

Chief Duncan's office had just called. Powers was to
call back forthwith.

Powers thought about this a moment. His smile had
vanished.

"Do me a favor," he told the desk sergeant. "Call back
Duncan's office. Tell them that I was in earlier, but I'm not

76

here now. Tell them I'm not on duty tonight. Tell them you're trying to find me."

"But I did find you, Captain."

"Just tell them you don't know where I am, okay?"

Outside it was nearly dark. Powers got into his car and began the long drive home.

7

BY 9:00 A.M. Powers had been waiting twenty minutes, but above the PC's door the red light remained lit. He wore his best and newest uniform. His wife had worked hard on it. Its creases were perfect, its buttons shone. He had stood by the ironing board cheering her on. He had worked on his shoes himself. He had polished them twenty minutes. He had polished them to a gloss. They shone like black glass.

The deputy inspector continued to open and stack the PC's mail. He did not look up.

Powers, pacing and fretting, stared up at the red light. He was in custody here. The red light was as restrictive as handcuffs or a jail cell. It was a means the PC used to exert his will through the door. There was no way that Powers waiting, or anyone waiting, could exert his own will back. The PC was untouchable. Waiting, Powers could not even sit down for fear of wrinkling his uniform. Men were geniuses at thinking up ways to unnerve other men, he reflected—"the games men play to give each other heart attacks," was the way his wife described it.

The red light winked out.

The deputy inspector got up and went into the PC's office. Left behind, Powers became as conscious of his appearance as a boy waiting for his date to come down the stairs. He straightened his tie, his hair. He tugged his jacket down so that it would lie smoothly over his gun belt and service revolver.

"The PC will see you now."

As Powers went through the door he saw that the PC's office was dark. The drapes had been drawn, and they were heavy drapes. A thin sliver of sunlight sliced across the rug. It cut the rug in two. Whether by accident or design it formed a barrier that Powers chose not to cross. He advanced only that far and stopped. The PC, in shirtsleeves behind his desk, glanced up.

Powers' opening line was rehearsed and he spoke it with assurance: "It was good of you to agree to see me privately, Commissioner."

But at once he became conscious of other men in the room. He felt their presence in the shadows behind him. With a stir of movement they came forward.

"You know Chief Duncan, I believe," the PC said. "And Deputy Commissioner Glazer of Public Affairs."

Powers, trying to reorient himself, said, "I was hoping to speak to you alone, sir."

"I have no secrets from these two men," said the PC. His eyes narrowed, he appraised Powers briefly, then shifted his gaze to Duncan. "And Chief Duncan, as chief of the patrol forces in this city, is your commander. Properly speaking, he's the one you should be reporting to, not me."

Duncan said, "Your twenty-four hours were up last night, I believe. In fact I asked one of my men to reach out for you, but he was unable to locate where you were."

Powers fixed his attention on the PC. "Commissioner, I've been offered command of the Fifth Precinct, as you know. Before deciding whether to accept the assignment, I determined to talk to people with knowledge of Chinatown, Federal agencies in addition to our own people. I've now talked to Immigration, the FBI, to Drug Enforcement. I've talked to our own Intelligence Division, and to the present commander of the Chinatown precinct. I've learned some things. I concluded that I would be derelict in my duty if I made my decision without talking over with you what I've learned." It was a rather lengthy speech, and perhaps a pompous one, and long before it ended the PC had begun stirring through papers on his desk.

If he wasn't going to listen, thought Powers, why did he agree to see me at all?

"Go on," the PC said, but his attention had been caught by something and he was reading it.

Powers stepped forward across the sliver of sunlight. He raised the volume of his voice, changed its cadence and added energetic gestures. He was like an actor in a play trying to control an audience that had begun to cough.

"There are now more Chinese living in New York City," he proceeded, "than in any other city, including San Francisco, anywhere outside the Orient. Most of them are honest, hard-working and very poor people. Most of them have escaped from Red China into Hong Kong, where they were exploited by the Chinese already there. So they kept going. They emigrated to the United States—they call this country the Gold Mountain—where they are still being exploited. There are at least two highly sophisticated organized-crime syndicates preying on these people and on the rest of the city as well. The syndicates are allied in some mysterious way to the major tongs, or perhaps they've taken over the tongs, we're not really sure. The syndicates run about twelve gambling dens that are open around the clock, and at the moment we allow them to stay open."

Duncan said, "I didn't know captains had received orders to criticize department policy."

"A statement of fact is not criticism," said Powers, "it is a statement of fact."

But the PC, who might have smiled or in some way encouraged Powers' recital, did not look up.

"The cash from gambling," Powers continued, "finances all their other illegal activities, especially drugs. The Chinese are now the largest importers of drugs in New York. The heroin comes through Hong Kong from Southeast Asia. Cash flow from the gambling and the drugs is so great that the Chinese syndicates are buying up legal businesses and real estate The syndicates are in conflict with each other—these recent killings seem to point to a struggle for power within Chinese organized crime itself—and they are in conflict with the Italians. That's what yesterday's assault on the candy store in Little Italy was all about, we think."

Chief Duncan interjected coldly, "There is no evidence whatsoever that the assault on the candy store was carried out by Chinese."

"Yes there is. I talked to witnesses."

"The detectives found no such witnesses, Commissioner."

"Maybe by the time the detectives got there, the witnesses were gone," said Powers.

"I don't believe this, Commissioner." Duncan turned back to Powers. "Why would the Chinese shoot up an Italian candy store?"

"The Feds had information that guns were being sold out of that store to Chinese youth gangs."

"If the Feds had such information, they would have acted on it. Why didn't they?"

"Ask them, don't ask me," snapped Powers.

The PC had glanced up sharply. He peered over his glasses first at Duncan, then at Powers. He peered at them almost with amusement, like a parent watching a squabble among children.

Deputy Commissioner Glazer said: "Are you saying that in just a year or two the Chinese have managed to establish their own Mafia here?"

"No sir. They already had their own Mafia in Hong Kong. They simply spread here, and the Chinese crime families appear to be both more sophisticated and richer than the Italian families ever were. The Mafia concept is not Italian anyway. It's Chinese. It was invented in China three or four thousand years ago. The Chinese crime syndicates are called Triads. What we are suddenly facing here are offshoots of the Hong Kong Triads."

Duncan said to the PC, "Commissioner, I've heard this claptrap before, and that's all it is, claptrap, which Chief Cirillo can verify, and I suggest we get him in here."

The PC agreed, and the chief of detectives was sent

for. All waited in silence until he came through the door, moving softly for such a chunky man, glancing around carefully to see who was present, searching for clues as to what the subject might be. The half-chomped cigar he affected everywhere else was missing here, Powers noted. Cirillo is another of the PC's eunuchs, he thought.

"Repeat what you just told us," ordered Duncan.

Powers paraphrased it. It came out, unfortunately, not only briefer, but also weaker.

"Where did you get your information from?" asked Cirillo.

"Well, first I went to the Drug Enforcement Administration, and—"

"Commissioner," Cirillo interrupted, "the DEA has been peddling that Chinese Mafia theory for years. There's absolutely nothing in it. And I wouldn't believe anything those clowns said anyway. About ten years ago they made a few cases in Chinatown. They haven't done a thing since."

Powers said, "According to Immigration—"

"Those guys," snorted Cirillo. He gave a short laugh. "Commissioner, that's the most corrupt agency in the country. It doesn't require any Chinese Mafia to bribe them. They take money from anybody. They ought to spend some time investigating themselves."

"That candy store was shot up by Chinese," insisted Powers.

"So you say," said Cirillo. "I'll look into it."

"Satisfied?" inquired Duncan.

Powers was not satisfied. He said stubbornly, "There is too much interconnected crime down there for it all to be free-lance."

Deputy Commissioner Glazer said, "The words 'Chinese Mafia.' I wouldn't go bandying them about too much, if I were you." His tone was both unctuous and anxious. "Those are dangerous words for us. The newspapers get a hold of those words, they'll go to town with them. The mayor will want to know what we're doing to break up the Chinese Mafia. People will be all over us. We don't need pressure like that."

Powers glanced around from face to face. He was surrounded, and nearly out of ammunition. The PC, scanning something on his desk, was not even looking at him. "Commissioner," Powers said, "you are asking me to take over what might be an impossible job."

The PC glanced up. "Captain Powers, as I understand it, you've been carping on what's wrong with this department ever since you made captain. Here's your chance to show us what you can do." He gave a cold smile. "So it's a difficult job. You wouldn't want an easy one, would you?"

This speech concluded, the PC's attention again flagged. The man had flipped the page of his appointment calendar and begun to study it.

"All right," said Powers, "I'll take Chinatown." His next lines depended for their effect upon the assurance with which he could project them, but because he was talking to the top of the PC's head, with Glazer, Cirillo and Duncan still in the room, he began talking too fast. "But I'll need time." Immediately he forced himself to slow down. "That's the first of my conditions."

But trying to correct his error was as useless as trying to correct an explosion. Since the action could not be reversed, one could not correct anything. And in any case, which rate of speech was the correct one? Only an assured man would know.

"I want you to guarantee me two years. And secondly—" Although it was possible to counterfeit most emotional states, hatred or love for instance, it was not possible to counterfeit assurance, which relied, like the structure of the atom, on the harmony of too many too-cunning particles. If any one were out of place, the thing self-destructed, and this was visible to all.

"I need what the Chinese think of as face. Face is not a Japanese concept, as you may have thought." A person who could not gauge a man's age within ten years or his weight within fifty pounds could detect the flicker of a muscle in his cheek, or the breath that came in the wrong part of a sentence. Voice timbre that changed to a minute degree sounded as blatant as trumpets. Assurance thrived only in the absence of passion, which was why it was so rare and so prized. It was an absolute, which hatred was not, nor love either. There was purity to it. It was perfect.

"Face is Chinese in origin," Powers concluded. "Chinatown has had a steady successions of captains in there. If I'm to be effective, I need more face than that. I'm asking you to send me in there as a deputy inspector."

The PC looked up. "Don?"

Duncan said: "We have seventy-six precinct commanders in this city. Every single one of them has his unique problems."

"Whether or not there is a Chinese Mafia," Powers said, "Chinatown is about to explode."

"You get six months," said Duncan. "Same as any other precinct commander. Six months to produce results."

The PC had stood up behind his desk. The interview was over. "Your need for extra rank seems exaggerated," he said. "I want you to go in there and suppress the youth gangs. At the end of six months we'll evaluate your performance, and if you've done a good job, we'll consider promoting you to deputy inspector then. And we don't want to read anything in the papers about any Chinese Mafia, eh? That wouldn't be a good idea. You get my meaning?"

Powers got his meaning. A man of real power, he saw, did not need to present his threats as threats.

A slight smirk had come onto Duncan's face. Powers saw it and his eyes blazed. He sent thunderbolts across the room, but failed to blast that smirk away. Duncan merely glanced down at the floor, still smirking.

"Am I in charge of the Golden Palace investigation?" Powers asked the PC.

"Chief of Detectives Cirillo is handling that investigation personally," answered Duncan. "The Golden Palace investigation is not your business."

"And the assault on the candy store?"

"That's not your business either. Your business is running the precinct."

The PC said: "We just want to see the arrest rate go

up, and the crime rate down." He came around the desk, his hand outstretched like a politician's. "I'm sure you'll do a fine job, Captain."

Powers, defeated, inclined his head and left the office.

He went immediately home. He lived in a three-story brick house in a row of similar private houses on a hill on Park Terrace West in the Inwood section of Manhattan. It was the same neighborhood and parish in which he had grown up, though not on a street as fine as this one, for his father had been a liquor salesman. He had bought his house during the fifth year of his marriage with a down payment borrowed from his wife's father. He had paid that loan off, and in two more years his mortgage too would be entirely paid off. The slate-roofed house had a small garden, almost all of which cowered under a weeping willow tree. The willow was stately, even noble, but under it grass struggled and mostly failed to grow. Even flowers would not grow, and Powers sometimes thought its domination of his garden resembled the police department's domination of his life.

During Powers' boyhood, Park Terrace West was where the rich kids lived, doctors' and lawyers' sons, kids whom he played with but secretly detested, and whose existence he imagined to be idyllic. From grade school on he had coveted the life style they would accede to, and therefore their houses, and he had brought Eleanor by to look them over in the early days of their courtship. By that time the neighborhood had deteriorated somewhat, most of the rich kids and their parents had moved away, and such a house was no longer impossibly beyond the dreams of a young policeman who intended to rise swiftly within the department. Powers' youthful ambitions for the most part had been in no way original. He had wanted to marry the best girl, and live in a big house on Park Terrace West, and he had achieved both those goals reasonably early in life, though not his third goal, which was to attain the rank of chief of detectives at least. He had hoped one day to be named police commissioner too, but had realized from the start that this would take luck. The PC was a political appointee. Merit helped a cop only as far as captain, a level one achieved principally by passing examinations. No high-ranking officer or commissioner could intervene. Powers' rise to captain had been inexorable. But all ranks above captain were appointed by whoever was PC that year. Each one promoted officers for his own reasons, or for reasons advanced by advisers who had his ear, mostly the latter. PCs came and went, but the advisers tended to remain. Cliques formed and, for as long as they lasted, reigned. Sometimes merit counted and sometimes scores were settled. Some officers advanced and some did not, and that was that.

Powers, entering his solid brick house, found his wife in the kitchen putting away groceries.

"You came home to surprise me," she said. "I'm to have the pleasure of making your lunch."

Powers smiled. Glum as he felt, it was nice that she was there and that he liked her so much.

"I came home to lay my head in your lap."

"I don't like the sound of that."

Hanging his jacket and gun belt over the back of a chair, sitting down heavily, Powers began to describe his interview with the PC.

"I feel like a fighter who just lost every round," he said.

"But you did take the job."

"I didn't see where I had any choice."

"It's a precinct," his wife said, moving behind him, and embracing him from behind his chair, her cheek against his. "You'll do fine. I know you will."

"It's an impossible situation in there."

"I'll make you an omelet. Then I have to leave."

Earlier Powers had gone to the public library on Forty-second Street where he had collected a number of books on Chinese history, on the Chinese language, on the Chinese experience in America. When his wife had gone out he put on his half-glasses, opened to the first page of the first tome, and attempted to wade into his new life's work. It was like wading through mud. He felt dull and unwilling, like a schoolboy forced to ingest a subject not only beyond his understanding, but also beyond any conceivable interest to him, now or ever. It was an emotion Powers thought he had seen the last of twenty-five years earlier. Like a schoolboy he wanted to rebel, but he would have to do the work eventually or go under, and he refused to go under—the instinct to survive was stronger than any other, stronger than humiliation, stronger than pain.

To help the people of Chinatown he would first have to find out who they were, and he kept reading.

The volume in his lap was as thick as a blacksmith's anvil and as heavy, as was its prose. Presently he put it down, and got up and went to stare out the window. What he needed was to talk, not study, to unburden himself of these violent emotions, principally anger, that churned around inside him. He wished his wife were there to talk to, and he resented her for being out of the house, focused on her own life, and not his.

She had worked as a nurse until their first son was born, and now that both boys were in college she had gone back to it. She managed an entire floor at St. Clare's hospital on Fiftieth Street, and at first she used to come home and regale him with tales of each day's heartbreaking cases. They were descriptions he did not wish to hear, and she soon came to understand this. The result was that she no longer talked about her work at all, any more than Powers talked about his. The world was full of malignancy, some of it deliberate, and one simply lived with this, one could not turn it into cheerful conversation, and had best not try. Her hours had now become as erratic as his—hospitals, like police stations, were busy around the clock. Each knew vaguely what the other's schedules were, they made their off-duty hours coincide as much as possible, and for the rest they came together at odd times as they could. But more and more Powers hated the fact that she wanted to work. He longed for the old days when Eleanor's life had revolved totally around him, and he hoped she would see this for herself without his saying so, though so far she had not.

For most of the afternoon he remained at the win-

dow, watching the cars go by. Despite himself he kept replaying in his head every line from that morning, reliving
his humiliation. In terms of moving men to action, humiliation may be the strongest of human emotions. It causes
not only the blood to boil but also the brain, so that a man's
paramount desire becomes to strike out in some way. Any
action becomes better than none. It was out of humiliation
that, late in the afternoon, Powers decided to risk more of
the same. He telephoned Carol Cone.

"I thought you might like to get your coat back," he
said when she came on the line. He had kept his voice bright
and cheerful so as not to scare her off. He could not stand it
any longer inside this house and himself. But to go out he
needed a destination.

"By now I thought maybe you had sold it."

He managed a light, confident laugh. "So just tell the
delivery man where to take it."

He had thought to meet her downtown, perhaps in a
restaurant near her network. But she was off that night and
on her way home, she said. To his surprise she told him that
she lived in Bronxville, a rich Westchester suburb. Why
didn't he come for a drink about six?

Why not indeed?

8

HER CAR was in the driveway, a $25,000 open Mercedes. He parked his four-year-old Mustang behind it and got out. He supposed it was her car. The plates read CC-44, her initials plus the number on the door of her house. Who else could it belong to?

Despite his age, he was no more sure of himself, as he approached this woman, than he might have been at twenty. Did the new sexually liberated generation, exposed (literally) to dozens of girls and women from adolescence on, approach them with more confidence? He didn't know. Hesitating still, Powers fingered the ostentatious car in front of him. Real leather seats. Chrome. Did she leave it out to impress him? He walked across the lawn and rang her bell.

She wore tight blue jeans and a loose blouse. He carried her raincoat clutched in his fist and it preceded him into battle like a weapon or a shield. It masked his vulnerability. It was something with which to ward off blows.

"Thank you," she said, and disarmed him. "Well," she said, "come on in."

The house itself unsettled him further. It was big. He had to come to terms with the idea that its owner was an unattached woman. She ran this house and household, occupied space in the world exactly the way a man did. He had never thought of a woman in this light before and it was difficult for him. She was not a man. She would not know how to fix a leaking faucet, and she would be subject to all of a woman's curious vulnerabilities. Or would she? She was too new to him. He could not be sure.

Did her house give any clues? In her living room stood two barber's chairs. They were low leather chairs out of some rich men's club probably. They shocked Powers. So did a Wurlitzer jukebox that served as her sound system. So did what it was playing: rock music.

"I was listening to the Bee Gees," she said. "Do you like the Bee Gees?"

As a conversational opening this reminded Powers of his adolescence, and as music the Bee Gees did not match his age—or hers. He was glancing around, trying to learn about her from the decor. But there was no one style here. Nothing matched. Real Persian rugs on the floor. Abstract paintings on two of the walls. Signed photographs on a table of Carol interviewing celebrities, including the President of the United States.

"Would you like a drink? What would you like?"

He looked her over. She wore a lot of makeup today too, and looked younger than he remembered. She had rather more bosom than he remembered as well. She had a nice figure.

"I'll have whatever you're having."

He followed her into the kitchen where she took a bottle of chablis out of the fridge. He followed her outside onto a terrace. Long shadows on her lawn. She opened and poured the wine. There was a short upsweep of grass and then flowers amid rocks. He stared into the cold white wine. She must pay a gardener plenty, he thought.

"Is that nicer than Chinese champagne?" she said, and he laughed.

There were certain questions that had to be asked immediately. Otherwise no relationship of whatever kind was possible. He began to ask them.

"Do you live alone in this big house?"

The house, she said, was for her daughter, because all children should grow up in houses, not apartments, didn't Powers agree? Her daughter, who was away at college at the moment, was eighteen. Carol added quickly, "I was married very young."

So she was sensitive about her age, whatever it was.

"You never remarried?"

No. She was perfectly willing to talk about her life, much of which, he supposed, had appeared in gossip columns. Her concept of privacy was not the same as his. She had been divorced fourteen years, and had since lived, she said, four years with one man, almost five with another. She had almost married the first one. They had taken out a license, a date was set. Powers did not ask what went wrong and she did not tell him. Instead she peered wistfully off into the middle distance.

"And you? Are you still married to the same woman?"

"Yes."

"I'm not even seeing anybody now," she said. "You're the first man I even felt like talking to in over three months."

He weighed these words. Maybe she felt sex-starved. Or found him attractive. It was possible. Maybe she still hoped to make use of him professionally. Maybe she was only making small talk. Powers felt like a student staring at symbols on a blackboard. He couldn't decipher any of them.

From time to time Carol leaned forward to refill their glasses.

"You've killed two men. What did that feel like? To kill somebody?"

Powers looked up sharply. "The first was a psycho who had already killed three people. The other was a guy sticking up a store." He stopped.

"We'll talk about it another time, maybe."

"Yeah. Maybe." He did not want to relive those emotions. It was too complicated to explain to someone who had not been there.

"Whenever you feel you can."

"Sure."

Carol jumped up. "Would you like to see my house?"

Her eyes looked to him either preoccupied or unfocused. In any case, overbright. He set his glass down with great care. The glass was fragile and so was whatever mood she was in. He did not want to risk breaking either. "I'd love to."

He began to trail her through rooms. She talked as steadily as a tour guide, but her voice had gone off fractionally. He watched her.

They stood in her bedroom, a bright airy room with chintz curtains at windows that were partly open. The bed was queen-sized—rather a large bed, he thought, for a lone woman. It was like an empty arena. It existed to be used. Without the two struggling gladiators, the grunts of combat, it did not make sense. In itself it seemed an invitation. He wondered if he was supposed to make a try here.

But she never stopped talking, and instead led him through a short corridor into what must have been a boudoir originally—a small room outfitted as an office. "Here's where I do a lot of my work," said Carol. Boudoirs have changed Powers thought, but women have not. All roads still lead to the boudoir, he thought. It was the place a man must reach. He could measure his progress toward it with a ruler. Afterwards, to determine the magnitude of his victory, he can make a body count.

There was a desk and typewriter. There were stacks of books and papers on the floor. Against the wall was a daybed, and Carol sat down on it. When Powers sat beside her, she threw him a shy smile.

"You are a beautiful woman."

"Well, thank you. What a nice thing to say. Thank you very much."

He decided to take up both her hands, but she disengaged them.

Powers was not sure what to do next.

"I feel there's something between us, don't you?" she said. "Maybe it's just that we've been shot at together. I don't know what else it could be, do you?"

Powers felt like a man whose letter was in the mail. His message would reach its destination eventually. Repeating it now could do no further harm.

He said, "I want to go to bed with you. I want to go to bed with you right now."

"No, I don't think so," Carol said. "That won't be possible." She frowned, then smiled, then frowned again.

Powers said nothing.

"It isn't," she added, "because I don't find you attractive. I find you very attractive. You're a very attractive man. As a matter of fact, I'm flattered to be asked. I'm sure any woman would feel flattered, an attractive man like you. Thank you for asking me."

Powers stared at her; his face felt set in cement.

"So tell me about yourself," said Carol nervously. "Did you go to college?"

The question hung there, as red and tender as a bruise.

"Did I go to college? What kind of question is that? What do you take me for? For some stupid flatfoot? Is that who you think you're dealing with? Of course I went to college. And got a degree. And law school. And got a law degree. You want to know something? Some cops can read and write. Try getting to know a few. You'd be surprised."

"You're a lawyer then. I didn't know that. I didn't know you were a lawyer."

"I've got a law degree. I'm not a lawyer, I hate lawyers."

"But I don't see why," she said nervously, triumphantly, "why you went to the trouble of getting a law degree. If you didn't intend to practice law, that is?"

"Because if a man wants a big career in law enforcement a law degree helps."

"Is that what you want, a big career? In law enforcement?"

"I have to shove off."

Carol, in a small voice, said, "I seem to have led you on. I'm sorry. I'm really terribly sorry. I didn't mean to."

Powers, on his feet, stepped toward the door.

"There's a very nice restaurant in the village. Would you like to go out to dinner? As my guest, of course," she added.

"You want to know something else? I can afford to pick up a restaurant check, too."

"Then you'll come?"

He strode out of the office, out of the bedroom and into the hall outside, where he got lost, and was obliged to wait for Carol to lead him to the stairs. At the front door he said goodbye and kept moving. As he backed out of her driveway, he caught a glimpse of her standing in the doorway. He thought he saw her wave but did not wave back.

LATER, POWERS in pajamas came to bed carrying a heavy tome on China. His glasses upon his nose, he sat down against the headboard.

"I always have enjoyed a little light reading in bed," he said to his wife beside him.

"Don't be worried, honey, it will work out."

She put her magazine down.

He looked at her. He saw where her knees rose up under the covers, her feet, the rumpled hills and valleys of the country he knew so well and in which he felt safe. He was glad to be home and in bed with her.

"I'm going to have an awful lot of studying to do," he said.

She reached to switch off the light.

"Study the Chinese tomorrow. For tonight, how about studying your wife?"

As she turned toward him, the tome fell off the bed onto the floor.

"Hey," he said, "you made me lose my place."

9

PRECINCT COMMANDER. Only one perk came with the job usually, a spot near the station house in which to park his car. Powers would have to learn where that spot was. For today he did not want to be seen searching—to search is to display weakness—and so he parked in a lot that would cost him five dollars plus tax until closing time.

Approaching the station house on foot, he was like a penitent approaching a shrine. It was as if the place itself had the power to heal, and would perhaps make him whole again. Since it was early, the sidewalk was in gloom. The sun was still stuck to the cornices high above. The produce stalls were still being set up outside the shops. Tanks of live fish were being carried out onto the sidewalks. Chinese kids wearing aprons were brooming out the insides of stores.

The station house stood in a row of tenements on Elizabeth Street. It was one of the oldest in the city, built in the 1880s. Except for the flag hanging above the street and the double-parked police cars—and waiting news crews—it was indistinguishable from the tenements around it.

The news crews, Powers saw, guarded the entrance in phalanxes, one to the right, another to the left. They lurked like beggars. They wanted something from him, and he had to decide quickly how much, if anything, to give. He felt like an athlete coming up to the starting blocks. He needed a good start at all costs. But the rules for his event had not been written. What constituted a good start, what a poor one? He did not know.

Since the illusion of confidence was more important than confidence itself, he quickened his pace. As he climbed the stoop, microphones were thrust into his face, and questions were slung at him sharp as knives. He knew he must not be seen to flinch—or get skewered either. Managing a warm smile, he ignored all questions, murmuring only, "I've got nothing to say now, I'll be glad to talk to you later when I've learned something about my new command, thank you, excuse me, thank you," and he trotted past them.

He had a satchel with him that he set down inside the door. He was inside the sanctuary, his station house. Though it had seen nearly a hundred years of crime and degradation it had also given scores of previous commanders this same feeling of sanctuary. How had their lives been, Powers asked himself. But he imagined he knew the answer. Precinct commanders were only cops with bars on their shoulders, and most of them, just like ordinary cops, were terrified of their superiors, and terrified also of running afoul of some citizen with clout. And so most previous commanders had cowered inside this place for most of the hours or years of their command. Cops on patrol from the beginning until now had had to make the life-and-death decisions by themselves, while their commanders had hid out in here; this was a commander's second perk, to evade responsibility, if he wished, totally. Which was the time-honored way to survive in the New York Police Department, Powers knew. A commander could do very little to alter crime patterns anyway, and a precinct would run well enough by itself. A captain who managed his paper work and who otherwise merely hid out was safer and probably wiser than one who came in determined to institute reforms, to improve the life of the community. On a realistic level a station house was not a shrine, not a sanctuary. It was more like a cavalry post. The commander was isolated inside his fort. To go outside was to court possible, even probable ambush, for there were hordes out there who didn't like him and who could overwhelm him if they wished.

A sergeant sat behind what was called the desk but was actually a counter ten yards long. Powers headed toward it across the broad-board floor over which so many platoons of cops had marched, so many prisoners been dragged. The boards rang to his footsteps. Stepping up onto the dais and behind the desk, he signed the blotter. No bands played, no salute was fired. Nonetheless it was with this banal act that he officially took command.

"They want to come inside, Captain."

Powers looked up sharply. It was the cop on security duty at the door. He stood with his back against it, holding it shut against the newsmen outside.

"No one comes in here," said Powers. His first order. He took a deep breath and felt much better. "Sergeant, send some men out there and disperse them. Do it gently."

He stepped across into his office. A small square room with a desk and two chairs. It had a single very grimy window. A barren place. It was like a stage without scenery, a library without books. New books would have to be written by him. Water stains showed like old sweat high up in the armpits of the room, and cigarette stains scarred the desk top. He opened each of the desk drawers. They were as empty as his future. He would have to furnish this place, ornament it with trophies. To close himself in here was for him not a realistic choice. He would have to go out into the community and bring back trophies of one kind or another.

He had avoided the first trap set for him, the press outside. He had made no rash statements. He was going to need cooperation to succeed—from the PC, from Chief Duncan, even from Chief Cirillo, probably. He could not afford to antagonize them further. When they turned on the TV news tonight they would not see his face for very long, if at all. They could not get angry over the few words he had spoken. The score was in his favor so far. No victories yet, but no defeats either.

Through the open door he could hear a platoon of cops lining up in front of his desk. The eight-to-four tour was about to go out. He went out into the muster room, mounted the platform, and looked down on about thirty men. One or two were in their forties. A few pot bellies. Most were young cops in their late twenties, men, he judged, with no knowledge of or interest in their constituents, the Chinese.

"Ten-hut," bawled the desk sergeant.

The men snapped to attention in two long ranks. They wore short-sleeved blue shirts and regulation caps—the uniform of the day.

Powers tried to decide what to say to them. Cops became very cynical very fast. They hated bosses—and Powers now was their boss—because bosses were men who hid out in offices, sticking cops with the risk, taking credit if there was any, avoiding, at all costs, blame. In addition, most cops counted their own experiences as real and vital and all other police experience, especially desk experience, as being in some way fraudulent. They would respond to and respect only street cops like themselves. Powers knew this, he knew that it was useless to talk to them in terms of sacrifice or service or trying harder. He'd have to prove first that he was a street cop himself. This would take time, but he'd best begin now. "Nothing I could say would impress you," he said, and made his voice go hard. "Just remember this. I was on the street more years than most of you have been on the job. For the time being, nothing changes. The sectors, the foot posts, remain the same. When I learn my way around the precinct, I'll order changes, not before."

He stepped back. "Sergeant—"

"Right face." It was the patrol sergeant this time. "Forward march."

The platoon filed out. The news crews, Powers noted through the door, were now across the street, filming the cops as they came out.

During Powers' brief address the midnight-to-eight tour had straggled in, rough men moving in pairs, pairs as united as brothers, as united as married couples, united in hostility against any common enemy, real or imagined. Some of them had paused to appraise him. Most, gear clacking like medieval knights, leather creaking like a sheriff's posse, had filed straight through and up the stairs to their lockers. They knew who he was but chose to ignore him. It was as if he didn't exist.

Powers gave them five minutes to collect up there, then climbed the stairs and in an open space called them together: thirty hostile cops in various stages of undress. He made the same speech again. A number of men eyed him carefully. Others avoided any eye contact at all. Most, as he talked, went on changing their clothes so that the noise of slamming lockers punctuated his sentences. At the end he nodded curtly, as if dismissing them, and went back down the stairs and into his office. He hadn't dismissed them at all, only himself.

The administrative lieutenant, Motherwell, stood with an armload of file folders beside the desk. He was a prissy, corpulent fellow. There was no time to accord him more than a glance. Powers sat down and opened the first of the folders. He saw he had 209 cops assigned to him, and eleven radio cars. Someone in the past had divided the precinct into eleven sectors, one for each car, and he began studying how they were laid out. There were foot posts as well. After a time he scanned the roster, looking for names he might know from the past. He found six that were familiar, none in any sense a friend. None could be counted on for help. He was completely alone here.

Motherwell still stood beside the desk.

Noting that the precinct investigative unit was headed by a Detective Kelly, Powers sent Motherwell to get him. There was a small alcove off his office and, while waiting, he changed to civilian clothes out of the satchel he had brought with him.

"Detective Kelly is here, sir," called Motherwell.

Powers poked his head back into the office.

"That will be all, Lieutenant."

He came out of the alcove with his brown sports coat over his arm. "How long have you worked out of this precinct, Kelly?"

"Twelve years, sir."

Kelly was in his mid forties. Florid-faced. A harder man than Motherwell. There was nothing else Powers could tell about him merely from looking. People were not furniture or trees. One could not judge their strength and/or utility at a glance.

"Speak any Chinese?"

"No sir."

"All right, Kelly, show me Chinatown."

On Catherine Street the detective led the way into a tenement where, just inside the door, they found themselves staring at a rat. It stood on the second step of the stairs. Kelly simultaneously stomped his foot and slapped the bannister. The rat scurried through a hole in the baseboard, and they started up toward the sound of humming. It sounded as if the entire building was vibrating. The stairs seemed to become more rickety the higher they climbed, and in the dim light Powers could see that lathes showed through the broken plaster wall. At the landing Kelly pushed open a door. About fifty Chinese women sat at sewing machines. The humming came from their machines. It sounded like the violin section of an orchestra. The women sat under neon lights and pushed bolts of cloth through under the needles. They were working fast. The entire floor was taken up by the machines, and there was no ventilation. Windows front and back had been boarded up, and the air was so foggy from lint that many of the women wore surgical masks across their mouths. Some had toddlers sitting on piles of cloth beside their machines. A number of ten- and twelve-year-old Chinese kids were working too. They heaped bundles of finished clothing into bins.

"This place is in violation of the fire laws, obviously," Kelly said. "It's also in violation of the child labor laws, the minimum wage laws, and health and safety codes. None of those violations come under our jurisdiction, as you know. These women probably work twelve hours a day. They get paid probably for eight hours a day. That's the way things are done in Chinatown. The boss punches out for all of them, after which they go right on working. The Labor Department may have a civil suit going against this place, provided they've been able to find out who owns it."

Lint hung in the air like snow.

"Who does own it?" asked Powers.

"According to our information, a syndicate of four Chinese businessmen, all of them directors of the Nam Soong Tong. We'd never find the documents to prove it, though."

"I see," said Powers.

"The clothing manufactured here is sold principally in the garment district uptown, which is controlled, as you know, principally by Jews. People think Jews own the sweatshops in Chinatown too, but they don't. The Chinese own them."

"I see," said Powers.

"There are about five hundred sweatshops like this in Chinatown," said Kelly. "The last I heard, the Labor Department had ten inspectors to check the entire city. That doesn't leave too much of a share for Chinatown. Very few of these women speak English. Most of them are probably illegal aliens. They know they are being exploited. They just can't do anything about it."

Kelly let the door swing closed.

"There are four more floors just like this one," Kelly said. "Want to see them?"

"I've seen enough," said Powers. "Where are the gambling dens?"

"Usually in cellars. I'll point them out as we walk along."

In crowded Chinatown, commerce flourished not only at street level, but also one level down. Most cellars, Powers saw, had been converted into businesses and shops, and from them staircases led directly up to the sidewalk. Walking along, he peered down stairwells into open barber shops and laundries, and also at the closed steel doors to gambling dens.

Then for an hour he sat parked in Kelly's car watching the entrance to the den at 61 Mott Street.

The sun was higher. It had dropped like a scaffolding part-way down the buildings, painting the walls in bright broad strokes, painting lower, painting quickly. The still gloomy sidewalks were already crowded. Faces hurried along, few of them white, which to Powers was still surprising and slightly confusing. This was New York, but the people who lived here belonged to a different world, one he had never looked at closely before.

He watched customers filing up and down the stairs to the gambling den. Though it was not yet 10 A.M. the place was in full swing. "This is amazing," he told Kelly.

Chinatown gambling joints did business twenty-four hours a day, Kelly explained. "The Chinese love to gamble."

"Did anybody ever ask why?"

"It's compulsive with them."

Powers frowned. He was looking for answers and understanding, not for platitudes, not for pat cop-phrases. Kelly might just as well have remarked that blacks had rhythm, and Jews a knack for making money. The response seemed all too typical of the police mind, which was not normally inquiring, and which sought only to nail something down, not to understand it. In fairness to cops, most of what they encountered, Powers knew, was so atypical of human behavior that it could not be explained, and it was therefore not possible to understand it. Evil, by its nature, was incomprehensible. Having discovered this generations ago, cops had long since quit asking the type of question that outsiders always posed first. Kelly personally could not really be blamed.

The detective said, "We used to raid these joints regularly. There are about twelve of them in Chinatown. We found very few records, obviously, and none going back more than one week. Still, we found enough to determine that their minimum profit was never less than $100,000 per joint per week. No taxes. I'm talking about profit—over a million dollars a week, over sixty million a year."

"Untraceable cash," commented Powers.

"Right. They ship it to Taiwan or Hong Kong and it

comes back laundered. It's now clean money. They can buy buildings with it, or import heroin with it—whatever they want."

Powers was beginning to be pleased with Kelly.

The cellar of 61 Mott Street was like an anthill. Traffic up and down. Asian men only. There were no whites or blacks, and no women.

"We're not allowed to raid them any more," said Kelly. "The Fraternal Organization complained to the Mayor. They said raids hurt business throughout Chinatown. The Mayor agreed. Word came down that when the Chinese operate a gambling den it's not criminal, it's cultural. Anyway, what good did it do? We never managed to arrest any of the big guys in the tongs, and the day after we would bust into one of these places they would be right back in business. Besides, it only led to two results. It cut off money from the gangs, so they increased their extortion of shopkeepers to make up for it. And it led to payoffs to cops. The only way we can raid them now is if we get permission all the way up to Chief of Detectives Cirillo."

Powers considered this. The dens were where Chinatown was most vulnerable to police pressure. They were arteries of money and vulnerable to tourniquets. But he couldn't touch them. The more he learned about Chinatown, the more constricted he felt. Already he felt like a man locked in a phone booth. He could see out. He could even call out, but he couldn't get out. The danger was that he would stifle to death before someone freed him—or beat himself to death trying to break through the walls.

He pointed with his chin, Chinese fashion, at 61 Mott Street. "Who owns this one?"

"There are a number of investors. The principal owner is Mr. Koy, the undertaker."

"That name again."

"He was once a sergeant in the Hong Kong police department."

Powers grasped at this. "He's one of us then." Perhaps he could use this Koy as his bridge into Chinatown, find an

103

ally in a fellow cop. "It ought to be possible to talk to another cop."

"He's not a cop like you or me, Captain. Drug Enforcement inquired about him through their bureau in Hong Kong. Hong Kong apparently has the most corrupt police department in the world. Up until about five years ago Koy had a vice squad. He enforced the gambling, prostitution, and drug laws in the Hong Kong red light district. He's supposed to have left there with a hundred million dollars in graft profits. There were supposed to have been five Hong Kong sergeants sent out to take over the rackets in the United States and Canada. They were called the Five Dragons. The head Dragon was Koy, who landed here."

The police world was full of rumors. It was a world in which bizarre behavior was commonplace. No rumor, therefore, could be discounted or challenged just because it was fantastic. To challenge it would be like challenging the virtue of another cop's wife. It would be like challenging his faith. Powers did not believe the rumor about Chinese cops in general, nor about Koy in particular, but for the moment he let the matter drop.

"Could one of us get into this gambling den?" He stared across at 61 Mott Street. He wanted to see what it looked like from the inside.

"Not without a warrant," said Kelly. "There's no way through those steel doors unless they open them. And they only open for Orientals."

"They only exploit their own, eh?"

"That's right. It's been going on in China for thousands of years. We're not dealing with a problem here, Captain. We're dealing with a civilization."

"I'm sick of that thousands-of-years line," muttered Powers. "Because this isn't China. This is New York. We're here to protect all the citizens of this community, Chinese or not."

"Well, good luck, Captain," said Detective Kelly.

Later they parked across the street from P.S. 130, a junior high school. They could see through the fence into the school yard, which was empty.

"What are we stopping here for?" Powers had seen too much or not enough. He was not feeling sociable.

"You wanted to see some gang members," said Kelly. "This is a good place to see them. They come here to recruit."

They waited.

"The noon recess begins at ten minutes to twelve," commented Kelly.

Presently from inside the school came the dull ringing of bells, and a few seconds later kids spilled out into the school yard. The leak almost instantly became a flood. Basketballs appeared. Kids raced back and forth on rollerskates. Perhaps 10 percent, perhaps more, were Asians, presumably Chinese. This school stood at the intersection of Hester and Baxter streets, two blocks outside Chinatown in Little Italy. According to Kelly, the school districts overlapped, and about 90 percent of Chinatown's kids attended junior high here.

"You are in luck, all right," murmured Kelly. "See that older guy?"

A young Chinese—he looked to Powers to be in his early twenties—stood peering through the chain link fence into the school yard. "That's Nikki Han," said Kelly. "He's the leader of the Flying Dragons."

"He's looking for someone," said Powers.

"Right. And I think I see who."

In the school yard a group of long-haired white students had begun tormenting a Chinese boy. The Chinese boy was almost shaven above his ears and to hide such a disgrace he wore a cap which the others were trying to snatch from him. Victim and persecutors were about the same age, about fifteen. The Chinese kid was dressed differently from the others too: black trousers, an open-necked white shirt. He looked like a waiter. Having lost his hat, he found himself inside a circle. Around him the hat was tossed from hand to hand while he lunged for it. There were tears in his eyes, and he seemed to be begging for his hat in Chinese.

Nikki Han went through into the school yard. As he

approached, the group around the Chinese boy broke up. The hat was dropped on the pavement and kicked away. The other boys melted backwards. The whole schoolyard had gone silent.

As Powers watched, Nikki Han picked up the hat, put his arm around the Chinese boy, and led him to a corner of the yard. They sat down on a bench, and Nikki Han, leaning close to the boy's ear, began talking earnestly.

"I don't know that kid," said Kelly. "But from his clothes and his haircut he's an F.O.B.—fresh off the boat. That's what the American-born Chinese call them. The kid's parents probably work twelve hours a day in sweatshops and don't have time to take care of him. Maybe one parent speaks a little English, maybe not. The kid obviously doesn't. Yet he's in class with American kids his age. The principal put him there. It's a junior high. What else could he do with him? But the kid can't keep up. He can't speak or read or write English. He doesn't know our alphabet, or our numerals. Probably his teacher makes a special effort to be nice to him. But it's hopeless. He doesn't understand a word she says. This is a very ordinary story in Chinatown, Captain. It's happened many times in the last few years."

The two police officers stared through the fence. Nikki Han, still talking earnestly, still had his arm around the boy. "To the other kids, this kid is a clod," continued Kelly. "So they steal his hat and make him cry. You just saw it. You know how cruel kids are at that age. By the end of a few weeks he's ripe to be taken over by one of the gangs. That's what is taking place now, I believe. Once he makes contact with someone like Nikki Han, it's all over. Nikki speaks to him in his own language. Nikki saves him from persecution. Nikki offers to put meaning in his life. All he has to do is join the gang."

Nikki Han and the boy got up off the bench, went out of the school yard, and walked down the street toward Chinatown.

"Now he's probably taking him to a restaurant," said Kelly.

"We'll follow them."

"Sure."

They gave Han and his recruit a hundred-yard head start, then trailed them into a restaurant on Canal Street called the Jade Urn, where they took a table on the other side of the room from the two young men. If Han knew they were there, it did not show. They watched him order lunch for himself and the kid.

"We might as well eat, ourselves," said Powers. "What's good here?"

Kelly, who had put on glasses, peered at the menu. "Try the candied chicken wings, Captain."

They waited to be served.

"Fifteen-year-olds are very useful," commented Kelly. "They carry the guns, for instance. Nikki never carries. We've stopped him many times. He's always clean. Some fifteen-year-old carries, and if we lock up a juvenile on a gun charge, most likely the judge lets him go."

Nikki Han was still speaking earnestly. The boy was grinning, and his eyes were bright. He kept nodding his head up and down. He was also wolfing down food. His chopsticks flashed. Powers admired the way he used them. He was like a doctor in surgery. He plucked morsels big and small from the center dishes, and never dropped one. He was an expert.

"The fifteen-year-olds also do the killing," commented Kelly. "They'll pull the trigger on anyone for Nikki. Fifteen-year-olds are mindless. They think he's a god, because he tells them he is. They believe him. He's been shot several times. Not by us. By other gangs. He shows young recruits his scars and tells them he can tense up his muscles so bullets won't penetrate. That makes him a god, and so they both fear him and adore him. If he says kill someone, they do it. Yeah."

Powers stared into his candied chicken wings. He was trying to absorb all Kelly was telling him.

"The gangs recruit constantly," said Kelly. "The older members get arrested, or killed. There have been about thirty of them killed in the last three years. Being a member of a Chinese youth gang is a dangerous occupation." He paused. "Or members get married and drop out, or simply scared and drop out. A gang is a volatile thing. It needs constant new blood. The gang leaders are all like Nikki, twenty-five or so. They are getting paid by the gambling dens and the tongs, and they are extorting money from shopkeepers. We figure they keep three or four thousand dollars cash a week each. They pay the younger gang members practically nothing, a hundred fifty a week tops."

Across the restaurant, the waiter placed the check face down beside Nikki Han.

"Watch," said Kelly. "He'll sign it 'Flying Dragons.' There."

Having scrawled something on the check, Nikki Han carried it toward the cash desk, where the owner waited, smiling nervously. Nikki walked with the arrogant, frightening swagger affected by gang thugs the world over. The smiling owner watched him coming. To Powers the smile looked like a gash in meat, like evidence of pain.

"Chinatown is terrified of all the gangs," said Kelly, "but particularly of Nikki's gang because it's the most violent. No restaurant owner would dare try to make Nikki pay. I shouldn't be surprised if Nikki asked for a donation, as well. There. What did I tell you?"

The smiling owner handed the gang leader two twenty-dollar bills. After handing one bill to the boy, Nikki reached for the door. The owner ran to help him. He bowed them out. Only when the door closed did he cease smiling.

"C'mon, that's extortion," said Powers. "We can arrest him for that."

"You need a complainant, Captain," said Kelly, "and that owner is not going to sign any complaint."

Powers had risen to his feet. He placed his napkin beside the plate. Though supposing that Kelly was right, he was hopeful. "We'll see," he said.

They went forward, where Powers introduced himself, showing his shield. "Those boys who just left," he said, "I noticed they didn't pay their bill."

The owner was again smiling nervously. "They flends, Captain. Velly flendly boys."

"How much protection money do you pay the Flying Dragons each week?"

"I no want tlouble, Captain."

"We have laws in this country to protect you," said Powers. "We can protect you against the gangs. But you have to ask us to do it. That's the law. You have to sign a complaint. For instance, if you sign a complaint against those two who just left, we could arrest them. Detective Kelly and I are witnesses to what happened. Ultimately they would go to jail."

The smile never left the owner's face. "Take too long, Captain. Many court appearances. Much delay. Too many gangs in Chinatown. I don't want trouble, Captain."

Powers found that his fists were clenched. He went out of the restaurant and stood with Kelly on the sidewalk.

"Every store and restaurant in Chinatown pays protection to one gang or another," Kelly said. "The Flying Dragons have Canal and Mott streets. The Ghost Shadows have Division and Catherine. Two other gangs are disputing control of Pell Street at the moment. The extortion payments aren't all that much. But most Chinese merchants don't have much."

Not ten feet away, Powers noted, Nikki Han leaned against a lamppost smirking at him. But the young boy was not in sight and had perhaps gone back to school.

THE COP on duty on the switchboard handed Powers a sheaf of telephone messages as he came into the station house. All were from newsmen, none from Carol Cone. All requested interviews he could not afford to give. He handed them back. "Refer these people to Deputy Commissioner Glazer's office," he told the switchboard cop.

"Er, Captain, a package came for you."

The cop wore a half-repressed grin.

Powers glanced around. The desk sergeant seemed secretly amused, too.

"It's on your desk."

Powers went across to his office and closed the door. The package that had made at least two cops grin—and how many others, Powers wondered—was a bouquet of flowers. It lay wrapped in green paper on his desk. Cops, he reflected as he searched for the card, have the mentality of teenage boys. They see flowers as sissy, or something. Flowers provoke mirth.

The envelope was not sealed. The card read: "Good luck in your new job." It was signed Carol Cone.

How many cops had read this, Powers wondered. Not an important question yet, but it would become one the first time some cop saw them together. That, plus these flowers, would be enough. Evidence plus an eyewitness equals a conviction. Any jury would agree. The news would sweep through the department.

She must be crazy, Powers thought. She risks all kinds of problems for me. She can't be trusted to be prudent, he thought. Watch out for her.

The flowers made him feel even more embarrassed about last night. He was frustrated in his career, yes, but not sexually, and he wondered why he had come at Carol so crudely.

He wanted to blame it on Carol, but was not sure. Had she attempted to seduce him and then, for some reason, changed her mind? Men did not often seduce women, Powers believed. Men were blunt and solid, not seductive at all. Whereas women dealt in emanations that were invisible to the naked eye. Women sent these emanations out like radio beams. Nothing showed. One could not even accuse them of it afterwards.

Powers reached for the flowers. Tonight he would take them home to his wife, no card attached. He would collect a kiss and a hug for his reward, and then perhaps take her out to dinner.

He took Carol's card, tore it into small pieces and dropped them in the basket beside his desk.

10

EVERY PRECINCT in the city had a patrolman assigned full time to community relations, usually a member of whatever ethnic group predominated there. In the Fifth Precinct the slot was filled by a fourth generation Chinese-American named Lawrence Lom. Lom's great-grandfather, along with thousands of other coolie laborers, had helped build the Union Pacific Railroad. Afterwards he had stayed on, moving to New York and, twenty years later, importing his wife and full-grown children from China. Lom, now forty-nine, had grown up on Mott Street. A portly, moon-faced man, he spoke perfect New York English, of course, plus halting Chinese—in Chinatown the Cantonese dialect was always called Chinese, as if there were no other. Lom had learned it partly in the streets, but principally in a Chinese school to which his parents had sent him two afternoons a week; they'd sent him religiously, spending too much of their meager earnings on it, but putting first things first. He had attended Chinese school the way Jewish boys in other parts of the city attended Hebrew school, the way Catholic boys attended catechism classes. But most of Lom's teachers had spoken the language of Canton poorly. Too many generations had gone by, the United States had been closed too long. There were no new Chinese coming in. The Chinese in New York were by no means being assimilated, and did not want to be, but they were, in Lom's youth, beginning to lose their language.

Lom had graduated from Brooklyn Technical High School, one of the two or three elite high schools of the city, for he had been taught like almost all of his race to revere scholarship and he was a brilliant student. But he was also Chinese, and he went to work as a telephone lineman, the best job he could find. Later he took the police department test because the job offered both security and a 33% raise in salary; of course, he passed it easily.

Upon being appointed, Lom was sent back into Chinatown, supposedly as an undercover cop, even though he had grown up there and, in the Chinese fashion, still called almost every man uncle. The Cantonese dialect has three words for it: *ah-bok*, which means older uncle; *ah-sook*, which means younger uncle, a title to be used when a younger man was either rich or a dignitary; and *ah-ke*, which means real uncle—Lom had a number of them in Chinatown also—and he was quickly recognized as a policeman. That was when he learned how shameful in Chinese eyes such an occupation was held to be. His parents were considered disgraced. To save family honor his father was required to make donations to both major tongs, and Lom himself was required to get out of Chinatown. He spent most of the next five years in midtown writing out traffic tickets from the back of a scooter.

Then the community relations program started. In every precinct a single experienced officer would serve as liaison between the community and the department. The rumor was that all community relations cops would soon be promoted to detective, and so Lom had applied and been accepted. He was sent back to the fifth precinct, and this time the Chinese simply absorbed him, the way their forebears had absorbed entire invading armies for four thousand years. They used him when they could and ignored him otherwise, and Lom used them also, as will be seen. He had been there now twenty quiet years.

With time he had become, perhaps, more cop and

less Chinese. He was a practicing Lutheran, as was his Chinese-American wife and their four children, and they lived in half of a two-family house in a section of Queens that was literally infested with other cops and their families. He belonged to the PBA, the police union, of course, but not, like other cops, to one of the ethnic, so-called line associations. There was a line association for Italian cops, Jewish cops, German cops, but not for Oriental cops because there were too few of them. So, Larry Lom, who had learned to play the fife in grade school, had become an honorary member of the Emerald Society, the line organization for cops of Irish origin, and he wore a kilt and played his fife and marched in all the parades in the Emerald Society marching band. He was still not a detective. Like many police-department rumors, that one had proven totally unfounded.

However, Lom had few other complaints. He had learned to sell himself to each new precinct commander as indispensable to the peaceful solution of any Chinatown problem that might arise. He knew most Chinese elders, and pretended to have access to all of them, which was often not the case. He attended most community functions from kindergarten graduations on up, and chairs were kept for him, though not usually on the dais. The Chinese community seemed to treat him almost as a kind of chaplain—one representing a faith that was not theirs; he was not to be taken seriously. If he realized this, he never said so and perhaps did not care. He lived a far better life than most Chinese. He worked only eight hours a day only five days a week. He had twenty-seven paid vacation days a year. He was rarely in uniform or in the station house, and he moved through the community more or less unsupervised.

He had convinced each precinct commander in effect that verbal intercourse with any segment of the Chinese community was not possible unless it took place in Lom's presence, and through the intercession of Lom. This magnified his importance, of course, but at the same time it reduced the commander's stature in Chinatown to the same level as Lom's, and Lom's rank was patrolman. The Chinese were among the most class-conscious people on earth, and each time a new commander spoke to them, not from a posture of command but through Lom, Chinatown took him at once for a fool.

On this particular morning Lom sat in an office on the second floor of the station house tapping out on an upright Underwood typewriter a long memo to Captain Powers. The typewriter had been used by a generation of detectives for booking prisoners, and all the keys stuck. Typing on it was like chopping wood—pulling the axe out after each stroke was more work than driving it in. Lom was writing thumbnail sketches of the ten most important men in Chinatown—Ting and Koy were both on the list—to whom he proposed to introduce Powers at their places of business during the next several days. The memo also promised that Lom would serve as Powers' translator and adviser at each of these meetings.

Detective Kelly stuck his head in the door and said, "Lom, they want you downstairs."

The two men went down the stairs.

A middle-aged Chinese named Quong waited just inside the station house door. He was ill at ease and therefore smiling. The smile looked pinned on. He was skinny. All his bones showed. He reminded Lom of one of those flimsy Chinese shacks he had seen in photos. They stood on stilts by rivers. They were made of sticks—you could see the skeleton. You could see Quong's skeleton too, he was that frail.

Cops moving in and out of the building paid not the slightest attention to Quong, brushing past him as if he weren't there.

"Very good to meet you, sir, thank you very much," said Quong to Lom in Cantonese. He bowed to the community relations patrolman, who did not bow back.

"Do you speak English?" said Lom.

Quong did speak English, though badly, for he had been a schoolteacher in China and before that had been partly educated by American nuns. His English was better than Lom's Cantonese. "What's your problem?" said Lom.

Quong, smiling more nervously than ever, apologized for taking up the valuable time of such an estimable gentleman as Lom. His problem was really such a small one, hardly significant—his son.

Lom brought him up to the second-floor office, closed the door, and listened for about fifteen minutes, then he went in search of the new precinct commander. Captain Powers should perhaps meet this man and hear his story. It would be educational for him, and he would surely applaud Police Officer Lom for bringing it to his attention. Lom knocked at the jamb beside Powers' open door.

Powers looked up from some papers.

"There's a Chinese guy upstairs," said Lom. "He's got a problem that's typical of many of the people of Chinatown. He speaks a good deal of English."

For a moment Powers looked ready to snarl at Lom. Already bogged down in paper work, he could not afford to get bogged down in particular Chinamen too.

But, instead, he followed Lom upstairs where Lom made the introduction: "Captain Powers, Mr. Quong."

Powers' hand shot out. Quong, smiling nervously, did not see it, for he was busy bowing.

"Is an honor, Righteous Worthy," said Quong. "Is very great honor."

When the bow ended Powers' hand was still out there. After a moment, Quong took it. He seemed as timid as a young girl, and he would not or could not meet Powers' eyes.

"Sit down, Mr. Quong," said Powers. "What seems to be the problem?"

Lom led the former schoolteacher back over his narrative. Lom did not care about Quong, but about the impression he was making on his commander and he directed Quong to speak in Cantonese, as this would establish him as invaluable translator. But Powers quickly became impatient—the interview was taking too long—and Lom was obliged to allow Quong to explain himself whenever possible in English.

Thus the story unfolded. In a farm village at the edge

of the Pearl River in Kwangtung Province, Quong had served as schoolmaster for more than twenty years, and had held the rank of learned scholar.

"The class structure in China is quite rigid," commented Lom to Powers. "Learned scholar is pretty high."

Quong had run a one-room schoolhouse for all grades up to age fifteen. He had taught the little ones to draw their ideographs; he had taught the older ones Chinese history and as much of the five classics as they would sit still for, and he had been an admired figure in the village.

Then had come the cultural revolution. The Gang of Four was in control. Learning became unpopular and men like Mr. Quong were suspected of deviationist tendencies. Rumors began to circulate: the schoolmaster might be sent somewhere for reeducation, or arrested, or driven out.

"When was the Gang of Four?" murmured Powers to Lom.

"A couple of years ago, Captain, a couple of years ago."

Quong was terrified by the rumors, because he feared for his young wife and small son. On a certain night, gathering a few possessions, he led them out of the village, trotting down the road toward Hong Kong more than a hundred miles away. Quong, in the lead, carried a stick to ward off the dogs. They woke dogs in every village they trotted through, but when alone under the moon were not safe either, and had to trot more silently than ever so as not to disturb the earth gods.

"Earth gods?" said Powers. "But he's an educated man."

"He's also Chinese," commented Lom.

After many nights they reached the coast at the edge of Deep Bay, across from the British Crown Colony, and a boatman, promising to take them across, took all of their money, then forced them out into shallow water when still about a mile from shore, and they were obliged to wade and swim the rest of the way, their possessions above their heads.

Once ashore they resumed trotting. They trotted three more nights toward Kowloon, where Quong's wife had a relative she had never met. They went to his house, a small flat. She addressed him as Third Uncle and he took them in. When told they had no money, he agreed to accept all of their jade and gold instead—two pairs of earrings and a brooch. In return, he gave them part of one room sectioned off by curtains. Quong was lucky. He found work as a laborer in a land-fill project, six days a week, twelve hours a day. He saved his money, for he had conceived the idea of emigrating to America, the Gold Mountain, and he made contact with one of the Triad societies that provided false immigration papers, paying the cost in monthly installments over a period of years.

The Triad society had an arrangement with the New York branch of the Nam Soong Tong. Passage to New York would cost fifty percent of Quong's earnings for the next ten years. He agreed.

The Quongs were flown to Vancouver, then led across Canada to Toronto where, with fifteen other Chinese men, women and children, they were crammed by white demons into the false bottom of an oil tanktruck for the drive across the border to Niagara Falls. The hatch was slammed shut and bolted from the outside. There was no light or headroom and very little air. They squatted in the dark hip to hip, arm to arm, unable to stand up or shift position. The temperature rose higher and higher, reaching, probably, 120 degrees. The truck was motionless for several hours. Some of the women fainted, and some screamed, but no one came to open the hatch. Hours later, the truck began to roll again.

They were let out in New York City, drenched by then with sweat and piss, and most of them half crazed from the claustrophobia and the fear.

Here Quong's face broke into a broad grin, and he reverted to Chinese.

"I haven't heard anything yet," interjected Powers, "that sounded funny."

"He crossed the border illegally, Captain," said Lom. "He put one over on the American authorities. He's proud of it."

"Great," said Powers. "He's an illegal alien. What do we do about that?"

But the grinning Quong had extracted his green card, which he was trying to thrust on Powers—who did not want to take it.

"I'm not an immigration officer, Mr. Quong. I don't have any right to ask to see your green card. What's he saying, Lom?"

"He says the Nam Soongs regularized him the next day. He went by tong headquarters and his green card was ready and they gave it to him."

Powers took the card, studied it briefly, and handed it back.

"Counterfeit?" asked Lom.

"I wouldn't be surprised."

"I guess he's a very naive fellow."

"He's a schoolteacher. He came halfway around the world to get here, more than twelve thousand miles. He trotted nearly all the way. His green card is none of our business, do you understand me, Lom?"

Quong, still grinning, had been peering from one face to the other. "Green card good," he said. "Velly good. Cost much money."

"Where do you work, Mr. Quong?" asked Powers.

"Velly good job, Righteous Worthy," said Quong, "velly good job."

He worked in a clothing factory on Pell Street. His job consisted of snipping off the loose ends of threads from finished trousers. He was paid five cents per pair of trousers snipped clean, and was allowed to work twelve hours a day, he reported proudly, thereby being granted the opportunity to earn much money and pay off his note. At first he tried to pay it off by gambling.

He could not gamble anymore, he said, and explained why.

One night he had begun to win at the fan-tan table in a gambling den on Mott Street. His run went on and on. The money piled up. He won enough to pay off the tong, and have money left over, and with this realization he came to his senses and pushed back from the table.

Here Quong paused, gave a rueful grin, and shook his head sadly.

As a big winner, he was entitled to a limousine home. It was explained to him that the owners always provided limousines for big winners, like himself, because they were pleased at his good fortune and wished to contribute further to his happiness.

With thousands of dollars in his pockets Quong climbed into the limousine, and told the Chinese driver to take him to Times Square. He had never been in a limousine before, nor to Times Square either. The car rolled along. He sat back on the plump cushions, and closed his eyes and contemplated his rosy future.

The door was yanked open. The car had stopped and two Chinese youths had him by the arms. They yanked him out at gunpoint and robbed him of every cent. They did not rob the driver, Quong noticed. The driver stood by watching, and once the robbery was over he got back into the limousine and drove off, leaving Quong on the sidewalk with his pockets hanging out.

"That's armed robbery," said Powers. "Did you report that to the police?"

"Is nobody's fault, Captain. I velly foolish man. I learn good lesson. I no gamble anymore." He had seen one of the boys later on Mott Street and was told he belonged to the Flying Dragons, who were very dangerous boys. "I learn a good lesson," he said again, and laughed.

"You said you had a problem with your son," Powers prompted, after a moment.

"Is not worthy of your notice, Righteous Worthy," protested Quong.

"Try me."

Quong's son had joined the Flying Dragons, he said.

The Dragons were gangsters. The boy wore new clothes. He was being led into a life of crime—had perhaps already committed crimes.

"And he's only fifteen years old," said the former schoolteacher, and he turned away blinking.

His wife worked in the kitchen of a restaurant on Mulberry Street, he said. She prepared vegetables for the chef and cleaned up afterwards, working from eleven in the morning until the restaurant closed at about midnight. So neither of them had had time to watch the boy. Recently Quong had punished his son. He had administered the beating, he said, by which the boy would remember his guilt.

"What did he say?" asked Powers.

"The Chinese rarely resort to physical discipline," Lom said. "He took a stick to the kid, and hasn't seen him since."

Quong paused. His manner brightened and he brought out a photo of his son for Powers to admire.

"Note how his ears are set close to the head," said Quong proudly. "And the lobes are long. These are signs of high intelligence."

Powers studied the photo. Was this the same boy he had watched being recruited in the school yard? He could not be sure. He handed the photo back.

"My son understands which are the four valuable things," said Quong hopefully.

"The four valuable things?" said Powers.

"Ink, ink slab, brush and paper, Captain," said Lom.

"I see."

Powers began to speak gently, and Quong to nod his head up and down as if he understood. Whether he did or not Powers did not know. There was no law against a boy, any boy, associating with other boys, even if the others might in fact belong to the Flying Dragons, Powers said. However, the law did state that boys were obliged to attend school to age sixteen, and this could be enforced, though not by the police. Truant officers enforced the truancy laws. Powers would alert the truancy office. Also, he would take every possible action under the law against the Chinatown youth gangs, because to drive them out of Chinatown was his first priority.

Somewhere in the course of this speech Powers saw he had lost Mr. Quong, who had pleaded for help, and instead was receiving words. Quong rose to his feet and, smiling and bowing, he began to back his way out of the room.

"Thank you, Righteous Worthy, for time and attention. Thank you velly much," Quong said, and was gone.

For Lom, the interview had gone well. "These Chinese gentlemen are so graceful, aren't they, Captain?" he commented.

Powers said nothing.

"I've prepared a memo for you, Captain," said Lom, and he not only handed it over but also stepped to Powers' side to point out details in his sketches of the ten important elders. "I think you and I should go call on them, one by one."

Powers said, "I wish we could do something for Mr. Quong. I wish we could give him back his son."

Lom agreed. "If the kid is running with the Dragons, it's bad news. Those guys'll blow you out of your socks. Shall I begin setting up our appointments?"

Powers folded the memo and gave it back. "Sure, set them up," he said.

AT THAT moment, young Quong was about to be formally inducted into the Flying Dragons. Together with Nikki Han and six other boys he trooped down the stairs into a Chinatown cellar. Two of the boys carried Chinese lanterns and Nikki Han carried four steel tent pegs about two feet long, some lengths of rope and a small sledgehammer. In the darkness under the tenement they lit the lanterns, which cast eerie shadows upon the walls. They were under a Chinese grocery. Young Quong, peering up, could see seeds and leaves that hung from the rafters, drying. He was wearing his new clothes and grinning, happy among his new friends. His hair was growing out. In a few weeks it would be long enough to tease into the bouffant style of the other boys.

He no longer felt alone.

Nikki Han tapped one of the tent pegs an inch into the floor. Pacing his distance carefully, he tapped in each of the other three pegs similarly, so as to form a square. Nikki Han then handed the sledgehammer to Quong saying, "Drive each of those pegs in halfway."

The dirt floor was trodden solid, and Quong had to swing the hammer hard. By the time all four stakes were planted, the fifteen-year-old was breathing hard, though still grinning. He felt himself a working member of the gang, and appreciated by the others, and he did not know about the ritual he was about to undergo. He handed the hammer back to Han.

Upon a command from Han, the other youths leaped upon Quong, tore off all his clothes, and threw him down naked onto the floor. Since he did not comprehend, he struggled, but he could not move. Hands held him spread-eagled. Other hands lashed his wrists and ankles to the four stakes. He was terrified. His ass squirmed uncontrollably on the dirt, and his head lashed back and forth. His frantic eyes sought an explanation, but none came. The lanterns were placed at his head and between his feet, and the other boys backed off into the darkness, and stripped to the waist, though he could not see this. Nor could he see them take out knives. For a time there was no sound, no movement. Quong's terror mounted.

From out of the darkness came first a maniacal scream, then a butcher knife—the lantern light flashed off the blade—and then the Chinese youth attached to it. The lantern light danced on his flesh and on his weapon, and he lunged for Quong's face, and drove the knife into the dirt beside his left ear.

Quong screamed.

In rapid succession other gang members, torsos glistening, flew screaming out of the darkness and planted knives and cleavers around the perimeter of the naked figure. Quong screamed louder than they. His sphincter muscles let go. Now as he twisted and squirmed he only soiled himself further. He began to babble, and his eyeballs rolled almost out of his head.

Nikki Han strode forth into the light. "Enough. Untie him."

Quong, quivering, got to his feet. He was handed a newspaper, with which he cleaned himself up as best as he could. Sweat ran down his breastbone, the muscles in his face twitched, and he was weeping uncontrollably. His clothes were handed him and he got dressed. "Give him the initiation ritual," ordered Nikki Han.

Quong was handed a paper written in Chinese and ordered to his knees. The boys crowded around him. One held a lantern high so that he could read. "As long as I live I am a member of the Flying Dragon Tong," he read in a trembling voice. "Even if I die, I am still a member. If I betray the tong, Heaven and Earth will destroy me. I will obey all the rules of the tong. If I don't I will die under the condition of being shot. The secret of the tong must be kept or I will die under a thousand knives."

The oath continued. "If one is found to be a traitor, the punishment is death. We are all brothers of each other. If a brother is in trouble or danger we must respond, or die under a thousand knives. The tong leader is the adviser of all events. If anyone tries to get rid of or kill him the punishment is death."

Having completed the oath, Quong was allowed to stand up. His head moved among the drying seeds and leaves, and the other boys stepped forward grinning, and began pummeling him on the back. His tears dried and he began to smile. They were all talking at once in Cantonese. Quong was now a sworn member of the Flying Dragons. He beamed with pride. His terror had been worth it. He was truly one of them now.

Nikki Han handed Quong a short-barreled .32-caliber revolver which he brandished this way and that, as if it were a toy pistol, which it was not. Like a small boy he pointed it at the far wall. "Tock! Tock!" he cried, which was the noise a Chinese child makes when playing at gunfire. "Tock! Tock!"

Nearly bursting with happiness and pride, Quong thrust the revolver into his belt under his shirt and all the boys trooped up the stairs out of the cellar and stepped into the sunlight on Mott Street.

LATE IN the afternoon Lom entered Captain Powers' office. Powers, in uniform behind his desk, looked up.

"Well, Captain," Lom said, "I've been able to set up the first of those appointments for us."

Powers, peering over his half-glasses, studied Lom. "I won't need you to come along, Lom."

"Excuse me, Captain."

Powers had thought the matter out. "I think it's better if I go by myself."

"But Captain—" Powers did not know these elders, Lom told him, nor understand the Chinatown power-structure, nor speak Chinese. Lom would be invaluable to him, as he had been invaluable to the dozen precinct commanders before him.

Powers shook his head, cutting him off. "I've made my decision on the matter, Lom." Another trap avoided, Powers reflected.

"But Captain," protested Lom, "what about my prestige?"

"Perhaps my prestige," murmured Powers, "ought to come first, do you think?"

When Lom made no reply, Powers said: "You know what I wish you'd do for me, Lom? I wish you'd find Quong's kid and have a talk with him. Maybe you can do some good. After that, go see Quong. Make him understand that his police department is doing everything for him that it can. Now hand me over your list, if you will."

"Yes sir," mumbled Lom, and he laid it down on Powers' desk and went out.

11

WILBUR D. LURTSEMA, producer of the Seven O'Clock World News Report, was a big man with a big paunch, who tended to bull his way through life belly foremost. He came bulling out of the men's room now, fingers still working at his half-zipped fly, and bumped smack into Carol Cone. His hands were wrongly placed to ward her off. As a result she caromed off him into the wall, and nearly went down.

Her eyes caromed too—from his face to his hands at his crotch. His fingers let go immediately, the job half done, and rose to straighten his tie. Lurtsema, embarrassed, was therefore irritated—an effect this woman had on him all too often. He longed for the good old days when journalism meant newspapers, and was a male profession. He thought grimly: a man can't even piss privately anymore.

"Willie," she said. "Just the man I wanted to see."

The other on-camera people called him Will, or Mr. Lurtsema. He hated Willie. He was fifty-five years old. No one had called him Willie since college—and even then only his pals—until this woman. Who was not a pal.

She said, "I need to see you and I run into you. What a coincidence."

It was no coincidence, he believed. More likely she had lurked in the hall outside the can waiting for him to come out, something no male reporter would have dared.

125

Appointments were supposed to go through his secretary. Everybody went through his secretary. But not her. He was one of the most important producers in television, but to her he was just another man to be manipulated, he believed. Her method when dealing with men was to catch them off balance, with their fly open if possible, and then to keep them that way until she got what she wanted. It was an outrage. She was an outrage.

He thought he could feel a draft, and he considered zipping himself shut right in front of her, blatantly, and screw women's sensibilities. But he belonged to an older school—as a boy he had been taught, among other concepts, gallantry. A man was not allowed to zip up in front of a lady. The next best thing was to hike his pants higher on his hips as a means of pulling the open edges together and he did this. He also turned sideways so that whatever there was to see would not be staring her in the eye.

"What do you want?"

"Let's go into your office."

In the office he would have to listen to another of her far-fetched ideas. The daily news conference was the place ideas were supposed to be tried out, give twenty other people a chance to shoot them down, but not her. In the news conferences she never opened her mouth. She much preferred waylaying him outside the can. One on one. A sexual confrontation of some kind.

Lurtsema had been managing editor of the old *Herald Tribune* fifteen years earlier, before it folded. He had the same job here, different title. In the newspaper business the news came first, then the editors. The reporters, despite their bylines, were largely anonymous and did what they were told. But in television the reporters were referred to as talent, same as rock singers. They and their goddam Q factors had far more clout than editors—who were called producers—and got far more money. The Q factor was the recognition quotient of a reporter's face as determined by secret polls of viewers. The networks paid heavily for the results of these Q polls. Carol Cone had an extremely high Q factor. She was a star. Lurtsema could not have fired her if he wanted to. On the other hand, she could probably get him fired, if she chose to make a stand on it.

He peered off down the corridor, a long, airless tube. It was like staring the length of the inside of a submarine. At the far end, where the torpedo tubes would be, was the set for the Seven O'Clock News, an airless place also, where each day's grim events were collected and fired out into the world, destined, like a spread of torpedoes, to traumatize whatever they struck.

"You can give me five minutes, Willie, can't you?"

She was, he saw, blinking her eyes at him. It was not a come-on to him personally, but rather part of a technique she used. He had seen her use it often enough—a technique that tapped the deep, sexual core of a man, any man. She —it—made men respond to her as father to daughter, as a man to his woman. She made men want to accord her any boon in their power. Her technique was as subtle as the perfume she wore, for perfume was also part of her arsenal. Or perhaps it was not subtle at all. Like perfume, she evoked responses over which men had little control. By pretending to an intimacy that did not exist, by seeming to make promises she had no intention of fulfilling, she made all males aware of her sexually—whether producers, sources, competing reporters, anyone. She made men want to step back and let her through the door first, and they did this and were always surprised when she never even turned around to say thank you. Her technique, to Lurtsema, was a lie, and she was a cheat.

She was two other things Lurtsema did not comprehend: a so-called journalist who had never worked a day on a newspaper, and what had become known as a sexually aggressive woman. Formerly she would have been known as a bitch in heat, Lurtsema reflected. She had bedded a lot of guys. Or he supposed she had bedded them. She had as many dates as a college girl, different guys every few weeks, and a college girl she was not, so how else did all those dates end?

You tell me, Lurtsema thought.

"Willie, your office is that way."

He strode toward it. He was trying to keep ahead of her so he could finish unobserved with his fly. But she kept up, prattling non-stop. He increased speed. It didn't help. He strode in past his secretary, practically running. He dropped into the chair behind his desk and bellied up tight into the kneehole and glared at her.

"Here's my idea," said Carol. She sat down and got comfortable. "The Chinatown problem."

"What Chinatown problem?"

Carol outlined it: "Gangs, gambling dens, tongs, the Golden Palace massacre—"

"What happened to your other idea, police misman- agement?"

"This one is better."

"It's a local story. It has no national impact."

"Every Chinatown in the country is the same."

"We don't know that."

He studied her. She must be forty, he thought, but made up she looked thirty, and she posed as twenty. Granted she looked terrific on TV, but mostly because the picture that went out over the air was not nearly as sharp as real life. The picture lied, though not to her, apparently. She looked at herself in the monitor every night and be- lieved what she saw there. The old movie stars had believed what they saw too, he supposed. But they had seen them- selves only once or twice a year. This woman saw herself every night. She believed what the screen told her, that she was still as delicious as a girl. To her, TV and real life were the same.

Her Chinatown idea was worthless. It was like a statue she had constructed in her own image. He was de- molishing it and he was pleased. He would take a hammer to it. It would lie in shards at her feet.

"You have to admit that the Golden Palace massacre is national," she said doggedly.

"If the cops ever break the case, sure. So far they got nothing. They haven't even found the getaway car, for chrissake. And apart from the massacre nobody gives a damn about Chinatown."

"It's a big story," persisted Carol.

But her eyes had dropped to her hands, Lurtsema noted. She had a habit, when reading the news on camera, of dropping her eyes like that. Then she would raise them, reading directly into the lens, looking suddenly extremely vulnerable, like a woman who was about to exchange a confidence, about to confess something. It was an incredibly effective trick, or at least so the ratings seemed to prove. The public responded to her in a big way, according to the numbers. To Lurtsema her trick seemed transparent. That it produced results out of all proportion to its cunning infuriated him. The only other thing he would grant her was that she read the teleprompter well; she never flubbed words. He would not grant her that Chinatown was worth a story.

"Well," she said, "let's get somebody in here from the police department to give us a Chinatown backgrounder. It's worth that much at least. It's worth a backgrounder."

"Get who in here?"

"The guy who commands the Chinatown precinct, what's his name—"

"He's not involved in the massacre investigation. Probably doesn't even know what progress they've made, if any."

Carol stood up. "Say you'll think about it."

Lurtsema shrugged. "Sure." He had no intention of thinking about it or her.

Carol went out. Without batting her eyes at him, or wiggling her ass. Lurtsema considered this a victory, and he was chortling as he got up from his desk and began pacing the room.

His secretary came in. "Yes, Margaret," he said.

Margaret, a twenty-two-year-old blonde, was about to speak when her gaze was caught by something that was not as it should be.

"Mr. Lurtsema," she said cryptically, and pointed with her eyes.

"Goddamn it," cried Lurtsema, furious with Carol

Cone, furious with himself. Turning to the wall, he yanked the thing shut once and for all.

Back in her own office, Carol stared out the window, and thought about Powers, a news source she wanted to see again. Potential news sources were regularly invited to Lurtsema's office for cocktails after the Seven O'Clock News had been taped. The sources were then grilled by producers and reporters for background information. Would Lurtsema invite Powers to a backgrounder? Maybe not immediately, Carol decided. But she was confident that eventually she could make any man do almost anything she wished.

12

PINNED TO the wall of Powers' office, a map of the Fifth Precinct hung like a giant Chinese butterfly with wings outspread. As a wall decoration the butterfly failed, for it was dead and its tone was gray. It gave no hint of the color and vitality of the living organism that it represented, and that Powers would have to snare somehow and subdue.

In front of the map stood Powers and seven other officers, most of them sergeants. Powers had a pointer, with which he repeatedly tapped one wing or the other.

All eight men were in uniform. Like military commanders plotting a campaign, their first job was to study the terrain, and they were doing it. Next they should move up armament—tanks here, artillery there—and then troops, and they should attempt to achieve surprise. But their armament was useless—a handful of handguns that, normally, they were not allowed even to draw or brandish, much less fire. As for surprise, the British redcoats of long ago were no more glaringly obvious, or alien to the community, than police blue.

"We can't do anything about the sweatshops," said Powers. "We're not allowed to crack down on the gambling halls. We can't get at—" he hesitated —"at the tongs." He had almost called them what he believed them to be, crime syndicates. The leadership of the tongs and the Chinese Mafia were the same, he was convinced, but he was not even supposed to think this, much less say it aloud. "But we can suppress the youth gangs," he continued. "We can save these restaurant owners and shopkeepers from being extorted." He looked all around, and his subordinates stared back. He saw they did not believe him. They accorded him silence, not faith. "We can try, anyway," he said, an admission of weakness he regretted as soon as the words came out, because the first adage of leadership was this: the leader must believe, or the led won't.

The officers before him had worked this precinct for years. The only newcomer was himself. The police department was not the army, and most lower ranks, once assigned to a station house, worked there the rest of their careers; only commanders were rotated. "As I understand it, most gang members are known to us by sight," Powers told them. "I want you to order your men to harass them. Every time they go into a store or restaurant to make a collection, I want a cop to go right in behind them. Stand right beside them. The cop will not understand Chinese. Legally speaking he won't have witnessed a thing. But I want the police presence felt. I want these victims to believe we are with them, that we will remove the fear they have lived under for so long. If we can convince them of that, maybe we can begin to get them to testify."

Again he looked from sergeant to sergeant. Again he listened to their silence. This was the best plan he had been able to think up, and he knew it wouldn't work. He saw they knew it too. "I want to know exactly when and where collections take place. I want regular reports made and an intelligence file built up. If we can pinpoint the collections in advance, we can have a cop standing there every single time." Every single time? There weren't enough cops in the precinct for that, in the entire division. "If threats are observed, if force is used, I want an arrest made."

This is crazy, he thought. Chinatown is in the grip of an octopus and I'm asking them to help me lop off the ends of a few tentacles. There are too many tentacles and each one can be replaced. What we ought to be doing is going after the creature's head. Kill the head and the tentacles will die by themselves. We're dealing with an organized criminal conspiracy and I'm not allowed even to say so, much less try to fight it. He thought of the PC and Duncan: arrest rate up, crime rate down. Okay, he thought.

"I want lots of arrests," he said. "I don't care whether they stand up in court or not."

Their faces remained resolutely blank. What Powers was ordering was the same type of arrests that occurred whenever the mayor ordered a crackdown on prostitutes. The prisoners, whether prostitutes or Chinese gang youths, would be swept into court in front of a bored judge who was probably sixty, and an assistant district attorney, who was probably twenty-five. Both had much more political clout than any police captain. The judge—almost any judge— could be depended on to start screaming about "bullshit arrests that are stinking up my courtroom." As for the young ADA, his only interest was to make a name for himself, to advance his career as fast as possible. He did not want his time taken up with arrests that would wash out, and he would denounce any police captain who caused this to happen. Neither the judge nor the ADA was likely to denounce the PC or the chief of patrol.

So the orders Powers had just given were risky in the way that climbing a mountain was risky. He was clinging to the mountain by a succession of small handholds, and the more he kept on, the more dangerous it became. Safety was down there, not up here, and the height got dizzying. Before long, one could no longer see the summit, or the ground either.

"I also want new foot posts," he said. "I want a foot patrolman at every gambling hall twenty-four hours a day. I want the bosses to feel weight too. I want to see if we can't hurt business enough to force the bosses to cooperate against the gangs. Any questions?"

No one answered. But Powers was a cop too, and believed he could read their thoughts. The principal police emotion was not love or hate, not boredom or fear. It was cynicism. Almost all these men, when they came into the department, had been idealistic young cops. They had soon changed. Much about people's lives, they learned, could not be explained, and almost nothing could be improved. It was hardly worth trying. Their own superiors had long since given up trying and were content to issue dumb orders. The real world was already set. It was as smooth and hard as a globe plastered in concrete. One could not get a grip on it. The world they had hoped to change did not exist, no world comparable to it existed either, and as a result young cops were left with nothing to believe in at all. Loss of idealism was like having a tooth extracted. It was painful, it left a hole, and nothing would ever grow there again. By the time they became old cops, thirty-five years old or so, they were as sour as men of sixty.

Powers' executive officer, a captain named Harris, said, "You want the gang members harassed. On what grounds?"

"Any grounds. Loitering, disturbing the peace, anything that comes to mind."

"What about their civil rights?"

"Screw their civil rights," snapped Powers. "Any other questions?" None were likely to be put to a captain in this mood. "No? Then that's all. Move out."

As stolid as men in pain they filed from this office. Cynicism was pain—the toothache kept recurring. In addition he had challenged them and challenge was pain too. They would obey his orders, and that was all. They had been wounded in action and were in no condition to do more. Was he in any better shape himself?

Powers took Lom's list, and began working his way through it at the rate of one Chinese dignitary a day. Most of the meetings took place at 3:00 in the afternoon. He introduced himself and usually was offered tea. The meetings were formal, always polite, and afterwards his host invariably bowed him out the door. Usually he managed to leave his home phone number behind, saying that in the event of problems he should be phoned directly. But no one promised special cooperation, and no one ever called him at home. He learned very little. He was making himself known, not coming to know them.

Most of the rest of each day he walked the streets, looking into shops, shaking hands with owners, smiling a good deal.

In a cellar-level laundry one day he again encountered Nikki Han. He had come down the stairs from the sidewalk, and had introduced himself. He had launched into his pitch: the police were there to help.

The owner and his wife, bowing and smiling, appeared nervous, and they kept turning to glance at the clock above their heads. For Chinese, their behavior was almost rude, and they wore smiles that were much too brilliant. Powers realized they wanted him to finish his speech and be gone and, since there were no customers in the place, he did not know why. Then footsteps came down the staircase behind him—a customer, he supposed, without turning around. But the laundryman's wife had recognized this "customer" at a glance. It was as if a mask had been ripped off her face. Underneath was terror. Her new expression was as ugly as a smear of blood. The transformation was as shocking as anything Powers had seen in Chinatown.

Spinning, the precinct commander stared at the figures in the doorway: Nikki Han and two others. The Chinese gang leader was wearing a tan polyester suit with bell-bottom trousers, clothes several years out of style. His confederates were similarly dressed. Italian gangsters, Powers thought irrelevantly, were far more mod, far more stylish. It seemed obvious that he had interrupted a scheduled extortion payment, and he glanced from the gang leader to the laundryman, who was almost imperceptibly trembling. The laundryman had been caught talking to a cop. He would be accused of squealing to the cops, that much seemed clear, and the gang would wreak who knew what reprisals as a result.

Nikki Han said something in Chinese—probably that he would return later—and backed up the stairs to the street, as did his two friends, or bodyguards, or whatever they were.

The Chinese couple said nothing. Their lips moved but no sound came out. Powers allowed himself to be bowed out of their laundry. There was no way, given the magnitude of their fear, that he could convince them that he would try to help, try to prevent whatever was to happen to them. Up on the street he peered about for Nikki Han, but did not see him and, although he waited a few minutes, the gang leader did not return. Powers, with a precinct to run, could not stand idle above the laundry forever, and this made him recognize still another of the disadvantages under which he worked. The gangs could outwait him any time. They had nothing else to do except make collections. They could outwait a whole precinct of cops.

He began to attend meetings of the various Chinatown Associations, the first of them the Mott Street Merchants Association, forty to fifty Chinese adults sitting in the auditorium of P.S. 63.

"We can put an end to protection payoffs," said Powers from the stage. "But we need your cooperation. The law requires that you sign a complaint. The law requires that you testify in court."

The people below him showed no reaction. They were like passengers aboard an airliner listening to instructions in the use of the emergency gear. What to do in the event of a catastrophe. But the idea was unthinkable. The entire subject was unthinkable. The listeners were not listening. They were only being silent.

"I know you are worried about wasting endless time in court," Powers said. "That's why I went to see the district attorney. He has agreed to appoint a special assistant district attorney to handle these cases as expeditiously as possible."

He paused, wetting his lips, hoping for encouragement. But there was none. "I know you are worried about reprisals. For those of you who will come forward and sign complaints, I will assign foot patrolmen to protect your places of business as much as is humanly possible. We will do everything we can."

Below him no one moved. Not an expression changed. They stared at him as though he was a comedian sent to entertain them. His first jokes may have failed, but perhaps he had better ones up his sleeve. At any moment he might bring forth a joke that would make them chuckle.

Powers turned to one of the men who had introduced him. "I am afraid that a number of these people don't understand English too well, Mr. Wang. Perhaps if you could translate my remarks into Chinese—"

There had been no reaction from Wang either. After staring a moment at Powers, he stepped to the edge of the stage and spoke three or four lines in Cantonese. There was still no reaction from the crowd. When he turned back to Powers he was smiling. "That does it," he said in English.

Powers said, "Did you tell everything? It took me about twenty minutes, and you about twenty seconds."

Wang nodded sagaciously. "Chinese is a very economical language, Captain," he said.

"I see," said Powers.

He addressed the Lee Family Association in the reception hall of the group's building on Mott Street. Tea and rice cakes were served, and Powers stood on the dais, the only white face and blue uniform in the room, the only one not named Lee, also.

He began to speak—by then he was half through a crash course in Cantonese at Berlitz. *"Joa san,"* he said. Literally this meant good morning, although it was 8:00 at night. But there were no words in Cantonese for good afternoon or good evening, and *joa san* would do, particularly since it was not an easy phrase to speak, for Cantonese was a language of tones. The same word pronounced in nine different tones had nine different meanings. *Joa* went down in tone on the *o*, and up on the *a*, and when he had spoken these words, after a kind of astonished moment of silence, the assembled Chinese began grinning and applauding.

Powers smiled back and added: *"M-goy nay,"*—thank you very much.

The people applauded again. They looked delighted with him, as if watching some precocious toddler learning to walk. Their reaction was so overblown that he wondered if he had not made a fool of himself.

"I want to prove to you that I am with you," he said, "that we your police department are with you. We want to stop the terror of these youth gangs. We want to end extortion in Chinatown. But we must have complainants. We must have people who will testify in court."

Although his speech continued, there were no more smiles, no more applause after that.

He met with Mr. Ting. He sat in Ting's empty restaurant in the middle of the afternoon, and Ting ordered tea brought to them by a waiter.

"I've come to you for help, Mr. Ting. You are perhaps the most respected man in Chinatown. If you would get behind my anti-gang program, it would have a chance."

Ting poured out the tea. "Me no pay plotection to gangs," he said. He had a high lilting voice. Close your eyes, Powers thought, and you might imagine yourself listening to an Irish tenor.

"You are a man of such stature," Powers said evenly, "that they do not approach you. But they did shoot up your restaurant. They came in here and killed five people."

"Not attack me, Captain," said Ting. "Attack rival gang. Is accident. Target rival gang."

Powers, who had been given no information on the progress of the investigation, did not know if this was true or not.

"Police department no solve case," said Ting. "Chinese people have no confidence in police."

Powers let this pass also. He said evenly, "Those weaker than you pay protection money every week, or else their shops are wrecked. In some cases they are assaulted. A few have been killed. You know that is true."

Ting rose from his chair. The interview was over. He was smiling politely. "Chinatown behind you, Captain. In favor all the way. What you do, you take gang kid into alley. You beat with club. You put bag over gang kid's head first so he don't know who hit him. Chinatown behind you one hundred percent. No civilian complaints."

So Powers went to see Koy, the last name on his list, the last person he thought his arguments might reach. The meeting took place in Koy's office inside the Flowering Virtue Funeral Parlor. The place reeked of incense. Attempting to create a casual, almost convivial mood, one cop to another, Powers began by describing his meeting with Ting. Koy immediately began to laugh.

"Put a bag over their heads and beat them with night sticks. Mr. Ting told you that?"

The man was about the same age as Powers, and stood about as tall. But he was finer boned, and perhaps twenty pounds lighter. And he did not speak like a cop at all. He spoke with a British accent. He spoke like a prosperous British business man.

"Ting knows very well we can't behave that way, and so do you. Sure, an occasional cop still beats up a prisoner from time to time. But the days when this department behaved that way as a matter of policy are over."

Koy not only stopped laughing, but he assumed a solemn mien. "You must forgive Mr. Ting, Captain. In most parts of the world they are not over. Not in China, not in Hong Kong. Mr. Ting fails to understand the subtlety of the New York police mind, as you perhaps fail to understand the subtlety of the Chinese mind."

The man wore glasses so dark that Powers could not see his eyes. The glasses annoyed him. So did Koy's manner. The man was talking down to him, waving four thousand years of Chinese civilization in his face like a stale fish, and expecting him to be impressed. But Powers was here to learn something, and perhaps to find an ally, not to get angry.

"I have talked to nearly every association in Chinatown," said Powers. "These people don't even ask me questions. They just stare at me. There ought to be questions at least."

"The Chinese are a very polite people, Captain. Certainly they have questions, but they fear you would not be able to answer them. Therefore, out of politeness, they do not ask them. No Chinese would ask them." Again the arrogant, patronizing tone.

Powers was like a hiker moving through strange country. He was obliged to ask directions because without them he might not find his way out the other side.

"What questions are you referring to?" he asked.

Koy commenced to lecture him. "Many commanders have come and gone in this precinct, Captain. How can the people of Chinatown give you any trust when you too might be gone in six months' time, a year's time? Suppose they sign a complaint against one of these gang leaders. The gang leader is arrested. He is out on bail within an hour, and moving up and down the streets of Chinatown every day after that. Perhaps a year passes before his case comes to trial, perhaps more. Even if convicted, he can be out on appeal for a long time. You promise you will protect the complainant now, but by then you might not be here. You may be an inspector in the Bronx, or police commissioner at headquarters."

"That's not too likely," said Powers.

Koy, reacting for once like an ex-cop, laughed. "Perhaps you will retire and move to Florida," he said, "and with your savings buy a hotel."

"I don't have any savings."

"I believe you, Captain."

"Help us with the gangs," said Powers. But he felt like a man asking for a loan that was not going to be accorded. "In exchange, we will leave your gambling joints alone."

"It is no secret that you are not allowed to touch our gambling houses," said Koy, chiding him. "You mustn't lie to us, Captain."

They stared at each other. Powers realized he would get no help from this man, though for a moment his hopes had been raised. But he did not get angry. Koy was more sophisticated, more intelligent, and obviously better educated than he had expected. He was also the most important man in Chinatown and Powers was trying to refocus his image of him. To do so it was perhaps best to exert a little pressure and see what happened.

"There are rumors about you on the street," Powers suggested. "I suppose you know that."

Koy sighed. "I've heard some of the old ones. Are there new ones as well?"

"I don't know which are old and which new. I just got here." He paused. "I'm not accusing you of anything. I was just—wondering."

A man entered the office carrying a teapot and cups on a tray. "How about some tea, Captain?" When Powers nodded, Koy began to pour.

"I understand," Powers continued, "that you were a policeman in Hong Kong. Your rank was station sergeant, I believe."

"True," said Koy. "The rumors add that I left there with an awful lot of money. I suppose you've heard them."

"Yes."

"I was a policeman and policemen have been subject to calumnies since the dawn of time."

"That's true," conceded Powers.

"And there's nothing much we can do about it, is there?"

"Usually not."

"Rumors against men like us are impossible to put down. All we can do is try to ignore them, don't you agree?"

"Yes."

"The rumors you have heard are certainly not true. But I did make some wise stock investments in Hong Kong. I acquired a modest amount of money and came here and bought this modest business."

"In five years you also took over the most important tong in Chinatown."

"It was time for new blood, Captain. I just happened to be there at the right time."

"What made you decide to leave Hong Kong?"

It was as if Powers had Koy by the throat and was shaking him. They both knew this. He was trying to shake a reaction out of him. But none came that he could read.

"Hong Kong is a small place," said Koy patiently. "A

man like myself, a former policeman, found it impossible to achieve significant business success there. Where else could I go? The mainland was closed off. There was no other neighboring country to expand into. I was obliged to go abroad and seek my fortune, like so many of my ancestors. I came to New York. Also like so many of my ancestors."

"I need help to stamp out the gangs," said Powers.

"I don't envy you your job, Captain. And I also don't see why you should be so concerned. The gangs do not bother non-Chinese. If the citizens of Chinatown wish to put up with them, why should you care?"

"Well, extortion is a crime."

"You must try to understand the Chinese mind. The Chinese have no sense of civic duty, and no tradition of charity towards strangers. To the Chinese, the Good Samaritan was a villain because he risked the security of his family to help a stranger. Whether you realize it or not, you are asking the people of Chinatown to do the same, to risk their families to help strangers, and they are not likely to do it."

"Well, what course of action do you suggest I take?"

But Koy said, "The Chinese are a very patient people. They seem willing enough to put up with the gang problem until it goes away. They fail to understand why you don't do likewise."

"How long were you a cop?"

"Twenty-one years."

How could this man have been a cop, Powers asked himself. Cops were men of feeling. Their enthusiasms and emotions, their fears, were close to the surface. Even their cynicism existed on a strictly emotional plane, youthful illusions gone rancid. Koy bore witness to none of this.

And Powers could not believe it. "Don't you have any feeling," he asked in a mild voice, "for the people who get ripped off every week?"

"The principal victims, as I understand it, are newcomers to Chinatown. Why should I feel for them? These people are not my family. They are not from my village. They must learn to protect themselves. There is nothing I can do for them. These youth gangs are merely unruly children. Teenagers. How can I control unruly adolescents? Do you have adolescent children, Captain?"

"I have two sons in college." It seemed almost a sacrilege to mention them in front of this man.

"I too have a teenage son in Hong Kong—from a previous marriage. I haven't seen him in a number of years. His mother writes to me about him. Since coming to New York I have married again. I have three daughters by the second marriage. One always worries about the young, Captain. But the Chinese do not turn to the police for help. The Chinese do not trust the police. Traditionally the law in China never protected anyone but landowners. The Chinese don't go to the police because they fear being blamed themselves. And they fear reprisals from the criminals."

It was incredible, Powers thought. A sergeant from a police department smaller than his own was lecturing him.

But he kept calm, and when Koy offered a second cup of tea, he accepted. They began to discuss the Chinese passion for gambling, and Koy had an explanation for it. Koy had an explanation for everything. Most Chinese worked such long hours, he said, twelve to fourteen hours a day, that when they had some time off their one desire was to raise their excitement level very high very fast. Gambling did this for them. But Koy did not admit, or even suggest, that he owned a gambling den himself. Also, he added, most Chinese owed big notes and gambled hoping to pay them off in a single night. But Koy did not admit or suggest that he held any such notes himself.

The undertaker showed him to the door saying: "Let's meet again, Captain. Drop in any time. We're cops. We understand each other."

No we don't, Powers thought, but he smiled warmly and shook hands. He had found Koy charming, fascinating, and more dangerous by far than he had suspected.

13

THE YOUNG blonde's head and bosom poked out into the waiting room. "Captain Powers?"

Powers looked up. Nice nose, nice lips, really nice eyes.

"I'm Margaret. This way, please."

Rising, he dropped the magazine onto the coffee table, strode at her elbow down a long airless tube of a corridor. "First time you've been up here?" she asked, but did not wait for an answer. She was very cheerful. Her mouth marched cheerfully forward in time with her feet. She must consider herself an expert at putting visitors at ease, he thought. It was as if cheer was a subject she had learned in college.

She was also tall and good-looking. In college, he would certainly have fallen in love with a girl like this, which was perhaps why he made no attempt to talk to her now. The Margarets of those days had always known how to make him feel clumsy, how to instill in him various forms of fear. There was fear in him even now walking beside her, he realized. Which was absurd—no girl this age could ever again cause his heart to flutter, cause him pain. That he was having an atavistic response to her anyway wasn't pleasant. The fears of a man's boyhood stay with him always, he supposed. A man must overcome them every day. The only girl who had never made him afraid, who had instilled in him confidence always, was his wife, and he had married her as quickly as he could.

He was not, however, afraid of Carol Cone. Margaret, showing him cheerfully into a conference room containing Carol and six men, introduced him only to Lurtsema, and cheerfully disappeared, stepping out of his life presumably forever.

If he was not afraid of Carol, this was because she fit into a different category in his mind—not girl, but wife. She was someone he might have lived with twenty years already. Wives were predictable. They tended to obey certain rules of conduct. Girls were not and did not.

The seven people stood with drinks in hand, waiting for him. Lurtsema, whom he had never heard of before two days ago, led him around and he shook hands with two other unknowns who were producers, and then with men whose faces were as familiar to Americans as the logos on breakfast-food boxes. The white-haired and avuncular anchorman, who was sometimes spoken of as a candidate for president, murmured a pleasantry. Then came two network correspondents only slightly less recognizable. Finally came Carol, who was wearing a suede dress that fit her rather snugly across the bosom.

He had expected she would be here. Was that the reason he had accepted Lurtsema's invitation?

Though a big slob of a man, Lurtsema's manners were almost courtly. But Carol cut his flowery introduction short.

"We've met before," she said.

"Yes, we have," agreed Powers, taking her hand. He shook it briefly and let go. "How have you been? Nice to see you again."

Feeling Lurtsema glance quickly from one of them to the other, he said to him, "Is that a bar I see over there?"

"Indeed it is," said the anchorman. "What would you like?"

Powers was wearing a dark business suit much like theirs, and took what they seemed to be drinking, whiskey over ice. Man the chameleon, he reflected, ever eager to blend in. The only man you trust is one who looks like you.

He had arrived prepared to pose as an expert on Chinatown. He was resolved to project an image as sober as any TV commentator. But he soon perceived that the various Chinatown atrocities, the murders, the relentless extortions, interested these people very little. Lurtsema's whiskey interested them, and beyond that, since they were important men, they wished to seem interested only in problems of world moment. Were the Red Chinese moving in? How strong was the Taiwan influence?

He was disappointed to see how eagerly they awaited his answers. Then he realized that TV was not interested in human suffering—on either side of the cameras, apparently —but rather in entertainment, and so he decided instead to entertain them if he could—the alternative being to bore them. There was a funny side to Chinatown, too, if you could keep your sense of humor. He had certainly found much to laugh about there. He would give them that, and he began by describing some of the scams by which illegal aliens entered the United States.

"One travel agent in Hong Kong advertises worldwide tours to Mexico." They were amused, and he continued. "Coolies come in on passports that identify them as bank presidents."

They were all laughing.

"Japanese passports work quite well. Japanese businessmen are above suspicion. Some Chinese guy in Hong Kong, as I understand it, owns about fifty Japanese passports. He rents them out. About fifty Chinamen at a time land in San Francisco, show their Japanese passports to immigration, walk right out onto the street. The owner is waiting at the taxi line. He collects his fifty Japanese passports and goes back to Hong Kong and rents them out again. That's how he makes his living. He's in the passport rental business."

An hour later Powers stood outside on the curb with Carol Cone. It was night and the cars were going by.

"You were good up there," she said. "You were charming. I was proud of you."

Proud of him? "Thanks for the flowers, by the way," he told her.

"Oh, did you get them?"

"I meant to call to thank you. But I've been so busy."

"Well," she said, after a moment, "I've got to be getting home."

She began trying to flag down a taxi, but they went by full.

Powers could not decide whether he wanted to walk away from her or not, and so stalled. "Do you commute by train, or what?"

"Yes. From Grand Central." She looked at him.

Again there was silence and he still couldn't decide what he wanted to do.

"And you?" she asked. "Do you have to get home to your wife?"

All right, she had inserted a key into the door for him. But he would have to turn it himself. Maybe she had. One never got old enough to be sure. One hated to risk rejection, which was as unpleasant now as it had ever been.

"My wife's working tonight."

"Oh, a career girl, eh?"

"Not exactly," he said, thinking: not like you. "Look," he said, "we could have dinner."

She nodded. "Where?"

He did not want to be seen with her by network people. Or by some cop. "How about the place you mentioned in your town? I have my car. You get a free ride home out of the deal."

They were smiling at each other. "Agreed," said Carol Cone.

The restaurant was candlelit. To read the menu Powers had to get out his half-glasses. This bothered him, and he did not know why. She knows I'm not twenty-five, he thought. But he felt better when they were folded and back in his pocket.

The waiter took their order and left.

"I'm sorry about the night you came to my house," said Carol conversationally. "I must have given you the impression that all I wanted was a fuck."

More and more women used that word now, Powers knew. But from a woman's lips it still made him flinch. Any woman's lips.

"I can get that any night of the week, no problem," said Carol conversationally. "If that's what I want. In this town? Are you kidding? Any woman can. You and I didn't even know each other. That's all it would have been, just a quick fuck. I've never been much interested in that."

Her face was lit by tottering flames, and she seemed to him almost as exotic as the Chinese. Her worlds were show business and big money, worlds he did not understand. If she also spoke a dialect different from his own, that was only to be expected.

"It wasn't what I wanted at all," Carol said.

"Well, I wish it had been."

"Why, for heaven's sake?"

"Because I was terrifically attracted to you, for one thing. And because I felt there was something between us."

"You would have been disappointed."

"I don't think so," he said firmly. A strange sort of compliment to give her, he thought.

She smiled back. Compliment received, and noted.

This was all so different from the time when he used to date girls. Then one complimented a date on her hairdo, not on how she might comport herself in bed. He was out of his depth. What was he doing here? Where did he think this would lead him? Was he fascinated by Carol, or by himself? He felt like a driver whose tires had caught in tram tracks. Instead of steering free at once he was letting the tracks carry him along, knowing they might sling him out at any time. It was dangerous. He might crash. It was also terrifically exciting.

During dinner, she brought forth her life for his inspection, course by course, like dishes out of the kitchen—he could sample any one he fancied. Catholic girls' grade school. Catholic girls' high school. Catholic girls' college.

Three similar casseroles, all faintly steaming. She had dined on them for years. He was intrigued. "I never went to school with boys in my life," she said. "I thought I wanted to be a nun. I knew nothing about boys until I married one. What are you grinning about?"

"I went to Catholic boys' schools. I never sat a day in class with girls. I wanted to be a priest."

She thought about it. "Maybe you did become a priest. A cop is a kind of priest isn't he? Cops believe in absolutes, just like priests. Good and Evil. The law. Cops decide what's sinful and what's not, just like priests. And they can lay on hands like a bishop. They can change a person's condition just by saying so: You're under arrest."

Powers, who had realized the parallel long ago, was amazed that she had perceived so much. He was very pleased with her.

"I got married right away," she said.

"I got married right away too."

"But yours is a good marriage. Or so I gather."

"Yes. It's the best marriage I know anything about. I never had a doubt that I wanted to do it, and I've never had a doubt since."

"You're very lucky. Most marriages are not that wonderful. Mine wasn't. I got pregnant the first night. I found that I didn't like sex that much, and I didn't like him that much." She stared at the tablecloth.

"Were you a virgin on your wedding night?"

"Sure. Weren't you?"

When Powers did not immediately answer, she said, "Weren't we all?"

"Well, I was a virgin until pretty late in our courtship," he conceded.

"You mean the two of you were—naughty?"

It made him smile. "Yes."

"I think that's very nice. Was she a virgin too?"

"She said she was. It took us about two weeks of poking around to make it, so I think she probably was."

Virginity in a young man of twenty-three had been shameful even then, and he felt his cheeks go hot, as if the candle flame on the table between them was too close to his face. To this day no one knew his shame except his wife, and he wondered what had made him confess it to this woman, whom he barely knew. And why had he put such information into her hands. It was information that, by its nature, she could have got nowhere else—information she could hurt him with if ever she wished to testify against him. He knew better than to do this. Every cop knew better. Information was a cop's first best weapon. One wielded it like a nightstick. One punished people with it. One clubbed them into submission. One put them in jail. Information to a cop was as valuable as money. It was the currency of the country every cop lived in. Like the trading beads of the Dutch settlers it might have little value in itself, but if you hoarded it for the best time and place, you could often use it to purchase astounding things.

In any case, you did not squander it. You did not give it away for no reason, as now.

"When I walked out on my marriage I only took two things with me, my baby and a steam iron. I never took a dime from him. I came to New York to start over. It was so hard, so hard."

She had worked as a model. She went to photography sessions carrying her baby with her in a bassinette. Since it was a different studio every day, no one complained too much. When the baby was old enough to go to school she had found work in television commercials. But she didn't want to be a shill, she wanted to be a newscaster, and so had started over still again. She had struggled and fought and put in the hours and had got where she was today.

Moved, he slid his palm across the rough-textured tablecloth until the side of his hand touched the side of hers.

"I don't regret my kid. I never have a minute. You've got to meet her. She's a great kid."

He felt admiration for her courage and compassion for her suffering—emotions akin to love—and he hooked his small finger inside hers, interlocking like a golf grip.

"It's nice to hold hands," she said.

"Yes."

Holding hands was like twisting electric wires together. With the connection made current could flow. Powers could feel it flowing now, or thought he could. He thought Carol could feel it too.

"What's your wife like?"

"She looks much like you."

"Is she dark?"

"She has blue eyes like you. Her hair is streaked blond like yours."

"And you're crazy about her."

"Yes."

"Most men at a time like this would tell me their wife was a bitch. Thank you for being honest with me."

"Carol—"

"I think I'm falling in love with you."

What was he to say to this? Was she being theatrical? Was she so lonely that it was perhaps true? Was she experiencing the equivalent of a teenage crush, and was she so unstable a woman that she would indulge herself, and call it love? His reaction was intellectual rather than physical because he was too old to accept such declarations at face value. He felt none of the hot and cold flashes, no headlong rush of emotion as in the past. Love he knew to be as unruly as a mob, as unpredictable as a riot. Love to his regret, he knew too much about. It was very expensive. It raised a lot of questions.

He didn't know her well enough to answer any of them but when he looked at her across the candle flame her eyes appeared to be moist, her lips were parted, she seemed to totally vulnerable, and he was perplexed.

Their bill was presented and paid. While they waited for change neither spoke. The change would change nothing.

It came, "What do you want to do now?" asked Carol with false brightness.

If the principal intimacy of lovers was their display to each other of naked pleasure, the next greatest intimacy was a display of naked pain, for pleasure and pain are so closely related it is sometimes impossible to tell them apart. Carol had shown him her pain, holding back almost nothing. The intimacy between them at this moment was certainly very great. It was almost as if they were lovers already.

He pocketed his money. If she wanted to play the role of teenager, then so did he, for it would be amusing. It also seemed safer than any other. "Let's go out to the car and neck," he suggested.

"Yes, let's." Smirking at each other like adolescents planning deviltry, they pushed back from the table.

His car was the last one left in the parking lot. They slid in on either side and kept sliding until their arms were around each other. Their knees knocked together, and then their teeth. Powers was unused to kissing in cars. So was she, he supposed. But it brought back nice memories. He had always enjoyed kissing girls, and he enjoyed it now. The next move, as he remembered, was to begin stroking her sweater, and then to get her skirt hiked up, but under present circumstances these notions were repugnant.

The chaste kiss ended, and Powers did not know what to do next, so he started another.

"Let's drive to Ardsley and look at the moonlight on the Hudson," said Carol. "I know a terrific place."

So he drove there, steering at her direction into a small park and nosing his car up to the low fence that overlooked the view. The moon was a little past full. Below them, wearing the lights of the great bridge like a necklace at its throat, flowed the dark river. It was a mile wide here, wider than most people's worlds, wider than ten Chinatowns. On its moon-dappled surface millions of silver dollars floated downstream.

It was a sight to stir blood that was already stirring.

"See," said Carol.

"Yes."

"It's beautiful."

"You're beautiful."

He embraced her, but this kiss was doomed to be interrupted, for a police cruiser was rolling silently into the park behind them. Without warning the cop turned his floodlight on. The beam landed hard as a blow. It struck Powers in the back of the head, glanced off and turned Carol's face ashen. It turned white everything it touched, dashboard, steering wheel, seat. It bled out all color instantly, and all intimacy, security, emotion.

In candlepower it matched an explosion, and was therefore as shocking. But it made no noise and so the shock did not last.

Powers and Carol turned blinking toward the light's source, and the cop, seeing he had surprised two adult taxpayers, hurriedly shut it off.

"He's now as shaken as we were," noted Powers. "He thought we'd be eighteen years old. Now he's worried. For all he knows I'm the mayor of this town, and you're my secretary. He may be in bad trouble." Powers began to laugh. "Shall I get out and reprimand him?"

Carol was laughing too.

"This park is closed after dark," boomed the loudspeaker on the cop's roof. He was certainly not coming over. He did not want to know who they were.

Powers started the engine. As he drove out of the park, he gave the cop a wave. The cop merely looked sullen; he gave no wave back.

"Did you ever sneak up on lovers in cars when you were a young cop?" asked Carol, snuggling against his arm as he drove.

"No. I had too much respect for lovers to do that."

"Are we going to be lovers?"

He looked at her, but did not reply.

"Where are we going?"

"I'm driving you home," he said, which did not answer her question. The answer to her question was that he did not know.

When he had rolled into her driveway, had doused lights and ignition, he kissed her again. Her big house loomed over them both, one of two looming presences he was trying to cope with. His marriage was the other.

He followed her into the house and up the dark staircase. In her bedroom they undressed separately. Beside her bed he found himself behaving exactly as if beside his own; not having undressed his wife in many years, why undress this other woman now? He didn't even look at her as she took her clothes off, though he did watch her a moment later when, naked in the moonlight that came in the windows, she threw back the covers. Then he was in bed with her, making love to her, and then she was weeping. It astonished him more than anything so far. She had screamed with pleasure—louder by far than Eleanor ever had—and a moment later she was sobbing just as loudly.

Jesus, he thought.

All he said was: "You're crying."

"Because I'm so happy," she sobbed.

Not knowing what to do or say, he stroked her arm, her shoulder, her face until she was quiet.

"You're beautiful, you know that?" she told him. The tears had stopped. "I love your neck. I love the way the hair is on your chest. And you're a very good lover."

He lay beside her. "How many lovers have you had?" The eternal male question. He was ashamed to have asked it, and he saw she did not intend to give a figure anyway. "Hey, I withdraw that. It makes no difference, and it's none of my business."

There were many mysteries to women, but this was one of the central ones, the one most of them would preserve at all costs.

"Not many," she said, moving across him. "And no one like you."

She lay on him, kissing him, and he found he wanted her again already. She kissed his eyes, his nose. "I'm crazy about you," she said, beginning to move. "And you're married, and you love your wife. What am I going to do?" Sweat glistened on her upper lip, and between her swaying breasts. She punctuated her efforts with more words. "Oh, I'm so hung up on you."

"Not just figuratively," he muttered. "Literally as well."

Her breath came in gasps. "Promise you won't just drop me. Promise I'll see you again. These next weeks are going to be agony for me. Promise you'll call me every day. At least until I get over you a little. At least give me a chance to get over you. If you have to drop me, promise you'll let me down easy."

He felt as virile as a boy.

"I love you," she said. "I love, love you, love you."

He was exultant. It was true he loved his wife, but he loved Carol too, somehow, at least at that moment. Because she loved him, and because—

"Promise me," she pleaded. "Promise, promise."

She was handing him a bill that would have to be paid regularly, a bill as recurrent as mortgage payments. But she was gorgeous in this light and totally open to him, body and soul, and his heart was near bursting that a night like this, a honeymoon night, could have happened to him again at his age.

"I promise," he heard himself say. "Oh Carol, yes, I promise."

14

AN HOUR later he was sitting up in bed in pajamas, half-glasses halfway down his nose, studying the volume open on his lap. He heard his wife come home, heard her crepe-soled shoes complain as she moved about down in the kitchen, and he stopped reading to listen to her. A cabinet opened and shut, and her shoes crossed to the stove. Then he heard her climb the stairs, and it pleased him to think that in a moment she would come into the room.

"I'm sorry," she said, "I thought you were asleep. I should have made two cups." She had entered carrying a cup of tea close to her lips, sipping as she walked. In her nurse's uniform, wearing her hair tied back, she looked tall and slim, but also rather tired.

"That's okay. I had some earlier."

She held out her cup to him. "Take this one. I'll go back down and make another."

He shook his head. "Sit down and drink your tea, Puss," he said.

She obeyed, sitting on the edge of the bed beside him. He watched her drink and felt content that she was home. After a time she reached down to take off her shoes.

"Well, what did you do with yourself all evening?" she asked, and began massaging her white-stockinged toes. "My feet hurt."

"Oh, I was out gallivanting," said Powers lightly, misleading her, avoiding the outright lie. To him each new lie would constitute an additional betrayal.

"Good." Her fond smile caressed him. "Did you get a decent dinner?"

In an expensive restaurant with another woman, he thought.

"It was okay," he said, still not lying. Lies didn't kill outright. They produced flesh wounds, like jabs from a pen knife. The victim later bled to death. In the long run they were as damaging as ax blows. They cut out chip after chip until the tree went down.

She leaned over and kissed him on the nose under his glasses. "Did you miss me tonight? Tell me how much you missed me."

She craned her neck around and peered at the book in his lap. "What are you reading?"

"Liang Shan Po."

"And what does Liang Shan Po have to say for himself?"

Powers grinned at her. "This you'll like. He writes that the rich man and the policeman are regarded by the people with equal suspicion. The outlaw, on the other hand, is regarded with sympathy, because he must have had an excellent reason for becoming an outlaw."

"Sounds like a Black Panther," said Eleanor.

"He writes of the 'holy mission of the outlaw.' "

"Are you suggesting that Liang Shan Po writes drivel?"

"I'm suggesting that the Chinese invented Robin Hood too."

"Those people sound awfully deep." She got up and began to get undressed. "What kind of day did you have? Any complainants?"

Powers, shaking his head, said: "Not one. So far, the new commander of the Fifth Precinct is as ineffectual as the last guy. Maybe more so. At least he amused them with his horse. They don't find me funny at all."

Eleanor, having undone the buttons on her white

dress, pulled it off over her head and threw it into the hamper in her closet. Her slip went into the hamper also, after which she patted her blond-streaked hair back into place. Over his half-glasses her husband watched her.

"Well, do you have a plan?" she asked conversationally. "What do you do next?"

He watched her remove her bra, pull her nightgown on over her head, and then reach up under it to take her panties off. Every night she got undressed the same way, and he always wondered why. She was not shy. In sex she enjoyed being nude. He had asked her why, but she could not tell him. Puzzling over it, he had decided that girls of Eleanor's generation—Eleanor herself, anyway—must have grown up with some deep psychological block about removing their last article of clothing. As if without it they became suddenly overly vulnerable. Back then, and it wasn't very long ago, her underpants constituted a girl's last bastion before catastrophe.

Of course Carol tonight had displayed no such fetish. She couldn't wait to get completely naked. Carol was rich, Carol was glamorous, and Carol was sex-starved.

Powers brought his knees together so that the book in his lap slammed shut.

"What's the matter?" Eleanor asked.

"What?"

"You looked sad just then."

"No, just thoughtful."

He dropped the book onto the floor. That story was over. He might never forget what he had read so far, but he would not read on.

His wife came toward the bed. "I think I've seen you somewhere before," she said. "Aren't you the hero of Chinatown?"

Powers smiled.

"That's better," she said. "I like you much better when you smile."

But his smile faded. "They sent me to Chinatown to suppress the youth gangs," he muttered. "They want no more massacres. They want the crime rate down, and the arrest rate up. But there's no earthly way to stop the youth gangs without going after the conspiracy as a whole. It's impossible. I'm going to fail. Six months from now, maybe sooner, they're going to fire me. Puss, I don't have any choice. I *have* to go after the Chinese Mafia. I have to prove it exists and I have to bring it down."

"If they find out," said Eleanor, "they'll ruin you."

"I'm ruined anyway. I have nothing to lose."

"Calm down," said Eleanor, sliding into the bed. "I'm on your side. How do you go about it?"

"I go after the biggest hood in Chinatown. I go after Koy."

"Poor Koy. The hero of Chinatown is after him, and he doesn't even know it."

"It isn't funny."

"I know it's not funny."

"I had a long talk with him this afternoon," said Powers. "It was one of the most disagreeable conversations of my life. Look, we know the tongs control the gangs, and Koy controls the richest tong. If there is a Chinese Mafia, then he has to be the leader of it. There is no one else in Chinatown with his stature. If I can nail Koy I can decapitate the conspiracy and then pick off the gang thugs one by one. Also, I'll have more face than any man in Chinatown— enough face, maybe, to turn Chinatown around."

"I like your face the way it is," said Eleanor. "And anyway, what do you have on him?"

"Nothing at all. I've been to every law enforcement agency in the city. No one has anything on him. He's absolutely clean."

"Then how can you be so sure he is dirty?"

"It's something a cop can read," said Powers doggedly. "Particularly in another cop—which is one of my problems, by the way. Being a cop himself, Koy will see me coming."

Powers reached to turn off the light, then slid down into the bed, and moved up against his wife, his sole support in a hostile world. There was no one else he could talk to like this, but tonight she had left him alone and he had betrayed her with another. "I wish you wouldn't work these four-to-midnight tours, Puss," he said.

"Hey, that's what I always used to say about you. What I still say about you."

"Dinner time is a bad time to be alone."

She thought about this. "I agreed to work four-to-midnight until the end of the month. After that, we'll see, okay?"

"I wish you wouldn't work at all." There, it was out. He had felt it for a long time and now, finally, he had said it. They were face to face, breathing on each other, and he held her close.

"We have two kids in college, Artie. It's costing us a fortune," she reminded him gently. "We need the money." She kissed him lightly on the cheek. "Now go to sleep like a good boy."

He held her in the dark, her exhalations beating regularly against his throat. He felt her fall down deep into sleep, and then the telephone rang on the bedside table beside his ear.

He lunged for it, trying to catch it halfway through the first ring, before it could awaken her, and he answered almost in a whisper.

But his wife's bedside lamp had gone on, and she sat up and watched him.

This long strange day was not over after all. "I'll be right there," said Powers and hung up. "They've found the getaway car from the restaurant massacre," he told Eleanor. "I have to go out." He got up and began to dress. "This has been some day," he said.

"Want me to come with you?" she offered.

It was tempting. But she had been on her feet eight straight hours. "They want me to make the identification. I shouldn't be too long. Go back to sleep."

"I'll keep the bed warm for you."

He grinned at her. "Can I wake you when I come back?"

"Don't you dare."

Dressed, he went around to her side, switched off her light, and then in the dark gave her a brief hug. He could barely see her in the darkness. He stroked her hair once, and then went out.

THE GETAWAY CAR, if it was the getaway car, was parked under a tree in front of a two-family house on a residential street in Queens. The street had been closed off to traffic by radio cars that stood sideways at both ends, red lights turning. Powers double-parked at the corner and walked in, heading for the spot where the police photographer had set up his lights. There were rows of passenger cars parked solid along both sidewalks, only one of which was floodlit.

Inside the nearest houses no one, apparently, slept. From the windows heads hung like grapes, and the front stoops were crowded with people in bathrobes. It was an attentive audience and it seemed to be waiting to applaud, but the play was proving less exciting than had been hoped; nothing seemed to be happening. The forensic van, Powers noted, was double-parked just beyond the getaway car, back door agape. There were about eight cops in uniform standing in the street, and a dozen or more detectives as well. One of the detectives was Chief Cirillo, who stood smoking a cigar, and Powers, after inspecting the car, approached him.

"Is that the car, Ralph?" Powers asked him, for they stood apart from Cirillo's subordinates, and they had known each other a long time.

But Cirillo, after puffing on his cigar said, "Last I heard, I was chief of detectives and you were a captain."

Powers looked at him.

Cirillo said, "The proper form of address, the last I heard, was Chief."

Powers looked away. After a moment he said, "Is it the car?"

Cirillo let this pass. "I don't know. You tell me."

Powers went back and studied the car. The license

plates were wrong. He walked around it. All four doors were open, and technicians were working carefully inside.

"Is it the car?" said Cirillo at his elbow, "the one you fired shots at?"

"It could be. It's the right model and year. It's certainly dirty enough. Who found it?"

"A foot patrolman found it," Cirillo said. "It was on his foot post. It's been on his foot post over a month."

"Finally it got dirty enough that he noticed it."

"Yeah," said Cirillo. "We've got some very observant cops in this department."

Powers peered into the car. A fingerprint technician was working in the front seat. "Got anything?" Powers asked him.

But Cirillo's head appeared in the opposite doorway. "You tired of being a detective, pal?" he said to the technician.

"No sir."

"In that case," said Cirillo, "you report directly to me, got that? You don't tell anybody else anything until I say you can. Unless you're tired of being a detective, that is."

The technician gave Powers a glance, shrugged and was silent.

Cirillo had moved off and was facing the other way, chewing on the cigar between his teeth, chewing on information Powers wanted. Powers went over there. "So how's the investigation going?"

Cirillo blew smoke at him. "What investigation?"

"The restaurant massacre."

"Oh, that investigation." Cirillo studied him. "That investigation is proceeding."

"What leads do you have?"

"We are following up all leads." He again blew smoke at Powers.

Powers said, "I am going home."

"You are not. You will sign a statement first. Detective McCoy will take your statement." Cirillo peered about under the trees looking for McCoy. "McCoy?" he bawled. A detective ran up whom Powers did not know. "McCoy," said

Cirillo, "take down Captain Powers' statement and have him sign it."

"My statement is that it could be the car," said Powers. "Some statement."

But he was obliged to follow McCoy to the hood of an adjacent car, where he held McCoy's flashlight on the form while McCoy, pushing hard on his pen, wrote out the statement. When it was finished, Powers signed it.

"One of my detectives ought to be here," Powers said, glancing around. "Detective Kelly. You seen him?"

"Some of the guys went around the corner for a cup of coffee," said McCoy. "I think he went with them."

"What do you know about the investigation?" said Powers. Cirillo, he noted was watching both of them.

"It's going well." said McCoy nervously.

"What did they find in the car?"

"Nobody tells me anything," said McCoy.

Powers found Kelly in a diner two blocks away, and took the next stool. "Cirillo is sitting on this case," muttered Powers. "I couldn't get any information at all."

"This car tonight is the first break in the case," said Kelly. "What do you want to know? You know that the back floor mat is caked with blood, don't you? And there's a bullet embedded in the doorjamb. What more can I tell you? They're going to tow the car in and cut the bullet out with power tools, in case they can still identify it. And the fingerprint guy got a partial off of the ashtray."

"I will have a coffee and a doughnut," Powers said to the girl. "You came away with more information than I did, Kelly."

"The fingerprint guy is Goldbarth. If I ask him something, he tells me. He was my first radio-car partner. He's a kike, but he's a good guy. And guts? Gutsiest cop in the department. We was partners almost five years."

Presented with a source of information Cirillo did not know about, Powers considered: "If your friend really did lift some prints, do you think tomorrow you could find out who they belong to?"

"Sure."

"I don't want to get your friend in trouble. Or you either."

"So Cirillo clamped the lid on. So fuck Cirillo."

Powers drained his coffee. "It's been a long day," he said. "I'm going home to bed." At the doorway he looked back. "Be, er, discreet."

"My middle name, Captain. I will take care of the little matter. Rest assured."

They grinned at each other, arch-conspirators. The most arch conspiracy of all: putting one over on the boss. But once in the street Powers' grin went sour. He hated to be beholden to a detective, or to display his weakness to one. And he didn't want to be Kelly's ally against the chief of detectives. He wanted to be chief of detectives himself.

BY 4 P.M. the next day, Kelly was standing in Powers' office handing over a fingerprint card. "That's the guy, Captain."

Powers, in uniform behind his desk, studied the card for a moment, then pushed it back toward Kelly. "Who is he?"

"His name is Hsu. There's two of them. They're brothers. A pair of pricks. We arrested them about three months ago. They don't speak English. They were slashing up chair seats in a restaurant on Canal Street. I guess the owner had missed a payment. Some cop walked in off the street to use the phone or something. He sees the owner cringing in the corner while these two pricks are destroying his restaurant. The cop arrested them on the spot, and we did an investigation, but the little Chink who owns the place was too scared to press charges. The DA washed it out. What else could he do?"

Powers, peering at Kelly over his half-glasses, nodded.

Kelly had just come from the Police Academy lab. "What else did you learn that I don't know?" Powers asked.

"Well, the car itself checks out. It was stolen in Brooklyn the night before the massacre. And the bullet in the doorjamb is from your gun. The car is definitely the car."

Powers studied Hsu's fingerprint card again.

"The curious thing is, Captain, we got these Hsu brothers as Flying Dragons. We watched them pretty carefully for about two weeks. We know where they went, who they hung out with. They're Dragons, all right."

Powers and Kelly looked at each other. "And the Dragons are affiliated with Ting's own tong," mused Powers. "So why did they shoot up his restaurant?"

Kelly said: "If we were dealing with white men, this would indicate that Ting shot up his restaurant himself." He shook his head. "Chinamen are too devious for me, Captain. With Chinamen it could mean something else entirely."

It could mean, Powers thought, that one of Ting's colleagues shot up the restaurant so as to discredit Ting. But who? Who profited? Koy did, Powers thought. Koy became mayor the next day. Am I thinking like a Chinese, Powers asked himself, or making no sense at all? Was Koy capable of something so monstrous? Don't leap to conclusions, he warned himself. Who else profited? But he did not know and had no way of finding out.

"Are you going to give this out to the press, or what?" asked Kelly.

Powers again studied the fingerprint card. No, he thought, let's give it out to Mr. Ting, and see what happens. What was likely to happen? He had no idea, and he did not try to explain himself to Detective Kelly. Pushing back from his desk, he put his cap on his head, but at the doorway he paused: "Better put the fingerprint card back where it belongs," he said. "And Kelly, thanks."

ABOUT FIVE minutes later and a block and a half away, he pushed through the glass doors and stood again in the theatrical lobby of the Golden Palace Restaurant. As he started up the great staircase, he had second thoughts. Suppose he ruined Cirillo's investigation? But clearly the secret could not be kept. The getaway car had been found, and you could not keep such juicy stuff away from 25,000 cops. It would spread from radio car to radio car, and then out into the city. Because the one thing true about cops was this: they talked too much. Cirillo would be obliged to hold a press conference whether he wanted to or not. Nor could the identity of Hsu be kept secret. The detectives searching for him would have to know his name, and as soon as a few detectives knew, again, every cop and then the city would know.

He was spoiling nothing except Cirillo's press conference, Powers told himself, and perhaps he would provoke Ting into a reaction that would bring the hierarchy of the entire Chinese Mafia out into the open. It was worth the risk.

He pushed through the upstairs doors into the restaurant. Waiters worked setting up tables for dinner. Ting was behind the cash desk watching them. Powers walked over.

"Good evening, Mr. Ting," he said. "Do you have time for a cup of tea?"

AT TING'S request a meeting of the Nam Soong board of directors was held the following day. The goddess on her dais stared out as impassively as before. The joss sticks smoldered again in their urns. To either side of the conference table sat the same sinister old men. A waiter had entered and was pouring tea, and the men were silent until he had gone out.

"Please continue, Mr. Ting," said Koy, who now occupied the place at the head of the table.

Ting, seated at Koy's right hand, said in English, "If, as the police claim, this Hsu is indeed affiliated with the Flying Dragons, then the motive for the attack on my restaurant becomes unclear." And he stared at Koy, although no one else did.

The accusation, if that's what it was, drew at first only silence.

"It has been my experience," murmured Mr. Hong, who was seventy-eight years of age, "that police theories too often resemble trees planted on hillsides: shallow-rooted and precarious."

A generalized, almost poetic remark—for 2500 years educated Chinese had tried whenever possible to mimic not only the wisdom but even the speech patterns of Confucius. Thus rash words were avoided as assiduously as rash conduct, for this preserved everyone's face, and it provided time in which the correct compromise could be worked out. Violence was for street hoodlums. Precipitate emotions were the mark not only of the uncultured man, but also of the unsuccessful one.

Hong had spoken for all the others. He had found a solution: the police were not to be believed, and further research was needed. Koy had expected no less from him; nonetheless, he was relieved. Hong and the others, having rejected Ting on the day following the massacre, continued to reject him. By now they had invested heavily in Koy, both in prestige and money. They would not abandon these investments easily. Their loyalty to Ting was less great than their desire for increased profits.

However, no profits had yet come in, and Ting's veiled charge had been made. There was pressure on Koy to produce—there would be stronger pressure after today— and he knew it.

"Mr. Koy can perhaps investigate the truth of the police theory," suggested the second Mr. Hong, the one with thick glasses and protruding yellow teeth.

"My information," persisted Ting, "is not official, and therefore perhaps more trustworthy."

He could go no further than this without support, and he did not get it. The old men around the table peered into their teacups.

Finally Mr. Lau said, "I thought we were agreed that these youth gangs were no longer under our control. Was it not for this reason that Mr. Koy acceded to the presidency of our association?"

It was a way of saying that the problem was Koy's; it

was Koy who must deal with it. If he dealt with it success-fully, then the subject would not be raised again. If not—

If not, thought Koy, glancing from face to face, they were perfectly capable of protecting their investments by other means. He watched Mr. Lau sip tea. The cup was raised in a mottled, trembling hand, but Koy did not make the mistake, because of this, of thinking Lau feeble. Nor were any of the others. Though old, they were by no means senile, and in some ways had grown more dangerous than ever.

Koy said, "Now that we know who is presumed to have taken part in the attack, perhaps it will be easier to find him and his colleagues." He paused but none of the eyes met his, and this signaled that the meeting should proceed to other matters.

"Now," said Koy, getting down to business, "it is in-deed fortuitous that we should meet today, as it gives us the opportunity to discuss certain of the charities we support, and also to hear Mr. Lau's report on his interview with Dr. Peabody at Yale University. As you know, we are attempting to endow a chair in Medieval Chinese History there. Mr. Lau."

Lau opened a dossier on the table in front of him, and in his trembling old man's voice began to speak. "Dis-cussions have reached the point where Dr. Peabody has asked me to recommend the names of three Chinese schol-ars. Meanwhile Dr. Peabody's committee—"

Perhaps the others were still listening, but Koy, star-ing at the tips of his steepled fingers, was not. It was proba-ble, once this meeting ended and they all returned to their offices, that Ting would send out men to find the Hsu broth-ers; it was possible that one or more of the others would too. All of them employed disciplined, unscrupulous subordi-nates who were good at such work; their gambling dens, their extortion, loan sharking and drug rackets required it. But the Hsus were only part of Koy's problem. He was sud-denly being pressed to expedite his other schemes as well. His investors were becoming impatient, and had just made this plain to him, though not a word had been said. He had been trying to work through intermediaries but it was taking too long to set things up. Now, clearly, he would have to do much of the work himself. To remain insulated was a luxury he could no longer afford. It would mean meetings with the Italians, and then a long and dangerous journey, and he was not happy about any of it.

As for the Hsu problem, it must be resolved immediately. Today's meeting had certainly meant bad luck for the Hsus.

15

A DIM, empty street. The streetlights were far apart, and some were out. None shone on the building, an abandoned warehouse near the piers. This was Brooklyn, just across the bridge from Chinatown. The hour was nearly midnight. For the third time Koy's Mercedes cruised past. He was driving very slowly, peering all around. Very few cars had gone by and no pedestrians. Again he saw no one, no lovers, no joggers, no dogwalkers. Such people would give this forbidding area a wide berth. The warehouse had an alley. He thought the buildings to either side looked abandoned too, but his policeman's instinct warned him not to count on this. There could be night watchmen on duty if the buildings still functioned. If they did not, then an infestation of junkies or derelicts was possible, perhaps probable. But on the whole he was pleased. As the site for what had to be done tonight, it was ideal.

The warehouse had been sealed, the front windows boarded up and the entrance bricked up with cinderblocks. Koy, who had noted this during the first pass, swung the wheel and his Mercedes flowed into the alley, which was not only dark, but also choked with refuse, a garbage dump between two high walls. His headlights beat against the stuff as if to tramp it down. He drove in until his bumper touched it, then stopped, extinguished lights and ignition and sat there, listening. When he got out he could not see at all—light from the street did not come this far in. Good. To anyone driving or strolling by, his car had vanished. It did not exist. He listened again, the way a priest might listen for instructions from God. But he heard nothing.

Reaching back into the glovebox, Koy got hold of a flashlight, flicked it on, flashed it around, flicked it off again. The alley was blocked by rotting timbers, ripped-out insulation, bedsprings and other such junk. In darkness he went forward. He was wearing a tan silk suit, and he moved with great care, stepping sideways between two discarded refrigerators, using the flashlight for quick glimpses only, clambering over a pile of wooden doors that looked like a deck of gigantic cards that had wafted down from the roof. The doors were unstable, shifting under him as he crept, and he was afraid they might collapse entirely.

Entrance was by a steel door toward the rear of the side of the building. The door hung by its bottom hinge only. Koy pushed it open and went in. His flashlight shone on steep, narrow stairs. The bottom two steps were missing. He went on up, shining the flashlight all around, wary of rats, and came out into a second floor loft illuminated like a church by the flames of many candles.

The loft had been gutted. Its contents, probably, had been chucked out the windows. That would account for the junk in the alley. Koy turned off his flashlight. He was standing in a single enormous room. At the far end, the candles stood on the floor, like votive lights around a shrine. The eight gang members were clustered there near a formerly boarded-up window that had been knocked out to admit air. Most of them squatted, or sat, on the floor, for there was no furniture.

Two of the boys crouched over a single comic book. Four others played mah-jongg between outstretched legs. Koy in the doorway could hear the movement of the mah-jongg tiles, which clicked like teeth. Another boy, his back against the wall, held a .9 mm Browning automatic in his lap. He kept cocking and uncocking it, sending out clicks louder than the tiles, as loud as coins dropped into a turn-stile, one-way fare for the longest journey of all.

Only Nikki Han, standing by the window, had perceived Koy's entrance.

"The Cho Kun is here," he called in Chinese. All the boys sprang to their feet. As Koy came forward out of the darkness, their faces split into broad grins, and they bowed.

Koy murmured a greeting in Chinese, and gave a wave of his hand, saying, "Let me have a word with elder brother"—this was the title by which the boys commonly addressed Han, their leader. As Koy and Han stepped over to the window to converse, the noise of the clicking mah-jongg tiles resumed, and the clicking gun. But at the same time the boys watched the men carefully.

"Do any of them speak English?" Koy murmured.

"One of them—you know him—Go Low."

Koy did know him. American born. About eighteen years old. Han's lieutenant. Reliable. Koy glanced toward him and nodded. All others were from Hong Kong. Good, Koy thought.

"Do they know why they were brought here?" he asked Han. His voice had dropped almost to a whisper.

"No."

Koy went over to the group playing mah-jongg. Go Low and three others. The boys stopped playing.

"Please continue," said Koy, squatting down, bringing his face to their level. The position was uncomfortable for Koy.

"You must be the new boy, Quong," he said conversationally.

The child stood up and bowed politely. "Very pleased to meet you, venerable sir."

He was quite small, hardly taller standing than Koy squatting. Koy recognized the younger Hsu brother. "And you're the boy who was shot in the leg," he said. "How is your wound?"

The younger Hsu sprang to his feet and swiftly undid his belt. His jeans collapsed at his ankles. He was grinning with pride. He was like a flasher sending shock waves through a girl. He was like a recruit waiting to be inoculated, the only one not afraid—head of the line!

The bullet hole had scarred over. Koy, having removed his dark glasses, became aware that young Quong's face was as close to Hsu's thigh as his own.

"Do you know how he got that, sir?" asked Quong in an admiring voice.

These kids talk too much, thought Koy. "No," said Koy, "I don't." Looking at Quong, he frowned.

Koy, who had seen a great many gunshot wounds in his career, probed the puckered hole with his fingertip. "Does that hurt?"

Quong answered, not Hsu. "No sir," said the boy in Cantonese. "Nothing hurts this guy. The bullet's still in there, and he doesn't even care. He's got balls on him this big. He's my best friend."

Koy peered at Quong. Had he ever been that young himself? Had he ever believed and uttered such puerile nonsense?

"It doesn't hurt at all," boasted Hsu.

Koy's gaze lifted, and he studied the two angelic countenances above him. One boy was a murderer, the other a total innocent, but their faces were the same as if the printing press of life had not come down yet on either. Their cheeks were entirely smooth, like paper too heavily glazed to hold the imprint of the ink. At their age the ink in the machine was invisible, but it was also indelible. A few years would bring it out. If either lived long enough.

"How about your hand?" asked Koy. He took Hsu's hand in both of his. The thing seemed to have frozen into a claw.

"That don't bother him either, venerable sir," said Quong admiringly in Cantonese.

Koy glanced around for the older brother. It took a moment to recognize him—it was the boy cocking and uncocking the automatic. Another bland adolescent face. It bore no trace of suffering, no resemblance to the youth Koy had last seen writhing and bleating on top of a dirty sheet on a bed in Queens. When Koy stepped toward him, the boy did not look up. He was working his gun. Like a boy masturbating, he was totally concentrated on what he was doing.

"Can you walk all right?" Koy asked, squatting down beside him.

The boy jumped up and bowed. "How do you do, venerable sir. Yes sir. Want to see?" He pranced about the room.

"Very good," said Koy. "You hardly even limp. What's your secret? Did you grow new toes?"

The boy sat down in the same spot and took up his gun again. "No sir," he said politely. "But it healed real good, and I got an extra sock stuffed into the front of my shoe where my toes used to be. I don't even miss them."

"Good," said Koy with a smile, "I'm glad to hear it."

Hsu cocked and uncocked the automatic.

"Lend me that for a minute, will you?" said Koy casually. He took the gun away from him and carried it to the window where he conferred again with Han.

"It's a shame," Koy said. He peered down at the gun, turning it this way and that without really seeing it, for he was disturbed by the decision he had come here to make.

"Yeah."

"Both of them have made really miraculous recoveries."

Han nodded.

"It's a real shame," said Koy. But every cop in the city was now looking for the Hsu brothers and Ting might have people looking too.

"The only thing didn't work out so good is they both got big habits," said Han. "It's been a problem taking care of those habits."

"It won't be after tonight," said Koy sadly.

"You leave it to me."

The gang leader looked eager. He wanted to do it, Koy noted, the sooner the better. He liked this sort of thing. Well, it had to be done. Life was a guerrilla action. One conformed like water to the terrain, or one did not win, and one probably did not even survive.

There was no way to get the Hsus out of the country on such short notice. They had missed their ship and there had not been another.

"I take no pleasure in it," said Koy. "Who will escort them to the land of pines?" In China most cemeteries were surrounded by pine trees. Koy had translated the euphemism literally from the Cantonese.

"I will," said Nikki Han avidly. In his own mind it was settled, and excitement seemed to come on fast. His eyes began to glow, his breathing quickened. To Koy he resembled a woman anticipating sex. He likes killing, Koy thought. He can't wait. He gets a sexual jolt out of it. No form of human depravity could any longer shock Koy. Nonetheless, he was revolted by Han, and he decided to dominate him, not indulge him. One dominated people by denying them pleasure, as every religion in the world had learned long ago.

"No," Koy said, "use the new boy, Quong." Han must be denied, and Quong's loyalty must be locked in. Once the child had killed, he could not turn back. "Let him prove his loyalty to the Flying Dragons," Koy said.

Han's disappointment showed promptly. His voice sounded as keen as a knife blade. "I'd rather do it myself," he protested. "Quong is tight with the younger Hsu brother and—"

But Koy's voice was sharper still. "You have your orders. I'm leaving now."

Handing the automatic to Han, Koy flicked on his flashlight, and for a moment its long beam could be seen searching for the exit door. It found it, and locked on, and Koy strode down the beam and out. From the rear, it was like watching a carpet rolled up behind him.

When the Cho Kun was gone Nikki Han began to shout commands in Chinese. The four boys playing mahjongg, one of them Go Low, jumped up. Low and one other grabbed the older Hsu's arms, while Quong looked on in surprise and confusion. Simultaneously, the two boys reading the one comic book ran over and grabbed the younger brother in the same way. The Hsus were dragged to the center of the candlelit area and were forced to kneel. Held crucified on their knees, they began glancing wildly about. They read the scene accurately and were terrified. In Chinese, in a low harsh voice, the gloating Nikki Han ordered Quong to take out his gun, to press it to the nape of the neck of the kneeling older brother, and the bewildered child did so.

"Now kill him," ordered Nikki Han.

But Quong did not react. The kneeling boy, struggling in the grasp of Low and the other boy, squawked like a parrot, and his head swiveled all around.

"Fire!" cried Nikki Han. "Shoot him! Pull the trigger!"

Perhaps Quong was remembering his own initial ritual. Perhaps they were testing him still again. He looked both confused and frightened. He did not know what was expected of him.

"Stink pig," cursed Nikki Han in Cantonese. "Dog vomit." He took two steps toward the older brother, who saw him coming and tried to struggle to his feet. When the muzzle of Han's automatic touched the nape of his neck, the boy screamed. But his scream was cut short. The explosion made everybody jump. The two boys holding the outspread arms let go, and the body pitched forward onto its face.

Han, automatic outstretched, moved on Quong, who appeared stupefied. The fifteen-year-old stared from the fresh corpse to the oncoming automatic. A thin trickle of smoke leaked out of its barrel as if to match the thin trickle of blood that leaked down the corpse's neck onto the floor.

"Kill him," the gang leader cried in an emotion-charged voice. He thrust the muzzle two inches from Quong's mouth. Han was having trouble catching his breath, he seemed in the throes of some sort of terrific excitement, and this contributed to Quong's terror because he did not understand it, only felt its weight. It would force him to perform an act that was unspeakable.

Quong began to cry. Tears ran down his tortured,

child's face. "I don't want to kill him, Elder Brother," he pleaded. "He's my best friend, Elder Brother. Don't make me kill my best friend."

"Fire," shouted Han. "Fire." Grabbing Quong's gun hand, he rammed it forward, so that the gun's muzzle pressed into the squirming boy's neck. "Hold him tight," Han shouted to the two youths tugging at Hsu's arms. "Kill him, or I'll kill you," he shouted to Quong, and his face was illuminated by a fierce joyous grin.

In the cluttered alley below, Koy had come over the piled doors, had passed between the discarded refrigerators. He had got into his car, and as the second shot rang out his engine was already turning over. Removing his glasses, Koy rubbed the bridge of his nose. After a moment he replaced them, backed carefully out of the alley, and drove home.

AT NOON the following day, a narcotics detective named Pete Spengler met with an informant in a bar about four blocks away. The informant was a junkie and, therefore, unreliable. Still, he sometimes came up with good stuff. His name was Carmelo, street name Johnny Blood. Although his clothes were filthy and he had not shaved, he looked in pretty good shape this morning, Spengler observed, not stoned anymore, not sniveling and begging yet either, which was his usual condition later in the day.

"Go ahead and drink that, Blood." Spengler said, as the barman put beers down in front of them. "It's got food value. The trouble with you is, you never eat." Both took a long swallow, and Spengler noted that Blood looked excited. "Why did you want to see me?" he inquired. Blood looked so excited that Spengler thought: he may really have something. "What have you got for me, Blood?"

"That's not the question," Blood said archly. "The question is, what do you have for me?"

I wonder what he's got, Spengler thought.

Spengler and the other narcotics detectives drew their expense money in monthly allotments. For this month, the detective was empty—he had already used it all up. On the other hand, he had made an arrest earlier in the week, confiscating—and neglecting to voucher—two five-dollar bags of heroin. They were in his locker back in the station house, where they lay like money in a savings account. They were like emergency rations. They were there to tide a man over.

Spengler began to bargain. "You got nothing," he stated flatly. That's what a cop did, he thought. Cops bargained with these germs. You beat them down. The alternative was to run out of expense money, and out of stuff as well, by the end of the first week.

"There was a shooting down the street last night," said Blood archly.

"Oh? Where was that?" Spengler asked, pretending disbelief and disinterest both. There had been no report of shots fired in this precinct last night.

"It will cost you to find out," said Blood.

Spengler thought about it. "Tell you what, Johnny, you take me there and if it pans out, I may have something for you."

"You're good," chortled Blood, rubbing his hands together. "You're a cop, but you're not a prick. Come on. It's down by the piers."

Blood led the detective to the deserted warehouse. "You go in there," he said archly. "You tell me what you find."

Spengler eyed the refuse-strewn alley. "You come in with me," he decided.

"I ain't going in there again," said Blood. "I wait for you right here. It's worth a spoon." A spoon was five bags. "When you come out, you give me a spoon."

Ten minutes later Spengler called in the precinct detectives from the gas station down the street and he waited for them at the head of the alley. "It's two Chinese kids," he told the first two to arrive, and led the way across the shifting pile of doors. "They can't be more than eighteen years old. It looks to me like some kind of ritual execution. When you make your notifications, you better notify the Fifth Precinct as well. Since it's Chinks involved, they might want to know about it."

By the time Powers and Kelly drove up in front of the warehouse, the street was crowded with police vehicles. A cop in uniform directed them into the alley. They mounted the stairs and came out into the second-floor loft. The police photographer had his lights up. Many detectives and uniformed cops stood around. There was no sign, thankfully, of Chief of Detectives Cirillo, who either did not realize the possible significance of these murders, or had not yet been told of them. Powers and Kelly approached one of the bodies.

"That's him," said Kelly, looking down. "That's the Hsu kid."

The medical examiner, bag open on the floor, knelt beside the body. They watched him work.

Powers, glancing across at the second corpse, said to Kelly, "Is the other one his brother?"

Kelly went to see. "I can't tell," he said, bending over it. "The face is gone."

Just then the medical examiner moved the body he was working on. The head flopped sideways, as if there were no bones in the neck.

"Jesus," said Powers.

"Bullet passed between the second and third cervical vertebrae," grunted the medical examiner. "Neck broken. Same as if he'd been hung. Ever seen anyone been hung?"

"Yes," said Powers. Corpses no longer made him nauseated, only depressed. A cop saw every kind of death there was.

"The other one is the same," said the M.E., throwing a glance toward the second body. "I already worked on him. Except in his case, the bullet also tore up the front of his face. You can't see what he used to look like so good. Hey, look at this, he's got a bullet wound in the leg, too. About a month or five weeks old, I guess. Maybe a little more. Somebody's sewed it up."

That's my bullet for sure, Powers thought.

"There's no exit wound, and no sign it's been worked on," said the medical examiner, probing the puckered thigh. "So the bullet is probably still in there. When I get back home to my place I'll extract it and send it up to ballistics."

To this guy, Powers realized, "home to my place," meant the morgue.

He went to stand at the window. He looked out at the river, at the water that sparkled in the sun. On the other side the skyscrapers of the financial district rose straight up like the wall around a medieval town. Overhead reached the three soaring bridges. The bridges seemed to him a symbol of man's vision, of his desire to join hands and to create, as opposed to his equally fantastic need to kill and destroy.

These dead kids might have been vicious murderers, he thought, but they were babies. What went wrong? And who did this to them? He wanted to get his hands on him, whoever it was. But how?

Kelly came over and stood beside him, and they looked back at the corpses. "Seeing dead kids is hard," the detective said. Powers nodded, and they stood side by side not as commander and subordinate but as two cops forced to look at this kind of thing far too often.

Ting is involved in this, Powers thought. One day after I give him Hsu's name, the kid gets whacked out. But Ting is old and out of power. He must have taken it to the tong. The decision must have been made high up in the tong, and the head man of the tong is Koy.

It *is* a Mafia, Powers thought, and Koy is the godfather, and I want him.

"Call up your friend in the lab," he told Kelly. "I want to know whatever ballistics turns up on these bullets."

"No problem, Cap."

"Now let's get out of here before the chief of detectives shows up."

They strode past the bodies and down the stairs.

16

POWERS STOOD in front of the desk of Chief of Patrol Duncan. Of the two uniforms, his own was newer, better cut, more freshly pressed, and for a moment this gave him confidence. Appearance counted. The visual expression of a man's will to excel counted. However, Duncan's uniform did surpass his own where it counted most, in the insignia on the shoulders, Duncan's shining gold, opposed to his own dull silver. If you stared at Duncan's three stars long enough, their candlepower had the power to blind.

Like a job applicant, Powers carried that morning's *Daily News* under his arm. But it was not folded open to the want ads. "I wonder if you saw this," he began, placing the paper on the outside edge of Duncan's desk. If he wanted it, let him reach for it. Powers was interested in scoring points, big or small, in any way he could.

The headlines read: COPS SEEK CLUES IN TONG EXE-CUTIONS. Beneath was a photo that showed the corpses being carried out of the warehouse, while a number of cops looked on. But Duncan, who could see the headlines from where he sat, only glanced at them, then leaned back in his swivel chair ignoring the newspaper altogether. "Chief Cirillo and I went out there," he said. "We heard you had been there earlier. We were surprised you didn't hold a press conference."

They stared briefly at each other.

Powers said, "If you got there before they wrapped them up, then you know it wasn't pretty."

"No," Duncan conceded, "It wasn't pretty. What's your point?"

"I've got one Chinese cop," Powers began carefully. "His name is Lawrence Lom. He's pushing fifty years old and his specialty is community relations. I don't think he's ever been on the street in his life. I need help. You've got to assign me a cop who speaks Chinese, who is Chinese, and who can do me some good on the street."

Duncan responded with a smug smile. The battle was joined, and he saw he would win it easily. "There are only six Chinese cops in the job. All of them were offered Chinatown at one time or another. The other five turned it down, and they all gave the same reason. They know everybody in Chinatown. They don't want to be seen as cops in Chinatown. The Chinese people despise cops."

Powers said: "Everybody despises cops."

"Their argument," said Duncan smugly, "and I agree with it, is that they are no good in a community where they call everybody Uncle. The Chinese are very big on calling people Uncle. As I understand it, they have three words for Uncle, did you know that?"

"Yes, I heard," said Powers.

"The three words mean Young Uncle, Old Uncle and Real Uncle." Duncan smiled patronizingly. "So you can't have any Chinese cops."

"There's a Chinese recruit in the Police Academy right now," said Powers. "I want him."

If Duncan was surprised by this news, his answer was no less automatic. "You can't have him. He'll give you the same story anyway." The subject, as far as Duncan was concerned, was closed. He came forward in his chair. He looked pleased with himself.

"I've talked to this guy," said Powers doggedly. "He didn't grow up in Chinatown, he grew up in Hong Kong. He moved to San Francisco when he was fifteen, and he moved to New York five years ago. He's never lived in Chinatown. And he's willing to work for me."

"I'll consider it," said Duncan. He began to rearrange papers on his desk. "I'm not promising anything." Duncan sent a smile out into the void, and Powers sent a glare. The two different tools, both unsuited to the job at hand, collided in midair, and crashed to the desk top.

"Considering it is not enough," said Powers. "You owe it to me. You've given me this impossible job, and I need him."

Duncan's smile had faded. He stared across at Powers, who stared back. Their stares strained against each other with equal force and weight. Stares as blunt as walls. In the absence of a cutting edge, no breakthrough seemed possible on either side.

"What are you planning, Powers?"

"Planning? Nothing. Nothing at all. I'm trying to break up the youth gangs, that's all. And I need help."

"I don't believe you."

"I want this Chinese cop," Powers said, "And you'd better give him to me or—"

"Or you go to the press," said Duncan, leaning forward across his desk. "If you do, you won't survive it."

"I didn't say I'd go to the press."

"With you there's always that possibility."

"I'm asking you please."

"You move through this department like a piece of heavy machinery, Powers. You want to know why you don't get ahead? That's why."

"Can I ask you something? Can I have this recruit sworn in secretly? I want to use him undercover. I don't want him to show on the Fifth Precinct roster. Can I have him assigned to me personally? Can I have him, or not?" And he added, though it cost him heavily in pride: "Chief, please."

THE POLICE ACADEMY firing range was in the basement. Powers came down the stairs and through the multiple doors whose purpose was to confine the tremendous daily noise as much as possible inside the range itself. The range was a place of almost perpetual gunfire, and most days the noise seeped out anyway, rising like smoke into the classrooms above.

Door after door closed behind Powers. The racket got louder, like a fanfare announcing his arrival. When he entered the range itself, the noise was deafening. Ten cubicles. Ten fire lanes, all active. He could see the backs of ten recruits practicing with revolvers. They wore gray training uniforms, gray baseball caps and, clapped over their ears, sound barriers. They were firing at will, the many individual reports blending into what was almost a single unending explosion. An instructor, hands clasped behind his back, paced like a football coach up and down behind them, sometimes stepping forward to correct someone's flawed technique, or to reel in and examine one of the targets.

Powers walked the length of the alley behind the shooters looking for the Chinese recruit, Luang, who was supposed to be there. But the men were all focused downrange, and he could not pick him out. From the front a Chinese face was distinctive, particularly down here in this private sanctuary of New York cops. But from the rear, all men looked much the same.

Powers approached the instructor, who saw him coming and lifted one sound barrier off one ear politely. "I'm looking for the Chinese guy," Powers shouted in under it.

"Lane three," the instructor shouted back.

Powers stepped over and tapped Luang on the shoulder. The shooter turned, smiled to see Powers, and stepped back out of his cubicle. He pulled the sound barriers off.

"Okay, it's done," Powers shouted at him. "Come with me."

Luang handed gun and sound barriers to the instructor, and followed Powers out through the doors.

"Any trouble?" Luang asked.

Powers thought about this, and decided to say: "No. None at all."

Twenty minutes later they stood in the office of the commander of the Police Academy, a one-star chief named Devaney. Powers knew him. He had once been a hard-nosed, ill-mannered street cop—rude, uncouth, insensibly brave. He had become prissy, pedantic and preoccupied. He looked like what he was, a headmaster.

Present also was the department's chief clerk, who held his bible outstretched in one hand while he read the oath off a card in the other. In this way Luang, who still wore recruit gray, was sworn into the police department.

"This is all highly irregular," said Chief Devaney. Like most headmasters, he was frightened by irregularity of whatever kind. He pushed a gun and shield across the desk at Luang. "You're assigned to Captain Powers personally. But you pick up your paychecks here in this office every two weeks. I'll have to ask you to sign for that gun. The shield, too. You sign here, and here."

Luang, leaning across the desk, signed.

"Well, I guess that's that," said Devaney. He looked unsettled. Something was happening that he did not understand. "I guess Captain Powers has some undercover assignment ready for you. Is that right, Powers?"

"We're in a bit of a hurry, Chief," Powers said gently. The headmaster of the Police Academy, despite his exalted rank, normally went no higher. The man could neither hurt him nor help him. Headmasters, unless you were a student in the school, were not forces to be reckoned with. "I'll be glad to talk it over with you another time," said Powers. "We'd better get going, Luang."

The Police Academy faced onto Twentieth Street. Outside they got into Powers' car, and in heavy afternoon traffic, started down Second Avenue toward Chinatown. The red lights were staggered. They moved slowly, steadily away from safety—what could be safer than a school, even a police school—into the battle zone.

Powers, trying to think it all out in his head, was silent for so long that at last Luang asked, "What's it all about, Captain?"

From Houston Street south they were in Little Italy. Second Avenue had changed its name to Chrystie Street. The store fronts had Italian names and sold Italian products. "Do you know Koy?" said Powers.

"The undertaker? I know who he is. I've seen him a few times. They call him the Cho Kun. As I understand it, he's the top guy in Chinatown right now."

Powers, who had stopped at a light, was still wondering how much to tell Luang. He turned to face him directly. "I want you to wake up with him in the morning, and put him to bed at night. I want to know everywhere he goes, everything he does, everyone he sees. I want to know everything about him."

Luang whistled. "You don't want much, do you, Captain?"

For a moment they appraised each other. Luang, Powers knew, was thirty-two, and stood under five feet seven inches tall. He was too old for a police trainee, and too short, and he ought to have been disqualified on both grounds. But he had wanted to be a cop so badly that he had instituted a class-action suit charging racial discrimination, and had fought his petition through the courts for over four years. In the interim he had worked as a prison guard at the City's house of detention on Riker's Island, while also earning a college degree nights from City University. He was not married.

So he was industrious, strong-willed, smart, knew prison from the inside, knew criminals up close—knew cops up close too, presumably.

And he was Chinese.

That was all Powers knew about him. Was it enough? Could Luang help him?

Horns were blaring, making Powers realize that the red light had changed. He put the car in gear and started forward. "Keep track of your overtime," he told Luang. "I can't give you money, but when this is over I can give you equivalent time off. And don't get made. I've got no one to replace you with."

"And don't get killed either," said Luang, and he grinned. "You forgot to put that in, Captain. You forgot your best line."

It made Powers smile.

For several blocks neither spoke.

"What's the point of this exercise?" asked Luang.

The point, thought Powers, was to break up the Chinese Mafia. But to say this to Luang was to place his career in Luang's hands, and he did not even know the man yet, much less trust him.

"To put Koy in jail, Luang. To put Koy in jail."

"On what grounds, Captain?"

"You sound like my wife," said Powers cordially. "On any grounds we can find. That's your job. To find the grounds."

"It sounds like an interesting assignment," said Luang. He sounded happy. "You know something, Captain? I think I'm going to like working for you."

17

DIMLY LIT side street. Tree-lined. Small trees of the upper East Side. Trees striving to live. Head-high bars around each one. Trees in protective custody, Powers thought, witnesses too valuable to lose. Driving, he checked the address—109 East 62nd Street—and matched it to the building itself, Koy's building. High-rise. New. Penthouses on top, probably. Uniformed doorman out front. Brocade and epaulettes. More brass buttons than an eighteenth century admiral. Glass doors. Luxurious lobby. Second admiral inside reading the *Daily News*.

Powers didn't stop. Rest of street mostly brownstones. Brass plaques beside several doors. Light through the meager leaves let him read two. Embassy of Pakistan. Embassy of Finland. Cop in front of third embassy. Powers couldn't read the plaque. Israel? Iran? This street and a few others constituted New York's embassy row. Very clean street. Total absence of plastic garbage bags piled out front, of litter against the curbs. Sanitation Department pickups here were regular and thorough, or heads rolled. In revenge the men skipped Harlem. Under the trees, signposts like planted spears. Signs like guidons. Threatening red signs: TOWAWAY ZONE. But soothing blue ones: EXCEPT DIPLOMATS. Diplomatic immunity, modern version, meant cars with DPL plates parked along both curbs from corner to corner. Immunity from that most modern of plagues, the municipal tow-truck.

Driving across to Third Avenue, Powers turned and started uptown. Big bright street. No parked DPL cars. No trees. Overflowing litter baskets on every corner. More litter blowing along the sidewalks. Stores. Movie theaters. Bus stops. People in line waiting for buses. Lines in front of the theaters, too.

At Seventy-second Street Powers pulled to the curb, threw the passenger door open, and Luang jumped in. Powers continued uptown.

"What makes you so sure it's Koy's house?" said Powers. To him a vital question. If you knew where a man lived you knew a lot about him. You knew where he could be hurt, and were close to knowing how to do it. "You've only been on him one day," he said. "You only tailed him there once."

"I asked the doorman, Captain."

Powers was like an archeologist digging for a city in hard-packed earth. Except that archeologists did not have to worry about alarming what they uncovered.

"That was risky, wasn't it?" he said.

Luang gave a smug grin. "Risky? I don't think so."

Luang's orders had been to measure the extent and area of the dig—to discover Koy's habits and patterns, to probe for his life style, which, like long-buried walls, would delimit what they were looking for.

"Why don't you tell me how you did it?"

"Sure, boss."

Luang had tailed the Cho Kun home. Or at least he supposed he had tailed Koy home. There were no short cuts in surveillance and the proper way to make sure, cops were taught in the Police Academy, was to tail him there several nights in a row, and then pick him up there several mornings. But Luang had decided he couldn't at this stage wait several days for each piece of confirmed information. Koy's car, a white Mercedes containing two other men—chauffeur and bodyguard, he assumed—had driven off. Luang had waited only long enough for the elevator doors to close on Koy, then had sauntered up out of the darkness.

"That Chinese guy that just walked in," he had asked the doorman, "he's an ambassador at the United Nations, right?"

New York doormen did not usually gossip about the great men who inhabited their buildings, the same great men who tipped them so lavishly at Christmas. They could be as correct as divorce lawyers, as tight-lipped as psychiatrists. At least until money showed. This particular doorman, gazing into the Oriental countenance before him, saw no money there, saw nothing of interest there ever, and so did not deign to acknowledge the question. He looked away.

"He makes great speeches," said Luang, wondering how far to risk pushing this. "So this is where he lives."

The doorman, insulted that such an individual should even approach him, much less believe a conversational exchange possible, was stung to reply, "In a penthouse. Him, his wife, and three little yellow kiddies. You a Chinaman?"

Tailing this close, Luang was bound to leave footprints from time to time. The important thing was to keep their indentations as vague as possible. "No, a Jap," he confided. "From the land of the Rising Sun." And he sauntered on.

"What a moron," Luang told Powers now, and he laughed.

But Powers stared pensively out over the wheel.

Three nights later Powers stopped on the same corner and Luang again jumped into the car.

"I don't know how it fits in, Captain, but he's certainly a devoted family man."

This was possibly important, for it suggested other ways and places that Koy could be hurt. "How do you know that?" asked Powers.

On Saturday morning Koy had come out of his building accompanied by a young Chinese woman whom Luang took to be his wife, because the two adults were pushing a carriage and a stroller, and had a third child by the hand. The bodyguard and chauffeur were waiting beside the car, but Koy spoke to them and they stayed there while Koy and his entire family went down the sidewalk and into Central Park. There Koy lifted the two older children into chair swings, pulled the bars carefully down across their laps, and then pushed them indefatigably until they tired of it. He kept both swings moving at once, leaping back and forth with the energy and mindlessness of a coolie laborer, the sweat running down his face, his shirt showing wet semicircles under the arms.

When the children at last had had enough, Koy sat with them in a sandbox, helping them make sand patties, and the proud, foolish smile—Luang could describe it no other way—never left his face.

"Go on," said Powers.

Later Koy did sleight of hand tricks for them, plucking coins out of their ears. Or he sat gently rocking the baby in the carriage, from time to time peering inside, his face illuminated by the same fatuous smile.

"All this is typically Chinese, Captain," said Luang.

The Chinese made doting parents, he told Powers. Their world revolved around their kids. They spoiled them. Always had. It was traditional. They loved big families. For centuries in China a man's wealth was measured by counting the number of children he had fathered, and how closely he was able to group them around himself. The Chinese simply loved everything about having lots of kids.

"Mrs. Koy," Luang said, "struck me as being American-born."

"Why do you think so?"

"I don't know, Captain. There was a quality about her." He sought a better word but couldn't find it.

She had seemed as American as the park itself—she was totally at ease there, and Koy in some vague indefinable way was not. Also, Koy had been totally focused on his children. For him nothing else existed except this world he had created for himself and when he gazed at his kids, he looked like a teenager in love. Whereas Mrs. Koy had pretty much ignored the kids. She had spent the whole morning reading a book.

"Where were you all this time?"

The answer was, draped belly down over a boulder in a high spot watching through binoculars, and suddenly something hard had prodded Luang in the small of the back. He sensed what it was even before he had rolled out from under it and sat up. A cop's nightstick. And the cop who owned it was glaring down at him.

"What are you, a peeping tom?"

Luang, recounting the story, laughed. "The rest of the department," he said, "carries nightsticks only at night."

"In Central Park they're allowed to carry them day-time as well," said Powers. "What did you do?"

Luang might have pulled out his shield and identified himself, but he was afraid of any commotion that might cause Koy over in the playground area to turn around. He had decided to slink away, saying nothing, if he could, and to his relief, the cop had let him go. He had looked back as he left the confines of the park, and the cop still stood on the boulder watching him.

"Are you sure Koy didn't see you?"

"Certain. He never took his eyes off his kids the whole day."

"Then what happened?"

"I waited in my car, Captain. About an hour later here comes Koy back from the park. He's pushing the carriage, looking exhilarated, like an American looks who has spent the day at Yankee Stadium watching the Yanks come from behind to win in the ninth. He looked high, Captain. High on love for his kids."

Powers didn't understand it, but filed it away. He was like a prospector who had found a strange rock. Better hold on to it, it could be priceless.

"The bodyguard jumped out of the car and helped him in with the carriages."

The reports continued, usually every other night, so

that, as Luang tailed Koy through the streets of Chinatown, Powers, figuratively speaking, walked at his side. Koy attended regular meetings at tong headquarters, and at the benevolent association building also, and some of these meetings, experience showed, were long ones, so that Luang seized the opportunity to pay his respects to whatever corpse was laid out in Koy's funeral parlor. In this way he was able to attach names and functions to the faces in Koy's entourage. There was the embalmer, Chang. There were two or three bodyguards who also served as pallbearers. There were several assistant funeral directors.

"That funeral parlor has got to be losing money, Captain. They don't change corpses in there twice a week. That place is a front for something else."

"For the gambling," murmured Powers. "And for whatever else he may be involved in."

"Like what, Captain?"

But Powers said only, "That's what we're trying to document."

Often Luang trailed Koy to the gambling house one flight down under 61 Mott Street. But always he waited in the street, for he feared approaching Koy too closely, and he also feared being caught in there in a raid carried out by some federal agency, or some other unit of the police department. The Fifth Precinct had formal orders to leave the gambling houses alone. Luang had not been a cop long enough to be willing to flout these orders. The risk to him was unacceptable.

"I'm surprised to find out how crowded Chinatown is, Captain," said Luang.

They were sitting in Gough's bar on West Forty-third Street, across the street from the *New York Times* plant. From snatches of overheard conversation Powers judged that everyone in the bar, apart from themselves, was a *Times* reporter or editor.

Luang had never spent much time in Chinatown before, he told Powers. It was as crowded as the Hong Kong he remembered, as crowded as the cities of mainland China were reputed to be. It was far more crowded than the rest of New York, and it was these dense crowds that enabled Luang to move as close as he did to Koy, who was usually accompanied by a bodyguard; often Luang was only a few paces behind them, or to the side. Also, he was using disguises. From his surveillance instructor at the Police Academy he had borrowed eyeglasses in various shapes, a pair of mustaches, and some different hats. He wore somber clothing, changed his appearance frequently, and was careful never to be caught looking at his subject directly.

Koy, on the other hand, seemed to sense that he was being followed, Luang said, and Powers on the next stool stiffened. Or perhaps, Luang added, he was only responding to the habits of a career policeman—but he eyeballed the sidewalks incessantly. Whichever bodyguard he had with him was like most of the other people of Chinatown who, on the whole, eyeballed nothing. Each man or woman formed a separate island moving alone against a river in flood. The Chinese, Luang well knew (and Powers knew this too, now), were impervious to the pushing and jostling of the crowds, to bumping against other bodies, to being guided to one side by hands so that the owner of those hands could get by. But Koy was proving to be no ordinary Chinatown citizen. The undertaker eyeballed everything, just like a cop, looking for the same face glimpsed too many times, for eyes that displayed undue interest in what he might be doing.

"Has he made you?" demanded Powers anxiously.

Luang shook his head. "I don't think so. I don't think he would ever expect to be tailed by another Chinese.

"Don't count on it," said Powers.

This bar was ten blocks south and two blocks west of Broadcast Center, where, less than thirty minutes from now, Carol Cone would get off work—a detail of which Luang was ignorant. But Powers, conscious of the time, kept glancing at the clock over the bar.

"And he's a gastronome, Captain. A gourmet. He shops for Chinese delicacies nearly every day. Everything has to be absolutely fresh for him."

Koy shopped at outdoor stalls on Mott and Canal Streets, dealing only with the proprietors, speaking only Chinese. He bought no produce or fish or pigeon or duck that he had not fingered first. He pinched the stuff, prodded it, often held it to his nose to check the freshness of its aroma. As he moved from stall to stall he seemed to construct that night's meal in his head, as did Luang behind him. He bought only Chinese products not commonly available outside of Chinatown: snow peas, celery cabbage and bok choi, a Chinese cabbage that had deep green leaves and yellow flowers—most of these vegetables had been trucked in that very day from Chinese-owned farms in New Jersey. He liked mushrooms, and also their counterparts, the tree fungi, called wood ears by the Chinese.

"The bodyguard, or whoever's with him, carries the stuff he buys," said Luang.

He bought water chestnuts and bamboo shoots, and he went down into Mott Street cellars and bought bean sprouts that grew there overnight in the dark. He bought the grayish-black fungus known as cloud ears, and lotus leaves and tiger-lily buds, also known as golden needles, which the Chinese savored for their pleasant musty taste. He liked abalone, sea slugs and crabs, and he favored roasted duck from a butcher shop at the corner of Mott and Canal, where the already cooked ducks hung by hooks in the shop window, making Luang's mouth water when he looked at them. He hadn't tasted such duck in many years, he told Powers; they were simply not on sale in the neighborhood where he lived.

"Another beer, Captain?"

"No thank you. I've got another appointment in a few minutes a bit further uptown. I've got to be going."

The next day Luang tailed Koy to City Hall. After Koy had gone inside, Luang ran up the steps and showed his shield to the cop on security duty at the door.

"I'm on the job," said Luang. "Where did the Chinese guy go that just came in here?"

The cop stared down at where Luang's shield had been, but it was already gone. Vanished. It was back in

Luang's pocket. Probably the cop was not sure he had even seen it.

Luang waited while the cop decided whether or not to answer. The cop was acting, Luang thought, just like that goddamn doorman.

"He's in with the mayor," said the cop.

"Don't burn me," pleaded Luang. The cop, frowning, stared out at the city over the top of Luang's head.

That night Luang reported to Powers in a Chock full o' Nuts coffee shop on Madison Avenue at Fifty-second Street, Luang having just seen Koy home. They sat on adjacent stools sipping coffee, watching each other in the mirror.

"Still nothing suspicious?" asked Powers. It was more statement than question. He was beginning to give up hope.

"He was an hour in with the mayor. Is that suspicious?"

Not suspicious, Powers thought, dangerous. He said: "The tong is a big contributor to the mayor's re-election campaign." Chinese political clout in New York was based on money, not votes—they didn't have many votes. The tong gave the money and Koy was the tong. An hour with the mayor—my God! Such a man, if he got wind of this tail, could ruin Powers with one phone call.

They sipped their coffees in silence. "If I could just focus in on something, Captain. If I just knew what I was looking for." Luang sent a pleading glance towards Powers.

But Powers decided he could not tell him.

There was a clock in this place too, and Powers kept watching it for the same reason as the last time. He was also trying to think out what to do. Continue the unproductive tail? Expand the area of the search? But that would be to increase his risks and he was already in too deep. And what about the risks to Luang's career, to Luang's life? There was only one obvious area to expand the search into, the riskiest of all.

But what other choice did Powers have?

"The next time he goes into his gambling place, go in after him."

Luang said nothing.

"Watch how he acts," said Powers. A note of urgency had crept into his voice. He tried to separate it out but couldn't. It was like trying to push unwanted sauce to the edge of the plate with chopsticks—wrong tool for the job. The sauce leaked back. Situations imposed their own laws, obeyed their own laws, not his. "Gamble a little if you have to. If you lose money, I'll pay you back out of my own pocket." He was still trying to control his voice.

"It's not a crime for him to be in there, or to gamble himself. The crime is running the place, and for that you need evidence that he signs checks, pays the bills, handles the house percentage, that he is part of the continuing conspiracy to violate the gambling laws."

Powers was afraid Luang would simply refuse him. If he did, then what? "In the past, people like Koy were too wary to be observed doing any of those things. But we haven't raided those places in so long that maybe he's become careless. If you observe any hard violations, we can go to the DA, maybe get a wiretap order." It was an idea, anyway, though a bad one. Normally applications for wiretaps had to be approved by the chief of detectives first.

Without looking at his commanding officer, Luang said quietly, "The chief of detectives—"

"You work for me, not the chief of detectives," Powers interjected. "Let me worry about the chief of detectives." He raised his hand to attract the waitress.

"May I have the check, please."

At the curb they stood beside Powers' Mustang, which was parked in a bus stop. There was no pressing need to move it. No cop was going to hang a summons on it because his police plate showed through the windshield. He watched a bus come to a halt in the middle of the street. The people waded out there and waited patiently to board it.

"It's settled then," said Powers. His voice sounded harder than he intended, but at least he heard no quaver. "Tonight's Monday," he said. "Think he'll go there tonight?"

In the Chinatown gambling dens Monday was the

busiest night of the week. If Koy wanted to count his money, it was the night to be there. On Mondays some of China-town's three hundred restaurants were closed. Waiters and kitchen personnel crowded around the tables all day gam-bling their week's wages. Their numbers were augmented by Chinese from the suburbs, for nearly all restaurants were closed Mondays there, and the gambling dens sent out buses to collect them and bring them into Chinatown. They were let out at the door to whatever gambling den had hired the bus. They too had been gambling all day.

"He's gone there every Monday night so far," said Powers.

Luang said nothing.

"He goes there about ten P.M., doesn't he?" said Pow-ers.

"I don't like to go down there without a backup," muttered Luang.

Powers knew what this meant. He looked at Luang, who studied the pavement.

"You're not on the Fifth Precinct roster," Powers told him, and the accursed urgency was back in his voice again. "There's no way I can arrange a backup on this short no-tice."

Luang's eyes rose, though only as far as Powers' chest. "How about yourself, Captain?"

All he wanted, Powers knew, was for his commander to share his risk—political risk and physical risk both. Since this was not an unreasonable request, it made Powers angry.

"I can't," he said. "I have an appointment I can't get out of."

Luang said nothing.

"Look," said Powers, "I'll try to get away from my appointment early. I'll try to be there by ten. But if I'm not there, go in with him anyway. Okay?"

Luang shrugged. "Okay, Captain."

Powers watched him trudge off toward the subway. When he was out of sight the precinct commander climbed pensively into his car.

A FEW minutes later he pulled up outside Broadcast Center, turned the ignition off and, while waiting, brooded. Why was he sending Luang into that gambling den? he asked himself. And why was he waiting here for Carol Cone? The risks were insane. He was not a gambler. He had always hated gambling. He and his wife had been to Las Vegas. Eleanor had loved placing bets. It made her excited just to think about it, and when she had occasionally won she was ecstatic. He himself had enjoyed watching the action, watching the people, but he had never bet a nickel—nor been tempted to.

So what was he doing now? He had half of his life savings bet on one table, and half on another, and he couldn't even watch both tables at the same time.

Carol jumped into the car beside him. When she leaned over to kiss him, he gave her his cheek. There were too many people coming out of that building who might know him, too many people going by along the sidewalk. He did not want to be seen with her in a compromising position. He did not want to be seen with her at all.

"How are you?" she said. "Oh, I'm so glad to see you. How are you?"

Immediately he felt ashamed. As her arms came around him he gave in to it. I am lost, he thought, and kissed her, and for as long as the kiss lasted did not care who might be watching.

He started the car. "Where are we going?" she asked, almost purring with contentment.

"I'll drive you home. I don't have much time. I have to get back to Chinatown."

"Okay. I'll make supper for us." As always, she sounded eager to go anywhere he wanted to take her. "Just so long as I have some of you tonight. I know I can't have all. Just give me some of you and I'll be happy."

In her kitchen, she stirred eggs in a bowl.

She was wearing a wraparound plaid skirt in dark colors and a brown blouse with a high white collar. The skirt was fastened in front by a huge safety pin and came down low over her boots. He watched her at the stove. As she worked she talked with animation of her job, of her life, of her daughter—who was home from college for a few days, by the way, and might walk in at any moment.

"You'll get a chance to meet her."

Powers did not want to be seen with Carol even by her daughter. Nor did he want the daughter to meet him in his current role, the role of philandering husband. He didn't want to be there when the daughter came in, yet couldn't say so and couldn't run.

"Don't look so glum," said Carol from the stove. She was laughing at him. "She knows I bring men home. She won't bite you."

This woman seemed able to read his thoughts, and once again Powers was amazed.

She prepared quite a nice mushroom omelet which they shared at the little table in the breakfast nook. They also shared a bottle of wine.

"What we have is not just sex, is it," said Carol. "I mean, lots of times we haven't made love at all."

"Two or three times, anyway," said Powers with a smile.

It was as if they had been married many years already. In marriage the best times were always like this, the quiet times. They were just finishing up, he had just speared the last mushroom and popped it into his mouth, when the back door opened and in walked the daughter.

"Hi. I'm Nancy."

She looked him over briefly, then turned to her mother. She had come home to take a shower. She had a date in a few minutes. Had her sweater come back from the laundry?

The mother was full of questions which the daughter answered in an excited way, while Powers appraised her.

A pleasant-faced girl.

Shorter, not nearly as good-looking as her mother.

A part of Carol's body that now had existence on its own.

To Powers the girl represented a complicating, disturbing intrusion into a situation that was already too complicated, into emotions that were already too disturbed; and his principal reaction to her was one he was not particularly proud of. Like most cops he had come to see truth in different terms than ordinary people. Truth was not really truth anymore. It was certainly not an absolute. There were many kinds of truth, and the only kind that counted, unfortunately, was the kind that could hurt you. To hurt you it had to stand up in court. In a certain sense Powers' affair with Carol had not become real to him until this moment—until the daughter turned up. Carol's testimony would be inconclusive, because she was a co-conspirator. But the daughter, to Powers, was a corroborating witness. If she testified to his conduct—misconduct—in court, the jury would believe her, and he would be convicted.

The girl came down again, having bathed and changed. "Very glad to have met you," she said. "I'll take my car," she told her mother, and went out. The door slammed behind her.

"What car did you buy her?" asked Powers, "a Rolls Royce?"

"Just a little Alfa Romeo sports car," said Carol, taking his hand. "She had to have something, and I could afford it. Please don't be hostile to me."

They carried the dishes to the sink, and as Carol stacked them in the dishwasher she spoke of her daughter. The car had been a present for the girl's eighteenth birthday. There had been another present also, a box of birth-control pills, together with a prescription so they could be renewed.

"She hadn't made love with her boyfriend up to that time," said Carol. "I wanted her to be able to, if she wanted to." She turned to Powers and said brightly, "They've since made love three times. She's told me all about how it was."

Powers, with dishes in his hand, put them down on the counter top.

"Are you shocked?"

He did not know how he felt. Was her love for her daughter incestuous? Was she reliving her own earliest sexual experiences through the girl? Or was she, perhaps, facing the modern world more realistically than he, preparing her child for the multitude of choices she would have to make, any one of which could destroy her? He could not say. He had never before known a woman without a husband, and he did not have daughters.

"I may have been a lousy wife," said Carol, "but I'm a good mother. I'm very close to my kid. We tell each other everything. She knows all about you, for instance."

"That's what I was afraid of," said Powers.

Carol closed the dishwasher door. If only all of life's unpleasantness could be closed off like that, thought Powers. When you open the door again, all unpleasantness is gone. Life sparkles like a set of dishes.

What a pity he couldn't do that with Chinatown. He thought of Luang, and glanced at the clock over the stove.

Carol, having washed her hands at the sink, was drying them on a dish towel. When she spoke it was in the matter-of-fact tone a wife might use, addressing her husband at the end of a busy day.

"Do you want to go to bed?"

18

THE SHOP window was dark. Behind the glass, porcelain gods and goddesses crouched in shadow, too many of them, as if heaven itself was overcrowded—as any Chinese heaven must be, Luang thought, overcrowded with divinities, overcrowded with Chinese. He had been standing at the window thirty minutes when at last, reflected off the glass, he saw the white Mercedes pull up in front of the entrance to the gambling den across the street. He saw Koy get out. The car and bodyguards continued on. Koy stood a moment, eyeballing both sidewalks. Luang did not turn around.

Apparently satisfied, Koy stepped over to the stairwell. Luang watched his reflected legs, torso and head disappear below the level of the sidewalk. Now he would rap several times on the steel door, Luang imagined. Now he was admitted. Now the door clanged shut behind him.

By then it was nearly 10:30. Koy was later than usual. Any special reason? Luang had no way of knowing. He peered around for Captain Powers, but did not see him, and so crossed to the opposite sidewalk where he stood above the stairwell, waiting for him a bit longer. The stairwell was like a mouth. It was like a dragon's gullet. It could swallow him up permanently, or incinerate him where he stood with sudden fire. He did not want to stand even this close to it, much less go down there.

Koy, meanwhile, had passed through the gambling room and climbed the staircase beyond, up past the restaurant that occupied the building's ground floor. The restaurant was owned by someone else. The floor above belonged to Koy, and was the nerve center of his gambling operation. His bookkeeper, he saw, was at work in the rear office. Next came a room in which his stickmen and pit bosses relaxed between tours—they worked one hour on, one hour off, because a great deal of money was involved and absolute concentration was essential. He looked in on them briefly: six men sipping tea and jabbering in Cantonese. Seeing him, they sprang to their feet. He nodded, and continued on.

The front room, which overlooked Mott Street, was a dormitory and security lookout. Since the basement gambling tables were busy twenty-four hours a day, so was this room, which was occupied by never less than six armed teenagers belonging to the Flying Dragons gang—Luang's dragon imagery was more apt than he realized.

Nikki Han, Koy saw, was on duty tonight. The other youths, most of whom were unknown to him, were recent arrivals from Hong Kong. Han was monitoring a bank of closed-circuit television screens—this modern dragon had multiple eyes as well as arms. The screens showed Mott Street in both directions, plus the stairwell and entrance to the den, the back courtyard, and the interior of the gambling room itself.

One glance into this room was enough to make Koy angry, principally because Nikki was monitoring all five screens by himself. The others only lounged on the beds, playing cards or reading comic books. Furthermore there were guns lying in plain view on tables: wobbly revolvers, automatics flat as books. They were as common—and as conspicuous—as ashtrays.

Koy began shouting in Chinese. He wanted the guns out of sight. He wanted the beds made, the room cleaned up and he wanted at least two other boys, at least three people at once, watching those screens.

All six boys sprang to their feet and began doing as

ordered, while Koy studied the screens over Nikki's shoulder. He had not intended to study them, but something had caught his attention. It was as if it had snagged his clothing as he walked past.

"Who is that? demanded Koy.

On the screen he watched Luang peering up and down the street.

"A customer," said Han. "Looks like he's waiting for somebody."

Luang disappeared from that screen but reappeared on another as he descended the gullet and approached the door. The screen gave a three-quarters closeup of his face.

"I've seen him someplace," said Koy. "I've seen him too much someplace. Find out who he is." Could he be working for Ting? Koy thought.

Striding back the way he had come, Koy went into the office to talk to his bookkeeper, while Han, behind him, continued down the stairs and into the gambling room.

Luang, still outside, had decided he would wait no longer for Captain Powers, and had rapped on the steel door. Powers would certainly be along soon. He didn't really need him now anyway. The need would come later, if at all, when he left the gambling den. If somebody followed him out of there he would need Powers plenty.

The small inset window looked to be made of reinforced glass. In it a face appeared. Like a television close-up, the face filled the entire screen, cheekbone to cheekbone, lips to eyebrows. Perhaps now it would begin to read the news.

Or breathe fire.

The lookout looked Luang over, but the door swung back quickly. The police officer had passed his first test. His Chinese face was his passport. Since he was not one of the millions of white demons who also inhabited this city and whose barbarian ways were unfathomable, he could be trusted. He was one of them. He could enter.

After passing along a short, dim hallway, he came in to a basement room packed with Asian men. It was like entering a furnace. The dragon's fire, and also its bad breath, were manufactured here. The only open spaces were the four gambling tables, and they were covered with money. They were like parks surrounded by trees. Men leaned over them three and four deep. The din was terrific. So was the smoke, the heat, the odor. Across the room Luang perceived joss sticks smoldering in front of a shrine. Along another wall he noticed hot teapots on hot plates. Long neon light fixtures were affixed to the low ceiling. They showed so much hanging smoke—tobacco smoke, incense, steam from tea—that Luang could barely see, much less breathe. But most of the heat was body heat. The strongest odor was the odor of unwashed Chinese men. Too many of them were crowded into too small a space. They were preponderantly low-income workers living in crowded tenements where it was not always possible to bathe, and now, as they gambled, most sweated nervously as well.

Luang trudged forward into the crush of bodies, into the smoke, into the miasma of odors. It was suffocating. He couldn't breathe. He had the notion that he must fan his arms. Unless he created space for air to collect around his face, he would suffocate.

The noise was oppressive too. He detected voices speaking Korean, Japanese, and at least four of the eight major Chinese languages, voices continually crying out in elation or disgust. Because of the tonal qualities of the languages, the voices were high pitched, the noise approaching a kind of sustained shriek.

The gambling tables were eight-by-four planks of plywood on trestles with green cloths clipped down over them. The game at one of the tables was thirteen-card poker. The racket there was compounded by the clack of chips, the rustle of money, and the roll of dice. This, Luang saw, was the small-money table, for the game was complicated and slow. According to the ideograph that hung over the table, the minimum bet was a dollar a hand, and the maximum, $100. Most of the gamblers appeared to be waiters and sweatshop employees, or else early losers. Their object seemed to be to amass a big enough stake to move on to one of the other three tables where the game was fantan, and the maximum bet was $2000. The fantan players, Luang saw, were betting both cash money and chips, and it took him a few minutes to work out the value of the chips. The red chips, he concluded, were worth $10, the red plaques $100.

Stacked chest-to-back around all three fantan tables, men pushed and jostled as they thrust themselves forward to make bets, and Luang did likewise, until the edge of the table pressed against his abdomen and he was at last in position to watch both the game and the room. Unfortunately he was also in plain view of Nikki Han, whom he had never seen before, and who now watched him carefully, studying what he did with his money and also what he did with his eyes.

Fantan was a simple game. Luang had played it since childhood, though never for stakes like this. A handful of buttons out of a bowl went down onto the table, and was immediately covered by a second bowl. Bets were made on one of four numbers, after which the buttons were raked away four at a time until four or fewer were left—the winning number—and immediately after that most of the money and chips and plaques were raked away also. Pit bosses paid off winners from bills folded in half between their fingers, holding back each time the house's ten percent cut.

Luang began to bet carefully, pushing forward one-dollar chips, hoping to be taken for the type of gambler, if there was such a type, who started slowly so as to test for omens. Meanwhile, his eyes roamed the room, searching for faces he knew, searching for Koy. The undertaker descended the stairs about twenty minutes later, moving through the haze, smiling, sometimes pausing to bow or to shake hands. Luang watched him closely. He appeared to take no notice of the action at the tables. He did speak quietly to the pit bosses for a few minutes, apparently asking questions, apparently quite satisfied by the answers. But he did not ask to see the books the pit boss was keeping. He did not touch money or chips. There was no indication that he owned or ran the place. Nothing a jury would believe. Luang's observations were insufficient and he knew it. There goes any chance of getting a wiretap order, he thought.

Moving to the hot plate, Koy helped himself to a cup of tea, and stood sipping it. Nikki Han came over and spoke in Koy's ear, while the undertaker surveyed the room, apparently idly. As Koy's eyes neared him, Luang studied his bet, but when he looked up from the table again he found Koy and Han both staring at him. At once the police officer dropped his gaze a second time. Did they continue to stare at him? Had Koy found his face too familiar? Would he now take action of some kind? Luang was badly shaken. His eyes felt like rubber balls—he had slammed them down hard onto the table top and they wanted to bounce back up again and give him some information. He craved answers that his eyes might supply, that they wanted to supply. The difficult thing was to restrain them, to smother their resilience, to hold them down.

Luang knew he was in trouble. He wondered how soon he could leave—should leave. The important thing to Luang was to wait long enough for Captain Powers to get there. Powers must be given ample time to take up his station outside. Like the gamblers around him, Luang too had now begun to sweat. He wanted Powers on hand when he came up the stairs onto Mott Street. Powers would be able to size up the situation at a glance, whatever Koy and his henchmen might decide to do. With Powers there he would be safe.

But Powers lay on a dark bed amid tangled sheets in a house twenty-five miles away. Carol Cone had one leg swung over him. Her hand on his abdomen had begun dragging its fingers through his curls, combing them out.

"I've been completely faithful to you since the day I met you, do you know that?" she said.

His fondness for her was so great it made him drowsy.

It was like being in a warm shower, and he did not want to get out, not ever. Though she lay on his arm, he was contentedly stroking that part of her back and hip that he could reach.

"So have you been faithful to me?" she asked after a pause.

What was he supposed to say to this? She knew very well that he slept every night in the same bed with his wife of twenty-three years. What could she realistically imagine went on between them?

"No, Carol."

"You haven't?"

"No, Carol."

Was she disappointed? Jealous? Or only searching for facts. What other reply could she have been hoping for?

Fumbling for his watch on the bedside table, he turned it this way and that, striving to read it.

The watch hands were whips that lashed out at him. They stung him, and he sat up. "I have to go," he said. He was shocked to see how late it was. "We have a case going in Chinatown. An important one."

"What case?"

"Well," he said, "just a case."

He realized he would have told Eleanor. Although Carol was slightly damp with sweat from her exertions, as he was, and had lain half stuck to him on the rumpled bed, still he couldn't tell her. Was it because she was a journalist? Or simply because she was a woman used to getting what she wanted? Even during moments of greatest intimacy, when her moans sounded like a great ship leaving its berth, even then he tended to see her principally as a threat. She could hurt him if she wanted to. She seemed not so much a woman in the act of love, as a real or potential adversary, and however much he might think himself in love with her, still he didn't quite trust her.

She took his watch from his fingers, sought its luminosity in her turn. "I don't believe in any case in Chinatown. Not at this hour. It's too late."

"Please, Carol."

She lay sulky and unmoving on the bed. "You just want to get home to your wife."

This irritated him. He reached down beside the bed and began to gather his clothes. He needed a shower—the first important job was to rinse the scent of lovemaking, Carol's scent, off his body—then he'd drive to Chinatown. At this hour he ought to make it in under thirty minutes. Though he did not really believe Luang needed him, he had promised to be there.

"You're always under control, aren't you?" said Carol, and the pain in her voice was so obvious that he looked at her sharply. "With you, everything is compartmentalized. You never go overboard in any one direction. You're never late for appointments. You always fulfill all obligations."

These words, as far as they went, were true, he believed, so that he felt a renewed belief in her love for him—if she had observed him that closely, she must love him.

"You have your neat little life where everything runs smoothly," she said. "You have your perfect house, your perfect job, your perfect little wife."

She caught her breath and muttered in what was almost a sob. "—And meanwhile, I'm going begging here."

He was stunned. It seemed the saddest line he had ever heard a woman speak.

"Carol, I do love you," Powers said.

He could not leave her in this state, at least not as abruptly as he had planned. He would have to soothe her first, beginning with a single kiss.

But the kiss grew in length, and then in intensity, expanding as if to fill the principal void of his life, and at the same time Carol's fingertips brushed against him almost beseechingly.

"Oh, Artie, make love to me. Please make love to me."

He thought he would do it, because Luang was in no real danger, but only thought he was. Luang did not need him. It was Carol who needed him. His obligation was to Carol, and so he could not go to Chinatown tonight, even if he wanted to, which now he did not. He wanted to be here on this bed with this woman.

She had begun to groan. She sounded as primitive as a cavewoman keening for the death of a child. Powers noted this because across the room a part of him stood watching these strange goings-on. It was that part that had always been able to see with absolute clarity even in the dark, to see through walls, to see for miles.

Why are you doing this, it asked him now. What is the compulsion? Is it simply a reaction to eleven years of frustration? What about Eleanor? What about Luang?

LUANG'S GAZE felt nailed to the green felt table, and his arms to his sides. His money rode for two more rounds because he was unable to focus on it. Amazingly, he won both times. His winnings were pushed toward him, over $200. He counted it again. What was he supposed to do with this money? Keep it? Did it belong to him or to the Police Department? But he was too confused and frightened to decide. There were now three men staring at him. Koy and his henchman had been joined by a Chinese youth of about eighteen who had come down from upstairs. Small, mean-looking kid.

Luang put the money in his pocket, no doubt compounding his crime in Koy's eyes: the winner would quit while ahead. And alive. And hope he could stay ahead. And alive. He pushed back from the table, pushed backwards through bodies which flowed forward around him, filling the space he had occupied even as he vacated it. He went out through the short hallway and up the steep stairs and out onto Mott Street. The night air tasted amazingly cool and fresh to him. He felt free, but wasn't. He took a deep, clean breath. But Powers wasn't there. Luang looked everywhere for him. He definitely wasn't there.

Downstairs Koy had pointed with his chin. Nikki Han

and the other youth, Billy Low, alias Go Low, began pushing their way out of the room.

Luang stood above the stairwell. There were still crowds of people on both sidewalks, crowds of cars in the street, though fewer of both categories than before. In a short time, a matter of minutes, all the tourists would be gone. There would be no one here but Chinese. Chinese custom would prevail. If a street altercation occurred the Chinese would veil their eyes. They would see nothing.

Again Luang's eyes raked the crowds in all directions. Again Powers was not there. Where could he be, thought Luang anxiously.

Crossing to the shop window he had stared into earlier, he stared again, like a young girl returning to her mirror to be reassured. On the darker street the glass gave a better reflection than ever. Too much so. Only a few seconds passed before Han and Low, in the reflection, came up out of the stairwell and peered around. And found him.

Luang took another deep breath, but this time forgot to notice the taste of the air. As he started up Mott Street, he was trying to think out what to do. He was trying to stay ahead of them until he had decided.

Should he head straight for the station house on Elizabeth Street? It was only about three blocks away. He could walk straight into the station house, showing his shield to the cop at the door.

But it would blow the investigation. Powers would fire him, and rightly so. A white cop, he was certain, would not feel this afraid. Luang was only about three weeks into the six-month probationary period faced by every new patrolman and could be dismissed for almost any infraction. He had waited a long time to become a cop. It was the best-paying job he had ever had. He was Chinese. He could not realistically hope for something better. If he lost this job he would wind up in a sweatshop. He would wind up a waiter. He would wind up gambling away his paycheck every week like those poor slobs he had just left, because a big night at the tables was their only hope in a hopeless life.

So he could not go to the station house, and if he happened to pass a foot cop on the sidewalk he could not identify himself and ask for help. He would have to get out of this on his own if he could, though he could not yet think how. He could not use his gun. That too would blow the investigation, and he would go to jail for it, unless they fired first. Two against one.

He turned right into Bayard Street. He passed a jade store, two restaurants, a narrow building that was a noodle factory. All were closed. Everything on Bayard Street looked closed. He squinted at the reflection in a shop window, watching the entrance to Bayard Street. Here came Han and Low—he did not know their names—swaggering along. They were about fifty yards behind him. They looked completely confident. They looked heavy with purpose, menacing.

He began to hurry. He came out onto the Bowery and looked across Confucius Square. The great thinker sat enthroned amid eight lanes of traffic, all pouring north past Chinatown without stopping. How could Confucius think in the midst of such bustle and noise? How could Luang think? Across the square was what looked like a Buddhist temple—if Luang couldn't think, then perhaps he should pray. Of course it was not a temple at all but a bank, and prayers could not help him now.

Across the square also stood a public housing project inhabited almost exclusively by Chinese. Luang conceived the notion that if he could reach these buildings he would be safe. The first job was to cross to the other shore. He waited for the lull and then ran, sprinting into the closest building. There seemed to be several banks of elevators, several stairwells. Luang yanked open the door to the first stairwell he saw, and took the steps two at a time, heading for the roof. It was sixteen floors up. By the time he spilled out the door into the night air he was breathless and nearly exhausted.

Now what?

But he had thought it out no further than this.

For a time he waited for them to come through the door after him. He had his gun pointed straight at the door. If they came through he would shoot them both down and take his chances on Powers, on going to jail. But nothing happened, and presently he went to the parapet and glanced down at the street.

There they both were, conferring on the sidewalk. They did not look up. Had they lost him inside the building? Were they waiting for reinforcements? He watched the street in quick peeks, ducking back after each one.

After about fifteen minutes he saw them run back across the square and into Bayard Street. When he had lost sight of them he sat down with his back against the parapet and his gun on his lap, waiting for his still pounding heart to slow down in his chest. He began to shiver from the residual fear, but at the same time a kind of smile came onto his face, born of hope.

He thought he would wait an hour on the roof to be safe, then leave.

After a while he fell asleep.

Powers felt none of Luang's fear, none of Luang's hope, only exultation and a kind of surging, overpowering faith. He believed in everything. Accompanied by Carol Cone, he approached as close to ecstasy as it is given man to get. His life became huge. He soared naked over the polar icecap, plunged into the warm waters of the Gulf. He could go anywhere, he could see God. He was stunned by the power of his love for this woman, who had made such rapture possible, who had given him this unending night. He would never let her go. He would build another room on the palace and install her there. Eleanor would understand.

So thinking, Powers too fell asleep.

THE MIDNIGHT-TO-EIGHT A.M. tour had not yet come off duty when Powers strode into his stationhouse. He was unshaven and looked haggard. His rumpled clothes looked as if they had lain in a pile all night. He stopped at the desk.

"Any calls for me during the night? Nothing at all? You're sure?"

The desk sergeant was sure. Powers went into his office, closed the door and phoned his wife, who came on the line sounding sleepy.

"What time is it? You didn't come home."

In theory cops worked midnight tours every third week. Their wives were used to sleeping alone. He said, "By the time I realized I wouldn't get home, it was too late to call." There was no need for an outright lie, "I was afraid I'd wake you."

"Did you get any sleep?"

"Not much," he said, which was true.

He shaved, changed to his uniform, then sat behind his desk with his face in his hands. The only woman he had ever slept all night with was Eleanor until now. He had awakened to find daylight streaming in the windows, and had jumped up and dressed. He left as quickly as possible, without even washing his face, refusing the coffee Carol wanted to make him. When she stood with him at the front door he gave her a quick kiss and quicker smile, for in fact he couldn't get out of there fast enough.

There were degrees of intimacy, he believed, and therefore degrees of infidelity. But to sleep all night with another woman seemed to him, at the moment, the ultimate betrayal.

At noon he met with Luang in the park in Brooklyn Heights. Women pushed baby carriages past their bench.

"I'm sorry I couldn't get there last night. How did it go? Any problems?"

Luang too had been awakened by daylight, and had found that his face and clothes were wet with dew. He felt stiff and sore as well. Putting his gun back in his pocket, he had gone down off the roof and home.

He said now, "No problems, Captain." The investigation could well be blown, but Luang was afraid to admit it.

"What about Koy?"

"I was in there over an hour, Captain. He stood around sipping tea. He talked to a couple of people. That's all he did."

Powers' lips tightened. Otherwise his expression did not change. A kid came by, throwing a yo-yo out in front of him. The string was too long, so that the yo-yo kept hitting the ground. Powers watched him. The kid seemed unable to understand why his trick didn't work.

That's me, Powers thought. I'm trying a trick too, and it isn't coming off. How long before Koy recognized that he was being tailed, and complained to City Hall? Forget Koy. How long before Chief Duncan ordered an investigation of Powers' use—or misuse—of Luang? At a time when the city was nearly bankrupt, when too few cops were on patrol in the streets, Luang represented a prodigious waste of police man-hours. Duncan didn't believe in any Chinese Mafia, and would have Powers up on charges. If convicted, he would lose his command certainly and might even be dismissed from the department.

Luang too brooded. Doubtless Koy was too smart to order a cop killed, but he might order Luang killed, not knowing he was a cop. Most likely Koy suspected he worked for a rival gang or tong. Therefore his police officer status would not protect him.

Powers knew he should call off this unproductive tail at once. Luang wished he would do it.

"How long before he makes you?" said Powers. "That's what I'm worried about."

Maybe I should tell him, Luang thought. But he was afraid he'd lose his job. "That's what I'm worried about, too, Captain."

They were like men imprisoned inside adjacent telephone booths; the wire between them had been cut. Meaningful communication had become impossible. Although they might continue to send visual signals across the void, these had all been misinterpreted so far.

"Stay with him a few more days," said Powers, "and —and be careful."

19

L UANG, following Koy's Mercedes, saw it pull up in front of a store on Mulberry Street in Little Italy. There were two bodyguards in the front seat. Koy and Ting got out of the back seat and stood on the sidewalk. The Mercedes continued on, turned the corner, and Luang lost sight of it. After Koy and Ting had entered the store, he cruised on past. It was an Italian espresso bar. He could see Koy and Ting inside through the plate glass. The waiter had come over and was showing them to a table.

Pulling in beside a fire hydrant farther up the street, Luang slouched down in his seat, and he watched the doorway in his rearview mirror.

It was early morning. He had his memobook open on his lap, and as he wrote down all he had noted so far, he kept glancing from the memobook to the mirror and back again.

About five minutes passed before a black car pulled up in front of the same coffee house. The driver ran around to open the back door. Two Italian-looking men stepped out and glanced around. They looked as self-conscious as bridegrooms. They kept pulling their suit coats down over their hips. Leaving the car double-parked, they went into the coffee house. The driver stayed with the car. Luang licked his pencil and wrote in his notebook: 10:00 A.M., 167 Mulberry Street, Italian espresso house. Black car pulls up, New York plates HT 1134. Two Italians. One about 45, the other about 55. The older one has head like a melon. Melon head very pale. Younger one thin-faced like a prune. Big nose. Tanned.

Luang closed the notebook, shoved it into the glove box and slouched so far down that only the top of his head showed above the back of the seat. He sat there waiting, eyes fixed on the mirror.

Inside the coffee house the two Chinese, having ordered tea, were already sipping it when the two Italian-Americans entered. The Chinese rose to their feet. Simultaneously, having recognized the two newcomers, the waiter had come out from behind the bar. He looked nervous, for the newcomers were important men in Little Italy. He was anxious to perform any service they might require of him. The result was five men standing together in a kind of embarrassed silence. They stood around the tiny table. It was circular, small as a tray.

The older of the two Italians, whose name was Marco, turned to the waiter: *"Due cappuccini."*

The waiter bowed like a Chinese. *"Si, Signóre,"* he said, backing away.

Marco said to Ting and Koy: "This is my brother-in-law, Mr. Casagrande."

There was no shaking of hands, and no one sat down. Instead Ting and Koy glanced at each other, after which their eyes became veiled, as if blinds had been drawn. "We expected you to come alone," said Ting.

Marco jerked his thumb toward Casagrande. "He was looking after my business while I was away."

Still no one sat down. The men stared at each other. It was clear that a detail had to be settled before this meeting could begin.

Koy and Ting, eyes fixed on the Italians rather than on each other, began a conversation in Chinese. This annoyed Marco. As he saw it, the Chinese took him and his brother-in-law for dumb clucks who could not understand their language and who, furthermore, could converse in no secret language of their own.

He turned to Casagrande. "Do you speak Italian?"

"I forgot it since I was a kid."

So had Marco. As the Cantonese tones rose and fell, his mouth hardened angrily. He could not even return the insult. He had been bested.

The discussion between Ting and Koy ended. Casagrande, they had decided, constituted a security risk, and this meeting, therefore, could not take place.

"I'm sorry," said Koy. "Mr. Casagrande is certainly most trustworthy. Nonetheless—"

A moment longer the four men, all still standing, stared at each other. Then Marco jerked his head toward the door. Casagrande nodded and went out into the street.

"I am sorry," said Koy apologetically, "but it is a business in which one cannot be too careful."

Marco gave a shrug. As the three men at last sat down at the small table, the waiter appeared with the two coffees on a tray. He began peering around for the missing customer.

"Put them both down on the table," ordered Marco. "That's right. Now beat it. Scram."

"*Si, signóre,*" said the waiter and he retreated behind the bar.

The three men, still staring at each other, ignored their cups. In the center of the table the fourth cup, belonging to no one, was ignored too.

"You're looking well," said Koy. "A bit pale, that's all."

Marco said, "Where I was, they didn't give you too much opportunity to take the sun."

"In any case," said Koy, "We are glad to see you. We have been waiting for you for a number of years."

"So who did you deal with while I was gone?"

"No one," said Ting.

"You waited for me?"

"It seemed wisest," said Koy.

Marco shook his head in a kind of grudging admiration. "You Chinamen are patient guys."

Koy, who detested being called a Chinaman,

frowned. "The river is patient," he said coldly. It was as if he had resolved to teach this dolt some important truths. "The sky is patient. Man must live in harmony with nature. If one wishes to be certain, often one must wait. Would you require the same quantity of merchandise as in the past?"

"More. I lost a lot of time. If the price is right. If the quality is as high."

Koy said: "The source is the same. Transshipment is still via Hong Kong. As for the price, that is what we are here to discuss. Once that and certain other points are agreed upon, then others can handle the details. We will not meet again. Much to our regret, of course."

Out front Casagrande paced up and down smoking. From time to time they could see him as he passed in front of the plate glass.

Luang through his rearview mirror watched Casagrande also. Then Marco came out. After conversing briefly, the two men got into their black car and drove down the street toward Luang. As they passed him, he slouched so far down in his seat as to be virtually invisible. But as soon as they had turned the corner he again raised himself high enough to watch the espresso bar through the mirror, and presently Ting and Koy came out and stood waiting for their car. Either they had phoned for it, or else it was due at a certain time. Luang started his engine and waited. When the white Mercedes appeared in his mirror he pulled away from the curb and drove up to Houston Street, where he phoned Captain Powers from a street-corner phone booth.

Powers said that he would meet Luang at once at the Drug Enforcement Administration offices on West Fifty-seventh Street.

There, for over an hour, the two men paged through photograph albums of major drug traffickers, as brought to them by a DEA agent named Wilcoxon. Each album, once viewed, was added to the stack that stood on the edge of the desk. It was becoming a tall stack, floors of a building headed for the sky, each landing a staircase climbed to no avail. Powers was like a man trapped in the stairwell of this skyscraper. He kept running up flights but the doors were locked at each landing.

Luang, finishing with the final album, handed it to Powers. "No," he said.

Powers hefted the latest thick sandwich. A moment ago it had represented hope to both of them, a prodigality of hope because it was the bulkiest yet, it could feed an army. Unfortunately it had proved to contain no nourishment at all.

"He meets two Italians in Little Italy," Powers said. "It's got to be drugs. It's got to be a major guy." He gestured toward the albums. "He's got to be in there somewhere."

But he wasn't, meaning that Powers' newest idea had failed as miserably as its predecessors. For all he knew, the Italian had been an undertaker just like Koy. Perhaps they had met only to discuss the price of coffins.

He stared at the stack of albums: another dead end.

"Come on, come on," said Luang. "Bring out some more albums." Luang, Powers had learned, was a man of incredible patience.

"There are no more albums," said Wilcoxon. "That's it."

"He had a head like a melon," persisted Luang. "That's what I call him, melon-head. When I have to remember someone's face, what I do is remember what his features remind me of. He's got a nose like a cork, got ears like a cocker spaniel. Well this guy had a head like a melon. The guy who waited outside looked like a prune."

"If you don't have prune-face in your book," said Powers, "that doesn't surprise me. Maybe he's new. Maybe he's just muscle. But melon-head you should have. Koy is not going to meet with anybody but an important guy."

"Any man active over any period of time," said Wilcoxon, "is in those books. Maybe he hasn't been active."

It was a small inside room. No windows. Airless. Powers paced it. It was like pacing a cell. A prisoner locked in a cell was locked also inside his own skull, and could concentrate on nothing except breaking out. Powers knew this.

Most prisoners, he had learned, yearned so hard to break out that the yearning became actual physical pain, and it was centered in their teeth. They began grinding their teeth, even in their sleep. Prisoners were men whose teeth hurt all the time.

"What did you say?" demanded Powers.

"He may not have been active recently," said Wilcoxon.

"Maybe he just got out of jail," said Powers.

Wilcoxon left the room. While he was gone Powers and Luang stared at each other, and Powers' hopes were blazing once more. Hope, the great arsonist. Calm down, he warned himself. You're just going to be disappointed all over again.

Reentering the office, Wilcoxon dropped a new album in front of Luang. "Here's a book of guys we've put away. Maybe one of them got out recently." His tone was apologetic. "We update these books every once in a while." He was like a man confessing a sin common to everyone in the room, making it, therefore, not such a bad sin. They were all guilty of it. If the DEA had not updated its albums in months, perhaps years, this could not be helped, and probably the New York Police Department had done no better. Law enforcement stumbled along on too little money. For the most part accuracy and efficiency were dreams that could not be paid for, and so did not come true. As cases moved from one jurisdiction to another, the records attached to them did also, usually by hand. Time then passed, usually a great deal of time, until hardly anyone remembered the original case, much less the whereabouts of the paper it had generated. One could not update files if the paper got lost.

Luang, who had been turning pages, rapped a glassine-covered photo with his knuckles, and said calmly, "That's melon-head!"

Powers jumped to peer over Luang's shoulder. "Bruno Marco," Luang read aloud. "It says here he was eligible for parole last January."

"I guess he got paroled," apologized Wilcoxon.

Powers said elatedly, "Koy and Ting meet Marco and—"

But Wilcoxon attempted to blanket what he evidently considered too much enthusiasm. "It's a nice bit of information, Captain. Unfortunately, I don't know what good it will do you. That's probably the first and last meeting between those two people."

Most cops were defeatist, Powers reflected. It grew up out of their vast cynicism. They were like players on a last-place team. They expected to lose. The world was a malignant place. Justice rarely triumphed.

It was amazing that cases ever got made at all.

Wilcoxon said, "The Chinese have the best source of supply. They got Southeast Asia tied up. Here in this country the Chinese import only. They have no distribution network. That's the way it was the last time we were able to hook into them. The Italians are their distribution network. The Chinese bring in the stuff via Hong Kong and Amsterdam. They make their deal with the Mafia and they arrange for Chinese couriers to deliver into Little Italy. They send some Chinese seaman ashore with a load off a freighter. He gets to take the risk and they pay him maybe a hundred bucks. Once it's ashore they pay some Chinese waiter another hundred bucks to carry it to the Italians. At some point the money changes hands. A lot of money. The Chinese dump it in there with all that cash from their gambling houses. There is no way you can trace it, no way you can find it. We catch a courier now and then. Big deal. There is no way you can catch a guy like Koy. He's much too cute. He never goes near the junk himself and rarely ever meets with anybody. Today's business deal with Marco —it fits. The Chinese deal only with Italians they have dealt with for a long time. If the Italian goes away, most likely they wait until he comes out."

There was no way, Wilcoxon told them, and never had been, to infiltrate the Chinese end of the operation. Ten years ago the DEA had managed to make cases against a number of major Chinese dealers. They had done it by sending in undercover agents who posed as Mafia buyers. Three or four major Chinese importers had fallen for it, and were still in jail. But with the Chinese the same technique never worked a second time. Most criminals, and especially most drug dealers, were morons. A successful technique, once developed kept working. Law enforcement kept dropping the same guys over and over again in the same way. But not the Chinese, who never repeated mistakes. Since those few ten-year-old cases, the Chinese had sold exclusively, it was assumed, to Italians they knew and could trust, and although the drug agency had continued attempting to infiltrate, they had never been successful again. Operations against the Chinese drug lords were now at a standstill. Nobody could think of a way to get a case going.

"I'll tell our guys what's probably going down," Wilcoxon said. "But don't expect too much."

Wilcoxon showed them out of the airless little office, walking them as far as the elevator. "If we manage to drop anybody," he said, just before the doors closed, "we'll send you a thank-you card."

Downstairs Powers and Luang stood in the sunlight in the plaza in front of the building.

"What next, Captain?" asked Luang.

But Powers' euphoria was evaporating fast. It was clotting like blood. Scar tissue had begun to form over it. The scar tissue was called reality. He believed more strongly than ever that a Chinese Mafia existed and that Koy was the head of it. And yes, he had begun to discern the edges of the case he might make against Koy. But, no, he still had no hard evidence, nor even hard information he could take to Duncan or Cirillo or the PC. And he did not have the resources to break up the Chinese Mafia without their help.

"If I had a few more of you," he told Luang, "I'd keep the tail going at least another week."

Luang shook his head. He did not like the sound of this. He wanted no more of Koy who, if he was protecting a drug empire, would stop at nothing. "I've got to have some time off, Captain," Luang said. Though nothing showed on his face, he was terrified of Koy, who would certainly order him killed, might already have done so. "The Chinese cop is not like you American cops," he said and gave a broad grin. "We Chinese like to eat. We devote a lot of thought to it. I got to have a decent meal, Captain. Maybe some butterfly shrimps. I can't take any more surveillance work for a while. Maybe a dish of stir-fried sliced beef with oyster sauce. Have you ever had that, Captain?" He tried the grin again, but this time it failed. "For me that is as close as you can come to ecstasy at a dinner table. You make it with black pepper, soy sauce, thinly sliced onions, chopped fresh ginger and—"

"Stop," Powers said with a smile. He had failed to notice Luang's fear—by American standards it simply did not show. "You are making my mouth water."

"I want to sit down at a table and eat with chopsticks," Luang said. He was grinning, pleading and sweating all at once. There were beads of sweat on his brow.

This time Powers did observe the mismatched symptoms but they only confused him. He could not figure out what they meant.

"And drink a pot of hot jasmine tea." Luang said. "I can't take any more hamburgers for a while, I can't take any more of these meals out of a paper bag." He watched anxiously for his commanding officer's reaction.

Powers, brooding, thought of Koy as the lord of a fortified encampment. Not only did he rape and brutalize his own subjects within, he also manufactured poison in there, and sent it outside to contaminate the wells for miles around. Stopping Koy was more important than Luang's dinner habits. On the other hand, there was probably very little more to be gained by tailing the man.

An idea came to Powers, a way to infiltrate the Flying Dragons and to go after Koy from inside the gang. For about a minute he was silent, mulling the idea over, kneading it like dough, watching it take the shape he wanted.

His hand clapped down on Luang's shoulder. "Take

a week off, and when you come back we'll try a different plan. It's one I think might work."

He did not notice Luang's vast, interior sigh of relief. "Thank you, Captain," said Police Officer Luang.

H E TOOK Carol to the movies in a village ten miles from her house, and at the ticket window the woman in line in front of them turned around, recognized Carol, and gave her husband a violent dig in the ribs—causing him to turn and stare too.

"Oh," he said, looking startled. "Oh, it's you."

Although this had happened before, each time Powers was both surprised and pleased. His pleasure was pride —for the moment this valuable object belonged to him. Carol gave the couple the frosted smile she reserved for such people and they advanced into the lobby where the man who tore the tickets at the door recognized her too. On came a friendly grin and he nodded to her, but Carol ignored him altogether and plunged forward into the darkness, Powers following.

They took places in the last row, and stared at the screen, and Powers tried to examine his emotions, which seemed to him unworthy. The ownership instinct was one of man's strongest and most base. No human being owned any other, Powers thought. Carol certainly existed independently of him, they weren't even married, so why did he continue to preen when she was recognized at his side?

He was experiencing many emotions these days that were strange to him. To be in love at forty-six was in some ways as vivid and compelling as at twenty-three, and the object of that love was just as irresistible, though she did not always seem as perfect. Because love then had blotted out all else, whereas now it had to compete for his attention. Often it produced sensations that only resembled those of the past, the way his face in the mirror only resembled a snapshot from his youth; the two faces were far from identical.

There were ritual aspects to love, and these were much the same as before. In fact Powers sometimes found himself engaged in the same actions and conversations as twenty or more years ago. Such experiences were not always thrilling. Often they were simply confusing. Take one of the more simple questions lovers always put to one another: age. He remembered the day he had asked Eleanor how old she was. "Twenty-two," she answered, with a touch of pride at being so old. Casual question, casual answer, as if he had asked how much change she had in her purse, and she had replied: twenty-two cents.

But two days ago in a restaurant he had put both his hands over Carol's and said, "Carol, how old are you?"

It was not a casual question at all. It was as if he were asking the contents of her bank account. Her eyes dropped at once to the tablecloth, and she looked about to cry, as if he wanted too much from her, more than she could give.

He had been circling the subject for days, the way, as a boy courting Eleanor, he had circled the subject of sex, edging ever closer to the big mystery. Sooner or later they would plunge in together, and it would be revealed for both of them.

Powers knew Carol was sensitive about her age, for he had watched her hide the clues, burying them deep. She had avoided this subject as Eleanor had avoided that one, almost desperately.

Powers said stubbornly, "Tell me."

"What do you want to know for?"

If he had met her years ago when such questions were important, he would have asked her, "Are you still a virgin?" A hesitation then or now, meant only that the answer she must give was the wrong one, would reveal tainted goods, threatened their relationship, might even end it.

"Please tell me."

Her guilty secret, she saw, could not be kept, though she went on trying. "What difference does it make?" There were always mysteries between couples she seemed to be saying. Her voice was pitched very low. And she was almost pleading. Why could he not accept this, and let the matter drop? Why crave the bad news that would make neither of them happy?

"I want to know," he said. Back then he would have wanted to know the answer to the other question too, because that was the way a boy fulfilled his function, was it not? Or so it seemed to courting males of whatever age—a boy's job was to undress a girl completely, strip her naked, leave her nothing.

"I am forty-two years old," Carol said. Her eyes did not rise.

Immediately he was satisfied. "So what's so bad about that?" he said cheerfully. "I'm not interested in eighteen-year-olds, you know."

"I don't see why you had to know so badly," she muttered, and now she sounded annoyed.

One's age, Powers told her somewhat pompously, was the single most important fact you could know about him or her. It set that person in a historical perspective. In the case of a cop, for instance, it told you who was commissioner and what the climate was in the department during his impressionable years in the job. It told you how far he had advanced in his career. In the case of a woman, it told you little things, the kind of clothes she had worn in college and the music she had danced to. And big things, such as what kind of world she had grown up in, affected by which specific political and social traumas. If you knew a person's age you could tell approximately how he or she was likely to behave under certain pressures. Powers nodded his head up and down vigorously. Oh yes, you could tell a lot about a person from his or her age.

"How old are you?" Carol asked.

To his surprise, he found he did not want her to know.

"Forty-six," he said.

"You have a hangup about your age," she told him.

Now in the dark in the movie theater, he became aware that Carol had shifted in her seat beside him, snuggling up into his armpit, so that he put his arm around her, and she in return grasped his thumb in one hand, his pinky in the other, holding the two fingers like someone milking a cow. His remaining three fingers and hand she draped over her left breast. Her nipple rose up promptly under the tissue-thin bras women wore these days—Eleanor wore them too —and he began to rub it gently, like someone polishing the brass ferrule on a walking stick, making circular motions which kept it caught within his palm.

So here he was feeling up a date in the movies twenty-five years later, and he found the experience as unsettling now as he did then. It was exciting, he certainly did not want anyone to catch him doing it, and he could not keep his attention on the screen. His attention was on Carol.

She slid her hand into his lap. "I see you're not concentrating on the movie."

"Neither are you."

"Let's go home."

He parked in her driveway, and as they crossed the lawn, she told him conversationally that something was wrong with her dishwasher, perhaps in the morning he could fix it. Seemingly she took it for granted that he neither had to go home nor wanted to, as if, in the jargon of teenage girls, he would be "sleeping over," as if sleeping over was as innocent for him as for children, and fraught with no more implications.

To Powers it was the biggest shock of the night and one of the biggest of his life. Had he really moved this far from Eleanor, from his marriage, his sons, his home, from all that he had cared about during more than half of his life?

They stepped up onto her front step.

"Carol—" He laid the words out rough as bricks,

sharp-edged, hard. "I can only stay about an hour," he said. And her head spun around.

She was really very perceptive, which was part of what fascinated him about her—that she was so quick. It was as if he had tossed her a heavy object. She had caught it at once and begun to examine it. It was like a diplomat's pronouncement. It had weight. He watched her turn it this way and that. It could be benign—or set armies marching —which?

"You stayed all night the last time."

She had unlocked her front door and switched on the lights.

"Yes," he said as they entered the hall, "and felt awful about it after." Did he really want to say this to her?

She turned swiftly to face him. "What's that supposed to mean?"

He was being forced for the first time to take a position, to dig in like a soldier on one hill out of several. But he could not decide which hill to choose, nor was he sure how strongly he wished to defend it. He did know that, for the most part, she focused only on her own needs, never on his, and this could not be allowed to continue. He had obligations both as husband and policeman, which she treated, for the most part, as though they did not exist.

"It means I'm still married, that I have a wife I care about, and sleeping all night with you feels to me about ten times more unfaithful to her than simply making love to you." He realized he was trying to explain the unexplainable. He couldn't really explain it even to himself. He just knew it was there, his guilt, his remorse, or whatever it was.

He found he was staring into the hardest blue eyes he had ever seen.

"Maybe," said Carol, "you had better decide which one of us you want, her or me."

Her words were as inflexible and transparent as glass. As brittle as glass also. "Please, Carol. I've known you a few weeks. I've been married to her for twenty-three years. You're asking too much too fast."

"Do you want to stay all night, or don't you?"

He shook his head gently, a gesture to smooth over the hard words, like a trowel smoothing out cement.

She said: "Don't shake your head. Say what you mean."

His jaw became set. "I'll stay an hour."

"I didn't invite you to stay an hour."

"Okay." He turned toward the door. "Good night, then."

When she neither moved nor spoke, he stepped out into the darkness. Pulling the door shut behind him he moved off across the lawn to his car, and though he scrutinized his emotions, he couldn't tell which ones he was feeling at the moment. It wasn't misery or disappointment or elation or grief. Perhaps it was relief. She had torn him in too many directions for too long and now it was ended, and perhaps he was relieved. He remembered having felt much this way on nights that various girls had thrown him over—the pain of loss did not begin until the next morning.

The grass was wet on his shoes. There was a big high moon. Standing beside his car he looked up at it, sucking in drafts of cold damp air. He grasped the Mustang's door handle.

He did not hear Carol's front door open nor her footsteps on the lawn. He did feel her bosom pressed against his back, her arms around his waist, her forehead against the nape of his neck.

"This is crazy," she murmured into the space between his shoulder blades. "You're right, I want you too much. I want you on any basis I can have you. An hour can be worth a lifetime. If that's all I can have, I'll take it. Come back into the house."

Arm and arm they recrossed the lawn, adding two more sets of footsteps to those imprinted so clearly ahead of them in the dew in the moonlight.

"WHAT'S THIS case you're working on?" she asked a little later.

"Oh, just a case."

"Don't trust me, eh?"

It was a joke, but not a joke—he had to tell her something, and it occurred to him that he could use her. He could get her interested in the story, so that if ever he needed it leaked—if, say, Duncan or someone tried to take administrative action against him—he could hand her the rest of it and she would tell it for him.

Carol had decided to use him too, if she could. There was no reason why he couldn't be a news source as well as a lover, and in truth there was no better place to worm information out of someone than in bed. Either from passion, contentment, or gratitude men were always anxious to accord women favors in bed, to give them presents. In bed woman was not queen, but king. If a woman could ask for diamonds at such a time, then why not for information?

"Of course I trust you," he said, trying to decide how much to tell her.

"What kind of case is it? Is it drugs?"

Now they were each attempting to use the other.

"Drugs, gambling, extortion, murder—you name it."

"Pretty big, eh?"

"Pretty big," he conceded.

"Is it the Mafia?"

"Not the Italian Mafia."

"The Chinese Mafia?"

"Headquarters says there's no such thing."

He felt her quicken, the way a woman did sometimes in the course of sexual arousal.

"But you think there is?"

"I'm obliged to believe what headquarters believes." That was all he intended to tell her.

She purred with contentment, and he thought it was because he was idly stroking her back, her hip, her behind. It wasn't. She was thinking not of Powers pressed naked against her, but of Lurtsema. She had her hook at last. The Chinese Mafia—a headline Lurtsema would go for.

Since she sounded aroused, Powers moved his hand

over her. Mat of hair as coarse as bark. She stirred, still purring.

"Who's the head of it?"

"Not a name you would know."

Carol was annoyed. She wanted to give herself over to what Powers as lover was doing to her, but couldn't until she got Powers as news source to give her a bit more information. She half rolled over, kissing him, and her fingers surrounded him, though only barely. From this she realized that the conversation was proving extremely sexy to both of them. It was kinky sex, in a way. It was like an erotic game they had invented to heighten their excitement. They might have played at being father and daughter in bed together, but this game was better. It was like sex between fourteen-year-olds; their innocent questions were not innocent at all, this conversation was dangerous and forbidden, and both of them knew it.

"But it is one man? A specific guy?" purred Carol, wanting to make him tell, and her cheek moved down him, crossed his abdomen cool as ice, crushed his curls. Her tongue darted out once, twice, and left a blind part of him questing it in the darkness.

"Yes," he said. His whole body had stiffened, and the word was almost a gasp.

"A Chinese guy. What is his name?"

"Oh Carol."

His hand cupped her upthrust buttocks.

"I can't tell you that."

"But he's big?"

"The biggest."

"A Chinese godfather," said Carol triumphantly.

"Yes. Yes. Yes. Oh, Carol, yes."

"The most important man in Chinatown?"

"Yes."

As he rolled her on to her back, she was in a state of such sexual excitement that she was almost overwhelmed by it. She thought the Chinese godfather must be the mayor of Chinatown, Mr. Ting, and she was satisfied she could find the rest out for herself, and in any case she could no longer concentrate on that story, she was working on this one. She wanted Powers now. She had a grip on him, and he was ready, he was always ready. He was like a teenager with her, a fact they had not discussed, but that no doubt surprised him as much as her every time. She had never had a more willing lover, he was always ready, and she guided him where she wanted him to go.

As he began to ride her she knew he wouldn't last long. He was too close to the edge for that, but so was she, her whole body tingling, her mind tingling too, delighted with what she had found out, delighted with Powers both as lover and news source, delighted with herself. She heard him begin to gasp and squeal, noises that came to her over and above the racket she was making herself. For once the tumult of a man's completion, this man's completion, was enough to release her own. She almost never had orgasms during sexual intercourse, only three or four times in her life, but now she experienced an unending, unendurable, agonizing, exquisite series of convulsions; she was so totally unraveled that she cried out, "Marry me, Artie, oh marry me. Divorce your wife and marry me."

ANOTHER SMALL, airless room. No window. A desk, two chairs, one beside the desk, one thrust into it. A filing cabinet that occupied an entire corner. Add two people and the room would be full, overfull. With two people, thought Luang, this room—any room—became a theater. The drama could take place. With only one person you had nothing, an actor without an audience, an audience without a play. Luang, hands on the backrest, stood behind the chair rammed into the kneehole. He had not sat down because the second person had not yet arrived. A Chinese newspaper, printed that morning in Chinatown, lay splashed open in front of him. It was a stage prop only. Luang was waiting, not reading. He was rehearsing his lines.

He wore his one business suit. It was six or seven years old, gray, threadbare, shiny, and in places as thin as paper. In Chinatown, where threadbare suits tended to seem reassuring, there were many like it. The Chinese asked that form be preserved. They did not ask for proof of prosperity. Some of the richest men in Chinatown showed no wealth ever. They owned blocks of buildings, but wore suits like Luang's. Ostentation was dangerous. There was a Chinese adage: If you do not wish your house disturbed by robbers, do not fill it with jade and gold.

Koy was an exception, of course, Luang reflected.

Koy wanted everyone to know how rich he was. But Koy was not your usual Chinese.

The door opened and a woman teacher led in the boy, Quong. A middle-aged Jewish lady, small. Taller than Quong though. Smiling, she had him affectionately by the arm. Quong wanted nothing to do with her. His expression was surly, and he kept trying to shrug his arm loose from her grasp like a hooked fish flapping against the floor of the boat, a reflex action, automatic, mindless.

"I'll send him back to class in a few minutes," said Luang.

Both Chinese watched the door close behind her.

Upon first noticing that Luang was Chinese, the boy's face had lit up, and for a moment he had ceased to struggle.

"Who are you?" he said now. His former surly expression had returned. Luang was perhaps Chinese, but to the pupil he was still the enemy.

Luang folded the Chinese newspaper, thrusting it back into his briefcase. Under it a nameplate now stood revealed. Luang had more than one prop and was using them carefully. The nameplate too had come out of his briefcase. It read: GUIDANCE COUNSELOR.

This meeting with Quong had been arranged through the school principal, Mr. Goldfarb, another middle-aged Jew. Goldfarb was sympathetic to the problems of his young Chinese newcomers. He was also aware of the threat posed to them by the Chinese youth gangs. If Luang wanted to interview Quong, this was fine with Goldfarb. But Luang had said nothing to him about passing himself off as a school guidance counselor.

"I didn't know they had Chinese teachers here," said the surly child. There were no Chinese words for guidance counselor. Supervising teacher was as close as he could come.

"I'm not a teacher," said Luang, and he nodded toward his nameplate. But the deception irked him. It was necessary, probably. If the kid was to lead him anywhere he had to pose as something. So he had had no choice. But to deceive another human being was evil, and law enforcement personnel, he already realized, did as much lying—maybe more—as the criminals they arrested. They played roles, as Luang was doing now, sometimes giving virtuoso performances—without ever warning the audience that the show was a show. They made promises to witnesses, to informants, that they knew they couldn't keep, and in the interest of taking felons off the street they swore out false search warrants and arrest warrants. If necessary to secure a conviction they often enough gave perjured testimony on the witness stand. All this was unfortunate. To combat fraud they multiplied fraud. Criminals, in the course of their depredations, murdered victims relatively rarely; cops murdered truth every day. They destroyed trust. They were guilty of one of the worst crimes of all, the proliferation of the lie.

Luang, staring at the boy before him, chased all these thoughts from his head, or tried to. They would never have occurred to a white demon he was sure, and if he was to do his job properly he had best not dwell on them. This kid would be easy to deceive, and nothing else counted.

"Say, it's good to talk Chinese for a change," he said jovially. He leaned on the joviality. He hammered it home. He drove it in like a spike.

"You don't talk Chinese like an American," conceded Quong grudgingly. He was trying to sound tough, one adult conceding a point to another adult. "You talk like us."

"I was fifteen when I came to this country," said Luang. "Same age as you." The memories were still sharp. Year by year the pain got duller of course, but when remembered it still hurt, the way a broken bone could still hurt long after it had healed. "I was homesick for China every day. Sometimes I walked along the streets crying."

Luang's pain must have shown on his face. The child saw it. His eyes went to the floor, and his chin quivered. "Then you know what it's like."

"Yeah." The vivid trauma of being fifteen. It was like remembering a car crash. One could still feel oneself going through the windshield. Fifteen was an age when a boy was more insecure, more vulnerable, and therefore more conservative than he would ever be again. He had discovered the real world, the one outside the home, its cruel rhythms, its harsh tones. Though shocked, he did not desire to change it. He did not know it could be changed. He desired only to adopt protective coloration so as to survive. Only the approval of his peers, it seemed, would save him. He wanted this desperately. He wanted it every day, every hour. He needed it more than food. He could not live without it.

"In classrooms I didn't understand a word," said Luang. All this was more than fifteen years ago, but he flinched from it as if from a blow. "School was so incredibly boring." True, but the least of it. After school was when a boy got his threshold of pain raised. How could you be accepted by your peers when you were Chinese in an American school and did not speak the language? It was impossible, but you hoped for it anyway, day after day.

"You feel so stupid," confessed Quong. "All the other kids look at you and you know what they're thinking. They're thinking you're stupid." He was trying to describe emotions that were so intense and immediate as to become for him indescribable. It was like asking a boxer to describe the blow that had stunned him. The boy was only fifteen, and it was like asking him to explain digestion, or sleep. The subject, though entirely normal, was too complex. At thirty-two, thought Luang, the answers would be only slightly easier to come by.

In his chair beside the desk young Quong was leaning forward, almost smiling, almost crying, on the edge of elation as well, thinking he had found a sympathetic listener at last.

I've got him, thought Luang, and immediately he became depressed. I don't care about this kid, he reminded himself. My one and only job here is to nail the undertaker, the Cho Kun. He said: "And a year or so later I got interested in girls. I didn't go to this school. The school I went to in

San Francisco was outside of Chinatown. There were no Chinese girls. The American girls wouldn't look at me."

"I'm interested in girls, venerable sir," said the boy eagerly. Luang noted the 'venerable sir.' Surliness was entirely gone. Chinese politeness was back in place. "But most of the Chinese girls around here were born here. They talk English to each other, not Chinese. They only want to make fun of me."

How like a young girl Quong was, Luang thought, reaching out to his supposed guidance counselor the way a girl reached out to a new boyfriend, timid, tentative—she had been hurt so often in the past. There was no equivalent relationship among males except perhaps for this one, a boy seeking a surrogate father.

Talking his way into the school proved easier for Luang than talking his way out. When he had sent Quong back to class, Mr. Goldfarb invited him into the principal's office. Goldfarb wanted to chat.

The white-haired educator evidently took him for a scholar, having learned that you could not judge a Chinese by his poverty or his clothes. Most Chinese were poor, and Chinese scholars, though highly honored by other Chinese, were usually among the poorest. Luang's threadbare business suit was as reassuring to Goldfarb as to most of Chinatown.

Goldfarb had long realized that the Jews and the Chinese held the same values, he said. Same clannishness. Same reverence for learning and the arts, for hard work.

He stroked his white mustache and chuckled. "I understand the Chinese are sometimes called the Jews of the Orient."

Luang nodded politely.

Goldfarb had tried to stop the gangs from recruiting in his school yard, he said. One day he went out there and confronted Nikki Han—ordered him to leave. When Han refused, the frustrated Goldfarb—to his own amazement—gave the gang leader a vicious kick in the balls. "I didn't know who he was at the time," said Goldfarb. "He doubled up on the ground. He puked his guts out."

Han's followers had helped him out of the school yard, while Goldfarb rushed inside to phone the precinct. A Detective Kelly had come around, had provided Han's identity, had described his reputation for violence. This had terrified Goldfarb, who feared reprisals. But there had been none.

"No," said Luang. "For the most part Chinese gangsters won't touch non-Chinese. They know you people will testify against them, whereas their own people are usually too frightened, and won't. That's why Chinatown crime is as successful as it is—and why it is expanding so fast."

"If I see Han or any of the others out there in my school yard," said Goldfarb, "I still will go out there and throw them out." But he sounded surprised by his own conduct, like a man who learns that he has committed an act of insane courage while drunk.

When the school bell rang that afternoon, Luang was waiting outside the fence in his car. He could hear the bell, then the drum roll of feet on the staircases. In a moment, he saw Quong, carrying a book bag, wearing now his Chinese cap, come running across the school yard and through the gate. The car door was yanked open and the boy, grinning with pleasure, jumped in beside him.

"Is this your car, venerable sir?" He looked around the car in wonder as if at the inside of a palace.

"This is my car."

"You're pretty rich."

The car was a Volkswagen Beetle, not new. It was older than Luang's suit. Certainly no American kid would have been impressed by it. But in Chinatown very few people owned cars at all.

"I went to school," said Luang. "I learned to speak English. I got a job, and I bought myself a car. You can do the same. Your first problem is to learn to speak English. I can help you there. I know a place that's run by the city for Chinese kids." Luang had spent the last several hours researching this. "I can get you in there. But only if that's what you want."

"Hey, I'd like that."

Luang, driving, thought he had never seen a happier-looking boy, and for a moment he felt less guilty.

"Well, what would you like to see? Would you like to see Central Park, the Bronx Zoo?"

Later in the afternoon they drove down Fifth Avenue. The office buildings were just letting out. Traffic thickened. Two-toned blue buses that plowed straight on. Yellow cabs that darted toward individuals who stepped out from between parked cars, hands waving frantically.

"You've been running with some bad kids," said Luang.

The boy had been gawking at the crowds, at the tall buildings. Immediately his defenses sprang up. Drawbridge raised, barbed wire out front. "They're my friends." He was as hostile as Luang had yet seen him. But it did not last. He turned pleading eyes on Luang. "They understand me."

"What makes you think they're your friends?"

Quong said nothing.

"They'll get you in trouble." His glance flicked sideways at Quong, who looked suddenly miserable. "Maybe they already got you in trouble."

"I don't know," the boy mumbled, his voice so low the Chinese police officer could barely hear him.

"This is Fifth Avenue here," said Luang cheerfully. "I guess you've never seen Fifth Avenue before." He was changing the somber mood, the mood of siege. He was pulling his troops back out of sight. He could not afford to alarm the boy too much.

"It's more crowded than China." There was gratitude in Quong's voice, relief. Detecting it, Luang was satisfied. Whatever the boy was afraid of, ashamed of, whatever he was hiding, it would come out. It was inevitable. He was like the Chinese maiden awaiting the arrival of the bridegroom she had never seen before. The only question was, how soon?

"Say, how about taking me home to meet your parents," said Luang. He would keep the pressure on. "I'd like to meet them very much."

This meeting proved not easy to set up. Both parents worked more than twelve hours a day, and were rarely off work at the same time. And so about a week passed.

The Quongs lived on the fifth floor of a tenement on Elizabeth Street, about one block north of the station house. Luang had to climb five flights of stairs. By the time he knocked on the apartment's front door he was breathing hard.

The Quongs had the rear third of what had been a living room. Their "home" was sectioned off by a curtain that ran along a wire. It was the preferred space in the room because it had the window, and was not a passageway—there was no foot traffic going through. For these reasons they were quite proud of it. On the other hand, one had to walk through the other two sections to get in or out, to use the kitchen or bathroom. Both other sections were full, Luang had noted, arriving. He had smiled and bowed to about fifteen persons on the way through. He was neither surprised nor shocked that such accommodations existed in New York. As a child in Hong Kong, and in China before that, he and his parents had lived just this way themselves.

The Quongs had a narrow single bed, which he supposed the parents shared, and a pallet on the floor for the boy. There were two straight chairs. A square of plywood lay on top of the bed—this served as a table. There was also a hot plate and a teapot, the tea already steeping.

"Tea, Mr. Luang?" said the mother. She was surely twenty years younger than the father, but she looked worked out to Luang, all the moisture squeezed out of her flesh long ago.

He was offered one of the chairs. Mr. Quong, lord of his own home, took the other, and his wife stood. She had her arm around her son, and was beaming.

Luang sipped his tea out of a porcelain bowl that seemed brand-new to him, and expensive as well, and he surmised that the Quongs had bought it just that day, believing their everyday cups unworthy of tonight's honored guest, the false guidance counselor, himself.

"He's a good boy," Mrs. Quong said, giving her son a squeeze. She grinned with pride—pride in her boy, pride that tonight she was entertaining such an exalted personage as Luang.

"Next year, he'll be speaking English," said the father. It was hard for Luang to concentrate because of the buzz of family conversations behind the curtain.

"More tea, Mr. Luang? Oh, I'm so relieved to think you're taking an interest in my boy. He's a good boy, but America is strange to him. I've been afraid he might get into trouble."

"That can't happen now," said Mr. Quong. "He's lucky and we're lucky. I used to be a schoolteacher myself, did you know that?"

"I think I will have some more tea," said Luang glumly. "It certainly is delicious tea. How do you make tea that good, anyway?"

By the time he went down into the street again it was nearly midnight, and he was so upset that he phoned Captain Powers at home, possibly waking him up—he didn't care. Powers told him to come right over, and gave directions. And so he drove through the night to Powers' house in a part of the city he had never entered before. It was at the opposite end of Manhattan island from Chinatown and to Luang, once he had seen it, it could have been the opposite end of the world. Powers' house seemed to him huge, solid, gracious, incredibly luxurious—a brick mansion to Luang, to any Chinese—and when he had parked out front he sat some minutes in his car merely contemplating it.

Powers, wearing a bathrobe and slippers, half-glasses perched on top of his hair, let him in.

"Do you want a beer? Something to eat? You want a cup of tea? What's the trouble?"

"I'll never make it as a cop, Captain."

Powers gave him a smile. "Of course you will. What's bothering you?"

So Luang spoke of lies and deceit—of deceiving the Quong family, of betraying their trust. "Mr. Quong wanted to tell me all about being a schoolteacher in China. He wanted to know all about my job as schoolteacher in New York."

Powers frowned. He had encountered Luang's reaction before—it had been his own reaction too, as a young cop. "Don't get soft on me, Luang."

"These people are so poor, Captain, and so hopeful. And the kid seems a decent kid. They are all depending on me, and it makes me feel like a snake."

"You're not a snake. You're a cop. You're doing your job."

As a young man—as a far younger man than Luang —Powers had confronted these same moral questions himself. He had concluded that there were just no answers. One had best not even look for them because the risk was too great. One risked becoming unable to function as a cop at all.

"The kid's got a gun in the waistband of his pants," muttered Luang glumly. "I could have arrested him for carrying. I didn't. I think he wants me to know he's got it. I think he wants me to ask him about it."

Powers said, "What are you waiting for? Ask him."

LATE THE next afternoon the school yard was crowded. There were skaters, Frisbee players. There were games going at both ends of the basketball court. Wooden bleachers rose up at one side of the court, between the court and the fence, and on the top row sat Luang with Quong.

"You've got a gun," said Luang. "I'm not blind, you know. Who gave it to you, your new friends? Did they make you use it yet? Did you shoot anybody yet?"

Tears popped into the eyes of the boy. It was instantaneous. Luang was astonished. Absolutely instantaneous. One second the boy was dry-eyed, and the next second his eyeballs overflowed with tears. A moment after that he was sobbing. Turning toward Luang, he threw himself into his supposed guidance counselor's arms. He wept copiously, wetly, the way a child weeps, and Luang embraced him, patting his head, murmuring: "There, there. It can't be that bad."

"It is, it is," sobbed Quong, and Luang suspected that indeed it was.

"Do you want to tell me about it?" said Police Officer Luang.

It happened that Nikki Han and Go Low had entered the school yard through the Hester Street gate about five minutes before. It was getting on toward dusk, the bleachers were on the Baxter Street side, and the school yard was teeming with kids. It was possible that the two Flying Dragons would not have noticed Quong and Luang at all, had not their attention been caught by the boy's racking sobs.

The noise of a child crying does not disturb other children. Children are people who have not learned to recognize most warning signals. They can sleep through alarm clocks. A police siren suggests excitement, not distress. Tears represent barked shins, not a cry for help. To them crying is as normal as pain, as normal as water—the one produces the other, though in minimal amounts only, like drops wrung out of a towel. There is no danger—no one is going to drown from it. In the case of Quong, a few kids threw glances toward the bleachers. But the glances glanced off.

But adults, having lived longer with fear, react instantly to any warning signal at all. Each one is a circuit-breaker. The mechanism will not function until the break is found and the gap bridged.

Nikki Han was twenty-five years old—old enough. Quong's sobs barely carried across the school yard, but they triggered every bell in Han's head.

Who was that kid and why was he crying?

"Look," said Han sharply. "That's the guy we followed."

"He's with Quong," said Go Low. "What do you suppose it means? Do you think it means anything?"

They were both American-born, and they spoke English to each other.

"That guy's a cop," said Han. "He's gotta be."

They backed out of the school yard, backed away while watching the bleachers carefully, making certain that their departure went as unnoticed as their arrival.

They were successful. Across the school yard Luang and Quong had their hands full with each other, for the boy's dreadful revelations had begun to pour forth. And so neither looked up.

A hundred yards down the street from the school yard, Han and Low began to run.

22

MIDNIGHT. Again Luang stood on Powers' doorstep. "Come in, Luang. What is it?"

Again Powers wore the homeliest of man's uniforms, pajamas and bathrobe. Again his glasses sat on his hair. Different uniform from the one he wears in the daytime, thought Luang. Different man inside it too, probably. Powers' bathrobe had become something he would recognize anywhere. He could identify it in court. It was as though he lived in this house, and Powers was his father—the notion was bizarre, but understandable: normally if you saw a man in his night clothes he was probably your father—someone you trusted totally, anyway.

"I just left the boy, Captain. I've been with him since three o'clock this afternoon. I just took him home. I couldn't leave him till now."

In Luang's voice was a note of quiet desperation. Powers detected it. He led the way into the living room. "Sit down. Can I offer you anything?"

Luang was wearing his gray suit, but had left his suit coat in the car. His tie was undone and his collar open. He took a small revolver out of his pants pocket, and handed it over.

Powers hefted it, studied it. Guns to Powers were not question marks, but statements. They were like presidents, they spoke with the power of their office. One had best pay attention.

"He gave it to me, Captain. He wanted to get rid of it. He's fifteen years old and absolutely horrified by what he's done." Luang looked and sounded drained. "He thinks I'm his guidance counselor. I'm supposed to tell him what to do next."

"Thirty-two caliber. One of those executions—"

"Take it to ballistics, Captain. The bullet will match. He shot one of the Hsu brothers. Nikki Han made him do it. Han shot the other. Koy ordered it. In any case, Koy was there a few minutes before the executions took place."

Powers began tapping the revolver against his palm. It was a cupping motion, aggressive, like making a snow ball, packing it down hard, preparing a projectile with which to inflict damage.

"Let's go wake up the district attorney," he decided.

Luang was surprised. District attorneys were elected officials. They were men of genuinely august rank, far higher than police captains. This one, in addition, had held the job through four straight elections. You couldn't just wake him up. But Powers went to the phone and did so.

The district attorney lived in a town house on Riverside Drive overlooking the Hudson River—about fifteen minutes away at this time of night. They rode there in Luang's Volkswagen, with Luang apologizing most of the way for the condition of his car.

The district attorney was waiting for them. As they climbed his front stoop he opened the door himself.

Another man in his bathrobe. Slippers with holes in them. Between slippers and bathrobe, red pajama legs. Luang was now totally confused. He was trying to relate the appearance of this man to the Chinese concepts of rank and face. A Chinese dignitary, even a minor functionary, would not have seen them at all at this hour. Or else he would have had them shown in by servants, would have made them wait, would have appeared only when decked out in all the finery of his office. Anything less was to lose face.

The district attorney of New York County had not even bothered to comb his hair, which was rumpled from sleep. He showed them into his living room, and while Powers talked he padded about trying to stuff and ignite his pipe. He was neither friendly or unfriendly. He said nothing at all until Powers had concluded.

A full minute of silence ensued before he began to speak.

"You got enough to convict the kid on the homicide charge." He said thoughtfully. "Maybe manslaughter—I don't know. You got the murder weapon and you got a voluntary confession to a police officer. The kid was not under arrest, so the fact that there was no Miranda warning does not enter in. On Nikki Han, legally speaking, you've got nothing. Even if the kid testified against him, it's the unsupported testimony of a co-conspirator. On Koy you've got even less. Your witness is the same co-conspirator, and he can't even testify that Koy gave the orders in his presence."

If this speech surprised Powers, it did not show. The district attorney puffed his pipe. He and Powers stared at each other through a cloud of smoke.

"A district attorney's first job," the DA told Luang in a kindly voice, "is to make the police bring in a legally sound case. I'm sorry to say that you don't have one."

"But we have enough for a wiretap order, don't we?" asked Powers.

"On whom? The kid? You already got the kid cold."

"On Koy. On his place of business, on his residence, and on the gambling den he runs." Powers, as always when under stress, had begun to pace the room.

"You have no legal proof he runs the gambling den, and there are no phones in the gambling den proper, as I understand it. So that's out."

"On his residence and his place of business then," said Powers stubbornly.

Luang saw that a negotiation was going on, and was surprised, though why? Everything else had to be negotiated every day. Why should law enforcement be different?

The district attorney said, "Legally it's pretty shaky. Wiretap orders must be based on the continuing nature of the conspiracy, as you know, and the court might hold that these murders were isolated incidents in the past."

"Come on, come on," said Powers, "you can do better than that."

"Also the law insists that, to be legally valid, a wiretap must be monitored, or you can't keep it open. Do you have enough Chinese-speaking police officers to monitor this around the clock?"

Both men stared at Luang.

"No," said Powers, "I guess I don't."

"Maybe," Luang said resignedly, "I can find a Chinese restaurant to send me in food." But he was not displeased. As a job, at least it sounded safe. It was better than tailing Koy through streets.

The district attorney said to Luang, "You understand that the law does not permit you to eavesdrop on general conversation. You have to keep switching the thing on and off." He was giving Luang a kind of genial course of instruction, and explicit orders at the same time. "As soon as you've heard enough to indicate that a general conversation is taking place, you may no longer eavesdrop. You may eavesdrop only when discussion of criminal activity is taking place." He turned back to Powers. "I'm sorry. I didn't make the rules. But they're getting stricter all the time. Make out your affidavit, Captain. Put down this police officer as the one who will monitor the wiretap. No one else may monitor it except for the person or persons specified in the affidavit. You know that of course." He tapped his pipe bowl down into an ashtray, then sucked the pipe stem dry. It made a sound like a tea kettle whistling. "Will you inform the chief of detectives? Or shall I?"

Powers had stopped pacing. He looked pleased. He was going to get his wiretap order.

"Do we have to tell him?"

"We usually do."

"May I ask you a favor?" said Powers. "Can we just not tell him for a few days?

Luang's glance went from face to face. This seemed an important point, but the significance eluded him.

"I don't work for him," said the district attorney.

"I don't work for him either," muttered Powers.

The district attorney gave a slight nod. "It makes no difference to me."

"Thank you," said Captain Powers.

A few minutes later Powers and Luang stood on the front stoop in the night. The door had slammed shut behind them. The light had gone out inside. The district attorney, presumably, had gone back to bed.

"We ought to pick the kid up before something happens to him," said Luang. "Can I run you home, Captain?"

Powers was watching the traffic for a cruising taxi. "We can't," he said. "It would notify them that we know something. We have to leave him out there. Thanks for the offer, but it's out of your way. You go home and get some rest. I'll find a cab.

Because Luang had seen Powers two straight nights in bathrobe and slippers, he decided that a kind of tacit intimacy now existed between them, a tacit permission to question his commander's decision. "If you ask me," he said, "that's taking terrible risks with that kid's life. If they find out he's talked to me, they'll whack him out so quick—"

Powers shook his head. His attention was divided. He was still watching for a taxi. "The answer is no."

Here came one, roof lights on, coming up the service road toward him. "Good night, Luang," he said. He stepped out into the street, flagged it down, got in and was gone.

POWERS SPENT the next morning with an assistant district attorney named O'Hara, twenty-four years old, brand new in the law-enforcement business, writing out the copious affidavits that went with a wiretap application. Late in the afternoon O'Hara took all this paperwork before a friendly judge, one of only a handful considered friendly enough by the prosecutors to be approached for this purpose—the rest being self-styled civil libertarians. This judge signed the wire-tap order, and O'Hara so notified Powers, who had returned to his precinct, by phone.

O'Hara also notified Telephone Company Security, whose men installed the wiretaps, running the intercepts, as requested by Powers, well outside of Chinatown into an office on the second floor of the Sixth Precinct station house in Greenwich Village. In this office Luang took up station at 9 A.M. the following morning. Powers waited with him until the first intercept was made, a call by Koy to a supplier of coffins. Both parties spoke in English and the call sounded, both to Luang and to Powers, entirely legitimate. It continued to sound legitimate as Luang cut back into it from time to time to make sure. The subject matter did not change, and after two minutes and thirty-three seconds the call ended.

As Powers left the station house many police eyes watched him go. The entire station house was already aware of Luang, Powers saw. Aware of the wiretaps too, and therefore brimming with questions for which there were as yet no answers available. Presently, Powers knew, some cop would manage to identify Luang and the situation would become clear to the entire complement of cops. There were no secrets in station houses. After that it was only a matter of time, perhaps days, perhaps hours, before news of Luang and of his wiretap—and of Powers behind it—leaked back to the chief of detectives. That is, Powers thought, I am already feeling the pressure of time. The wiretap order was for thirty days, but he had far less time than that, and he knew it.

Koy's wife made five phone calls from home that morning, one of them lasting forty-two minutes. She spoke each time in English, always to women. She had not been identified in the wiretap application as part of the continuing criminal conspiracy. Luang had no right to eavesdrop on her conversations at all, and did not do so, except to cut in from time to time to make certain that the phone had not been taken by Koy. In addition, as he noted in his log, there were seven incoming and six outgoing calls from the funeral parlor. He could put a name to Chang's voice. The embalmer spoke only Cantonese, and sounded like a moron. Since he was not listed in the affidavit either, Luang cut into his calls only briefly, making sure that the voice on the line stayed the same. Two other calls were made by one of the assistant funeral directors, and the rest were by Koy, who mostly spoke Cantonese. All of the local calls sounded innocent. But there were also two calls to Hong Kong, to different numbers each time, and these seemed more promising, principally because Koy had at once commenced speaking in a language Luang was able to identify, but could not understand: Hakka.

Luang spoke Cantonese and Shanghainese. He did not speak Hakka, one of the most difficult of the major Chinese dialects. Neither did any of the other six Chinese police officers, he knew. Not one of them even spoke Mandarin. New York, up till now, had been a Cantonese town, as far as Chinese-Americans were concerned. Mandarin was the official language of Red China, and also of Taiwan, and one heard more and more of it in the streets of Chinatown today. But Hakka was another story. The Hakkas had been the original indigenous people of China. They were forced out of their own country by invaders from the north about a thousand years ago, and moved to the south where they became known as the guest people. For the most part they hadn't mixed with local residents then, and still didn't. They had a reputation for trusting nobody but each other.

Traditionally they had been the adventurers, the seamen, the pirates, the criminals of China.

Luang realized that Koy was probably a Hakka.

In the afternoon Koy made more calls—the log showed six of them, two more to Hong Kong, two to Canada, one to London, one to Amsterdam, all in Hakka. The first came at 3:03 P.M. and the last at 4:41, at which time Luang phoned the Fifth Precinct. Powers rushed right over.

"Hakka?" he demanded. He had closed the door, closing the two of them into the small office. He had hung his uniform jacket over the back of a chair, and he was pacing. "Hakka?" he said again.

"The language of Chinese banditry for a thousand years," said Luang. "As far as Koy is concerned, it fits in, doesn't it?"

"That's not the point, Luang," said Powers. He looked and sounded extremely agitated. "That's not the point."

"I know," said Luang. "Since I don't speak Hakka, I can't monitor him. The minute he starts talking Hakka, I have to shut the tape recorder off."

"Don't you understand Hakka at all?" Powers was almost pleading with him. "Don't you understand it even a little?"

"Not a word, Captain."

"This is crazy."

"China is a big country. We have eight major languages. So what? Europe has about twenty."

Powers was pacing hard, head down. "We've got to find somebody who speaks Hakka."

"That's not going to be easy, Captain."

There was no Chinese-American cop they could use, and if they picked some Chinese-American off the street, he would most likely feel more loyalty toward a fellow Chinese than toward the police, and also more fear—Koy was, after all the Cho Kun. An individual off the street would be more likely to go straight to Koy with the news than to help make a case against him.

This deplorable tendency had been amply proven during past gambling cases. The department's public morals division had often employed informants who would enter the gambling dens, make their observations, and afterwards testify against those individuals they were able to identify as employees. Not once had any informant ever identified a single big shot in the gambling hierarchy. Nothing but low-level arrests were ever made—this was still another reason why crackdowns on the Chinese gambling dens had been curtailed. To the police commanders involved, it had seemed clear that owners and operators of gambling dens were men of respect in Chinatown; they were also dangerous. To finger one of them would subject the informant to swift, vicious reprisals.

It was useless to imagine that an ordinary Chinatown citizen, no matter who he was, could be trusted to monitor the wiretap on Koy.

"Wait a minute," cried Powers. "I've got an idea." He was suddenly beaming. "I think I know where some Hakka-speaking people can be found."

A crazy idea, as yet insubstantial, he tossed it this way and that. But possible, an idea that might work.

"Stay on post. I'll be back."

From an office down the hall Powers made a number of phone calls. He could scarcely believe his luck. Gathering up the notes he had made, he ran down to his car and drove to the district attorney's office at 155 Leonard Street. By then it was supper time and the district attorney, waiting for him, looked annoyed. He listened impassively as Powers outlined the situation. Trustworthy Hakka-speaking people were needed to monitor the wiretap, and he had found them. He had their names right here.

He pushed the new names across the desk. But the district attorney, who sat with his lips pursed, his fingers steepled, was shaking his head negatively. "All we have to do is add these names to the existing wiretap order," Powers said.

"Wiretaps must be monitored by law enforcement personnel," the DA declared. "These names you have given me, they're women, and they certainly would not be mistaken for law enforcement personnel. I don't know if a judge will sign this." But he was already beginning to change his mind, Powers saw. A half-smile was creeping onto his face. Powers' plan amused him. He looked willing to try it.

"They are not law enforcement personnel," Powers persisted. "They're retired missionary nuns who speak Hakka. Their integrity is beyond question. There have to be exceptions to these rules from time to time. The law can't

256

be that strict. Now would you please sign this thing and let's get it to a judge."

And an hour later Powers led the two old women into the station house. He knew heads would turn and stare. He watched it happen—the cop on security duty at the door, the desk sergeant. Powers wanted to laugh. He was like a practical joker observing the results of his joke—his joke on this station house, on the police department, on law enforcement, on the world.

"Right this way, Sisters," chortled Powers, and the two aged nuns, dressed in the flowing black habits and starched cowls of many years ago, followed him looking neither right nor left, great frail blackbirds with sharp white beaks.

In all that large room, as Powers and the two women crossed it, no one else moved. About ten officers and detectives stared. Their shoes seemed screwed to the floor.

What were these women doing here?

Station houses, every cop knew, were not cathedrals. They attracted neither worshippers nor tourists. They were as forbidding as cemeteries, as repugnant as garbage dumps. They were monuments to human degradation. One avoided them out of an almost superstitious dread. Even neighborhood people sometimes crossed the street to walk by, they crossed their breasts, as if the building itself had unknown power, gave off some vague occult emanation. No one strolled in off the street out of idle curiosity. No one strolled in at all except cops whose gear creaked, rough men, hearty, ribald. Most visitors were dragged in, hands manacled, cursing and screaming, or else stunned and bloody. They were sometimes accompanied by their victims, who were likely to be stunned and bloody also. Women visitors could be either one category or the other, prisoner or victim. If prisoners, they were principally shoplifters or whores. They could be axe murderesses too, but this was rare. If victims, they had suffered usually at the hands of their husbands, either legal or, more often, common law. The more impermanent a relationship, the more violent.

These were the categories of women cops were used to in station houses, and so now they froze and gawked, eyes like radar disks.

Nuns in station houses were totally outside every cop's experience. The two old women now parading past them could not have aroused more shock, created more questions, started more talk if they had been stark naked. Chiefs Duncan and Cirillo, Powers knew, would hear about this in an hour. There would be no keeping of secrets now.

Upstairs he threw open the door on Luang. The phones were still at the moment, and the Chinese police officer, wearing jeans and a sweater, sat with his feet on the desk reading a book. But he jumped quickly to his feet, and his gaze switched from Powers to the nuns. Unlike the men downstairs, he showed no surprise at all, so that Powers wondered: is it because he is Chinese? Have the Chinese seen so much more than we that nothing surprises them anymore?

In this room Powers' joke had fallen flat, and he did not know why.

"Sisters," he said, "this is Police Officer Luang. Luang, this is Sister Mary Bartholomew and Sister Mary Jeanne. They're retired nuns. They were missionaries in China for many years, and they speak Hakka. Show them what to do."

Sister Jeanne said, "Oh, Captain, this is so—so—"

She must be eighty, Powers thought, and she's as excited as a girl.

Sister Bartholomew was more pensive: "I do hope we can be of help."

As Luang began to explain the intercept console, the tape recorder, Powers excused himself. "I'll be back a little later, Sisters."

But once in the corridor he hesitated, for he could hear Luang's voice through the door.

"I'll work the machine, Sisters. All you have to do is tell me the gist of the conversation. If it's just ordinary conversation, the law says we can't listen."

Inside that room, Powers reflected, three people were engaged in eavesdropping. Outside the room, one more: himself.

Privacy, invasion of. An intellectual concept. A legal concept. In most of the world privacy did not exist. To the Chinese, it was unknown. Both here and in China they lived packed too close together. When families were separated by curtains hung on wires, if that, every fart and belch was common property. Yet in New York, although conversations in the street were not protected, the privacy of those carried electronically had been declared by the courts to be inviolable, as privileged as marriage, sacred, like love—a concept that was not even rooted in customs and morals. It was entirely new. In the days of open lines, party lines—not very long ago—it was unheard of. No one supposed that telephones were or ever could be private. A wiretap would have offended nobody.

Whereas now a villain such as Koy had to be tracked according to rules as refined as those that governed a banquet. The table had to be set just so, the guests arranged just so. A single breach of etiquette and all the foregathered food had to be dumped into the garbage-disposal unit, the wine poured down the sink, the guests sent away hungry.

"But if the subject sounds promising," said Luang's voice through the door, "we listen, all three of us, and you tell me what it's about."

There came a muffled, nervous giggle. Sister Bartholomew, Powers thought. A homely sound, encouraging to him, wholly pleasing, as if God (if there was a God) would surely reward the efforts of these noble ladies. Reward them, reward him, reward the wiretap.

Cops often set a thief to catch a thief, Powers reflected. The old adage was also conventional police technique. That's what informants were all about. He had gone one better. He had set two virgins to catch a crime lord—man's oldest and most revered symbol of purity manning the ramparts against the powers of darkness.

Powers went down to his car, parked in front of the station-house door, and drove home.

23

THAT MORNING, wanting to look his best for an appointment with Carol Cone later in the day, Chief of Detectives Cirillo had himself driven in his official car by his official chauffeur to a barber shop he favored on lower Broadway opposite City Hall. His chauffeur was a detective named Harold Sutherland—Mafia dons were not the only New Yorkers customarily driven about by armed men, nor the only ones who enjoyed lying under hot towels. As Cirillo went inside and mounted the tonsorial throne, as he lay back and closed his eyes, he was confident that no one would shoot him—few Mafia dons could share this confidence, their mortality rate in barber chairs being rather high. There was a second difference. As the manicurist, a young woman with dyed hair, kneaded the chief of detective's gun hand, as she soaked, massaged and pared his nails, Cirillo was on duty and being paid by the City. He was half asleep, half aroused and on duty all at the same time.

Sutherland, meanwhile, sat parked out front where, also at city expense, he waited.

If questioned, Cirillo would have maintained that this was the department's image he was grooming here, not his own—for the department's TV appearance later: he only wanted the Department to look its best on camera. Besides, he was underpaid by civilian standards, and a little barbering on City time was a perk that came with the job. Harold's presence in the street could be justified also. The chief of detectives' car contained some expensive radio equipment, which Harold was both guarding and monitoring; in addition, like any cop on patrol, he was presumed to be eyeballing all the sidewalk he could see. Let a crime be perpetrated within eyeshot of Harold, and he would be out of that car in an instant, gun drawn.

In fact, Harold had all frequencies turned down as far as they would go, except for the rarely used confidential band, because he had the *Daily News* spread open on the steering wheel and was reading. Harold was one of those individuals who required absolute concentration in order to read at all.

Cirillo, who was fifty-one years old, wore an exquisitely cut gray suit made for him by an exclusive Madison Avenue clothier—in return he had provided the store with about ten minutes of free security advice on his own time. He had provided it after hours, on the day he had driven up to the store in his police car to collect the suit.

Now, freshly scented, shaved and coiffed, his fingernails lacquered, he came out to the car. Harold folded the *News* and started the engine.

Sliding into the front seat, Cirillo nodded at the radio. "Anything come over, Harold?"

"Not a thing, Chief."

An hour later Cirillo's intercom buzzed and his chief secretary, a captain, announced the arrival of Carol Cone.

Cirillo straightened his tie, shot his monogrammed cuffs so that his gold cuff links showed, and was ready for her. He met her at the door.

He had expected to greet a three- or four-person crew. To his surprise she was alone. A sexy, brassy broad in a tight suede dress, but alone.

"Where's the cameras?" he demanded, giving her a wolfish grin. Though he pretended to be joking, he was annoyed. "I get all dressed up nice and there's no camera. What is this?"

"It's called preliminary reporting, Chief," Carol assured him. "The cameras come later."

Cirillo's annoyance began to recede. He liked looking at her, she was a celebrity, and her presence here made him feel important. In addition, she was a woman, and therefore easy to manipulate. All he had to do was give her whatever story she had come for. If he played his cards right, she'd be back again tomorrow to interview him on film.

"What's on your mind?" he said, stepping behind his desk. He ogled her up and down, exaggerating it, oozing charm. "I mean, I know what's on my mind, but what's on yours?"

He gestured to the chair beside his desk. She took it, crossing her legs, giving him a flash of thigh. Then she looked up at him, blinking her eyes—provocatively, he thought. A definite come-on, he decided, once he had thought about it a moment. She's too old not to know exactly what she's doing. He puzzled over what it meant.

"I like your suit, Chief."

He nodded, and grinned. "Yours fits nice too," he said, and gave her bosom another exaggerated stare. Compliments of this nature were the kind women liked best, Cirillo believed.

"It's about Chinatown, Chief." And again her glance, her half-smile, the way she leaned toward him in the chair seemed to him provocative. If he played his cards right, he thought, he might get more out of this than a bit of television time. The notion did not surprise him. In New York he was just as much a celebrity as she was, and a man of power as well. Women responded to power, as everyone knew, and they responded to cops too, which only cops knew. Women were always jumping into bed with cops. Some of them called in fake crimes just to bring cops to their doors. Cirillo had never bothered to think it out, but certain women were as attracted to cops as others were attracted to baseball players. Probably it was the dark side of the policeman's life that drew them. Cops were society's hunters—and sometimes killers. They carried guns. They represented force and public safety at the same time. Perhaps all women secretly wanted to be raped by a cop because he would protect them while he was doing it. This idea appealed to Cirillo's sardonic sense of humor, and he smiled at Carol.

"Chinatown, eh?" he said.

As an inspector, he had commanded the public morals division's gambling raids in Chinatown, he said. PMD was a kind of headquarters-based vice squad.

"Did you work on drugs too?" asked Carol. She had her notebook out.

Cirillo frowned. Why had she asked that?

No, not drugs, he told her. He intended to accord this subject one sentence and go past it, like a train rushing through a station. She would get only a glimpse, not enough to tempt her to return. Drug addiction was practically unknown in Chinatown, he said. There, that was the one sentence. And it was true, too. So was prostitution unknown, he added. There were almost no Chinese prostitutes or pimps. Prostitution was a low-profit business, and Chinese criminals were not interested in low-profit businesses. Gambling, on the other hand, was big, the Chinese weakness, and Cirillo had raided a lot of joints.

"What about Chinese organized crime?"

"There's no such thing, doll. The Mafia in this country is still run by the Italians."

Partly to get her off this dangerous subject, partly just to be funny, he began to tell her gambling stories. He would charm the pants off her, as the saying goes. In her case literally, he hoped.

He talked of police battering rams knocking flimsy tenement walls in on rooms full of Chinese gamblers. "You should have seen the surprised faces on those Chinamen," chortled the chief of detectives. "Their steel door is still standing, but the whole wall is down."

Carol grinned encouragingly, pen poised. To Cirillo she seemed an appreciative audience. She waited for whatever pearls he might drop next.

He used to station men in the back courtyard, he

said. "All those Chinamen would go pouring out the back door right into the arms of my guys. Worked every time."

"You'd think they'd know better than to run out the back door," encouraged Carol.

"The back door is instinctive with people," said Cirillo. "When a man is caught in a raid, you can't tell him not to run out the back door."

Cirillo, laughing at his own joke, realized that Carol seemed less amused than previously, and had not written anything down in some time.

"What about drugs?"

"No drugs. Not in years. I told you that before."

"I've been hearing stories about a Chinese Mafia," she said.

"There's no evidence of that at all," stated Cirillo immediately. "Who could have given you that idea?"

"It's something I heard."

Cirillo thought he knew where she had heard it. He asked carefully, casually, "Have you talked to the precinct commander down in Chinatown yet?"

"Yes."

"And?"

"Well, he seems like a nice fellow, but he doesn't say much."

They looked at each other, both nodding carefully, casually.

"He's a good cop." said Cirillo, looking for a response. But he got none; Carol did not reply.

Cirillo decided she was not stupid. He had best make a small concession. "Chinese organized crime, maybe. In a minor way. Chinese Mafia, no," he said.

Carol uncrossed her legs, and Cirillo got a second look up her dress. It made his shirt collar feel too tight. "Maybe you're thinking about the tongs," he said. "In a way the tongs might be considered organized crime, since they control the gambling. The other big crime down there is extortion by the youth gangs. But we're beginning to break that up now."

"And murder," said Carol.

"Yeah. Once in a while they knock each other off."

She had a way of gazing at him half smiling, the tip of her sharp tongue showing between her teeth. Cirillo imagined how she would look with her hair spread out on a pillow.

"Well, the tongs then," said Carol. "Who should I see about the tongs?"

Cirillo leaned back and studied her. She was sending forth conflicting messages. He read her as an intensely sensual woman who was also a celebrity, and therefore proud. She would come this far toward him, and no further. If he wanted her he would have to make his play.

"Why don't I get some men in here to talk to you, honey," he suggested. "The inspector who has PMD is a fellow you should talk to. And the intelligence sergeant in charge of my Chinatown section as well."

"Fine," said Carol.

Cirillo nodded at her, grinning broadly. "And after you finish with them, why don't you and I go out to lunch? I have something on for lunch, but for you I can break it." His hand hovered over his intercom button, as if to signify that the two offers went together.

Carol's smile was late. "Lunch would be swell, Chief. I'm sure you and I have lots to talk about."

Cirillo punched the intercom. "Reach out for Inspector Appell and Sergeant Torres," he ordered. "Get them in here forthwith."

About five minutes later the two men entered Cirillo's office. "Pete Appell, Sergeant Torres," said Cirillo, "meet the best-looking broad on television. She wants to know about Chinatown."

After showing them all into his conference room, Cirillo went back behind his desk, ordered his secretary to reserve a table for two at Il Cortile, one of little Italy's finest restaurants, then began to catch up on the messages and paper work that had accumulated during the morning. He bossed about 2500 detectives. a force bigger than the entire police departments of most of the world's cities.

In the conference room, Inspector Appell was mostly

silent, whereas Sergeant Torres proved a journalist's dream. He had more and better facts than the chief of detectives, and was delighted to disgorge them. He had headed the Chinatown section for five years. The intelligence had piled up and no one until Captain Powers a few weeks ago, and now Carol, had even talked to him.

"Did you go to Chief Cirillo?"

"I sent him a memo after these recent killings. I haven't heard back yet."

"I see."

"The Chief's a busy man," interjected Appell. "He's got the whole city to worry about. Chinatown is only a small part."

"You're right," said Carol.

"I'm only a sergeant," said Torres.

Carol began to fill pages in her notebook, scribbling quickly. Her questions became ever more explicit. She made Torres prove every important statement.

How did he know the Chinese were taking over real estate formerly owned by Italians? Answer: Gino's Roadhouse in Queens, a mob hangout, had just become the Shanghai Palace. And a "social club" on Mulberry Street in Little Italy was now a gambling den. The two sides seemed to have come together, as was proved by certain recent funerals: Mafia chieftains at Chinese funerals, tong officers at Mafia funerals.

"Give me a specific case."

A year ago, when Big Bob Fong died, the *consiglière* and one of the *capos* of the Gambino family were both there. They were photographed by both the NYPD and the FBI, and knew they would be, but they had been sent to Fong's funeral to show respect.

"So now we have a Chinese Mafia," said Carol.

"You could call it that," said Sergeant Torres.

"I wouldn't call it that at all," said Inspector Appell.

Torres caught the ball on one bounce. "Actually I wouldn't either," he said.

"We don't have enough information to call it anything of the sort," said Inspector Appell. He looked to Carol more and more nervous, as if he knew Torres was talking too much but didn't know how to shut him up.

"And," suggested Carol, probing carefully, "the god-father is this Mr. Ting, the mayor of Chinatown."

"Ting is out," said Torres. "The new mayor is a man by the name of Jimmy Koy."

"Who's he?"

Torres began to recount gossip. It was law-enforcement gossip, but it exactly resembled Hollywood gossip, and for the same reasons. The police were as constrained as studio heads to operate within certain defined limits, whereas the hoods were like film stars—rich, notorious, and unpredictable. They were likely to do any crazy thing they felt like. They were fascinating, and so gossip accreted around them and was propagated by the police as a means of making themselves and their profession seem more interesting. Koy, explained Torres, was a former Hong Kong police sergeant who had escaped from there five years before with an enormous amount of money. The sum had grown in legend in recent weeks, and Torres put it at 500 million dollars. Preposterous thought Carol, writing the number down, but she liked Torres' next remarks—that Koy had come here to take over the Chinatown rackets. He seemed to have succeeded too—most of the turmoil there, including most of the killings, coincided with his rise to power.

Carol became more and more elated, kept probing, kept turning pages in her notebook, even though most of what Torres told her about Koy was only speculation. Whatever his past, there were no open investigations on him at this time, as far as Torres knew. Koy had as yet made no mistakes that would bring one down on himself. He was considered a political leader and his role as a crime lord was still largely invisible, as the Chinese themselves were still largely invisible. Police pressure normally came only in response to pressure, and there had been no great pressure to clean up Chinatown as yet. Half the people there were illegal aliens with no vote, and almost all Chinese tended to keep their mouths shut about what was done to them.

Inspector Appell had fallen entirely silent. He believed they should be telling this woman nothing, but wasn't sure. Nor did he know how long they were supposed to go on talking to her. Chief Cirillo had put them in here with no briefing. They had best stay put until Cirillo himself ended the interview.

In the next room Cirillo kept glancing at his watch. The hour of his table reservation was long past. At last he strode to the door and threw it open, terminating the interview. Inspector Appell, he saw, looked relieved, whereas Torres looked ready to go on blabbing to this broad for a week.

"Can I see you a minute, Chief?" said Appell.

"No," said Cirillo, "you can't." Even as he dismissed them both, he turned to Carol, giving her his biggest smile.

"Well, honey, are you hungry yet?"

"I'm famished, Chief," said Carol, "But—"

But she was terribly sorry, she would have to take a raincheck on lunch. She had never lunched with a detective chief and had looked forward to it, but unfortunately she had lost track of the time completely. Those two men he sent here were so interesting. She had filled half her notebook, and she flipped the pages to show him. At the same time she batted her eyelashes at him. She was so sorry she had to run, she said.

And she was gone, Cirillo, standing in his doorway watched her hurry out through his anteroom, out into the hall, without looking back.

Carol, as she waited for the elevator, could hardly believe her luck. She was on to a big, big story, and she had avoided lunch with Cirillo—two triumphs in a single morning.

Out on Centre Street she flagged down a taxi, and rode up to the Drug Enforcement offices on West Fifty-seventh Street, where she was received by the agency press officer, a man named Joyce. Joyce told her she ought to build her piece around the agency's director, a great guy and a swell interview. A lot of reporters had failed to interview the director lately. She should go to Washington to meet him. He, Joyce, would be glad to set it up. Carol said she would surely do this before she was finished, but in the meantime she wanted to talk to someone familiar with Chinatown. So Joyce summoned Agent Wilcoxon to brief her.

"Any special aspect of Chinatown?" Joyce asked, while they waited.

Carol had to be careful. She did not want any one agency knowing too much about the direction in which her story was heading. Not because someone might stop her. If anyone tried, her network would scream freedom of the press, as if there were no other. No one could stop her. But possible sources could be made to dry up, and if parts of her story were leaked to other reporters, its impact could be diminished.

During the next hour Wilcoxon described how Asian heroin was grown in the so called Golden Triangle where Burma, Thailand and Laos came together, three thousand feet up in the mountains, one of the few areas in the world where the combination of soil, climate and altitude permitted the opium poppy to be grown at all. This region was controlled by remnants of the army of Chiang Kai-shek. These men had retreated there in 1949 and, afterwards, as the sole available means of supporting themselves, had gone into the opium trade. Every regiment was a private army now, each one headed by formerly high-ranking officers who had become indistinguishable from the terrible Chinese warlords of the past. These men moved literally tons of heroin down through the jungle on mule back to Bangkok, eventually shipping most of it out of Thailand to Hong Kong. The new warlords of the Golden Triangle were not only Chinese, but principally Hakkas and Chouchows who dealt only with other Hakkas and Chouchows at every step along the route to the United States, where the principal port of entry was believed to be New York. In recent years about 80 percent of New York heroin had come from Southeast Asia, Wilcoxon said.

"How do you know this?" Carol demanded.

Because it was different heroin. The DEA labs tested all the purchased and confiscated heroin that the agents brought in, and were able in most cases to determine exactly where it had come from.

"You really should go to Washington to see the director," interjected Joyce. "I know he'd love to talk to you."

Carol ignored him. "Does this agency have a case going against Koy?" she asked Wilcoxon.

Looking surprised, Wilcoxon shook his head. Koy was too cute, he said. No one had ever been able to nail him yet.

Carol could pick up a great deal of information in Washington, Joyce said, from the director. An interview with the director could be set up on very little notice.

Wilcoxon began to talk about Koy, repeating the same gossip Carol had already heard. She wondered how this gossip would compare with the facts, whatever they might be, and also she wondered how the gossip had originated.

Carol thanked them, put her notebook in her purse, and left. Joyce walked her to the elevator. "When shall I tell the director he can expect you?"

"Soon," said Carol. "Very soon. Tell him I'm looking forward to it." The elevator doors closed like scissors, snipping the forced smile off her face, excising Joyce and his director from her life.

In the taxicab riding back to Broadcast Center she plunged eagerly into her notebook. She was terrifically pleased with herself. The pages flipped like playing cards, like the sound of sustained applause.

She decided tomorrow she would make some telephone calls into Chinatown, try to set up an interview with this Jimmy Koy. It occurred to her that she should perhaps clear it with Powers first, for if he did have a case going against Koy, she might disturb it, might not only warn Koy, but even put one of Powers' men in danger. But she decided not to do it. Powers was getting more and more nervous lately and she didn't want to risk upsetting him any further.

NIKKI HAN, Go Low and two other Chinese youths entered the school yard at about three o'clock the following afternoon. They were looking for Quong, and spotted him.

The boy was seated halfway up the bleachers, wearing his Chinese cap, his English grammar open on his lap. He was poring over it, struggling to decipher information he needed to know, but the words were impenetrable to him, as dense as bamboo around a pond. He was also waiting for Luang, and kept glancing up, hoping to see him, his attention divided between the grammar book and thoughts of his guidance counselor. He felt slow-witted, happy, heavy with expectation.

As Nikki Han approached the bleachers, Quong, though uneasy, came down onto the pavement to greet him. The other boys, till then unnoticed, sidled up to him from three different directions, isolating him from other children in that part of the yard. He became even more isolated when they began to move him toward an empty corner hidden by the bleachers from the school building. However, the attitude of the four Flying Dragons was effusive and friendly, with much backslapping, and Quong was no longer as afraid of them, as he had been initially. He even became relaxed, joking back with them, though at the same time keeping an eye open for Luang. He was concerned that the guidance counselor, if he entered the school yard now, might go away without being able to find him.

Upon reaching the empty corner behind the bleachers, the attitude of Han and the others changed abruptly.

Han said, "That Chinese guy we saw you with, who was he?"

Quong immediately became tense. "Where?"

"You were on the bleachers with him."

"My guidance counselor." Quong again used the words "supervising teacher."

"There's no Chinese guidance counselor in this school. Where's the gun we gave you?"

The boys began patting him down, looking for it. They seemed to know they would not find it. Quong became terrified.

"I lost it."

"Hey, guys," said Nikki Han, with pretended amusement, "he lost it." It was the last amusement Quong was ever going to see.

Go Low said, "That's what happened, he lost it."

A third boy said, "He just—lost it." The four Flying Dragons, having surrounded Quong, began batting him back and forth with their bodies.

"He lost it."

"Well, what do you know about that?"

Nikki Han had him by the ear, twisting his head sideways. "Do you know what we do to informants?"

Surrounding Quong, they marched him out of the school yard. Although no force was used, it was clear to Quong that he was in custody. He glanced in all directions for Luang, but Luang was not coming that day at all. He was sitting with the nuns on the wiretap in the Greenwich Village station house, and had as yet found no way to notify the boy that he would be out of circulation for a few days. In an hour this detail would make no difference to anyone. Quong, meanwhile, was looking for him desperately, for Mr. Goldfarb—anyone. But there was no adult in the school yard, only other kids who, if they glanced his way at all, saw nothing amiss. Predators had singled him out to make a meal. The rest of the herd went on grazing. Quong was marched through the school yard and out the Hester Street gate. He was too scared to cry out. It was as if his vocal cords had been cut. He was so scared he could not even speak.

24

POWERS AND his wife sat at dinner at a table under a chandelier in Ting's restaurant.

"This is my precinct," Powers said. "Which means I have to be seen here more or less around the clock. It's called showing concern."

"More tea?" Eleanor poured it into both cups. "I'm a little gun-shy about eating in this place, though. After what happened to you here the last time, I mean."

Powers' own memories of that night were focused at this moment on Carol Cone. The machine gunning was over. His affair with Carol was not.

He said, "Besides, I want Ting to think I'm keeping an eye on him."

"He hasn't so much as glanced this way since we sat down. Somehow I don't think he's as afraid of you as you might like."

"It's not funny, Eleanor."

"You don't have to snap at me."

Powers looked across at Ting, who stood armed with menus at the door. "I could have sworn he was straight," he said, "a victim, like nearly everyone else in Chinatown. Until he went with Koy to meet that Mafia guy."

"You can't really be sure who Ting met, or what was said," Eleanor told him. "Maybe you're leaping to conclusions."

"I don't think so."

"The police mind is always so certain when it thinks it has discovered evil."

A deeper remark, Powers reflected, than perhaps Eleanor knew. With his chopsticks, he pushed unknown ingredients around on his plate, for he was not hungry. Instead he watched Eleanor eat, and brooded about the nature of evil, a popular topic these days, especially among liberal intellectuals, of whom this city was so full. Such persons talked about evil in abstract terms, which cops never did. To cops evil was not abstract. It was physical, and usually extremely bloody. Often it was repulsive, often it stunk—you had to hold your nose to get into the room with it. To cops it was also commonplace. They came upon it every day, and thought about it more than they wanted to, and struggled with insights about its nature—insights denied to those moral philosophers and political philosophers who only talked so much about it, without ever having had to clean up after it. It was cops who carried the corpses out. That was the principal difference in outlook between cops and thinkers. It was also the reason cops took evil so much more seriously, so much more personally, than thinkers did. And yet the most evil-prone among us, Powers reflected, devoted only a minuscule percentage of his time to committing evil, probably less than one percent a day. However, the tendency in him to commit evil was most likely constant, and therefore so terribly dangerous to other people that it had to be extirpated, and the only way the person's deplorable tendency could be extirpated was by extirpating the person himself—which was what cops did. That was the line of work they were in. So yes, to cops and to Powers evil was not abstract, not intellectual, but physical and personal. To a cop evil always came down to himself against one evildoer at a time. A cop could not war against all the evil in the world, only against those few individuals who, in the course of his career, would cross his path. Those he could fight. Those he could extirpate, and if he was a good cop he would keep trying to do so with all the energy and passion at his command until the last minute of the last day.

For me at this time, Powers thought, the person to extirpate is Koy. Ting too, if I can get him.

The check was presented. Standing, Powers began pulling money out of his pants pocket. "It's not only important that I be seen in Chinatown at odd hours," he said to his wife. "But also that I pay all my dinner checks with extreme conspicuousness."

Ting came over and shook hands with both of them. "It was a lovely dinner, Mr. Ting," said Eleanor. She gave him a warm smile.

Powers both noted the smile and resented it.

Powers realized that he was impatient with his wife. They were frequently impatient with each other these days. Together they went down the broad staircase and out into the streets of Chinatown, where Powers glanced at his watch.

"I know it's late," he told Eleanor. "But I want to stop in at my wiretap on the way home. I hope you don't mind."

"Mind?" Eleanor shook her head. "How long do you think I've been a policeman's wife?"

Sister Mary Bartholomew, Powers noted, as they came through the door, had cheeks like crepe paper. Looking at her face protruding out of her starched cowl was like looking at age squeezed out of a tube. The headphones were clamped over her habit over her ears, and the clamp looked as if it hurt, as if the headphones had flattened and elongated her head to match her cowl-squeezed cheeks. Powers was reminded of an accident victim he had seen once, lying on the pavement, head like a crushed suitcase. As she listened, the old woman made notes in the log book with one hand while with the other she worked the console, cutting in and out of the conversation. She seemed amazingly efficient, which surprised Powers, though he wondered why— the nuns of his youth had exuded efficiency as much as piety, maybe more; had instilled both values, as if they were inseparable, into little boys like himself: God loved you for praying and doing your chores. It was as if all the rest of life had no moral value whatsoever. If one prayed efficiently and performed chores piously, then God's love was assured, and

Powers wondered if these two nuns had proclaimed this same message during their years in China. If so, had the Chinese swallowed it as wholeheartedly as he had?—and all the other little boys too, as he remembered.

The call she now monitored had begun just as Powers and his wife entered the office. The second nun, Sister Mary Jeanne, had glanced up from her breviary and, like the classroom nuns of long ago, had imposed silence by giving them a stern look and pressing her forefinger to crimped lips. She had then resumed reading her breviary, and was reading it still, which reminded Powers of another message received from nuns. God preferred prayer to idleness any day. God was against wasted time.

Eleanor had taken the chair in the corner. Powers waited with arms folded for the call to end.

Removing the headphones, Sister Bartholomew turned around smiling. At the same time Sister Jeanne's breviary closed over the holy picture which served her as a placemark.

"We sent Officer Luang out to dinner," Sister Bartholomew explained. "The poor man was starving. This is the log of calls that have come in, Captain."

Powers, as he studied the log book over her shoulder, was brooding again about evil, for nuns like this had taught him that moral values never changed, and he had found them instead as unstable as most of the rest of life, no more constant than football—the rules of both changed slightly every year, until, after a number of years, it became a very different game. He had known dozens of nuns like this in childhood. They were revered as the most saintly of human creatures. They—and the Catholic Church itself—had propounded the notion that virginity was the highest station to which man and, especially, woman could aspire. Today virginity was becoming scarce even among high school girls, and above a certain age was considered almost dishonorable. Nuns had become anachronisms, faintly ridiculous. He wondered what these two old ladies felt when they considered the subject, if they considered the subject. Did they ever talk about it to each other, ever suppose that perhaps they had wasted their bodies, if not their lives?

"They seem to be mostly routine business conversations," said Sister Bartholomew, studying the log beside him. "That's what Officer Luang thought, too."

One of their number had once told Powers that it was evil to say the word damn, heavy baggage for a nine-year-old who wanted to sound tough, and for four or five years he had believed this. He wondered what that nun, or either of these nuns here, would think to hear the language that issued routinely from the mouths of some women today, from the mouth of Carol Cone, for instance.

Sister Jeanne said, "The perpetrator did call his wife in Hong Kong."

Perpetrator. It made Powers smile to hear the police word spoken by an elderly nun.

"You ladies must be tired," said Eleanor. "This isn't exactly God's work, is it?"

"Oh, it is, it is," said Sister Bartholomew. "If this Mr. Koy is as bad a man as your husband says he is."

"His wife doesn't live in Hong Kong," said Powers. "His wife lives on Diplomats' Row on the Upper East Side."

Sister Jeanne, shook her head. "He called her wife in Hakka."

"And she talked back to him as if she was his wife, too," said Sister Bartholomew. She pointed to the log book. "Anyway, there's her number in Hong Kong."

Sister Jeanne said, "He's going to go there as soon as he clears up some unfinished business here in New York."

Powers looked questioningly from one nun to the other, but neither had any further information to give him.

Sister Jeanne said, "And it's lovely to hear Hakka spoken again. It's been so many years since we were there, so many years."

Powers puzzled over the notion that Koy was on his way to Hong Kong. But all he said was: "Let's close up for tonight, Sisters." Last night he had driven them home himself. Today there'd been time to make other arrangements. "There's a radio car downstairs to take you back to the convent. And a radio car will pick you up in the morning, also."

But Sister Jeanne had become busy at the tape recorder. "I'm turning the machine off," she said. "It wouldn't be legal if it recorded a conversation with nobody monitoring it."

"Fine, Sister," he said. "Good night."

As soon as he had showed them out the door, Powers rushed to plug the machine back in.

"You heard Sister," said Eleanor. "That's illegal."

Powers grinned at her. "Who's going to turn me in?" he asked. "You?" He took her in his arms because he realized he could trust her with his career, with his life, with anything. As she put her head on his shoulder, he thought of Carol, whom he loved, but still didn't trust much at all. He still had not trusted her even with his unlisted home telephone number.

"If any more conversations come in tonight," he murmured into his wife's ear, "they'll be on there. It's Sister Jeanne's fault. Sister Jeanne just forgot to turn the machine off."

"She probably did it on purpose," said Eleanor. "She struck me as a woman with no respect for the law. Unlike some people I could name."

"True," said Powers. "She should be prosecuted."

"I don't think anybody is going to prosecute a seventy-five-year-old nun, though. A forty-six-year-old police captain, now. That would be another story."

"You're right," said her husband, and he kissed her on the nose. "Come on, let's go home."

He switched the light out, and locked the door. They went downstairs and as they walked out through the muster room Luang was just coming in.

"We've closed down for the night," Powers told him. They stood out on the stoop. "In the morning have the Sisters review today's tape. Maybe they missed something."

In front of the station house the two nuns were climbing into the back of the police car. Powers, Eleanor and Luang watched it drive away with them.

"Go home and get some rest," Powers told Luang. He was amazed at how fond of Luang he had become. He liked him more every day. "I'll see you tomorrow."

When Luang had gone off he and his wife got into the Mustang and started home, driving out of Greenwich Village and into the seedier neighborhood close to the waterfront. At West Street, Powers turned north under the old elevated highway, now closed and condemned. There were gaps in the pavement overhead where he could glance up and see sky. Weeds and bushes had taken root in the decaying concrete up there. Vines dangled over the edge like hair. Beside the car the steel supporting stanchions passed by, making rhythmic thumps, each one a single drum beat, a gasp of fear. The steel was corroding fast, his headlights showed, rusting away, the stanchions getting thinner, like old nails, like old men. The world changed. New York changed. Maybe, Powers brooded, even his own life changed, was changing now, and he glanced at Eleanor who reclined on the backrest, eyes closed, half asleep. She didn't know that Carol Cone existed. She was unaware of the sword that hung over her life.

On Powers' left the piers extended like fingers into the Hudson. There were cargo ships tied up, but some piers were empty, and from time to time he caught glimpses of the black water, flowing like a bride toward its marriage with the sea a few miles farther on. Close to midtown came passenger piers and Powers saw that three cruise ships were in, their sharp, lopsided prows extending over the road so that he was almost driving under them.

Evil, Powers reflected, could not be defined as the opposite of good, because good being an absolute, was in itself indefinable. Both concepts had to be reduced to some level at which human beings could comprehend them before they could be discussed at all, and so perhaps it was fair to define evil as a betrayal of trust. The degree to which a human action was evil bore, therefore, a direct relationship to the type and sanctity of the trust violated.

He glanced across at his wife.

"Will you work an eight-to-four tomorrow?" murmured Eleanor.

"An eight-to-four?" He would tour his precinct in the morning, then spend most of the afternoon at the wiretap. In the evening he had been invited to a community meeting and had to attend. Three hours on a dais. "No, an eight in the morning to midnight is more likely."

At Fifty-seventh Street he swooped up the ramp onto the West Side Highway. On his right was a long narrow park. To his left ran the river. It was almost at eye level, and only a few yards away, black and empty, tumbling tumultuously through time. Nothing floated on its mile-wide surface except probably garbage. It was this sumptuous river that had made New York into the most important city in the world. Dutch traders had come up this river, and after them the wooden ships, and then the ocean liners of almost every nation you could name, bringing wave after wave of immigrants who came ashore and moved out into the country, riding other rivers and later the trains, filling up the whole continent. The monumental impact of the Hudson River on America and thus the world could not be overdescribed, though it had little importance today. Today the foreigners came in by airplane, or across the Canadian border in the false bottoms of tanker trucks, and were betrayed, usually, by their own kind. Foreigners had always come to New York and every wave of them had been exploited by someone, but it seemed to Powers that no group had come here more foreign than today's Chinese, who had the misfortune to arrive when the immigration was over, when there was simply no place left for them anywhere, nowhere to go, no one to look out for their interests except—Powers hesitated to say it, or even to think it—himself. It was a responsibility he had accepted, but did this make him better than other men or as capable of betrayal as anyone else? He glanced at his wife, whose eyes were closed. Though he was driving very fast, she was not concerned, thinking her life was in the best hands possible, his own. How much evil was he capable of, really? He did not know. He had never really been tempted until now.

At Dyckman Street he exited from the highway, then turned north up Seaman Avenue past Isham Park, where he had sometimes played as a child. He had to get out of the car to open his garage, then climb behind the wheel again. Eleanor did not stir.

He steered into the garage. His headlights shone on the whitewashed wall one foot away. He switched them off. Eleanor was sound asleep. He kissed her on the lips.

"Wake up, sleeping beauty," he said, "You're home."

About ten minutes passed. Eleanor had trooped up the stairs to bed. Powers' eye, as he passed the front door, had been caught by that day's mail which, having fallen through the slot, lay scattered on the floor like fragments of his life. Gathering up the letters and bills, he had carried them into his study where he stood now, opening envelopes.

The phone on his desk rang. It rang also, he knew, upstairs on the table beside their bed where Eleanor perhaps already slept—she was a woman who could fall asleep in seconds.

Instantly Powers grabbed up the phone. Like a fighter he had responded to the bell—muscles tensed, senses alert, brain suddenly crowded. The precinct, he thought. A catastrophe. A cop shot. Or else one of his sons. Who else would call at this time of night?

"Hello," the female voice said, "are you all right? How are you?"

It was the worst catastrophe he could have imagined: Carol.

"Don't worry," she said. "If your wife had answered I was going to say I was from the network checking out some facts."

He could think of nothing sufficiently noncommittal to reply. He could think of nothing to reply at all.

Eleanor might already have picked up the bedside

phone. She might pick it up even now to see who had called —what the emergency was. She would hear Carol's voice, at first be puzzled by it, then comprehending.

"Let's go away together," he heard Carol say. "Let's go to Antigua. I know a neat place there."

Powers was stupefied, terrified.

"Do you know Antigua?" she asked.

"I've never been there, no." He was listening for any sound Eleanor might make, her breathing, the click as she hung up.

"Or Bermuda. That's nice too."

His fear was like antelopes galloping across a plain, feverish eyes, drumming hooves, headlong, out of control.

"I'll give your suggestions some thought and call you back on it."

"You can't talk freely," she said. "Okay. I understand. Sleep well. I'll talk to you tomorrow." She hung up.

Now what, thought Powers. At some point his chest had begun to heave. He could barely breathe, was close to tears. If he went upstairs what would he find? Eleanor grimly waiting for him?

If so, what would he say?

But perhaps she hadn't answered at all. Perhaps she was in bed leafing through a magazine, waiting to ask him who had called, was it an emergency? When he came into the room she would inquire idly: "Who was that?"

If so, what to answer? He couldn't even think of a convincing lie.

A marriage was as delicate as a pane of glass—it could split or shatter at the slightest sharp blow. A split down the middle could not be fixed, it was in there permanently, and the glass itself was now more fragile than ever. It could only be replaced, not repaired. Or you could stick tape over it, hold it together one day after another, learn to live with it, like learning to live with a deformity or a terminal disease.

He went to the stairs and stared upwards. What would he find up there? He turned back toward the study, where he waited half an hour, then climbed the steps like an old man or a toddler, one at a time.

The light was out in their bedroom—a good sign, he supposed. From outside the door he listened to her breathing, the way, years ago, he had listened to his small sons breathing. Eleanor was either asleep or pretending to be, so he went in.

He lay in the dark beside his wife. After an hour or two he convinced himself he was safe. She seemed to be sleeping deeply. If she had intercepted Carol's phone call, she could not have feigned sleep like that.

In the morning, as soon as he reached his station house, he phoned Carol at home.

"Don't you ever do that again."

She said in a little girl's voice, "Don't scold me."

Last night's titanic fear, now reduced to bite-sized morsels, poured out of him in chunks, like breakfast cereal out of a box.

"That phone rings all over the house," he said. "It rang right beside my wife's ear. Don't you understand that? She might have picked it up. She might have listened to all that talk of Antigua. How could you do a thing like that, how could you?"

Carol's voice was even smaller this time: "Please don't scold me."

But he could not stop.

"I won't do it anymore," said Carol, sounding close to tears, her voice scarcely a whisper. She sounded so contrite that Powers' mood changed, and he began to soothe her.

"I'd love to go to Antigua with you, but it's impossible," he said, and asked himself why he was mixed up with this woman, who dealt only in emotional extremes. She had him perpetually on the edge. No woman had ever pushed him about like this. "I'll see you tonight, and we'll talk about it," he said gruffly, and rang off.

THE TWO nuns had switched roles, Powers saw. Now it was Sister Jeanne's head in the padded vise. Her protruding cheeks hung like the folds in drapes. It was Sister Bartholomew, wrinkled and smiling, who looked up from her breviary.

"Nothing yet, Captain," said Luang, coming forward.

As Powers studied the log, the next call came in, and was intercepted by Sister Jeanne. Cool as a detective, she sat listening, pen poised. But after a moment she put the earphones down, and switched off. "He's talking to his wife in Hong Kong again."

"No, no," said Powers quickly. "Keep listening. His wife is here in New York. He may be talking to a drug contact."

The old lady obeyed, again clamping her black veil to her ears. Her eyes watched Powers as she listened, and almost immediately she began shaking her head. "He's telling her he'll see her very soon, and his son. He wants to sit with her in the garden. Now he's asking about the health of relatives."

She switched off. She did not ask Powers' permission, nor did she hesitate. She knew what the law was, and obeyed it. The nuns of his childhood had all been equally decisive. When you know what the Word is, Powers reflected, life becomes brisk, predictable. And you become arrogant. Arrogance and moral certitude are the same. One can not exist without the other. It is choices that make life uncertain, that make men clumsy.

"Maybe it really is his wife, Captain," said Luang. "One of them. It's in the Chinese tradition. Many rich Chinese take more than one wife. Especially if business keeps them away a long time. How long since this guy's been back in Hong Kong, five years? So he took a new wife here. Who's to know?"

Sister Bartholomew nodded. "He's right, Captain. We saw it often in China. It was one of the most pernicious moral problems we missionaries faced. It impeded many conversions. There was one man—a good and just man in every way, except that he had two wives. He took instruction, and wanted to be baptized. But we couldn't baptize him. He even gave us money to build our church. We told him he had to get rid of one of his wives first, and he refused to do it. He later died. We felt badly about it. We prayed for him and said masses for his soul, but he was a man with two wives, and I don't know what good it did."

The old lady shook her head darkly, sadly.

This story cast a pall upon the room. These holy nuns believed in a God who operated by the book, who had set up a place called hell, who had sent the rich Chinese gentleman there to burn for all eternity, and his two wives with him no doubt; and if all this was true, then the story was a grim one. Until well into his teen years Powers, as a product of women like this, had held these same beliefs, a notion that appalled him now. But so had everyone around him, adults as well as children, or so it had seemed at the time.

Was the world really that simplistic thirty years ago?

Sister Bartholomew said brightly, "Whatever unfinished business the perpetrator was waiting for has been taken care of. He's leaving for Hong Kong the day after tomorrow."

"He mentioned his flight number in one of his calls," said Sister Jeanne. "I copied it down. I figured that was all right because it wasn't personal."

"Let me see that."

Powers transferred the information into his notebook, then paced the room, head down. "By the time Koy gets back," he said to Luang, "our wiretap will have run out."

A phone in the room began to ring, and Powers, who had left this number with his desk sergeant, picked it up.

Another Chinese corpse had been discovered, the sergeant said. Same place as last time. A kid. Looked like another execution. No, the corpse had not yet been identified.

"I'll go out there and take a look," said Powers. As he put the phone down, a stricken expression came onto his face, for he knew intuitively what he would find.

Luang said, "What's the matter, Captain?"

"Sisters," Powers said, "we're going to have to leave you alone for a while. Something has happened. Any calls that come in now may be vitally important. I think you would be in your legal rights to record all of them, even though they might seem to be innocent." He didn't know whether they would obey him or not, but couldn't worry about that now. "Luang, you come with me."

The drive to the Brooklyn warehouse took twenty minutes, during which Powers spoke not one word. Relax, he told himself, but he remained hunched over the wheel. You can't be sure. There are a hundred and fifty or more Flying Dragons, and several other gangs as well, maybe five hundred members of Chinatown youth gangs in all. They're always killing each other. This corpse could be anybody.

"Where we going?" asked Luang.

But his fear made Powers deaf as well as mute, and he did not answer.

They crossed the Brooklyn Bridge in blinding sunshine. "It's sure a nice day," said Luang.

No answer.

They pulled up in front of the warehouse. Five blue-and-white police cars parked outside. One ambulance. One medical examiner's car. Chief of Detectives Cirillo's car.

Ten or twelve pedestrians had gathered on the sidewalk as well.

A cop stood guard at the head of the alley. To him the corpse inside was just another corpse. "You should post a permanent guard on this place, Captain," he joked.

Powers and Luang went on through. The alley was unchanged since their last visit, except that somebody had rearranged the pile of doors. Probably a scavenger had sifted through them, Powers thought. The pile was more unstable than ever and he clambered across it on his hands and knees. At the back of the alley the steel entrance door still hung by one hinge. The bottom of the staircase was still missing. They went on up. At the far end of the loft, near the one open window, stood the group of cops and detectives. The body was there also, lying like a third Hsu brother, with the same medical examiner as last time kneeling over it. Powers did not recognize the corpse and had not expected to. He stood aside to give Luang a clear view.

Luang said, "Quong," and gagged. Stumbling to the corner of the loft he began to vomit onto the floor.

The medical examiner looked up at Powers. "I couldn't say which shot caused the boy's death. He's been shot in each ear, in each eye, and in the mouth."

Powers nodded. He was looking across at Luang.

"The one in his mouth missed his mouth." Like a nun enforcing silence, the medical examiner put his finger to his lips. "It hit him here under the nose."

"He saw too much, heard too much and talked too much," muttered Powers.

Luang came back wiping his lips and stood over the corpse with tears in his eyes.

"The poor kid." Luang's control let go, and he began weeping. Tears coursed down his cheeks. Powers, trying to offer comfort, put his arms around him. He held him into his chest as he had held his sons when they were small.

"He must have been so scared," sobbed Luang. "So scared, Captain, so scared."

Cirillo called, "Can I see you a moment over here please, Captain Powers."

Luang wiped his eyes on his sleeve, and Powers went over to Cirillo.

"I hear you got a wiretap going," said the chief of detectives. "I want to know what it's all about."

"It's about this kind of thing." Powers gestured vaguely toward the corpse. Now the pressure starts, he thought.

"Tell me more."

When Powers did not answer, Cirillo said, "I got a call in to the district attorney to find out. But maybe you can save me the trouble of waiting for it."

Powers said, "No, you better ask him." He was in no mood to be browbeaten by the chief of detectives. He began to blink. "I have to go now."

"I'm not finished talking to you yet."

"I'm sorry, you'll have to talk to the DA."

He got Luang and they left the building. Powers stumbled going down the stairs. That's when he realized that his own eyes too were full of tears. He could barely see. In the street Luang caught up with him and asked bleakly, "What do we do now, Captain?"

Luang went back to the wiretap, and Powers to his office where he sat blaming himself for all three executions. It got dark outside, and still he counted up the blunders he had made and wondered what to do next. Finally he signed out and went home. He did not want to see Carol. The decision was instinctive. Hers was not a lap where he could lay his head. Whether stalking a woman or a bear—this was one of the first lessons primitive man ever learned—weakness was likely to be fatal. The stalking hunter must appear to be hard, ruthless, cruel. Doubt was out, mercy unmanly. Remorse was counter-productive.

And so Powers sat at home at the kitchen table eating soup. One could afford to show weakness only in the cave, though not very much even there. It was late, and his wife in her bathrobe stood by the stove cooking him a hamburger.

"Don't blame yourself," said Eleanor. "It's not your fault."

"I set him up though, didn't I? I put Luang on to him. And I was the one who decided to leave him out there."

"Eat your soup."

"You should have seen what his skull looked like," said Powers. Today he had learned a new definition of evil. "His skull was mush. He was fifteen years old."

"You'll feel better tomorrow." Her bathrobe was like chain mail—his misery kept glancing off it. He wanted sympathy and wasn't getting any.

"Koy ordered it," Powers muttered. "I have to believe that. It's as if he was sending me a message personally."

Eleanor frowned. "There's nothing personal about it. He may not be responsible at all. He may not know you exist."

Every man could remember a time when he was loved precisely for his weaknesses—by his mother, who was stronger than he was. As an adult he went on seeking the same relationship whenever he was hurt, but he never found it again.

"Your witness is dead," said Eleanor, "and your suspect is on his way to Hong Kong. That means your investigation is dead."

Wives usually remained friends with their mothers, having no substitute. Whereas husbands did not, having assigned the role of mother to their wives. Wives, realizing this, were offended, even insulted, and when their husbands came to them in pain usually refused to mother them—as Eleanor refused to do now.

"When he comes back you'll never get your wiretap renewed. That's what you're brooding about, isn't it? Do you really care about the dead boy?"

"Of course I care about the dead boy," snapped Powers. "I've seen a lot of ugly things since I've been on the job, but that's the ugliest, and I mean to get the man behind it."

Eleanor at the stove slid his hamburger onto a plate. "How?"

"If he's going to Hong Kong, I'm going with him," said Powers. He added lamely, "He'll be less on his guard there." But so far he had only bungled every aspect of this investigation. He was like a man in a dark shop who, while fumbling for the light switch, kept knocking precious vessels off shelves. They crashed to the floor all around him.

Eleanor was annoyed. It seemed to her that a grown man, when hurt enough, or disappointed enough, reverted to the emotional level of a small boy, a syndrome that did not exist in women. Although there was a little girl hidden inside every adult woman too, it almost never showed, no matter what the stress.

"You'll stick out like a sore thumb amid all those Chinese. He'll spot you from a mile away. Besides, how would you get there? The City's broke. I can't see the police department springing for your ticket."

Powers looked up from his soup, and their eyes met.

"Oh no," Eleanor said, "you're not using our money."

Her husband shook his head. "No, of course not."

THE FOLLOWING morning the police commissioner, in shirtsleeves, sat behind his desk signing papers, when the deputy inspector, his chief secretary, entered the office to say that Captain Powers was on the phone.

"What does he want?"

"It's personal and confidential, he said."

The police commissioner barely hesitated. "Tell him to speak to Chief Duncan." Having accorded Powers approximately ten seconds of his time and brain power, he resumed scanning the long memo—something about the reorganization of the Bronx detective command—that had reached the top of the pile before him.

So by noon Powers was at police headquarters in front of Duncan's desk. He told Duncan he had confidential information linking Koy to the murders in Brooklyn and to other Chinatown rackets as well, and—

"The Chinese Mafia again," Duncan interrupted.

"I haven't used that phrase with anybody."

Cirillo, who stood to one side, said, "You used it with that television broad, and she used it with me."

Powers, surprised, said: "I did not." What had Carol said and done behind his back? He looked from one man to the other. But he could not worry about that now.

He began to explain that he wanted to follow Koy to Hong Kong.

Duncan interrupted. "Are you crazy? I can't authorize that."

"I'm not asking you to authorize it. I'm asking you to go to the PC with it."

"You have no police powers in Hong Kong," scoffed Duncan. "You have no contacts."

"He'd be less on guard there," Powers persisted. "And I do have some ideas—"

"You don't speak the language. You don't know the city. You wouldn't have a chance. It would be wasting your time and the City's money."

"It wouldn't cost very much."

"Too much."

"I've worked out the costs and the possible advantages. I've written you a forty-nine on it—" Power's attempted to present the memo, but Duncan ignored it.

"Let me tell you my plans when I get there."

"The answer is no."

"But—"

"The subject's closed."

Powers spun on his heel and strode toward the door.

"Come back here," said Cirillo. "I want to know more about that wiretap."

"I want to know why I wasn't informed about it," said Duncan.

Powers, at the door, said, "You'd better talk to the district attorney." Though he might have walked out slamming the door, he did not quite dare to do it.

There was a long pause. Finally the chief of detectives said: "I spoke to the DA last night.

"What did he say?"

291

"That it was too sensitive to talk about over the phone."

And when you offered to go over and see him in person, thought Powers, he refused to see you.

"So why don't you tell me."

The two men eyed each other.

There was no other explanation, thought Powers. The elected district attorney of New York County did not need to answer to Cirillo. To prove his stature, or because he was annoyed, or to humiliate Cirillo perhaps—who knew why?—he had decided to protect the wiretap, to protect Powers.

"I'm sorry," Powers decided to say. "I can't help you." And he went out. Behind him a fist—either Cirillo's or Duncan's—was slammed down on the desk. He heard it through the door, but felt no satisfaction. He was trying to figure out a way to follow Koy to Hong Kong.

From a pay phone in the lobby, he dialed the district attorney, and to his surprise was accorded an immediate appointment. Ten minutes later, having walked briskly up Centre Street, he stood in front of the man's desk and again explained where he wanted to go and why. All he needed was money.

"Why come to me? The police department has far more money than I do."

"You have a special fund you can draw on for cases such as this."

The district attorney stepped to his window and stared out. "But I think it's a crazy idea too. I don't see what you imagine you can do when you get there. It's his city, not yours. And if he spots you—you wouldn't be the first individual to disappear in that place."

Powers had his hands on the DA's desk, leaning forward over it, and he was pleading. "Why is he going to Hong Kong? He hasn't been back in five years. We know there was an open investigation on him there until a short time ago. He's taking a risk to go back. Something important must be about to go down. Whatever it is, it's connected with Chinatown here."

The DA had turned from the window. He studied him silently.

"Look," Powers pleaded, "It's the only chance we've got."

The district attorney shook his head again. "I have too little money to give you any of it." But after a pause he added: "I'll do this for you. I'll call the PC and tell him I think you should go. I won't lean on him. I'll simply tell him that much. I think you are being foolhardy, but in a way I admire you for it. If you go, be careful, and good luck."

THERE WAS a leather box on Powers' dresser. It held cuff links and tie bars that his sons had given him over the years and that he never wore. Flipping open the cylinder of his off-duty gun—the other was in his locker at the station house—he ejected the five bullets into the box with the other jewelry, then went downstairs to the laundry room where, because he could not bring it with him, he hand-cuffed the gun through its open cylinder to a water pipe. This done, he was ready to leave the house. Eleanor was already waiting with the car in the street, and he went out through the garage, slung his suitcase into the trunk, and they started for the airport. All the way out he was afraid he might observe a crime in progress. Without his gun he felt totally impotent. If they came upon a crime, what action would he take? Should he intervene anyway?

At the Pan Am terminal he kissed his wife goodbye and watched her drive away. He had an hour before takeoff and knew he would need most of it, and after checking in and passing through security, he phoned Carol Cone.

"Look, I have to go away for a while," he said to her. Since late yesterday, when the okay had come down, he had been deliberating how—and how much—to tell her.

"When do you go?"

"Today."

"I don't like the sound of this. Are you really going away?"

"Yes."

"You don't seem unhappy about it."

"Well, I have to go." How he hated the telephone, which promised so much more than it gave. It was as if its capacity to convey emotion was limited by the thinness of the wire. It was unsuitable for any message more complicated than you could send by Morse code.

"How long will you be gone?"

"A week, a month. I don't know." He hoped it would be for long enough so that he might decide where his life went from here. Perhaps whatever hold this woman had on him would be broken.

"Will I see you before you go?"

"There isn't time. I leave in about an hour."

Communication by telephone was simply not normal, and perhaps was not even possible. One interpreted the sounds and one measured the pauses. These were the only clues to whatever messages one hoped to exchange. Powers measured Carol's pause now and judged it to be an unhappy one. But her next words betrayed no emotion at all.

"Where are you going?"

There was no reason not to tell her. "Hong Kong."

"Is your wife going with you?"

"No."

"You're sure?"

"Yes."

"Don't make me interview you. Why are you going to Hong Kong?"

"Because the guy I'm chasing is going there."

"Then the police department is sending you."

"Yes."

"It seems odd."

"Well, maybe it is. But the PC approved it."

"The man you're chasing—it's the same one you told me about the other night?"

"Yes."

"What's his name?"

"I can't tell you that."

Another pause. Powers wished he could see her face,

watch her chest move as she breathed, touch the life that was in her, instead of guessing at the timbre of a few words that, these days, might just as easily be coming from a machine.

"What hotel will you stay at?"

"Why? Are you going to call me up?"

"Sure."

"The Hotel Mandarin."

"Well," said Carol, "I have to get off. Have a good trip."

Powers stared at the dead phone in his hand, and thought that it isolated those who used it into worlds as small, as sterile, and as separate as their individual phone booths. It was perfect for causing pain.

He spent most of the next twenty-four hours in the air, staring out the porthole at vacant sky. The plane set down in San Francisco and Tokyo to refuel and he did not leave the transit lounge in either place. It was midnight in Hong Kong when he checked into the Mandarin. The Chinese bellhop led him to his room, stood his suitcase upright on the low baggage rack, accepted the tip and left, and Powers pushed open the sliding glass door and stepped out onto the small balcony. The air was balmy, and the city quiet. All around him slept millions of Chinese and he looked off across the black water at Kowloon and the mainland. There were ferries crossing, and cargo ships anchored here and there in between. It was noon New York time, he was not particularly tired, and he came in off the balcony and began pacing the room. He felt very much alone.

As SOON as she had hung up on Powers, Carol dialed the Flowering Virtue Funeral Parlor still again. She had left messages each of the last three days, but Koy had not returned them.

Again a Chinese voice answered. "Boss no here."

"Is he on a trip?"

"Gone oversea, mebbe."

"He's gone to Hong Kong?"

"Mebbe. Hong Kong mebbe."

Carol rushed down the hall to see Lurtsema. Her story, she told him, had just gone to Hong Kong and she wanted to go there after it.

"Why don't you let me give the assignments around here, Carol? That's my job."

"All right. How about giving me this one."

She had, once again, walked into Lurtsema's office uninvited. She was once again usurping Lurtsema's role and he did not like it or her. But instead of saying so he pointed out that such a journey was costly, nothing was prepared for her at the other end, and that the focus of her story was here, not there. Besides, they had a news show to put on every day, and needed her on it. The answer was no.

So Carol took the elevator up to the tower, where she walked in on the network's executive vice president for corporate affairs, to whom she complained that Lurtsema's well-known antagonism toward female talent was hampering the network's news-gathering capability once again. The vice president said he would look into it, and Carol was satisfied, for she knew television. She knew where the power lay. She knew all the peculiar rules of this extremely peculiar game. She had only to go back to her office and wait, and she did so.

The vice president phoned down to Lurtsema, heard him out, and then advised him cordially to give Carol Cone any goddamn thing she wanted. When Lurtsema asked why, he said, "Because her contract is up in three months, and NBC has already made her an offer. Do I make myself clear?"

"Perfectly," said Lurtsema huffily. "Why don't you give her the job of producer, in addition to the one she's already got?"

Having made his decision and his point, the vice president, who was always smoothing someone's ruffled feathers, was obliged to spend the next ten minutes smoothing Lurtsema's, which he succeeded in doing, more or less.

In any case, air tickets to Hong Kong arrived on Carol's desk that very afternoon, and she sat down and tried to decide what preparations she ought to make first. What contacts could she use? Did she have the right clothes?

Part
Three

26

KOY, meantime, was circling the globe in the opposite direction, moving fast, making local stops. Some stops were business-mandated. He was setting up his organization. At others he only changed planes and airlines so as to leave a trail that turned cold as he made it. He flew more or less in a straight line. There was no need to exaggerate. But he had no reservations and no through ticket—he bought each ticket in cash just before boarding each plane.

The essential thing was to stay off any one central computer. Instead he would appear—briefly—on many. Computers had memories that were almost human—the press of new customers caused the memory of old ones to recede; very soon it obliterated them. It would take law enforcement weeks to figure out where Koy had gone and when, much less why, and if any single computer lost his name, it would be impossible. Past fugitives stepped in and out of streambeds to throw bloodhounds, if any, off the scent. Modern man—Koy—stepped in and out of computers.

This was a precaution only. He had no reason to believe any agency of any country was interested in him. Old cases, like old clothes, went to the bottom of the trunk and were rarely seen again. He had lain quiet, after all, five years. Law enforcement had fewer computers than airlines and, to be blunt about it, even more new business. Case closed.

He knew of course of the existence of Luang, not his name or function, just that he had turned up in two widely separate corners of Koy's life. It was bizarre. It defied explanation. It was surely not coincidence. It was probably Ting's work, and he had men working to find out more. That a New York police captain was singlemindedly pursuing Koy almost on a free-lance basis would have seemed to him inconceivable. He knew law enforcement and it did not work that way. The idea simply never occurred to him.

He landed in Heathrow Airport, London, at 8 A.M. Because it enabled him to get in and out of airports quickly, he traveled light, only a single piece of hand luggage plus $10,000 in hundred-dollar notes in an envelope in his breast pocket. His journey was a long one—more than 25,000 miles —and he would be able to replenish his funds only in Hong Kong. He also carried two passports, which would further confuse the computers. He planned to use them more or less alternately, beginning with his Hong Kong passport, made out in the name of Koi Tse-ven, here in England. The name on his new American passport, unused until now, was Jimmy Koy. By marrying an American citizen, and by completing the required years of uninterrupted United States residency, he had qualified for naturalization, which, among other benefits, gave each new American the right to choose whatever new name he wished to be known by. And so Koi Tse-ven had become Jimmy Koy—legally—and had taken out a passport in that name.

For five years Koy had not budged—had waited for citizenship, had waited for the return of Marco, his distributor, had waited for an incident that would enable him to take over the Nam Soong Tong, for he needed the tong's sanction in order to move goods in and out of Chinatown. The first two events had occurred but not the third, preventing the fourth, until at last Koy had felt obliged to create the incident he needed—the restaurant massacre.

This had been somewhat out of character for him,

because it was an impetuous act. He was a man of immense power in the only true meaning of the term—being rich, shrewd and most of all patient. Until then he had always considered patience the most important of his three great gifts because it alone permitted optimum use of the other two. But New York had come to feel like a jail cell to him. He came to see himself as a virtual prisoner. He was a man who obeyed no laws except those he set personally, and those he set he could also change. At last, instead of condemning himself to further patience, he had allowed his restlessness and especially his vast energy to overcome him. He had sent the Hsu brothers into Ting's place.

The result was that he now could move forward again—had to move forward. For the first time in a long time he felt completely happy. He felt as eager as a sprinter bolting from the starting blocks. He felt rejuvenated, a middle-aged man granted a new life, a new career, the chance to earn a second fortune. He was on the move again.

In London he walked out through customs, bought himself a ticket to Amsterdam, and walked right back in again. Within an hour he was in the air, and less than an hour after that, stepping in and out of streambeds fast, he was in a taxi between Schipol Airport and the city. He rode past fields of wet green grass delineated by canals. In the distance, here and there, windmills poked up. It was the flattest, wettest-looking country he had ever seen. The taxi driver who dropped him off at the Rijksmuseum had deposited a thousand others there this year, and would not remember him. He went inside and stood in front of Rembrandt's "Night Watch," one of the most famous paintings in the world, but to Koy only a landmark, neither more nor less, a place to meet someone. He was not interested in Western painting, and this one, a grouping of seventeenth-century Dutch burghers occupying an entire wall, seemed to him heavy and gross, lacking the refinement and delicacy of Chinese art. Chinese artists, to Koy, painted with butterflies' wings; Western artists painted with tree stumps. The one was subtle, with three or four thousand years of civilization behind it, and the other was as violent as the violent games—football, hockey, rugby—that the foreign demons so much admired.

Waiting, he stared dutifully at the painting, his mind elsewhere, the perfect tourist, a tall Chinese wearing dark glasses that rendered him, like film stars, both conspicuous and anonymous—definitely someone, though who? His hands hung crossed at his crotch, as demure as a Greek's fig leaf, as protective as a fighter's cup, though the blow, if any, would not fall there. Behind him he heard tour groups moving in and out of the room, heard the painting described by guides in many languages, none of them Hakka.

Having traveled three thousand eight hundred miles overnight, Koy was early by five minutes, and Hung Hsui-ch'uan, the Hakka Chinese he had come to see, was late by the same amount, having had to cross the city through traffic by taxi. They came together with proper smiles and bows, formally, almost distantly, speaking Hakka. There was no handshake, no embrace, no touching, even though they had grown up together in the same village in China, had served as station sergeants together in Hong Kong, and had not seen each other in five years. Hung had been part of the combine—Koy's combine—that had dominated the Hong Kong police department. He was one of the five dragons. Koy would meet the other three in Hong Kong in a few days, but Hung could not go because there was a warrant outstanding for his arrest.

In Amsterdam, where the Chinese community had always been dominated by Hakkas, Hung had established himself in the import-export business against just such a day as this. He moved legitimate goods to and from many ports, including Hong Kong on one side of the world and New York on the other. For Koy's purposes he was both ideally placed and, up to a point, totally trustworthy. Betrayal, in the normal course of events, would not come via Hung. However, life did not always proceed according to one's wishes. Hung too had his investors, had payrolls to meet. He and his people had waited a long time. Money had been spent. Profits were wanted. He would follow Koy's lead only as long as these profits seemed assured, and he was perhaps growing impatient. They were boyhood pals, and he would abandon Koy, would switch allegiance to another, only with regret.

Koy, therefore, would tell Hung no more than he needed to know. The two men began to stroll through the museum, being careful to determine that no one tailed them from room to room, sometimes standing a long time before individual paintings to be certain. But they noted no evidence of any interest in them whatever, and the business discussion both had come for at last began. By the end of the week, Koy said, each piece of the organization would be in place, which would be a satisfaction to all of them.

"You're going to Thailand next?" said Hung.

"Yes."

"You'll see the general?"

Koy shrugged. "It's been arranged."

"He's not happy."

"So I understand."

"Whoever you sent didn't get the job done."

Koy said nothing. Hung was not so much criticizing him as pointing out that they were all under pressure that would be relieved only when the goods started to flow.

"The general expected you before this," said Hung.

"You yourself were unable to go," Koy pointed out.

When Hung was silent, Koy said, "The first shipment should reach you here in under a month."

"As fast as that?" said Hung in surprise.

The bane of the narcotics business was that the merchandise was condemned nearly always to move so slowly. Most large shipments had to be welded into the entrails of tramp steamers which then set out at five knots per hour on journeys of many thousands of miles. This tied up great amounts of capital for months at a time. In these days of high interest rates it was a problem. A very expensive problem.

"Yes, as fast as that," said Koy, but he did not elaborate.

Hung clapped his hands together in delight. "You've

thought up a way to move big shipments by air, haven't you?"

"I think so," said Koy. Business being a serious matter, he did not so much as smile.

"Are you going to tell me what it is?"

"No," said Koy.

Hung began to laugh. "You are one smart son of a bitch," he said in English.

"If we can move the new system into Amsterdam," said Koy, "of course you and your people will be part of it." Age and overuse dim all emotion in the same way that they dim a man's eyesight and hearing. Nonetheless, Koy had once been extremely fond of Hung, and some of this fondness remained, so that he added, "I wish you could come on to Hong Kong with me."

"Me too." Hung's voice was wistful. "It would be swell to see all the guys again."

Koy lunched alone on the terrace of the Excelsior, Amsterdam's most expensive restaurant, which stood at the confluence of two canals. The banks of the canals were planted in rhododendron and mountain laurel, both in bloom now in late spring, so that the colors of the flowers were mirrored in the water at his feet. The red brick buildings of the city were reflected too. Koy watched the launches go by, watched the fracturing of the colors into slivers of shattered glass. When the boats were gone, he watched the mirror reform itself over and over again as no true mirror could ever do.

It was an elegant lunch in an elegant place and he was enjoying it. He was pleased to have seen Hung again, pleased that the Amsterdam-New York connection, the final stage in the journey of the merchandise, was firmly in place, and he was in no immediate hurry to move on, for at his next stop he would have to deal with the general in Thailand, and it would not be this simple. Koy was like a director shooting his movie out of sequence, last scene first, because it was more economical and efficient that way, and also because it gave the director (Koy) and the cast (also Koy) confidence to start with something easy. One scene at least was already in the can. But the most vital scene of all had to be shot next; it would be a good deal more complicated, and it was time to move on to it. Koy paid his check, caught a cab out to the airport, and boarded another plane.

Twenty-two hours later, freshly shaved and fed, still wearing his tan silk suit, he landed at Bangkok's Don Muang Airport, cleared customs and crossed to the domestic side, where he bought a ticket aboard a propellor plane for the local flight to Chiang Rai, about 600 miles north, the last major town below the Burma-Laos-Thailand border and the closest to the Golden Triangle any airline flew. It was steaming hot in Bangkok, but much cooler on the Chiang Rai plateau, where Koy was met by a Chinese Thai wearing army fatigues and thong sandals, who handed him a letter, then led him outside to a jeep. Koy, after tossing his small suitcase into the back on top of what looked like an M-16 automatic rifle lying on the floor, opened and read the letter. Bad news. The calligraphy was crude, and in some places illegible, which was neither here nor there perhaps. But the news was very bad indeed.

Koy had been as far as Chiang Rai, but no further, about ten years before. A Hong Kong police sergeant at the time, he had done his business at the airport with a one-eyed Chinese general known as Sao Mong Khawn, then the principal opium warlord of the region, and afterwards had gone back. This time he was to deal with the new warlord, Khun Sa, because Sao was either dead or deposed, and he had expected to meet him either at the airport or in the city. But Khun Sa had refused, according to this letter, to leave the hills. He would await Koy at his headquarters in the jungle.

Koy tried to decide what to do. He could not argue with a letter, and if he sent a message in with the driver and waited in a hotel it might take days for an answer to come back. With important appointments in Bangkok and Hong Kong, he did not have time for that. Were there other warlords who could supply the merchandise? Yes, but none had access to the same quantity as Khun Sa, and it was this quantity Koy needed. Besides, it was nearly harvest time and he was not in contact with them.

Still trying to decide on a course of action, Koy ordered his driver to take him to an outdoor marketplace, and they moved through traffic through the town. Traffic amounted to a few buses, some taxis, and many pedicabs and bicycles. Small, busy people in broad straw hats. The buildings were low and flat, with the roofs of Buddhist temples rising above them like blisters on paint.

His decision, whatever it turned out to be, was an important one. Not because he dreaded the brutal trek into the jungle to Khun Sa's encampment, though he did, but because at stake was the most prized commodity of all in any negotiation between Chinese: face. To go all the way to Khun Sa's doorstep was to grant him an immeasurable amount of face. It would make him impossible to deal with. His price would rise by hundreds of thousands of dollars. Worse, his attitude would change. He would become superior, contemptuous, and his own attitude toward Koy would be transmitted to his underlings in the form of bad jokes and carelessness, with a consequent risk to the security of Koy's organization. Attitudes were transmitted from person to person more casually than disease, and faster, and often with more deadly results. Attitudes were far more critical than bullets, which killed one man at a time. Attitudes could wipe out whole armies.

The open market, Koy saw, sold principally food. There were pyramids of fruits on mats on the ground, durians, lichees, mangos, rose apples, mandarin oranges. There were wicker baskets of green vegetables, and chickens and pigeons that hung in squadrons from hooks. Tables held simmering caldrons of boiled rice, of soups, of various steaming curries whose odor cleared Koy's nasal passages as he strolled by.

Face was as precious to Koy as to any Chinese, and his own, if he went in there, would diminish even as Khun Sa's rose. It would practically vanish.

He bought some lichees and broke them open and munched their sweet flesh, spitting out the seeds, and reviewed what he knew of Khun Sa.

There were in those hills, under that triple-canopy jungle, tigers, elephants, cobras and other wild creatures, and there were at the moment four or five private armies in opposition to Rangoon. All purported to represent noble or semi-noble causes, such as independence for various hill tribes, of which there were six or seven. The major tribe was the Shan, and Khun Sa called his group the Shan United Army even though he and his chief lieutenants were not Shans but Chinese. Formerly an enlisted man in Chiang Kai-shek's Kuomintang army, Khun Sa had evidently succeeded the one-eyed general and was now a general himself, self-appointed. He was about fifty, and commanded about ten battalions of about three hundred men each, with which he pretended to be making war on Rangoon so as to free the Shan tribe from the yoke of Burmese oppression. This rallied popular support. Khun Sa's real business, however, was opium, though he also smuggled gemstones from Burma into Thailand as a sideline. The purpose of his private army was to protect his mule caravans from the other private armies, and also to war on them in order to hold his territory astride the main smuggling route. He was said to conscript his men in the hill villages, assigning them seven-to-twelve-year enlistments. He paid them in kerosene tins of rice, plus thirty bahts a month, and ruled through terror. He executed anyone who crossed him, and he moved a great deal of opium. He once organized a caravan 300 mules long to carry sixteen tons of raw opium down from the poppy-growing region further north to his own refineries near the Thai border—he had about fifteen mobile refineries. But another army attacked the caravan and there was a pitched battle which left more than 200 dead.

Koy in the marketplace had come to a stall selling rough clothing and heavy rubber boots, and abruptly he decided that he wanted to meet this man Khun Sa. There were ways to preserve face whatever the situation. He had never been humiliated in his life and did not intend to be now. He would teach this Khun Sa lout something about face. He bought the clothing and boots he needed, stowed them in the cardboard box in the floorwell of the jeep and got back into his seat.

A few minutes later they were out of town and rolling north along a rutted track, and Koy stopped the jeep, got out and changed to the work clothes he had just bought, repacking his suit in the cardboard box. Then they were in the jungle. The trees closed down on top of them. The bushes sometimes brushed the sides of the jeep. Driving was like punching a fist through a sleeve. The sky could not be seen. It was as if a storm were coming. There were many insects. Koy had just spent most of four bumpy hours in the propellor plane, flying low over mountains, landing four times, he had not slept in a bed in two nights, and as they bounded along he began to feel distinctly unwell.

With the road climbing all the time, they passed through a village belonging to one or another of the hill tribes—Shan or Lisu or Karen or Akkha, Koy did not know which, or care. The village was poor. Thatched huts surrounded by fields slashed out of the jungle. Small lean people in baggy black pants and broad straw hats, sometimes with straw baskets containing produce strapped to their backs. Then more jungle. The track came out at a high lake, and wound around it. Fishermen stood one-legged like storks on long flat barques, spare leg wrapped around an oar or pole, poling themselves along while manipulating their nets with their hands. On the bamboo posts that anchored the nets birds perched, some of them one-legged also. They swooped toward the water, roiled its surface, then rose again, gullets working, swallowing triumphantly.

And still more jungle. It was as if the earth had put on too many clothes—sweaters, vests, overcoats. In crushing heat the jeep pitched and yawed like a boat. To Koy the ride seemed unending. He was holding himself down, gripping the tubular chair frame in both fists. It was impossible to talk to the driver, whose dialect was a corrupt form of

Yunnanese; Koy could not even understand how much farther they had to go.

At length the guide stopped the jeep and jumped out. He grabbed the rifle and Koy's suitcase, and signaled him to follow. The forest lay on a slant. They started up on foot, Koy carrying the cardboard box containing his suit.

This was a teak forest here—the trees were as tall as towers, 150 feet or more above the forest floor, and from them dropped great dangling leaves up to two feet long, leaves big as awnings. Then the teaks ended, the trees became shorter, the undergrowth thick and knotted, and they were forced into a dry streambed, the only trail through it. Koy had long since soaked through his work clothes. He was dripping with sweat. This stream would be a torrent once the monsoons came, and as he stumbled upwards, he realized that the rains were due any day. The stream would be impassable. Khun Sa's headquarters would be unreachable, unless there was another way in.

There probably was, thought the sweating Koy. The one-eyed general he had dealt with last time had been a reasonably cultured man and a graduate of the same military college as Chiang Kai-shek. But this Khun Sa would be a lout, you could count on it, and he began brooding about him. What else but lout could he be, holed up in these hills now for over thirty years? A king with a mini-kingdom, but a lout in all other respects. Face would be everything to him, as it was to Koy, the Chinese curse. To a Chinese, face was everything. His face was his fortune. It was face that made business success possible. It was only face that made the rest of life possible. In a New York office Khun Sa would keep his visitor waiting two hours for no other reason than to gain face at his expense. He was doing the equivalent to Koy now. The worst of it was that Koy would stumble out of the jungle bedraggled, exhausted; and Khun Sa, being fed, rested, and freshly bathed would stroll forward to meet him, smiling warmly no doubt, and to his assembled subjects the man would gain face until he assumed godlike proportions, and the visitor, Koy, would seem no more important than one of the hill peasants who grew the opium. If this face carried over into the negotiations that followed, and of course it would, this would be a disaster for Koy.

The streambed was full of boulders that had to be skirted, and loose round stones that skittered away under foot. It was like walking on billiard balls. Koy, climbing grimly, was as resolved as ever that this loss of face must not happen, though he could not imagine at the moment how to prevent it.

About thirty minutes later the guide pointed ahead. A building was visible through the trees. They were almost to the encampment, and the stupefied Koy, now that he listened, became aware of voices.

Employing parts of various Chinese dialects, he ordered the guide to go forward alone and to announce the imminent arrival of the Cho Kun, Mr. Koy.

Sitting down upon a rock, he waited until he had caught his breath and had stopped sweating, then changed back into his tan silk suit, into his reasonably clean shirt and Dior tie. He combed his hair. Leaving his hiking clothes and boots behind, he stepped forward into the encampment.

A clearing under teak trees. Some sunlight came through but not much—the clearing would not be visible to the American-supplied, Thai government helicopters that patrolled these hills, usually with American drug agents aboard. Eight or ten buildings. Bamboo walls, thatched roofs. A corral full of mules, and another of elephants. A shed under which stood two jeeps and a truck—as to whether an alternative route led in here, the answer, obviously, was yes. The most imposing of the buildings had a veranda all the way around, on which waited five men. The driver stood in his thong sandals in the dirt talking up at them, at one of them in particular, who must be Khun Sa.

There was a post—an execution stake from the look of it—driven into the forest floor in the center of the clearing exactly where, in a cultured place, a flagpole might stand. Koy crossed in front of it and approached the veranda, approached Khun Sa, eyes never leaving him, as if approaching something beautiful, or something dangerous.

A short stocky man. Close-cropped, graying hair. Worn army fatigues and a red beret with a military crest. Broad, flat, Mongol face. Broad, flat, mirthless smile. Began an immediate speech of welcome in Yunnanese. Strong peasant accent. Koy would have understood an educated man, for the Yunnan dialect was close to Mandarin, but Khun Sa's accent was so thick as to be unintelligible. Could he speak no better? Was he doing it on purpose? If so, for what reason? Face again? He had looked astonished to see the New York fashion plate, Koy, step out of the jungle. His jaw had dropped. Surprise, both men knew, automatically conferred face on the man who caused it. Meaning Koy had regained a certain amount of lost ground, which almost made him smile. Almost. It was too early to say how much ground, and matters of face were too serious for smiles of any kind.

He was invited onto the veranda and there introduced to the other men, all Chinese, Khun Sa's lieutenants. One was chief of staff; he went by the Shan name of Phalang, which meant thunder. Koy had heard of him. He was reported to be Khun Sa's enforcer and executioner, a man hated and feared by the troops. A second man controlled the roving refineries, a third had charge of the business side of the operation—Koy understood him to be Khun Sa's nephew, and he was said to have excellent connections with corrupt Thai officials. The fourth man was Khun Sa's link to the peasant farmers in the inhospitable hills further north —his source of supply. Up there thirty or forty villages grew nothing but opium. It had been a traditional cash crop for hundreds of years, though never before on a scale as large as now. Not that the farmers ever earned much from it. Khun Sa's men drove hard bargains. In fact, they would not bargain at all. They bought raw opium for the equivalent of 2000 bahts a kilo, take it or leave it. If a farmer said no, they burned his fields.

Khun Sa clapped his hands and servant women appeared with tea and rice cakes. The six men sat at a table on the veranda, and the other five, excluding Koy from their conversation, talked and joked in their peasant Yunnanese.

It was as if Koy were not there. They were like teenagers reminding an outsider of his status. They were like adults spelling out words so that any child or mental defective who also happened to be present would not understand.

To allow this conversation to continue without him was to lose still more face, Koy saw. Speaking a mixture of pidgin Mandarin and pidgin Cantonese, he interrupted. He began to brag about his relationship with the late one-eyed general years ago, when these five men were younger and of less exalted rank. It was a way of suggesting that Koy had dealt with generals at a time when these others were still assigned to load the mules, and it was, he saw, so perceived. The late general had been a great man and a close friend, Koy said, and his memory was no doubt greatly revered here. Khun Sa jumped up and gestured impatiently with his chin. Koy followed him down the dirt street to a shack made out of wattles and straw. The others had trailed along. All six entered the shack. Inside in the dark sat the one-eyed old man. All his teeth were gone and he was grinning at nothing.

Khun Sa said, "We feed him heroin in his soup. It keeps him happy. He feels no pain." Khun Sa's accent, Koy noted, had suddenly improved.

So much for Koy's privileged relationship with the "greatly revered" general. He had again lost much face.

As they stepped out into the daylight, Koy said with pretended piety, "Being so old, he is of course very close to the gods."

Khun Sa said nothing.

"The Chinese revere the old for that reason," said Koy.

"This way," said Khun Sa.

They entered a warehouse made of stout logs, with armed guards out front. Cases of transistor radios, steam irons and other appliances—all destined for the Rangoon black market—were stacked to the roof tree. Khun Sa lifted two five-liter kerosene tins onto a table. They were filled to the brim with raw gemstones, rubies in one, emeralds in the other. Khun Sa, as gleeful as a child, lifted handfuls above the cans and let them sift through his fingers like loose rice. The gemstones, Koy knew, having been mined in Burma, were bound the other way, to the black market in Thailand.

Khun Sa was showing off, gaining face every minute. He selected a green stone resembling, both in size and in the irregularity of its surfaces, a walnut. It was clotted with impurities. After studying it a moment, he handed it to Koy as a gift.

The room fell silent. All wondered what Koy, now studying the stone in his turn, would do. To accept the lavish gift was to lose face. But to refuse it was an insult.

"Such wealth as this," said Koy, "is indeed proof that fortune has favored Khun Sa. May the gods continue to smile on him." Pretending that no gift had been made at all, that the emerald had been handed him only to inspect, Koy tossed it casually back into the kerosene tin. "What's in the warehouse next door?" he said, and stepped quickly outside before that emerald, or another, could be offered to him again.

The adjacent warehouse, equally stout, equally guarded, was Khun Sa's arsenal. It was stacked with some of the best weaponry unlimited funds could buy. Koy, as Khun Sa handed over gun after gun for his inspection, was furious. In this game of face he was not staying even, might at any moment lose definitively, and they were still a long way from negotiating for the merchandise he needed. He thought he should never have come to this place, at least not alone, he had been swayed by the nearness of the harvest, had been overeager and impatient, errors he had never committed in the past, errors frightening to him in their implications for the future. He had believed he could overcome Khun Sa on his own ground, another grave error, and he was paying for his arrogance in the hardest of all currency, face.

Behind Khun Sa, who described each weapon, Koy was obliged to tour the arsenal, to handle Soviet Kalashnikov rifles, Moisin-Nagant pistols and U.S.-made M16s. There were grenade launchers, bazookas and recoilless ri-

fles. There were wooden crates of ammunition. Koy understood that some of this stuff had been donated by the
Russians because Khun Sa's army opposed Rangoon, and
some had been stolen in raids on Burmese Army arsenals,
although not lately. The Russians had stopped giving arms,
and the army arsenals were better guarded. Lately everything had had to be bought abroad with hard currency
earned from opium—Burmese money was worth nothing
outside of Burma, and the Thai baht was not much better.

As a result every new bullet, by the time it got here,
cost nearly one American dollar. Khun Sa's voice, reaching
the end of this explanation, had taken on a plaintive whine
so that Koy thought: the man is dollar-poor. This was information that could be used, the first of its kind, but Koy,
lifting a British Webley revolver out of a bin, merely digested
it. He thinks we have deliberately held up the flow of dollars
he needs, Koy thought. That's why he is so angry. Koy pretended to examine the revolver. He did not look up or give
any sign.

Just then came a distraction—a commotion outside
in the clearing. All hurried out the door to see what it was,
Koy still holding the revolver into which Khun Sa, or someone, had previously inserted six dollars' worth of bullets.

Men were dragging forward a soldier in fatigues and
thong sandals—this seemed to be the uniform here, although how they could tramp through cobra-infested jungles in open sandals was beyond Koy. Now the soldier was
being lashed to the post, and Koy realized that Khun Sa, in
still another exercise in face, was about to provide him with
an execution.

"Deserter," said Khun Sa grinning. He seemed
hugely pleased with himself. "Went back to his village.
Caught in bed with his wife."

This execution, Koy saw further, was to be a beheading, for the condemned man had been lashed in such a way
as to hang forward off the post at a forty-five degree angle,
and the executioner, carrying a great scimitar of a sword,
had stepped into position. His assistant grabbed a handful of

the victim's hair and yanked the head downwards, nape now exposed to the blade, head turned sideways, cheek up, the terrified staring eyes facing Koy but seeing nothing.

How many chops would it take, Koy wondered. For the human neck was as thick as the bough of a tree and almost as resilient. It seldom ceded in less than six or seven sword blows, not counting the misses, the glancing strokes off the shoulder or the mastoid area. The victims were usually dead or at least unconscious before the final ones of course, often with their eyes still open, so that when the head finally dropped to the dirt and rolled, the eyeballs became covered with a film of dust, and one kept expecting the head to start blinking to clear them.

To be made to witness this barbaric spectacle would constitute, for Koy, the final loss of face, and he knew this. Doubtless Khun Sa expected that the sight of a human head bouncing at his feet would cause him to vomit up his tea and rice cakes. This would not happen. Any man twenty months a policeman had seen far worse, and Koy had been a cop more than twenty years. But his strong stomach would not save him with Khun Sa, who would have proven his life-and-death power over every man there, including Koy. Somehow, it seemed to Koy, he had to do something to thwart this execution, either to stop it or to perform it himself, or he would have no face left.

About fifty men had come out of the various buildings. Though they surrounded the execution post, they seemed only mildly interested, as if willing to accord this event which was of such moment both to the victim and to Koy, five minutes of their time, no more. Perhaps they had seen it too often. They seemed as jaded as American television viewers who had watched too many so-called world championships. They had lost faith. They no longer believed in the uniqueness of anything.

The executioner, sword raised high over his head, awaited a signal from Khun Sa, who was laughing about something with the man called Thunder. Victim, executioner and assistant were all held fast, as if in a frieze, a tableau of death. There was no other sound in the clearing except the two generals giggling over their joke, and nothing at all moved except for Koy's mind, which was racing. For he had recognized the moment as the best he was likely to get here. It was time to act, and he stepped between executioner and victim, directly under the upraised sword.

Now he had delayed the execution by a few seconds, but he had not yet decided what else he should do.

He might shoot the condemned man with the revolver in his hand, spoiling the fun for everyone and usurping the role of Khun Sa, who had decreed a different execution. And with this act of arrogance (still another one) he would also be declaring his own stature here. Or he could take the sword and behead the condemned man in the executioner's place. The wretch was a goner anyway, and either alternative was acceptable to Koy. Or perhaps he could buy the man's life and freedom. He chose the one action by which he seemed to give himself two of these options instead of one. The gun went into his pocket. Stepping forward, he asked the executioner to hand over the sword. Only a second had passed, but the blasé event had turned suddenly into tense theater; no one breathed. Then the executioner's upraised hands came down, he handed over the sword, and Koy raised it himself over the condemned man's neck.

"As the guest of the august Khun Sa," he intoned in a loud voice, speaking the closest approximation of Yunnanese he could manage, "I request permission either to slay this malefactor for him, or to buy the worm's life, for although he is without value to Khun Sa, he can be useful to me."

If Khun Sa said kill, then Koy would obey, and he was already thinking about it, because a different set of imperatives would then apply. It had to be done cleanly. He was hoping for three strokes or less. But beheading a man with a heavy sword was a difficult athletic feat for which he was untrained. If he got blood all over his suit, if he butchered the job (literally) then in terms of face he was worse off than ever.

"Buy?" said Khun Sa. His flat Mongol eyes darted this way and that. He had been totally surprised by Koy's action, a loss of face in itself, and for the second time today, and he did not like it. He was trying to think out what to do or say, but he was so unaccustomed to resistance of any kind, that his mind worked slowly. Koy saw this. From under the upraised sword he called out:

"Five thousand dollars for the worm's life."

"Dollars?"

Koy rammed the sword point into the dirt and the bait onto the hook. "American dollars."

The blade stood quivering. Koy's whole being quivered also, though nothing showed, for he realized that behaving this way he could get himself killed. Approaching Khun Sa, he withdrew the envelope from the breast pocket of his tan silk suit, and fanned out the bait.

Khun Sa displayed no emotion. His greed, if any, could not be seen. "Come into my office," he said, and strode off without looking back.

They sat opposite each other. Light entered principally through chinks in the bamboo walls—slices of light that lay white and irregular across the desk, like elongated noodles.

Koy counted out five thousand dollars and placed it to one side. He emptied out the revolver and pushed it toward Khun Sa butt first, standing the bullets in front of him like stacked chips in a poker game. "I want one ton of morphine bricks delivered in one week's time to an address in Bangkok you will be given. Do you have access to that much?" It was, Koy guessed, the largest single order Khun Sa had ever received. It would require gathering ten tons of raw opium up in the hills, necessitate a caravan of at least two hundred mules down to the labs on the border. The labs would have to work day and night.

Khun Sa's head inclined in the slightest of nods. It was as if he had become suddenly thoughtful, suddenly mute. He was perhaps counting his money.

Koy had judged him to be, on a long-term basis, entirely unreliable. In a month or a year, perhaps sooner, someone would kill him, and it would become necessary to make a new deal with his successor, or else find a new source of supply. Which would take time. Koy's plan was to make a huge initial purchase, and transport it immediately to Hong Kong. There it could be stockpiled in perfect safety. The stockpile was vital. No business was sound if conducted without an adequate reserve against shortages.

"Payment will be in American dollars," said Koy.

"On delivery."

"No, half on delivery." Until the merchandise was out of Bangkok, Khun Sa must share the risk. Otherwise he or his agents might be tempted to hijack the load or to inform on it in exchange for the reward. Chinese or not, Khun Sa, to Koy, could not be trusted. "The other half one week later."

Again the almost invisible nod from Khun Sa.

They began to haggle over money. They were talking about a million dollars in cash. Koy's figure was under this amount, Khun Sa's over, and he offered to refine the morphine into number four heroin in his own labs as part of the deal. But Koy refused, being determined to refine it himself in Hong Kong, thereby controlling the quality of the finished product. This detail settled, they reached agreement on price quickly, for Koy was more than willing to pay Khun Sa a small premium to get exactly what he wanted.

"Now," said Koy, "I must go. Please instruct someone to drive me back to Chiang Rai in one of those jeeps outside under the shed." It was the final test of how much face Koy had regained.

Khun Sa picked up the five thousand dollars, counted it, put it in the pocket of his fatigues, and gave one last nod. Out on the veranda he called out orders, and they strolled together to the shed, soon joined by the original driver, who came running up.

The condemned man stood sheepishly beside the jeep. Koy, in his dark glasses and tan silk suit, stared at him, as did Khun Sa and the driver.

"The worm is yours," said Khun Sa. "What will you do with him?"

The temptation was strong to throw him back like a too small fish, saying: I don't want him after all. It would be Koy's last and best victory of the day, Khun Sa's final loss of face. He would be enraged. And if he beheaded the worm as a result, what was this to Koy? But it was against all principles of good business to deprive business associates of face. Only a lout like Khun Sa behaved that way, and Koy refrained.

"Get into the jeep," he told the worm, and they drove out of the encampment.

About ten kilometers farther on he stopped the jeep and told the worm to get out, warning him if he valued his head to stay away from Khun Sa and his so-called Shan United Army. Whether or not the worm understood he could not tell. Nor did he care. It had been a good day and, although he had saved his life, the worm was no concern of his.

EIGHTY PERCENT of the Thai population were farmers, fishermen, loggers, and of the rest nearly half were Chinese. More than three million Chinese lived in Thailand, some of them for generations, all of them retaining their Chinese identity. They considered themselves Chinese, not Thais. They controlled most retail shops and many of the important factories, businesses and professions, often secretly, hiding behind Thai fronts, or even behind their own Thai names—those who had become naturalized had been obliged by law to adopt Thai names. They even controlled many government agencies and services, always facilitating the rise of other Chinese. It was not so much political as racial—they favored their own.

They controlled most of the country's wealth.

They had always controlled the movement of drugs through Thailand of course, trusting no one but each other. Either as morphine or heroin, the drugs came across from

Burma near Mae Sai in Thailand's remote northern jungles, where Thai border patrols were thin or nonexistent, and were conveyed south to Bangkok in convoys of armed trucks; from there small shipments left the country by air, strapped to the bodies of couriers, and large ones waited for ships at Klongtoey, Bangkok's port, eight miles farther south. Or at least that had always been the pattern in the past. Koy meant to change it. The key was to move major loads out of the country fast, and as soon as he had checked into Bangkok's Oriental Hotel, he was visited in his room by a Hakka Chinese, now a Thai citizen, who went by the name of Hla Nu. Koy had known him as a child. Nu, who was about sixty, had fled from China to Taiwan in 1949, and had emigrated to Thailand shortly afterwards. He was part of Koy's Bangkok organization, he held the rank of superintendent at the Bangkok Central Post Office, and after an hour's conversation the two men came to certain agreements, contingent only upon a meeting, which Nu would arrange, between Koy and a man named Praleep Kitcharoenwong on the following morning on a river bus out on the Chayo Phraya, which ran in front of this hotel. It was the safest meeting place either man could think of. A meeting there would seem accidental, and therefore innocent, to any ordinary eyes, and no observer could move up for a closer look without being observed in his turn.

The next morning was cloudless, as always just in advance of the monsoon, with a damp heavy heat. By 10 A.M., when Koy strode out through the hotel gardens, the temperature was already over 100 degrees, and it would go higher. He wore his dark glasses, of course, and a loose net blouse that hung outside his trousers. He walked along the embankment to the wharf at the head of Siphrava Street, paid five bahts for a ticket, and jumped aboard the stern platform of the first river bus that backed in to take on passengers. The bus left the wharf with a lurch that nearly toppled Koy. Propellor churning, it gained speed quickly. Its bow cleaved the current, its stern leaving a heavy wake.

A long low barque with a canvas roof and no sides, it

already carried about twenty passengers, most clustered in the rear where there was less spray, either sitting in rows on iron benches or standing on the platform, waiting to jump off at the next stop. Koy made his way forward past the craft's source of power, a naked automobile engine that looked twenty or more years old and that must have come out of some long-dead Cadillac or Rolls. A huge thunderous thing, it throbbed and shivered amidship as it drove the boat upriver, and it was intensely hot, far hotter than the day itself. It sent off waves of superheated air that Koy could feel against his face as he turned sideways to step on past. It was hot enough to cause severe burns to anyone that an errant wave might throw against it, for he noted that it turned spray to steam in a fraction of a second. Drops of spray sizzled and vanished instantly, even as they struck it.

Forward of the engine were more iron benches. Koy chose a place in the second row next to the low gunwale, as arranged, wiped it dry with his handkerchief, and sat down to wait for this Praleep Kitcharoenwong. Moving upriver through the heart of the city, the bus veered in toward shore every few hundred yards to take on or discharge passengers. There were many temples on both sides of the river, most with golden domes glistening in the sun, and there were many shacks on stilts as well: rickety open things that hung over the water, housing whole families, the Bangkok version of New York's Chinatown tenements. In places the green lawns of the tourist hotels came down to the water, and in others the river ran past mud banks where the sewage and garbage of the city had washed up in rounded dunes. The poverty of Bangkok did not disturb Koy. Sitting out in the breeze and the spray he was cool enough, and was enjoying the ride, and then a young man sat down beside him and started a conversation in halting Hakka. This was Praleep Kitcharoenwong, whose family had come here from Koy's native village many years ago, before Praleep was born.

"You speak Hakka very well," said Koy, studying him.

"My parents taught it to me, Uncle." The young man had good manners, anyway.

"Your father and I were classmates at a school called the Pavilion of Literature when we were boys."

"He died of illness some years ago."

"—And after that we went to the Dragon River Middle School together."

"He sometimes spoke of those years, Uncle."

A great deal rode on this young man. Koy had wanted to size him up. He had wanted to hear him speak Hakka. It was almost like betting on a horse. One could take all precautions, but there was no sure thing.

Koy got down to business. "Do you think you can do what is asked of you?" Praleep was a Hakka, his ancestral village was the same as Koy's, the scheme itself was sound: all together, the odds could not be better.

The young man, sensing that he had passed inspection, became more self-assured. "I am sure of it."

"You do not need to know what is in the mailbags," said Koy. "Neither the ones that come into Bangkok, nor the ones that go out. And if something should go wrong, you do not know anyone's name."

"That goes without saying."

"Good."

Koy got off at the next wharf and caught a taxi back to the Oriental, where he checked out.

Praleep Kitcharoenwong returned to the Central Post Office where he worked, and dreamed about the business he would buy, and the house he would buy after that. He believed he would soon be a rich man. His job, to which he had been newly assigned by Hla Nu, consisted of driving a postal truck that carried letter mail in sealed bags between the Central Post Office and the nose cones of airliners. Mailbags, whether entering or leaving Thailand, were not exposed to customs inspection at Don Muang airport in any ordinary sense. Normally Praleep drove his truck right onto the tarmac. He would park under the plane's nose and exchange on the average ten outgoing bags of letters for ten incoming ones. The bags weighed over a hundred pounds each, sometimes more, were handled by forklift, and if a customs inspector came out to watch at all, he merely counted the bags against the manifest, he did not open them. He did not need to, for one could smuggle nothing significant in letters and the bags carried post office seals. Praleep understood that duplicate mailbags had been prepared that were identical to real ones in every way, except that they were bigger—big enough to contain a real mailbag, plus twenty or fifty pounds of contraband. Between downtown and the airport, when meeting certain specified flights in the future, he would pull off the road for a few seconds and open the doors of his truck. Men would leap aboard and he would close them inside. The risk was really minimal—his exposure would last literally seconds. Further on he would stop to let the men out—again his risk would last only seconds. Depending on which way the contraband was moving, the men would either drop the real mailbags inside the false ones they had brought with them, or dump the real mailbags out of the false ones, which they would carry away. The false bags would always contain contraband sewn into the bottom. At all times Praleep would have the requisite number of mail bags in his truck.

At first, as Praleep understood it, all such traffic would be between Bangkok and Hong Kong, meaning that some Hong Kong postal driver was performing the same function there that he performed here. But if the scheme worked it would be expanded to other countries. And it should work. It required the collusion of only one or at the most two post-office people at either end. That was the beauty of it. That and the fact that the pay was so good in exchange for so little risk.

He had not been told the nature of the contraband he had agreed to help smuggle, and did not need to be: cash in one direction, obviously; morphine or heroin in the other. He had no qualms about helping to smuggle narcotics, and in fact felt almost patriotic about it. The heroin was destined for Western Europe and the United States where it would poison only foreign demons, not Chinese, for a change. It was the foreign demons who had introduced opium dens to

China. During the more than one hundred years that most of China lay in an opium stupor, foreign demons had systematically raped the country. Well, it was their turn now.

These were Koy's thoughts too, whenever the morality of the heroin trade occurred to him, which was not often. That afternoon he caught his flight to Hong Kong. All was in order, he was on schedule, and his organization, pending meetings in Hong Kong, was now almost entirely in place.

27

WHERE TO start? When in trouble, thought Powers pacing his room in the Mandarin Hotel, you turned toward your own. You did not need to be part of an ethnic minority—or an ethnic majority like the Chinese either—to know that. The principal brotherhood to which Powers belonged was the New York Police Department, but by extension this included all other police departments as well. Possibly because cops constituted the most despised minority on earth, they not only clung together fiercely, they also tended, like the Protestant churches, to be ecumenical about it. The brotherhood was both vast and generous. Most times it admitted not only all cops, but also all law enforcement agents of whatever kind worldwide. As with any religion, there were bound to be sects that had fallen away. Rites differed with the jurisdiction, dogma differed, but not much. In general all held the same faith. Their priests were all sworn, all ordained. All believed in the one true god. Nearly all would help out, once you identified yourself, would let you use their facilities, so to speak, anything from the bathroom to their power of arrest. In theory, those whose jurisdiction was closest to your own usually would help most—unless they were competing against you on the same case. Because the various agencies were also like sports teams in the same league. All wanted the glory of victory, but only one could get it. Whoever made the arrest would be champion.

On the morning after his arrival, Powers did turn toward his own—he made a phone call to a man named Gaffney, special agent in charge of the Drug Enforcement Administration's Hong Kong bureau, the only American police presence here, and explained briefly what he wanted. When Gaffney, sounding neither friendly nor unfriendly, said come on over, Powers hiked up a street that seemed to him steeper than anything in San Francisco, up past the Hilton Hotel, past the American Consulate, up to 26 Garden Road, the Peak Tram building. Out of its entrails, even as Powers watched, a cog railway car loaded with tourists began its climb up the steeply forested mountain toward Victoria Peak, whose presence looming over him Powers could feel, even though he could not see it. The peak wore a ball of fog or cloud around its neck like a scoop of vanilla ice cream.

The DEA office was on the twelfth floor, and security was tight. Powers came off the small elevator into a small alcove, and was examined through a spyhole before being admitted. The door was steel and, once he had entered, the Chinese clerk barred it shut behind him—which made Powers wonder exactly what role Gaffney played here. The office had become a vault, and he was inside it. Something immensely valuable must be kept here, but what?

Gaffney was about forty. It turned out he had once been—briefly—a New York City detective. He sat behind his desk with an American flag to one side of his head, and the Drug Agency shield to the other. Across from him sat Powers. Both wore open-necked sport shirts.

Powers, though still holding back his Chinese Mafia theory, began to describe the case he was trying to make against Koy.

But Gaffney interrupted: "Do our guys in New York know all this?"

It was a more aggressive question than Powers might have hoped for. Gaffney was like a boxer shuffling forward at the bell. He had already landed a solid jab.

"I brought the matter to their attention. Nobody seemed much interested."

"So they don't know. It's a drug case, and that's our jurisdiction, not yours, particularly here."

Powers was already on the defensive, already back-pedaling. "Fine. That's why I came to you. I'm asking you to take over the case. Or at least to help me out. Will you do it?"

Gaffney was shaking his head negatively. "That's not my function here at all. I'm a federal agent. I represent the DEA in Hong Kong. I have no police or investigatory powers of any kind. I'm a guest here. I can't take a step without advising the Hong Kong Police Department of what I'm doing. If I try to work on my own and get caught, then my guest status will be revoked, and I'll be kicked out, and that would be very bad for my career in the agency."

"What exactly then do you do here?"

"Is that some kind of snide remark?"

"No. I'd really like to know."

Gaffney was not even head man in Southeast Asia— region 16, he called it. The regional director worked out of regional headquarters in Bangkok. "Which is probably where this Koy is right now," said Gaffney. "You should have cooperated more with our guys in New York."

Gaffney's principal function, it seemed, was to sit in this office with his small staff and a great deal of cash money provided by Washington, and wait for informants to contact him with news of major drug shipments. He paid tens of thousands of dollars to such men, who were usually drug traders themselves, often direct rivals of whomever they informed on, and then turned the information over to whichever police department had immediate jurisdiction and hoped that arrests would be made and the merchandise confiscated. The DEA made no attempt to advertise the presence of Gaffney, or his counterparts in offices like this one around the world. Gaffney said there was no need to. He nodded sagaciously, indicating that the system as it now worked, worked perfectly. The advertising was done by word of mouth. The magic was in the immensity of the sums he was able to pay—it spread from one informant to the next. Gaffney really had as much business as he could handle. The barred door, the vaultlike quality of this suite of offices was necessary to protect the great stacks of cash that he sometimes kept on hand, and also the filing cabinet containing the names of the recipients of American largesse.

"So you see," he concluded, "I can't help you."

Powers said, "You can't help me."

Gaffney's attitude changed slightly. He had made all his points. That Powers had disregarded proper channels. That he, Gaffney, handled a lot of money and was therefore a man of great stature. This much accomplished, his police sentiments came into play. "I'd like to help," he said. "I'm a cop too, and that guy Koy is dirty. Everybody knows it. This office was after him years ago, before I came here. We got nowhere at the time. I don't know if you have a better chance now, or not. But my function here is liaison."

"Where can I go?"

"The one place you don't go is to the cops. The Royal Hong Kong Police Force is about two percent British and about ninety-eight percent Chinese, just like the city itself, and it's the most corrupt police department in the world. If you go in there and ask about Koy, the word will get back to him within an hour. And once that happens your life is in danger."

"They kill cops here that easy?"

"Here you're not a cop. You're a tourist."

"You can't help me. I can't go to the PD. What do I do?" Powers was almost pleading.

"If we had known he was in Bangkok," mused Gaffney, "we could have set something up. We have a bigger office there. My regional director—"

"We don't know he's in Bangkok," said Powers. "We know he had a reservation to London. We know he comes into Hong Kong today. We don't know where he went in between. I had every airline in New York trying to track him. They couldn't find him." But Powers' tone had become desperate. "What do I do?" he asked again. He had known all along he could do nothing here by himself. Alone, it was hopeless. He had counted on the fierce loyalty of cop toward cop. The loyalty of the tribe. He had counted on the brotherhood. Where was the help he had counted on?

Gaffney was tapping a pencil on the desk. "You had a corruption commission in New York a few years ago," he said. "The Knapp Commission. Turned the NYPD upside down, I heard. How many agents did they have?"

"About fifteen. Why?"

"There's a corruption commission here too. The Independent Commission Against Corruption. It has about eleven hundred agents. New York knows nothing about corruption compared to Hong Kong. If I were you I would go to the commission. The chances are they still have an open file on this guy Koy. They might be willing to help you. See Sir David Wynne-Jones. He runs it." Gaffney reached for his telephone. "Do you want me to call him for you?"

Powers could only nod.

After dialing, Gaffney spun his chair toward the window, and leaned back with his feet on the windowsill, the telephone at his ear. He talked to Sir David for some time, amicably it seemed. Powers could not hear the words. At last spinning back towards his desk again, Gaffney clapped down the phone. "You may be in luck," he said. He was smiling. "Sir David sounded quite interested. He's sending his car for you."

"Thank you," said Powers humbly. "Thank you very much."

But Gaffney ignored Powers' gratitude, for his mind had gone on to something else. "All these Brits have official cars," he complained. "Our government doesn't provide me with any car. I meet informants in dark places in the middle of the night and I have to use my own car. But these Brits all have cars, even men I outrank by two or three grades."

Powers smiled, because he was feeling a new onrush of hope. "Life just isn't fair, is it?" he said.

At Commission headquarters at 10 Harcourt Road

twenty minutes later he was shown into the office of Sir David Wynne-Jones, and such was the appearance of the room, and of Sir David himself, that his onrush of hope petered out on the spot. It was as if all of his money had run out through a hole in his pocket, every cent he had in the world. He felt suddenly destitute. Sir David, who rose to shake hands with him, was a man of about fifty-five or sixty with muttonchop sideburns, and he was wearing a bush jacket, knee socks and short pants. Powers looked at him in dismay. Street cops, and Powers was a street cop, were used to appraising all contacts on very little evidence, almost instantly. They had to. It was how they stayed alive. Powers now appraised Sir David and wanted to weep. He was in the presence not of a police official but of an aging safari guide or lion tamer, and such a man could not help him.

"Captain Powers," murmured Sir David.

"Sir David," said Powers in response. He managed a smile, the best smile of which he was capable at that moment. It felt like a crack in a pane of glass.

In appearance Sir David was no more a policeman than this room was a policeman's office. On the wall behind his desk was the stuffed head of a lion. There was a leopard-skin rug in front of the desk, and a hollowed out elephant's foot served Sir David as a wastebasket. On other walls hung spreads of horns of various African beasts, and their hooves, hollowed out, served as ashtrays on Sir David's desk.

"Are you a career policeman, Sir David?" asked Powers. However rude the question might sound, he was as compelled to ask it as he might have been compelled to cough or sneeze.

"Colonial administration," Sir David replied. "Spent most of my career in Kenya, what? My job now is to clean up the Royal Hong Kong Police Force, what? To paraphrase Winston Churchill, crime is much too important to be left to career policemen, don't you know. No affront intended, Captain."

Affront? Powers scarcely heard him. He stared at the really bad hand he had dealt himself. He studied it. He was focused totally on himself. The brotherhood wasn't going to help him. The brotherhood couldn't be found and perhaps didn't exist. He had only one card left to play, and it was not an ace. It was not even a face card. It was represented by this silly-looking big game hunter. It was about a ten, maybe even lower. But he had no choice left except to play it.

"Yes, well," he said, hesitating. And threw it onto the table. "Sir David, I have a bit of a problem," and he began to explain what it was. Again he did not speak of the Chinese Mafia, but only of Koy. He was trying to make a case in New York against Koy, who was suspected of complicity in several murders and in countless cases of extortion and other crimes, and also of directing a drug importing empire. But there was no legally admissable evidence against Koy on any of these things. He had trailed Koy here hoping to find evidence or information that could be used against him in New York. News of a specific drug shipment, proof of the transfer of large sums of currency, the names and whereabouts of accomplices.

"Indeed you do have a problem," said Sir David, when he had concluded. "Don't dare show your face in New York again without some results, I shouldn't wonder." And he gave a rather odd smile. He's not going to help me, thought Powers, trying to read it. It was the smile, Powers thought, of a proud father who, seeing his son in trouble, declined to help him on the grounds that it would strengthen the boy's character to get out of the mess by himself. If he could.

"There's nothing personal between me and Mr. Koy, Sir David," Powers said hurriedly. "I don't know him. I only talked to him once. I'm not out to get him in any personal sense. But he appears to be a dangerous criminal at the head of a dangerous organization, and there has been a lot of violence. A lot of teenage boys are getting it in the neck—literally."

"Yes. Time-honored means of execution out here," said Sir David, and he began stroking his muttonchops with both hands. He was listening, but with what interest Powers could not tell. Would he help? Could he help? Assuming he wanted to. Did he see Koy as a trophy he might hang on his wall?

Sir David, stroking his muttonchops with both hands, was grinning. Did the grin mean something or not? What might it mean?

Suddenly it vanished. Sir David jumped up and began to march up and down behind his desk, from wall to wall. He marched to a soldier's cadence only he heard, and snapped into each turn with an abrupt about-face. As he marched he did deep-breathing exercises.

Observing such conduct, being now utterly and totally dependent on what this man might decide to do, Powers felt close to tears.

Sir David stopped in his tracks. He fixed Powers with a hard eye. "I had a look at the fellow's dossier while you were on your way over here, what? Just to refresh myself. I helped set this corruption commission up some years ago. His case was one of the first to come to my attention. I must confess that I took a personal interest in it at the time. Not a good idea for an administrator, what? Nonetheless, I did." Sir David nodded his head vigorously up and down.

Powers was like a man falling through space. He lunged for the one dangling life line within reach.

"Could I possibly see that dossier?"

"Can't show you the dossier. Crown property, what? Confidentiality and all that. Not a shred of proof in it anyway. Fellow could sue us for libel if I showed it around. How much do you know about him, anyway?"

"Not very much. I was told in New York that he left here with five hundred million dollars."

"Nonsense," said Sir David. He gave an exaggerated guffaw. "What rot! He left with maybe twenty million. Thirty million tops. Still a lot of money, of course. All those station sergeants made fantastic amounts of money, and Koy made rather more than the others because he organized it all. But not five hundred million."

Sir David began marching again, taking more deep breaths.

"But I just don't see," said Powers, "how that much money could be available to a cop. In New York, gamblers used to put cops on pads at a thousand dollars a month and that was considered big money."

"Humph," grunted Sir David. "You don't know the Chinese, what? Ever hear of the Triads?"

"The Chinese Mafia."

"The Black Societies, so the Chinese call them. The British call them Triads because in their nomenclature and ritual they accord magical properties to the number three and to certain multiples of three. Gangs of vicious criminals are what they are. In Hong Kong we're blessed with about forty different Triad gangs, maybe eighty thousand members in all. Organized crime here is highly organized indeed. The Triads control all gambling, prostitution, pornography, drugs, loan-sharking, extortion, street gangs. Even the bank robberies. If you want to knock over a bank you have to get permission from your Triad, and afterwards you have to share the loot. Triad groups are always fighting for territory against one another, pitched battles with two-handed meat cleavers, usually. There was a fight the other night, as a matter of fact. The police got there too late. Found blood on the ground, and a human arm severed just above the elbow, and a cleaver lying next to its outstretched fingers. Ordinary people are terrified of the Triads, of the very name. They don't want to hear the word."

Sir David resumed his marching, but went on talking. In Hong Kong, it was a criminal offense to be a Triad or claim to be, or to attend a Triad meeting, or possess Triad books, accounts, writings, seals, or insignia, or give any aid or comfort to any Triad society. The origins of the Black Societies, Sir David said, went far back into early Chinese history. With the passage of years they had become more and more criminal, and more and more sinister. Their initiation ritual involved the drawing and drinking of blood to signify blood brotherhood, and the swearing of the thirty-six oaths of membership.

"The usual claptrap," said Sir David. "The thirteenth oath reads something like this: if I should change my mind and deny my membership in the family, I will be killed by a myriad of swords."

The new member was given the rank of soldier, was equipped with secret codes and hand signs for recognizing other members, and was obliged to prove himself. "They give him some obscene act," said Sir David, "and he performs it. Beat up some merchant, execute an informer—they hang informer chaps up by the thumbs and make knife cuts all over him—the myriad of swords. Lovely people, these Triads, what?"

Sir David went behind his desk, sat bolt-upright in his swivel chair, and stared at Powers. "Your man Koy was a Triad. He was the son of a banker in Canton. Came here when he was about fifteen years old. His father enrolled him in the King George the Fifth school. Very posh school, what? Same school British civil servants sent their sons to. Don't know how Koy ever got in. The British didn't mingle much with the Chinese at the time, called them wogs, don't you know. The father must have pulled hell's own strings. Of course the boy was an extremely bright student. That's not speculation. We checked on that."

Most of what happened next was entirely speculation, however. Sir David couldn't document any of it. Apparently Koy joined the Hung Pang Triad, a Hakka group. All the Triad ranks were numbers, not names, except that the top man was called the Cho Kun. Koy moved up in rank. He started as a 432, then became a 426—the strong-arm man in a Triad group.

"You might call it the first of the gazetted ranks," said Sir David.

Very quickly Koy became a 415, the idea man or counselor, and then a 412, the underboss. Then he was the Cho Kun.

"He may have been only twenty years old at the time," said Sir David. "We have no way of knowing exactly. Then he joined the Royal Hong Kong Police Force, and the cops and the criminals became one, and the sky became almost literally the limit."

"I still don't see how he came to amass so much money," said Powers.

"Got in on the ground floor, what?" said Sir David.

When the war ended the population of Hong Kong was about 600,000. About three quarters of a million refugees came in during 1949 and the spring of 1950 alone. After that the refugees only kept coming, until today Hong Kong held over five million people. When Koy was a young constable the police department was expanding fast, meaning that he quickly got promoted to sergeant and then station sergeant, the key rank, with command of a district vice squad. He didn't want any promotions after that. The economy was expanding fast. Koy saw the opportunity, and went after it.

"He seemed to be quite a remarkable individual," mused Sir David. "Intelligent, multi-lingual, and absolutely arrogant. I suppose it was the arrogance that caught my eye when his dossier finally reached my desk. According to our information, he conducted his affairs quite openly. Openly enough to stick in any law officer's craw. Corruption is a way of life in the Orient. Bribery, kickbacks, extortion—they're all time-honored to the Chinese. The drug trade is time-honored too. Drugs have been a way of life since the first opium dens nearly two centuries ago. Your man was no ordinary corrupt officer. He commanded his vice squad in Wanchai, the red light district here, and he taxed every bit of vice that went on in his district, what? Taxed perfectly legitimate businesses as well."

The population of Hong Kong went over two million, over three million, over four million. Koy set up syndicates not only in his own district but in four others as well, each of them run by a station sergeant who was known to him. All were Hakkas.

"Say you wanted to start a vice operation somewhere," said Sir David. "Gambling, prostitution, an opium divan, whatever. Well, you first had to buy an unofficial license from the district sergeant, plus you had to pay regular weekly fees. It was all beautifully regulated."

The chief collector in each district was a Triad and a civilian. He used sub-collectors. The chief collector kept the books. Whichever policeman would come by to inspect the books and collect the money was called the caterer, and he would distribute the money to all the other policemen via sub-caterers. The station sergeants got the most money, each receiving about $40,000 a month on the average.

Powers hearing this, gave a long low whistle.

The divisional superintendent, who was the gazetted officer supervising the station sergeants, and who usually was British, got much less, about $16,000 a month.

Sir David said, "When I say Koy and his station sergeants taxed everybody, I mean everybody. Street hawkers had to pay forty cents a day or the police would not allow them to operate. Perhaps that doesn't sound like much, but there are eighty thousand street hawkers in Hong Kong, and the income from that scam alone amounted to thirty-two thousand dollars a day."

These station sergeants had all grown up in the job, as Koy had, and their income only expanded as Hong Kong expanded. Drug importers had to pay licensing fees, loan sharks had to pay, and loan sharking was a very serious business because of the gambling. If one borrowed money from loan sharks to cover gambling losses, interest rates were ten percent per day—and the station sergeants all got a cut of that. As the new public housing complexes went up, bus companies came into existence to transport the residents into the city. The police would demand a fee for allowing the buses to operate. The housing estates had to be decorated by contractors. The police would charge the contractors a fee for allowing them to work in the buildings.

"And so it went," said Sir David. "It wasn't all bad of course. The police were so tightly tied in with the Triads and with vice that whenever a particularly heinous crime occurred they could solve it very quickly. A Chinese who commits a crime wants three things afterwards; he wants a woman, he wants to smoke some opium and he wants to gamble. The police would go to their contacts in the brothels, the opium divans and the gambling halls, and they'd come up with the chap immediately."

Being a policeman in Hong Kong was so lucrative that very soon most British gazetted officers were corrupt as well. In desperation, a number of new ordinances were passed. One brought into existence the Independent Commission Against Corruption, and another made it a crime to possess assets beyond what could be explained by a man's ordinary source of income.

"That was the key law for us," said Sir David. "We were able to go after the station sergeants, and we nailed many of them, although none of the Dragons. The usual sentence was two years in prison, plus monetary fines based on how much it was estimated the fellow had stolen during his police career. Some of these fines totaled almost a million dollars, which the ex-sergeant in question usually paid in cash immediately. Of course a number of cases never came to trial. Fellow committed suicide as soon as he realized he'd been caught, what?"

After a short pause, Sir David added: "Terrific loss of face involved with getting caught. A man's most precious possession is his sense of shame, the Chinese feel. It's what distinguishes him from the animals. So these fellows shot themselves. Very Chinese, what?"

"It's very cop, as well."

"I beg you pardon?"

"What you're talking about is part of the police psyche, not just the Chinese psyche. American cops are always killing themselves when caught, too. I've known several personally. Cops, even corrupt cops, can't cope with guilt, for some reason."

"I see, yes. Well, we went after your man Koy too, of course," continued Sir David. "I directed the inquiry myself. Shouldn't have. It was not particularly difficult to develop additional information against him. The trouble was that potential witnesses were terrified of him. Nobody would give evidence. We were able to learn that he had a net worth running into the many millions of dollars. But the money was not here in Hong Kong, and we were unable to discover precisely where it had gone. It was like trying to prove murder without a corpse. Meanwhile, the police force was extremely resistant to this Commission, as you can imagine. There were covert meetings, and then a huge outdoor rally in the stadium in Kowloon. Good deal of muck was thrown at us and our efforts. There was a protest march on police headquarters, followed by a police strike and the threat of violence. The governor was obliged to declare a partial amnesty for offenses committed before that day. Your man Koy was one of those who benefited from the amnesty. Our case against him at the moment is closed.

"Can you reopen it again?"

"Negative. Amnesty is amnesty. And in any case I'm left with still another problem, I'm charged to focus on official corruption and your man is no longer a Hong Kong official, what?"

The two men stared at each other. After a moment, Powers said, "If he's come here to set up narcotics shipments through Hong Kong, then you can bet that he will make use of former police cronies. At least one of these former cronies must still be a police constable or sergeant. There's your hook, if you want to use it. That's official corruption, isn't it?"

Sir David, looking thoughtful, almost troubled, was again stroking his muttonchops with both hands. Suddenly he began to grin, so that Powers thought with elation: I've got him, he's going to help me after all.

Sir David stood up. "I've taken a personal interest in this man, as I've said. Not the proper attitude for an administrator, but there it is. When is he due in?"

"We had his flight number leaving New York, but we lost him in London. However, according to our wiretap information, he arrives in Hong Kong today on Pan Am flight sixty-six at ten minutes after three."

"Probably coming from Bangkok," said Sir David, reaching towards his intercom. "Let me make some arrangements here, and then let's go out to the airport and have a look at him, shall we?"

WHEN KOY deplaned in Hong Kong that afternoon he was watched from an office whose window looked down on the customs area. The lights were out in the office, and the watchers, Powers and Sir David, stood well back from the glass. Koy proceeded normally through customs. They saw him present an American passport—at this Sir David's eyebrows rose—and his one small bag was not opened. As he passed out of customs, they were able to continue to observe him by crossing the upstairs corridor into a second office whose window looked down into the main arrivals hall.

They saw him met by one woman and three men, all approximately his own age, all extremely respectful. There were smiles enough to light up the hall, and much bowing, as if he were a visiting dignitary or politician, much honored but unknown to them personally. There were no kisses, touches or handshakes. One of the men did relieve Koy of his satchel; the man holding it stood rocking back and forth on his heels, beaming with pleasure.

"Humph," said Sir David, "summit conference. Captain, you may have happened on to more than you knew."

"Summit conference?" Powers was amazed at the authority that now emanated from this man, who no longer seemed silly at all.

"I can't be sure of course. It's been a number of years since I last saw any of those chaps. But I think you're looking at four of the so-called five Dragons, including the chief Dragon of course, Koy himself. Only chap missing seems to be Sergeant Hung. He was the most vicious of the lot, but not the smartest. We had him tight. We had his passport and everything. But somehow he escaped from the Colony. We never found out where he went and so were never able to extradite him back here. Whatever this summit conference may be about, I dare say Sergeant Hung won't be coming to it. Maybe he's dead. Maybe somebody shot him. I hope so."

"Who's the woman?" inquired Powers.

"Mrs. Koy, his wife."

"You're sure?"

"Oh yes. When he resigned and left Hong Kong his wife and son remained behind. We were able to block travel documents for her for almost a year. She couldn't leave. He sent money regularly. He still supported them. We were able to learn that much. He sent them money and therefore honor. That's very important to the Chinese. He sent them face."

"Was there ever a divorce?"

"Not that we know of. Why?"

"Because he's got another wife in New York."

Sir David laughed. "I don't think the bigamy statutes cover two wives if you keep them thirteen thousand miles apart."

Below them Koy, the woman and the three other men started out of the arrivals hall toward the street.

"Let's go back to my office," said Sir David.

This decision provoked agitation in Powers, who glanced from Sir David to the departing Koy and back again. "You're not going to let Koy just walk away, are you?"

"I have some men tailing them," Sir David said sharply. He gave a snort of annoyance. "We're not New York here, but we're not completely incompetent, what?" And he led the way out of the office and down the stairs into the arrivals hall.

"I'm sorry," said Powers, but he was talking to his back.

"We'll set up a major investigation. You'll be kept informed."

"I'd like to take part." Powers followed him outside toward his official car.

"Negative, I'm afraid." Sir David's voice had become overly hearty, impersonal "You'll have to be satisfied with watching from the wings, so to speak," said Sir David.

28

CAROL CONE, floating first class above the Polar icecap, sipped Moët et Chandon champagne, listened to the Bee Gees in stereophonic sound in her earphones, and studied the collection of clippings, articles, treatises and books about Hong Kong, and about crime therein, that had been gathered for her by an unknown network researcher.

She was unable to decide what her motives were. Was she making this trip for the sake of a story or only to be with Powers in a place where, at night, he would not have to leave her to go home to someone else? Or perhaps her purpose was to bring this affair to a head. She was not good at sharing. He would have to choose between Carol Cone and his wife. She wanted all of him or nothing.

The clipping in her hands at the moment was about rape. The Hong Kong version of an old story. Interesting version. A thirty-one-year-old man was in the habit of approaching girls on the street and claiming to be a doctor. He was Chinese, as were the girls. He offered to cure one girl of an upset stomach, and told another that she was even more gravely ill—she appeared to be suffering from blood clots and an ulcer, and her hymen was broken. Unless she agreed to treatment he would prescribe, she had only a short time to live. These girls and others withdrew money from their bank accounts to pay this "doctor," then followed him to an apartment building where he "cured" them. After a hot bath the girls were told to lie naked on the bed, and submit to body massages followed by the most critical part of the treatment, the miracle drug that never failed, sexual intercourse. Of course several doses of this drug were invariably required. One or another of the girls did question him from time to time. But the treatment was absolutely necessary, he told them. The alternative for the girl was the hospital, and an abdominal operation. After treatment he would present his bill, usually one hundred Hong Kong dollars, and the girls paid it.

Carol, reading this, shook her head in disbelief. The case had gone to trial. Two of the many girls had testified. Both were twenty-one years old, and immediately after filing their complaints had been examined medically. The examinations showed they had been virgins until only hours before.

Was sexual ignorance that great among the Hong Kong Chinese, Carol asked herself. Among the Chinese in general? Were twenty-one-year-old girls normally still virgins?

This article Carol put aside, picking up a booklet which purported to be a history and description of the Triad gangs. Most gangs seemed to have escaped virtually intact from mainland China to Hong Kong at the time of the communist takeover in 1949. So the criminals had run too, Carol reflected, just like the bankers, industrialists, and politicians. So what else was new? Thumbing through the booklet, she saw that a number of sections had been marked in red for her attention, and one of these caught her eye. It outlined Triad methods of selling girls into prostitution. Young girls who had run away from home were prime targets. The Triad groups were constantly on the lookout for such girls, who would be quickly raped, and in some cases gang-raped. This was referred to as "sealing" or "stamping" the merchandise, and usually it reduced the girl to a state of such catatonic shock and shame that, when she was brought to a brothel and sold, she did not resist. The price paid for her became her debt to the brothel. She could not leave till she paid it off, and this took considerable time, because she was credited with only thirty percent of the money she earned, and had to pay living expenses out of that. Another method Triads used was to sell their own girl friends. The Triad member would convince his girl that loan sharks were after him, she had to save his life by turning a few tricks and giving him the money. He would then take her to the brothel, and unbeknownst to her, sell her to the brothel owner. Once inside, she would find herself unable to get out until she had paid back her purchase price.

Carol had no idea where the researcher had found this stuff. She had no great interest in people on the research level, but this one, she guessed, had been a woman, for much of the material had a definite feminist slant. It was all very subtle. This type of thing was just what communist film-writers had been accused of more than a generation ago, Carol knew. They had proselytized not by speech-making, but by selection of material. Carol herself was a militant feminist who fought for women's rights only when the woman was herself. There was no place for feminism in her work. She was interested in success as demonstrated by the size of her paycheck and the degree of her celebrity, and such success was based strictly and solely on the broadest possible appeal to viewers, an appeal almost political in nature. That is, not offending people was more important than pleasing them. There was no room in television—not yet, anyway—for a woman who wished to stand as a symbol. Other women, as far as she was concerned, would have to fight their own battles. She had made the initial penetration, and made it possible for them to follow. It was up to them to widen the breach themselves. Her Q factor and her ratings proved that millions and millions of Americans invited her into their homes each day, accepted her as being just like them. She did not wish to disabuse them. If they knew, for instance, about her affair with Captain Powers, a married man, most of them would tune her out. She thought of Powers, who would be surprised to see her. She smiled. He would be astonished to see her. And, she hoped, very, very pleased. It was certainly the farthest she had ever traveled to see a man—13,000 miles.

A steward in a white jacket stood at her place carving slices of rare roast beef—the airline had decided it was dinner time. She was like a child again—someone else was deciding when and what she would eat—and at the same time she was like a queen—before her champagne glass was even empty it had been refilled. The Japanese gentleman beside her downed another whiskey. Carol only sipped, and watched the bubbles percolate, and contemplated luxury. She rode pampered above the clouds and it cost her nothing. The world's ultimate luxury had changed. It was no longer the yacht but the expense account. One bought goods and services without even asking about price, and was just as rich afterwards as before.

After dessert and coffee she finished her champagne. She began to feel a bit high. Pushing the button, she dropped the seat rest back as far as it would go, stretching out, snuggling in. Here in first class she lay almost in the horizontal, which was extremely comfortable, yet not really comfortable at all. It was like lying out in a dentist's chair, attached to various tubes and implements—the earphones, the tray, the seat belt. Like a patient she was fixed in place.

Twilight fled ahead of them. It lasted an interminably long time. It was like a lover, beckoning the loved one to follow. It was like Powers teasing her, staying always just out of reach. The only trouble was he didn't know he was doing it. At last it got dark. Sockettes and eye masks were passed out. Carol employed both. The steward arranged the foot-rest under her calves, arranged her pillow; he put a blanket over her. He was like a lover tucking her in. She saw lovers everywhere tonight, and wondered why.

Masked, she floated through total darkness at 600 miles an hour in a jet-propelled capsule that seemed motion-less, even soundless. She concentrated on sleep fiercely. She was determined to sleep at all costs because tomorrow in Hong Kong a film crew would be waiting, and she might have to film her standup, or one or more interviews. She wanted to look her best. She could not afford to look less than her best, and she began to worry about a makeup man. It was vitally important that there be a makeup man on hand. Would they have found her one or not? Suppose they hadn't?

The Japanese beside her had begun to snore. All day she had watched him drinking too much. Lifting her mask she peered at him. Dead asleep. Slobbering slightly. She wondered what to do. Call the steward? Change seats? It was like lying awake in a dormitory. But she couldn't change seats. This dormitory was full.

His snore was both a sneeze and a whistle. She was sharing a double bed with a Japanese she didn't know and paying heavily for it. It wasn't her choice. She had been given none. She had been assigned to his bed, or him to hers, as in a well-run whorehouse. His near arm was balanced on the armrest, and with her elbow she knocked it off. He came awake with a start, and glanced around, but could not find the culprit who was hiding under her mask, feigning innocence, feigning sleep.

Sleep was what she wanted, but it would not come. The Japanese gentleman, she sensed, was peering around, trying to decide what had awakened him. Consider it a miracle, pal, Carol thought. It will be a miracle if I ever doze off, she thought. Tomorrow she would look a wreck. She would go on camera after twenty-four hours without sleep, and it would show in her face. At her age she could not afford to miss a night's sleep like this. It would make her whole face sag.

She began to wonder where her career would be ten years from now, twenty. As she became middle-aged, and then an old woman, would the network keep her on, or get rid of her? With one or two exceptions, the famous movie actresses of her childhood had all disappeared from the screen at a far younger age than she was now: Lana Turner, Rita Hayworth, Hedy Lamarr. For most, tragedy had promptly followed. A number of them became shoplifters, or alcoholics, or suicides. Of course newswomen were not actresses. It was a totally different category. Or was it? One pretended that looks did not count. But perhaps they counted far more than anyone wanted to admit, especially herself. Was there a place in television news for the experienced older woman? Walter Cronkite had become a father-figure, and then presumably a grandfather-figure. Could the same thing happen to a woman? Could it—would it—happen to her?

There were no answers to these questions because Carol belonged to the first generation of women such as herself. One could not examine any track records. There were no track records. Not one of these women had yet reached menopause. It remained to be seen what would happen to them then—what would happen to her.

As she fought to fall asleep, Carol asked herself why this subject of age had so preoccupied her in recent weeks. For the last hour it had occupied every room and closet in her head. Was there some reason? She had known since adolescence that, like any baseball player, she was using up finite resources. The best part of her life would end after a set number of years, same as a shortstop's. And after that? She did not know. She had never yet squarely faced that question, or tried to resolve it, and when on occasion it was brought to her attention she had turned it aside with a flippant comment, or an arrogant one. Live for today is my motto, she would say with a grin. Or she would tell people, usually men, that she did not expect ever to have to face the problem—she simply did not expect to live very long. If depressed enough she might suggest—without ever actually using the ugly word—that there was always a way out. One could always simply "end it."

The Japanese gentleman was snoring again. She could not get away from him. She lay beside him. Call girls must experience this all the time: to be stuck there, unable to leave, the man snoring. To be frank, it had happened to her once or twice, when she would spend the night with a man she scarcely knew. Lots of men snored, even the most attractive ones sometimes. But this was different. She had not invited this Japanese gentleman into her bed, or even her life. She could not make him turn over. She could not pass it off as payment for pleasure received. There was no way to escape the rhythmic, rasping noise, no way she could ever get to sleep. Pushing the button, she snapped her chair upright, ripped the mask off her eyes, and stared at the villain. Who snored on, oblivious to her rage. Breathing hard, she found the earphones and clamped them back on her head, and turned the volume up high. The snoring vanished. Rock music drowned it out. But she was now so upset that the music sounded like a bombardment. It sent cannon balls blasting into her skull through both ears to bounce around in there. There ought to be a husband or lover in the chair next to her. Powers—her daughter—someone she loved. Why wasn't there? Why was she always so alone? Tears came to her eyes. It was intolerable. She was not going to get any sleep at all. Tomorrow she would look awful. She would look fifty. She stared blinking out the porthole into the void of night 35,000 feet above the Arctic Ocean. Total darkness, total emptiness, total nothingness, total cold. She was weeping hard. She was half drunk, exhausted, and terribly worried about her face, and about what would happen to her when it was gone.

29

TO ORCHID KOY the ride home seemed as endless as a day in school. She was like a schoolgirl being moved about at the behest of others. First stop was the Peninsula Hotel in downtown Kowloon where one of the ex-sergeants was registered. All of them trooped inside for the rite of afternoon tea. The Peninsula lobby at tea time was the place to be seen in Hong Kong, and had been since before World War II. After ordering tea and Western pastries, they stared around, stared into the babble of languages. The place was crowded, all tables taken, people waiting: European and Asian tourists, some British officials, mostly prosperous local Chinese.

At the sight of some acquaintances across the lobby, Orchid waved, attracting their attention. She wanted them to know she had her husband back. She wanted Koy to know she had not spent five years in a cloister. He quickly glanced that way, but saw no one he knew, and appeared disappointed. So she had new friends—after five years, what did he expect? He seemed almost jealous, and this pleased Orchid. It gave her hope, though perhaps it didn't mean much.

After tea the remaining two ex-sergeants had to be returned to their hotels through what was now rush hour traffic—the interminable afternoon continued. Only when this was accomplished could Orchid, if she wished, at last move off the jump seat to a place beside her husband. But she hesitated. The distance was greater than it looked, as was the danger. It was like crossing a busy intersection. One had to think it out first, then dash across. It was not something that could be done gracefully. One called attention to oneself. One looked clumsy doing it.

"Sit here," said Koy.

She did so—there, it was done. Only now she didn't know quite what to say to him, and so reverted to the deportment of her girlhood. She chose silence. She faced her destiny with naked eyes and frightened heart. She became like an old-style Chinese woman: she submitted with shyness, with downcast gaze, to the benign glance of her lord. She thought of their house that she had kept unchanged for him for five years. How would he find it? She herself was unchanged also, though she had aged more than it had. How would he find her? What were his feelings for her? What altered circumstance in his life had brought him back to her?

Now there was only the armrest between them, but it seemed to rise to the ceiling like a wall. Her emotions, unperceived by him, seemed to bounce back on her side. The armrest was like a river. She could see him without being able to reach him. One needed a special implement to get across, a bridge, a boat. But she could find no bridge, though she looked, and all the boats were on his side.

Hong Kong traffic got more intense every year. From time to time as they moved slowly along the streets, Koy murmured that this or that had changed. He spoke in Hakka, the language of their courtship, and she answered in Hakka. Although she also spoke Cantonese and Mandarin, she had never learned much English. She answered in monosyllables because it was best to avoid all risk. Perhaps he did not wish her to speak. She had no confidence in herself. In his presence at last she realized this. There was none left. Confidence was like a candle that had gone out. Only he could relight it. She could not give confidence to herself. No one could. It had to come from another. Sometimes she could feel him staring at her, and she kept her gaze averted because she was afraid she might see, mirrored in his eyes, the woman she was: one who still did not speak English, and who as a result could not move easily in the same circles he did; a woman now closer to fifty than forty. A certain Chinese proverb had been much in her mind lately: the husband will pick a plum blossom as his wife becomes a prune. Nothing could be more normal than that.

Beside her Koy did not trust himself to speak either, for to speak would be to betray how hard his heart was beating. He wanted to take her in his arms but couldn't because of the presence of the chauffeur. Public displays of affection, to a Chinese, were the worst form of bad manners and he had no intention of losing face in front of a chauffeur he had never seen before this day.

Even after they had entered their house, a mansion on a hill overlooking Repulse Bay and the South China Sea, he was constrained to act correctly, distantly, for some time longer. It was nearly dusk by then. The house had once been owned by a Pan American vice president in the days when Pan Am owned the only long-range flying boats able to cross the Pacific, and the internal airline of China as well. The chauffeur had carried Koy's bags upstairs to the room Orchid had ordered prepared for him. When they heard his footsteps pattering down the back stairs, Koy turned toward his wife and in the dim light of the hallway, a yard of air between them, took both her hands. But they gazed at each other like the strangers they had perhaps become.

They had been married when she was fifteen years old, and he two years older. Already speaking English, he had come back from Hong Kong to her village to claim her. He was the first boy in Orchid's life and she the first girl in his, but from the traditional point of view it had been a bad marriage for both, for she was only a village shopkeeper's daughter. The streets of her village were not even paved, and she brought him no dowry. His father totally disapproved, and as a result he had been obliged to leave Canton, to take his bride to Hong Kong to try to make his fortune there—the young couple would have been ostracized by both families and by most friends had they stayed. To the Chinese at that time, and still today, there were a number of good reasons to marry, but love was not among them. To be sincere in love, it was written, was to be grotesque.

But suppose he had married some other girl in the traditional way, one chosen by the two families, Koy sometimes asked himself. What might his career have been? Probably he would have become a banker in Canton like his father. Instead he had landed in Hong Kong with a frightened fifteen-year-old girl to take care of, still a boy himself, with no money and no prospects, and he had fought his way up the only path he had seen open before him. As a businessman he had achieved undreamed-of prosperity. He had wanted to be respectable too, but had never had time. Prosperity had been due principally, he believed, to the rules of conduct he had set himself, and to which he had adhered rigidly. He believed in *li*—which might be defined as the rightness of things. What was not *li* was not done. He learned to extract small amounts of money from the many, rather than large amounts from the few, and thus avoided the making of devoted enemies. These amounts were always stipulated in advance, and never exceeded, and in exchange he gave his clients what they paid for. He provided the protection he promised—protection from street marauders, from rival entrepreneurs, and from the police. Whenever possible he shied away from violence, which he had identified from the first as a bad business technique. Only occasionally was it essential, and even then he ordered it reluctantly, being careful each time to keep it at two or three removes from himself. He left such assignments to those with a talent for it: Sergeant Hung here in Hong Kong, and in later years Nikki Han in New York.

Now in the dim hallway Koy had reached at last for both his wife's hands. She seemed to give them up reluctantly, like small change she did not really want to part with, and there was no expression on her face that Koy could read. Her face was like a road with no traffic on it, which disconcerted him completely. There ought to have been something. He started to speak, but was interrupted by footsteps on the staircase and then by the appearance of a teenage boy who came down upon them, out of control, bounding like a loose soccer ball.

"My son," said Koy.

The boy was seventeen, and he pulled up short to see his father. He was dressed in blue jeans and a leather jacket, the international teenage uniform.

But his manner was surly. He was not interested in Koy and he was in a hurry to get out. "Hi," he said. "Will you be here long?"

His mother reached to straighten out the collar of his shirt. "He would not come to the airport to meet his father," she chided. "He said he was too busy."

Koy was trying to feel joy to see his son. This was the only son he had—the three children in New York were all girls. But the boy was so distant it was difficult to feel anything at all. "I expected to see you," he said.

After a short silence the teenager said: "Perhaps I did not believe you were really coming. When you went away I was a child. Perhaps I did not believe you were still alive."

"We'll spend some time together now," said Koy heartily, but he had been stung by his son's words. "It was not my wish to leave you when I did, nor to stay away as long as I have." He was trying to explain himself, he realized, not so much to the boy as to Orchid.

"I have to go," his son said sullenly. When he was halfway through the door, he muttered "I'll see you later."

Koy, both perplexed and hurt, turned back to his wife, but she did not move to console him. "He's running with a bad gang," she said. "I told you that on the phone. I can't reach him. You're his father. You have to do something."

There were a number of reasons why Koy had returned to Hong Kong at this time. This was one of them. "I'll try," he said. He frowned.

Koy was unusual among Chinese, and he knew this —he was a man who valued females. He thought females were, or could be important. This was contrary to the Chinese tradition. There were many adages and sayings which perhaps sounded comical to Westerners but which the Chinese took seriously. For instance "It is more profitable to raise geese than daughters." Or, "When fishing for treasures in the flood, be careful not to pull in girls." But Koy respected both his wives and valued all three daughters, whom he intended to educate in the best schools.

Nonetheless, he was not immune to the four thousand years of civilization that had formed him, and the firstborn son was special to every Chinese. This was especially true of Koy because the boy was so late in coming. He had thought for many years that Orchid could not have children —that he might die childless. When she had at last conceived she had wanted to go immediately to an astrologer to ask if the child would be a son, and Koy, wanting to know also, had not dissuaded her. But the astrologer after studying the stars had found only confusion, so she went to another seer who sought the answer in the entrails of a freshly killed duck. The answer there was confusion too, and they had had to wait eight more months to find out. His son's birth had brought him great joy. The problem now was to decide how best to straighten the kid out. Could it be done here? Should Koy bring him to New York, enroll him in some tough school there?

"When are you going back?" Orchid asked.

"I can't stay long in Hong Kong. Business—"

"Take him with you," Orchid urged. "The boy needs a father—badly." After hesitating, she added, "Take me with you. I need a husband." Her eyes dropped to the floor and she added almost inaudibly: "Badly."

"Well," said Koy, "it would not be suitable for you in New York. Still we'll talk about it later, all right?"

Orchid, who was wearing a white linen suit cut in the Western style such as any woman might wear to meet her husband at the airport, excused herself. She wanted to change before dinner, she said. Left alone, Koy pushed through the scarlet satin curtains that hung in the doorway and entered the principal room, and to his surprise it was just as he remembered it. The cushions on the carved wooden chairs were covered with the same scarlet satin. The tables were blackwood, and the overhead beams were painted blue and red. Here and there stood statuettes of various household gods and goddesses, and these were the guardians of happiness, money, and long life. On the walls hung picture scrolls of landscapes brushed in black ink upon white silk. The air was sweet to his nose—sweet with perfumes of soaps and oils. The floor was of tile, and latticed windows opened onto a court and onto a round, lighted pool where goldfish swam, their sides flashing in the light like birds in the sun. He turned back into the room. There was a mantelpiece on which stood two high brass candlesticks. Between them hung a painting of the sacred mountain of Wu T'ai, and under it stood a pot of yellow orchids, the imperial color.

It was Orchid who had chosen this house, and its ownership was in her name. Secretly, knowing Koy would not approve, she had consulted a geomancer or *feng-shui* expert before deciding to buy it—she had told him this afterwards. The Chinese believed that the universe was based on the interaction of two opposing forces, Yin and Yang, negative and positive, and that good *feng-shui*—living in a place where the combination of natural forces was harmonious—brought good fortune to a family. And although Koy no longer believed in gods and goddesses, or Yin and Yang —or astrologers—still he was pleased that his wife, when choosing a home, had decided to take no risks that could be avoided.

Koy went through into the next room, which was a kind of chapel. There were a dais and altar at one end on which stood an incense burner with vases of flowers to either side. The wall above was nearly covered with red and gold tablets that commemorated the family dead. If the Chinese made poor colonizers, Koy thought, it was because the wandering souls of their ancestors kept calling them back to pray in front of ancestral tablets such as these.

That night Orchid wore a floor-length satin robe of imperial yellow embroidered with small pomegranate-red flowers. Into her still jet black hair she had set an exquisite piece of jewelry—a small flower of seed pearls that seemed to grow out of leaves of thin green jade. They sat at dinner a long time. Koy could not take his eyes off her. They talked of their son who had been expected to join them, but had not come home. Koy would have preferred a more neutral subject. There were too many problems in his life, and the only one he cared about tonight was this woman opposite him. Tomorrow would be time enough for the others.

The servants padded about on rope-soled shoes that were noiseless upon the tiles. There were eight courses, eight surprises, eight delicious rest periods in which to savor the preceding dish and to imagine whatever might come next. Orchid's cook, in the best tradition of Chinese gastronomy, brought to this dinner the excitement of a sporting event. Each dish was a distinct contrast in color, texture and flavor from all the others, and each was cooked differently, for the first was stir-fried and the next braised, the ones after that steamed, lacquered, salt-baked. These were all rare dishes Koy had loved in the past, delicacies whose ingredients, for the most part, could not be found in New York, or could not be found fresh. Orchid was spoiling him, as she always had, and he remembered how, when they were adolescents, she had known how to find and bring to him the small, yellow-fleshed, sweet summer melons that grew on dung heaps in her village. She would search for them under the leaves, tapping them with her finger, for when ripe they sounded as hollow as a drum, and they would break them open and feast on them together.

Tonight the centerpiece dish was explosive fried lobster. The heat under the lobster and the flavored oils in which it cooked had been increased until the shells were almost red hot, whereupon a cup of cold sauce was poured over them. This caused a near explosion of the shells, allowing the flavored oils to penetrate the flesh, and at the same time creating a new and delectable sauce to which a lightly beaten egg was added in a thin stream. The flesh itself, enhanced and augmented by all of these flavors, was exquisite, and to suck the sauce from the shells was considered one of the peaks of Cantonese gastromic delight.

But by the time the explosive lobster was served Koy and his wife had fallen silent. Neither was much interested in the food. They were concentrated on each other, and the remaining dishes went back to the kitchen largely uneaten.

When the last had been cleared away they sat in silence sipping tea. They could hear the servants trotting through the house making final preparations for the night.

Orchid went upstairs, there to bathe and perfume her body, taking special care of the seven orifices, as any Chinese woman would. Koy remained in the principal room studying the painted scrolls that hung on the walls: bamboo leaves that were delicately drawn against dark rocks, plum blossoms that mingled with chrysanthemums. The precision and delicacy of these paintings pleased him. They seemed to be related to his own life. A powerful painting, like a powerful man, must be informed and controlled from within. Then only may it be called genius.

When Koy went upstairs, he found his wife sitting in front of a dressing table. He watched as she unwound her long black hair and combed it out using a Chinese wooden comb perfumed with the fragrance of a cassia tree.

An hour later, calm at last, contented, they lay in the dark holding each other close.

"I had forgotten what it was like to have a husband," Orchid murmured. This was as close as a proper Chinese woman could come to expressing any emotion related to sexual love. In all the Chinese dialects, the word for tradition and good manners was the same, and sex as a subject had always been proscribed. It could not be discussed between men and women, not even between couples who had been married many years.

"And I had forgotten how skilled you are," said Koy, employing the Chinese euphemism for sexual intercourse, "at the game of clouds and rain."

Orchid clung to him. "Don't go away again," she said. "Stay with me here. There is enough money. You know there is. You need never work again."

This was true, but Koy did not work for money. Poor people worked for money. Rich people worked for something else, and Koy knew this. They accepted challenges. They challenged themselves. Koy himself worked for power and prestige, the gold and silver currency of the man who had everything. Both were ephemeral. Both, therefore, had to be exploited immediately, ruthlessly. He could not stay here in Hong Kong. In addition, he had another family in New York: a younger wife, three tiny children.

"I must go back to New York," he told Orchid. "I can't leave it."

But he wished he had never got involved with any other woman than this one. If only he had not been so lonely. His conduct could be explained of course; it just couldn't be explained away. If only he had not met Betty Eng who, being a fourth generation Chinese-American, had seemed to him an exotic creature such as he had never known before. She had caught him, obviously, in the classic middle-age crisis. She had made him remember his lost youth. He had experienced with her emotions and sensations he had thought he would never know again. His passion had become love—or at least it could no longer be distinguished from love. And all this time it had been impossible to bring Orchid to New York to join him, for the Corruption Commission held her passport, and financial holdings in her name had been blocked. In New York the inevitable had happened: marriage. But when he thought of it now, holding in his arms the first and truest love of his life, Koy felt ashamed.

Orchid's hand lay over his heart. She said: "It is said that contentment is best achieved by not running after it."

"That's true."

. "I don't want to lose you again."

"Nor I you," said Koy, and he knew he meant it.

Orchid knew he meant it too, and in her elation sat

bolt upright on the bed, her hair hanging to her breasts. "What will we do tomorrow?" she cried, as excited as a child. "What will you buy me tomorrow?"

The young girl he had married used to ask him to buy her the coarse sweets street vendors sold, the red sugar cakes, the sesame toffee, the rice-flour dumplings stuffed with sweet bean paste. They had stood in the dusty street eating the stuff. Orchid had spoken in the same voice then, employed even the same phrases, and beside her in the dark Koy laughed because he was so happy. "Tomorrow I'll buy you anything that is in my power to buy you," he said, and pulled her down to him.

OUTSIDE, a short distance up the darkened street, a surveillance truck was parked next to a telephone pole. Wires led from the truck to a junction box high up on the pole. The Chinese detective, who had been smoking a cigarette on the lee side of the truck, cigarette cupped carefully in his hand, ground the butt out underfoot and climbed back into the truck.

At Corruption Commission headquarters, Powers sat across the desk from Sir David.

"I'm told there have been no telephone calls in or out," said Sir David. "I imagine they are tucked in for the night."

"You can give your guys a rest. He's with a wife he hasn't seen for years. He won't budge until morning."

"My detectives are Chinese," said Sir David. "There is no need to relieve them. The Chinese are very good at waiting." He rose stretching, and stepped out from behind his desk. He was still wearing the bush jacket and the short pants. "But I agree with you, there's no point in our staying on here. I think I shall go home to bed, and I suggest you do the same. I'll have a car brought around to run you back to your hotel."

30

WRUNG OUT and cranky, Carol landed at Kai Tak airport and was met by a tall Chinese named Austin Chan, who took her bags and led her out to the street to the bureau car, a green Mercedes, for some reason hurrying her along, briefing her while they walked. Suite at the Mandarin, okay. Sound man, okay. Light man, okay. Camera man, okay. Car, okay. He was like a checkout clerk stuffing groceries into the bag faster than her eye could follow. Was he trying to palm something? If she was smart she would pay attention. It was like too much fine print at the bottom of a contract—suspicious. There was bad news there somewhere. Makeup man, okay, said Chan, beginning tomorrow.

"Tomorrow?" said Carol sharply.

And the network's resident Southeast Asia correspondent was not here. Most unfortunate, Chan said. Had to go out of town. Had to go to Taiwan on a possible story. She would find the flowers he had left for her at the hotel.

The man's absence did not surprise Carol. Bureau chiefs were always furious when she—when any New York talent—invaded their territory, because it seemed to prove that New York wanted a story they had overlooked. They felt they were being criticized and upstaged both. They used to make her life a misery, and sometimes blocked her from the story she was after. Now they didn't dare. Now they usually left flowers, then left town—town in a huff, and flowers out of fear that she might try, once back in New York, to blight their careers.

"What about my interviews?" asked Carol.

Interviews all set up and ready to go, said Chan. But there were problems.

"Problems?"

"It certainly is lucky your plane was on time. The police commissioner can't see you next week. His schedule is too busy. But I was able to get him to set aside time this afternoon. The crew is already there waiting for you."

The police commissioner, whose name was Richard Worthington, represented the longest and most important of the interviews she had come for. Today was Friday. She had asked Chan by telephone to arrange it for early next week, giving her time to prepare for it, and time to talk to Powers about it first. The police commissioner had evidently rejected Chan's request. The bureau chief, had he been here, no doubt could have done better.

"Can't you call him back and put it off till Monday?"

"I'm afraid not."

"Have you explained how important the network is, the exposure we'll give him?"

"Yes, but he said that the only time he had was today."

No American police chief would have posed conditions if offered an interview with Carol Cone. Naturally the one here did not know who she was, and evidently Chan had not managed to get her stature across. And where was that bureau chief?

"I'm to get you to police headquarters on Arsenal Street as fast as I can," said Chan.

This was impossible. "If you think," snapped Carol, "that I'm going to jeopardize my career by going on camera looking hung over, you have another thing coming." But her jeopardy was double. To miss interviewing the police commissioner was to jeopardize the story she had come here for. Her very professionalism was pulling her in two directions at once. And she still wanted to talk to Powers first.

Her bags had been passed to the chauffeur who locked them into the trunk. She slid into the back seat, and was not surprised when Austin Chan took his place up front, where he soon began to converse glumly in Chinese with the chauffeur. Carol was sorry she had snapped at him, and was at the same time convinced she had read his rank correctly. He was the bureau chief's lackey, and the police commissioner, knowing this, had been able to push him around with impunity. Carol began to grow extremely angry at the missing bureau chief.

The Mercedes moved away from the airport, and entered the tunnel underneath the harbor. She was thinking it out, and by the time they drew up in front of the Mandarin had made her decision.

"I'd like you to come upstairs with me," she said to Chan.

As they waited for the elevator she looked about the lobby for Powers, but did not see him. It was just as well; she did not have time really to talk to him, and two minutes in his arms might simply undo her, break the string that held the package together. She was so tired and upset she might start crying again, and the only result of that would be new ravages on her face.

Once in her suite, ignoring the bureau chief's massive bouquet, she marched through into the bathroom and took a good look at herself, tilting her head at various angles. With her hands she moved her hair about. She studied her appearance as critically as she could.

Her eyes were nice eyes, she decided, and they were hardly puffy at all. She did not look all that bad. Given an hour or so in which to bathe, change her clothes and put on makeup, she concluded, she could get through this interview.

Returning to the sitting room, she instructed Chan to telephone Commissioner Worthington, and inform him that her plane had just landed. She would be along in about an hour. He was to wait for her. "Be extremely forceful," she advised Chan. "Don't forget you have the network behind you." Closing the door on him, she set the bath water pounding and began to get undressed.

She used up every bit of the hour she had allotted herself. For twenty minutes she lay in the bath, wallowing in hot, hot water. This was followed by twenty minutes on her hair, manipulating like a woman with three hands the blow dryer, the comb, and the hair spray can. The result was like crusty meringue, but every hair was in place and the unnatural stiffness would not show on film.

The final twenty minutes went into work on her face. The foundation went on in layers. It was like repainting a used car. She painted, then buffed, then painted again and buffed again. There was no other way to achieve the gloss she was after. She wanted to look like the newest model in the showroom, as if she had never been used, not once, and she very nearly succeeded. There, not a dent showed. Very lightly she brushed rouge onto her cheekbones—just a hint of it, the barest suggestion, as light as a dusting of sugar on top of a cake. Then the mascara. Then the eyebrow pencil, and the pencil outline of her lips, lines as definite as curbs along a street. She was ready.

In the car she had her notebook on her lap, preparing the interview she meant to conduct. The key line of questioning concerned Koy. She wished she could have talked this out with Powers. At what point did she introduce Koy's name into the interview? Early? Late? She was still trying to decide as the chauffeur steered them in past the sentry post and across the courtyard, and drew up in front of the headquarters building. A Chinese police constable in a green uniform opened the car door.

Upstairs in an interview room that had been prepared for them, Chan introduced her to the members of her waiting crew, all of them Chinese, and about five minutes after that two deputy commissioners walked in, followed almost immediately by Commissioner Worthington himself.

A tall skinny Englishman. About fifty years old. Bald. Not friendly. In fact, downright hostile. Kept referring in the conversation that followed to "you pressmen." Evidently neither liked nor trusted "pressmen." Was hostile to Carol for three reasons, she judged: because she was press, because she was a foreigner, and because she was a woman. A woman's place, to this man, was elsewhere, and the police could do their job much better if civilians, male or female, would mind their own business. Civilians were meddlers.

In major American cities, according to Carol's experience, police chiefs who dared talk this way no longer existed. Modern police chiefs had become as affable one and all as candidates for public office—which was virtually what they now were. They accepted civilian control totally, having no choice. They had learned to stand firm with the public even against their own men. Any other stand, they knew, would get them fired.

Carol was trying to appraise her man so as to judge how this interview should proceed. The camera was not yet rolling, and she was feeling him out. What were his responses likely to be? But he bristled at nearly every question. Triads? The Royal Hong Kong Police Force had them well in hand and any evidence to the contrary was an invention of irresponsible pressmen.

Carol was beginning to enjoy herself. This would not be an easy interview, but she thought it would be a good one. Blinking her eyes, flashing Worthington her warmest smile, she tried flattery: "You certainly are a man of strong opinions. I like that."

But he only stared at her, as if he found her distasteful. Carol was not offended. She was working. Nothing he might do or say could affect her personally.

"Have the Triads been exported to New York?" she asked.

"Rubbish."

"Would you care to elaborate on that?"

"No."

Beside him the two deputy commissioners sat stock still. They had not yet budged in their chairs or spoken one word.

"In New York," said Carol, "it is said that the Chinatown street gangs are made up almost entirely of youths from Hong Kong."

"It is said. Who said? Explain yourself."

"Well, our police department intelligence division thinks so."

"They told you that?"

"Yes."

"What you are seeing there is young hoodlums from China. They may have passed through Hong Kong—illegally, I might add—on their way to New York. But they are not from Hong Kong, they are from China."

"I see," said Carol. She turned toward her crew. "Are you ready to start filming?" she asked. Because the police commissioner seemed to be growing more and more testy. He seemed to be trying to prove to her that she was wasting his time. At any moment he might decide to break the interview off. Carol had made her decision. It was best to get something—anything—on film before it was too late.

"What else do you intend to ask me?" demanded Worthington.

"I thought we might just chat on film for about ten minutes, if that's all right with you."

"I warn you, if you ask any question about points we haven't gone over I shan't answer them."

It was a threat Carol would have to consider. To give herself time, she beamed him another warm, fond smile. There were several questions about Koy she must ask, and the best thing would be to surprise Worthington with them toward the end of the on-camera interview. She mulled this over. His reactions should prove interesting. But suppose, instead of answering, instead of reacting, he just got up and stalked out? Would this cripple her story, or kill it? Could she afford to take such a chance?

"Well, as a matter of fact, there is one other line of questioning I would like to pursue," she said. "Does the name Jimmy Koy mean anything to you?"

Worthington simply stared at her. She set her mouth into a thin hard line and stared back. If this was a contest of wills, she was determined to win it. The man was rude, she thought, as nearly all policemen everywhere used to be in the days when each one was a law unto himself. Except perhaps in outposts like Hong Kong, such cops had proven, like certain species of wildlife, unable to withstand the stresses of modern civilization—the pressures of racial minorities, the Supreme Court decisions, the television scrutiny. They were like those types of organisms that could function only in near-total darkness. They were not complex enough. Without darkness it was impossible for them to reproduce themselves.

Unable to stare Carol down, Worthington spoke. "What do you want to know for?"

"Because he appears to have set himself up as the overlord of organized crime in Chinatown."

"More rumor," snorted Worthington.

"I did my homework, Commissioner," said Carol. "I went to the New York Police Department, to the FBI, to Drug Enforcement. It's more than rumor. It's what the police agencies there believe and are operating on." An exaggeration that Carol covered at once. "Which doesn't make it fact. Fact is what I'm trying to ascertain. I've come thirteen thousand miles to ask you what the facts are as you see them. Now can I have those facts, or not?"

About a minute passed during which they again matched cold stares. Then Worthington, with an elaborate sigh, sent one of his deputies out to get Koy's dossier. When the man had gone, there was silence, and this silence endured. Carol buried her face in her notes, as if studying them. She did not want to stare, or be stared at, any further, and she did not wish to risk damaging the mood of conciliation that had evidently come over Worthington.

She did not know where the deputy commissioner would go, nor what he would do, and did not consider such details important. In fact the man returned to his own office and told his secretary, a Chinese constable, to phone down to personnel for Koy's dossier. At personnel, a second constable received the request, and a third retrieved the actual folder, and hand-carried it back to the deputy commissioner's office.

The entire transaction took less than ten minutes, and was accomplished at no cost at all, except that three Chinese constables now asked themselves why this sudden interest in Koy. Two of them had worked in the Wanchai district when Koy was station sergeant there, and the third had once worked for Sergeant Hung. They would arrange to meet in the hall later, when they would ask each other: what does it mean? An investigation into Koy's activities must be under way, that much was clear. Was he perhaps back in Hong Kong? They would find out. Perhaps they should warn him.

When he had the dossier in his hand, Worthington consented to read Carol certain facts from it: Koy's date and place of birth, date of appointment to the force, commendations won, dates of promotions, date of resignation.

"All this is immaterial," said Worthington. "The man has been absent from the Colony for five years."

"He's here right now," said Carol.

Worthington only stared at her, but the stare had a different quality to it. It contained surprise, and Carol felt for the first time that she had impressed him.

He had closed Koy's dossier and was tapping it with his finger. He looked thoughtful.

"Will you read me those same details on camera?" asked Carol.

"Mind you," said Worthington, "I shan't denounce the fellow. We have laws against that here. The enquiry into his official conduct was not pursued. As far as the Hong Kong authorities are concerned, he can go and come as he likes."

"I'm not asking you to denounce him," said Carol. "I'm asking you to repeat on camera all that you have just told me."

Once again their eyes met, only this time Worthington's right cheek twitched. It was almost a smile. It was an admission that a kind of armed truce existed between them.

It meant, Carol felt, that she had won his respect, and she didn't know why she should care, but she did care. She was thrilled. It meant also that she would leave this office with almost exactly the footage she had hoped for, footage that meant good television, and this was a second thrill. Twice thrilled was perhaps the maximum allowed one human being in one afternoon, and she could hardly wait to meet Powers and tell him what a triumph she had had. They would have dinner together.

And then?

She smiled to herself, feeling suddenly thoroughly confident, thoroughly happy. The night might prove lovelier than the day.

IT WAS past 8 P.M. before Chan dropped her off in front of the Mandarin. Powers had not yet come in. She left him a message that stuck half out of his box. It gave the number of her suite, but not her name. It was signed "An old friend." She did not mean to be coy, but rather wanted to surprise him. She wanted to hear the gladness in his voice, see it on his face. She didn't want it wasted on a piece of paper.

Upstairs she luxuriated in another hot bath, replaying in her head today's footage. She would not see it until she got back to New York, but did not need to. In addition to her interview with the police commissioner she was covered as far as intros and wrap-ups were concerned. She had filmed various versions of each in a number of scenic parts of the city, including one sequence in Koy's old red-light district, and another aboard the ferry boat traveling from Hong Kong Island to Kowloon.

Although she was very pleased with herself, this pleasure began to cool at about the same rate as the water in which she lay, for her phone still did not ring. Soon the bath was almost cold. Should she add more hot? Her toes curled over the faucet—she would not even have to sit up. With an abrupt movement she erupted from the tub, water sluicing off her.

By 9:30, dressed, she was irritably pacing the sitting room of her suite, and growing increasingly hungry. She ordered a meal sent up: minute steak, salad, yogurt. When it came, she signed for it, wolfed it down, and resumed pacing, her irritation rising. Crossing to the phone she checked one last time with the front desk, and was told that her message was still in Powers' box. He had still not come in. Furious, she ordered her message yanked.

In the bathroom she stared again at her face, seeking additional reassurance, but not finding it. She was like a man checking the contents of his wallet. How much was left? How much longer did it have to last? She was really showing her exhaustion now, she decided. Which was normal—she had run the marathon today. It was just as well she wouldn't be seeing Powers tonight. Swallowing two sleeping pills, she went to bed, and slept until 10 o'clock the next morning when she was awakened by Austin Chan's phone call. He was waiting downstairs with the crew. Carol phoned Powers' room, but he had already gone out. The day had just started and she was angry at him already. Don't be such a bitch, she told herself. It's not his fault.

She took her time dressing. Chan and the crew could wait. That's what they were being paid for.

It was Saturday, and she accompanied her crew throughout the Colony filming more scenery: the exterior of a police station, the border with China, the exterior of banks. When she would put the piece together in New York, this scenic footage would run beneath voiceover commentary as she described parts of her story for which no accompanying footage existed—the history of the Triads, for instance, or the structure of youth gangs.

It was an enjoyable enough day, and a profitable one, and it was dusk when Chan again dropped her at the Mandarin. Expectant and excited, she hurried inside, and again phoned Powers' room. He was again absent. This time she left a message that gave not only her room number, but also her name, and when she had mounted to her suite, and had begun once more to pace her room, her eyes filled up with tears of frustration. She did not know how much longer she could stay in this place, nor how long he could. But time was certainly short. Minutes, hours, more than a whole day had been wasted so far. Time continued to be wasted that could never be replaced.

POWERS, meanwhile, had driven with Sir David up into the New Territories to a country restaurant. They stood now in a second-floor office overlooking an outdoor patio where a banquet was in progress. Illumination came from candles burning inside lanterns that hung in the trees. About forty men, all Chinese, sat around a horseshoe-shaped table gorging themselves on delicacies. There had been nine different dishes so far—Powers had counted them—and, as waiters moved forward with the tenth, the man who occupied the place of honor at the head of the horseshoe—Koy—rose to his feet to propose still another round of toasts. From the office, watching and listening through cracks in drawn blinds, they could hear the toast and also understand it, for Koy spoke in English. He spoke too loudly, and with the excessive care of the man who knows his wits are addled. He was so drunk he could barely stand up.

"With true friends," he said, having raised his cup, "even water is sweet enough." Everybody was laughing. "And this is not water." In Cantonese, Koy added the simplest of all Chinese toasts: "Dry cup."

Peering through the blinds, Sir David said, "Our man does not look much like a master criminal at the moment, does he, what?"

"What are they drinking?" asked Powers.

"Probably Moi Tai. It's a distilled spirit. It's almost pure alcohol. Those men down there are old police cronies of Koy's. You're looking at a drunken police reunion. Ever seen one before?"

"A few," said Powers.

"The Chinese say that when a man is drunk his spirit is calm."

But the party itself was not calm. Below them was much boisterousness and hilarity, as each man in turn rose to offer a toast. They were drinking from small lacquered cups. After each toast the cups were emptied, and then were refilled for the next one, as the toast made its way around the table.

"We have no way of knowing what may be going on down there," said Powers, presently. It had become impossible for him to keep the urgency out of his voice. Two days of tailing Koy everywhere, two days of tailing the other ex-sergeants also, had produced neither evidence nor information. Conversations over the tapped telephone lines had been so innocuous and so brief that it was impossible to tell even why Koy had come back here, much less to determine what his future plans might be.

"They could be setting up deals down there," said Powers. "We wouldn't even know about it."

"Try to be a bit less anxious, Captain," advised Sir David. "The Chinese never talk business while eating. Gastronomy is as important to them as to Frenchmen. It's sacrilege to talk business while eating. I have men moving among the waiters, and we'll get their reports later. But I doubt we'll learn very much. What we are looking at is neither more nor less than what it appears to be, what? Same type reunion you have in New York, I expect."

"Police reunions are scary, aren't they?"

"Indeed they are."

"Cops are scary. They all have guns, and they get so drunk."

Koy had risen late each of the two mornings. Coming out of his house with his wife about noon, he had seemed to notice the surveillance trucks—a telephone truck the first day, and a moving van the second—for he had studied them closely, as if aware of what their function might be. However, each time his wife had distracted him, taking his arm and dragging him toward the limousine. The limousine had taken them no place suspicious—to restaurants, to shops, to a cemetery where they left offerings and bits of torn colored paper on the graves of ancestors, and finally to the American consulate on Garden Road where Koy entered alone and where, Sir David was able to learn, he applied for a visa for his son.

Neither Sir David nor Powers had considered this detail significant. Plenty of Hong Kong kids of college age went to college in America.

As for the other former sergeants, all three had moved about the city from bank to bank carrying attaché cases, and it was presumed that they were either depositing or withdrawing cash, presumably the latter. One imagined they were about to buy something, but who knew what. Without knowledge of the total sums withdrawn, one could not even guess. Their business could be completely legitimate. Hong Kong banking laws were strict, Sir David said. Not only was it impossible to learn more without a court order, but such orders were extremely difficult to get.

"Even if you get one," snorted Sir David, "it wouldn't do you much good."

Hong Kong had no currency controls of any kind, he explained. The Colony was blessed with over 900 branches of 105 different banks, whose cashiers cashed drafts for $100,000 or more several times every day in the ordinary course of business, and never looked up. Southeast Asia, according to Sir David, was a cash society. Enormous amounts of cash money were always moving around. The Chinese—who were the preeminent businessmen of Southeast Asia—had not in the past trusted checks. If you wanted to do business, whether to hire a cargo ship, or build an apartment complex, or buy a factory, you most likely arrived with the cash in an attaché case under your arm. It made money impossible to track. It made the job of the police, and especially the job of Sir David's Corruption Commission, extremely difficult.

Powers lifted one slat of the blinds with his forefinger. The flickering lanterns below lit the sweating drunken faces. The men looked as garish as circus clowns, as feverish as men terminally ill. "We are not getting anywhere," Powers said.

"Patience, Captain," said Sir David. "Try to emulate the Chinese a bit, what? Try to be a bit more patient."

Powers said nothing. It was very hard to be patient when his career, and to some extent his life, rode on whatever game certain of those men down there might be playing —a game whose object was to him impenetrable, whose outcome he seemed unable to influence in any way.

"It's getting close to midnight, Captain. Shall I run you back to your hotel?"

The ride back was via super highway, much of it elevated. Sir David sat in his corner, a reading light drooping over his shoulder, thumbing through memos and reports that had piled up during the day, while Powers stared into ten miles of third-floor windows, into small rooms crowded with large Chinese families and much hanging wash.

At the reception desk he was handed Carol's message. It was then midnight. He studied the message and at first did not comprehend it—he thought she must have phoned, which was not so surprising. Then he realized she was here —here in Hong Kong—which was more than surprising. It was astonishing. It was electrifying. His heart began pumping hard, and his hands turned moist, symptoms, he realized, that were more associated with fear than with elation. Did this mean he was afraid of her? Or merely shocked, and after a long day, both tired out and somewhat bewildered. If she was here, what did this mean?

He studied the message again, and did not know what to do about it. He knew he was preoccupied by Koy and the investigation, and thought he wished to remain that way. Carol was a separate problem, one he would have to cope with, obviously, as soon as he returned to New York. But not before. Not here in Hong Kong. Not now. Not right this minute.

And yet he wanted to see her. He could, if he wished, be in her presence in a matter of seconds, and in bed with her, most likely, shortly after that, a prospect that presented itself almost unexpectedly, and left him feeling not only slightly breathless, but also with a sense of wearing too-tight trousers. When he glanced at his watch a second time the hour still read midnight. Carrying key and message toward the elevator bank, he pondered this new equation, this new strain on his life. He should not be surprised that Carol had come to Hong Kong. She was rich, self-indulgent and capricious. She could afford to come here on a whim, and had done so, just to see him, he supposed. What other reason could she have? She wanted him, or said she did. And not just casually—she wished to take him away from his wife, or said she did. What did he mean to do about that?

Powers rode the elevator up and when it reached Carol's floor he stepped out into the hallway. As he walked along searching in the dim light for the correct door number, he was at the same time searching in his heart for a correct course of conduct. He either loved Carol or was infatuated with her—even at forty-six the two emotions were too close together to tell apart—but he had not come to Hong Kong for that, and believed it would be better for them both if he stayed away from her. Since any big decision seemed too big to make right now, he decided on a small one instead. He would rap softly on her door one time, and once only. If she answered, this would mean that their meeting tonight was meant to be. He would not fight what was foreordained. If she did not answer then he would go down two flights to his own room and go to bed. It was the type of game he had sometimes played as a child: he would let God decide.

He had reached Carol's room—when he stared from the number on the message to the number on the door, the two numbers matched. Raising his knuckles, he rapped once—softly—as promised.

No answer. Although he put his ear to the door, he could hear no movement inside, so he rapped again, slightly harder this time.

Still no answer. Turning, he gazed back toward the elevator banks, and tried to will his feet to take him there. But they refused. What to do?

He rapped solidly three times, and on the third knock Carol pulled the door open.

"Oh," she said, "it's you. Come in."

31

SHE WAS dressed in sweater and skirt and wore oversized horn-rimmed glasses, a surprise. He had never seen her in glasses before. He glanced past her into the lamplight at the end of the sofa: papers and clippings littered the cushion, the floor. He had interrupted her studying. Studying what?

"I didn't know you wore glasses."

"When I do the show I wear contacts. Oh, I'm so glad to see *you*." She made the "you" echo. He had noted this before, her ability to make an individual word sound as intimate as a caress. The whole weight of her body seemed behind it. It surrounded him like arms in an embrace.

Powers forgot about the evidence trying to find its way through to him, the pool of light behind her, the strewn sofa and floor. He kissed her mouth, her ears, the point of her chin. The only evidence that counted was her presence here in Hong Kong. She had come 13,000 miles to be with him—any jury would say the same—this famous, rich, beautiful woman who could have anyone, but wanted him. He was terrifically pleased with her and impressed with himself.

"I've been here two days," Carol said. "I was beginning to be afraid I would miss you completely."

Holding her by one hand, he walked half around her, looking her over.

"Two days? Why didn't you—but there was no message."

"I know. My mistake. I wanted to surprise you. What a silly idea. Surprises are for children. I should have realized."

It was quite a long speech. The grinning Powers hardly heard or understood it. He could not stop looking at her.

But at last his attention reverted to the evidentiary litter.

"What are you studying?"

She picked up the Triad booklet and handed it to him. "The Chinese Mafia. Would you like to know how the Triads induct young girls into a life of prostitution? Ask me how."

"Chinese Mafia?"

Powers held the booklet. He examined both covers. He peered down at the headlines on the floor. It was like studying the faces of playing cards, and finding them different from those he was used to. It raised questions. What kind of game do you play with cards like this?

He had two immediate reactions, disappointment— she hadn't come all this way just to see him—and alarm.

"What do the Triads have to do with you?"

"It's for a piece I'm doing. I'm mixing business with pleasure. Am I glad to see *you*."

But this time the word didn't echo. "Business?"

"Sure. I wanted to come to see you, but I saw no reason why the network shouldn't pay for the trip."

Powers' fatuous grin was beginning to dry out on his face. It began to feel caked on, like a mud pack.

"What's this piece all about?"

"About the emergence of a Chinese Mafia in Chinatown, about the gangs, the tongs—and how the root of the problem is here in Hong Kong. It's a good story. Don't you think?"

Powers sat down. There was more to this than one interview with Cirillo. "Please tell me more."

There was no smile on Carol's face now, either. As she sat down on the sofa facing him, she looked thoughtful.

"I mean," said Powers, "Your story parallels my investigation. When it airs will it compromise my investigation? That's what I ask myself." And what about compromising his career?

Carol shook her head firmly. "That won't happen."

"The network will want to run it. Right away. Suppose my investigation isn't concluded by then? Do you think the network will hold back for that reason? I don't."

Carol carefully set the Triad booklet down on the end table. "I don't see where my story compromises your investigation in any way."

"Well, I think it might."

"Listen, in New York I interviewed a lot of people. I mean, it's my story. I did a lot of work on it. It's not exclusively yours. I mean, you don't own it."

"It's a criminal investigation."

"I don't see what you are getting so upset about," said Carol.

"How did you get on to it in the first place?"

"You told me about it, didn't you?"

"That's right. And where did I tell you about it?"

"I don't remember."

"Yes you do. It was in bed. Don't you think that when you use bedroom talk, you violate a confidence?"

"This is my story. I earned the right to it. I got machine-gunned in a restaurant, and after that I did the work."

"How bad is this thing?" said Powers. "Who did you go to see in Chinatown, before you came here?"

"I tried to see Mr. Koy, but—

"Koy? Who told you about Koy?"

"You didn't, that's one sure thing. You can't blame that on bedroom talk. I found out about Koy on my own."

Powers had begun to feel frantic. He was being crowded by several disasters at once. "All you've done is warned Koy that he's the subject of an investigation."

"I haven't warned him of anything of the sort. I

haven't seen him yet. I'm going to try to see him here Monday or Tuesday."

"Don't you go near Koy," shouted Powers. "If he finds out he's being investigated, you're liable to wind up in the South China Sea."

Carol tried for a jaunty laugh. "You're exaggerating now, he wouldn't dare. My network—"

"Your network wouldn't be able to do a goddamn thing about it. They wouldn't know where to start looking. That's what the word disappear means. No trace. For all they would know, you ran off to India or somewhere with one of your many lovers to contemplate your karma."

"I don't have many lovers."

"Oh no?"

"Is that what's bothering you? Are you jealous? For someone who's jealous, you don't behave very possessively toward me, if you want my opinion."

"I'm not jealous. You took information you learned in bed and you're using it against me. If that's not a betrayal I don't know what is. Who have you interviewed here in Hong Kong?"

"Well, the police commissioner yesterday—"

"You didn't go to the police. Oh God."

"Sure. Why not? Didn't you? Who else was I supposed to go to?"

"This is the most corrupt police department in the world. Some constable will tell Koy—has probably already told Koy. They'd sell him the information if nothing else. It isn't enough you want to get yourself killed. You want to get me knocked off too. Jesus Christ, how could you?"

"I didn't know," said Carol in a small voice.

"And what about my wife?" cried Powers. "What about my marriage?" He was pacing and fuming. "Have you thought about me at all? Have you considered what my wife is going to think when she sees you presenting this story on television? Her husband goes off to Hong Kong, and you go off to Hong Kong, and we come back with the same 'story,' as you call it. Do you think she's stupid? Do you think she can't put two and two together?"

"If you want to know the truth," Carol shouted, "I couldn't care less what your wife thinks."

"I know," said Powers. "I know." His voice had dropped almost to a whisper. "If you ruin my marriage, I'll never speak to you again. If you ruin this investigation, same thing. My whole career rides on this investigation. Don't you realize that? Did it never occur to you?"

"I intended to talk to you before I did anything here. I just couldn't find you in time, that's all," said Carol. "I still say it's my story as much as yours. I earned the right to it. Where are you going?"

Powers strode toward the door. He yanked it open. "I'm going somewhere to try and think this thing out."

"You go out that door, and—"

"Right," said Powers, and stepped out into the hall and slammed the door shut behind him.

Waiting for the elevator he stood with knuckles pressed into his temples on both sides, pressed hard. He wanted to scream or to weep, but did not do either. There was still a chance this wouldn't get back to Koy. There was still a chance it wouldn't get back to Eleanor. Not much chance in either case, but some. He knew he would get little sleep this night.

HIS PHONE had just rung, waking him up. The sun came through the glass doors and stung his eyes.

"Did I wake you?"

"No."

"Have you had breakfast yet?"

"No."

"How about meeting me in the coffee shop? We'll have breakfast together."

Silence.

"Look," said Carol, "I'm sorry about last night. I'll meet you in the coffee shop in thirty minutes, okay?"

After a pause he heard himself say: "Okay, thirty minutes."

When she came into the coffee shop her face, in the early morning light, looked doughy. She can't have slept much either, thought Powers. His anger and fear had passed in the night. This morning the story did seem as much hers as his. As she said, she had been machine-gunned; this did seem to give her certain rights. She had not set out to hurt him, and perhaps had not done so. Law enforcement was no exact science. One learned to be fatalistic about it. Cases seldom went according to plan. Carol might even have supplied the pressure to break this one wide open. It was possible, or so he told himself.

At any rate, she seemed contrite, and this pleased him. What's done was done. He didn't want to fight with her. Their lives were bound together, were as inextricably intertwined as coarse-fibered rope—you could not pick the strands apart no matter how you tried. They belonged together, at least today. And by sticking close to her he could keep her from going near Koy.

"What are you doing today?"

"Nothing," she said. "Today is Sunday."

"We could go sightseeing."

"I did a lot of thinking in the night," she said. "From now on we'll just be friends, okay? I'm not going to go to bed with you anymore."

"More coffee?" said Powers, and poured it out. It was amazing—she surprised him constantly.

"Because I'm just not in love with you anymore," said Carol. She was buttering a piece of toast. "It's over."

"Fine," he said. "You're not in love with me anymore." He was amused—this was the way teenagers talked.

"I've already been sightseeing."

"We could go shopping."

"Yes, we could go shopping," conceded Carol. "I haven't done any shopping yet.

They nodded at each other. They flashed each other tentative smiles, the way teenagers did, and Powers asked his teenaged question.

"How come you aren't in love with me anymore?"

She responded briskly, as if she had feared he would never ask, as if she had rehearsed her lines in advance. She responded around mouthfuls of toast. She considered herself a special person, she said, and began enumerating her virtues. She was more intelligent, better looking, and more successful than other women. Any man ought to be proud to have her, and to consider himself lucky. She did not have to accept second-best at anything. She was also a woman who, when she loved a man, gave everything, held back nothing. She loved totally, and expected to be loved back in the same way. But Powers didn't prize her enough, and as a result the flame of love had extinguished itself inside her. It had gone out.

She spoke of herself as if describing someone not present. She spoke matter-of-factly, and she did not sound immodest to Powers, since everything she said about herself was, to him, true. But he was distracted by the thought that he could never have spoken of himself this way, probably because he had been raised to hold modesty as one of the most admirable and also most manly of virtues. And partly because he simply did not think of himself in such terms anymore. Only young people were forever contemplating and measuring their virtues and their faults, because they were uncertain of where they stood in the world. Whereas Powers knew where he stood or at least imagined he did. He considered himself neither a good man nor a bad one. He did not think of himself often at all and, when he did, saw himself as one compelled by background, by training, and now to a large extent by inclination, to act in certain ways. If some woman—if Carol—chose to fall in love with him, this to Powers was startling. It was not something he had earned or deserved. It was purely and simply a miracle. Love was a miracle. And if he had been under the sway of Carol Cone for so long, it was partly because somehow such a miracle had taken place between them. It was this state of love between them, this miracle, that so captivated him. Of course the miracle was all bound up in the apparent perfection of the woman herself, but basically it was the miracle rather than the woman that he found so difficult to let go. He knew he had fallen in love for the last time. It would never happen to him again.

Carol, he realized, was still explaining why their relationship, being no longer satisfactory to her, had changed. She liked Powers very much, and was sure she always would. She was simply no longer in love with him. If he wished her to believe that his feelings toward her were stronger than she had supposed, then he should prove it. He should divorce his wife and marry her.

"Carol, that's not what you want," Powers said. "If I did that, you'd run a mile." Having perceived a good deal in the last few minutes, he felt surprisingly calm. The miracle was either there or not there. Neither one of them could change that, whatever she might think or say. Her words, far from threatening him, only fascinated him more.

She was not trying to break up his marriage, Carol said. A good marriage could not be broken up by her or anyone else. If his marriage, or anyone's marriage collapsed, it was a failed marriage already. Perhaps his own marriage was over and he didn't realize it yet. She had had some experience in the matter. "It's happened to me twice before," she said.

"What's happened to you twice before?"

"Two marriages ended over me." Had he detected a note of triumph in her voice? Was she bragging?

"You mean two husbands got divorced? But they didn't wind up married to you."

"I seem to have the misfortune to keep falling in love with married men. I never promised I would marry either one if they got divorced. I'm not promising you either. If you want me, get divorced, and we'll see."

This conversation ought to be traumatic to me, Powers thought. Why isn't it? And then he realized—or thought he did—that the miracle, for the moment at least, no longer existed. He was free at last to walk away, provided he did it quickly.

"Finish your coffee," he said. "And let's go see the

shops." He was smiling, and somehow felt quite happy. He felt he was very close to discovering one of the central mysteries of life. Could the miracle come back again? He did not know and could only wait to find out.

They walked along Gage Street through an outdoor market choked with stalls, with cart and pedestrian traffic. The street was narrow. The buildings pressed in from both sides. The stalls were pushed out to the curbs, all neatly stacked with produce they could not name: chive shoots, angled luffa, flowering white Chinese cabbage, matrimony vine, leaf custard. Ducks, pigeons and other birds hung by the feet at eye level, necks dangling, and at the curbs stood washtubs in which food fish swam lethargically. It reminded Powers of Mott Street in Chinatown, except that it was even dirtier, even more crowded. The air reeked of rotten food, and sudsy rivulets ran in the gutters. As they moved through the market, they listened to the voices of hawkers, watched vegetables weighed on hand-held balances, watched marketing women prod the fruit, prod even the live fish held out for their inspection. Above their heads balconies hung off every floor. The balconies were crammed with plants, with birds in cages. Bamboo poles stood out from windows like flagpoles, and bore the universal flag of mankind, drying wash.

They rode the Star Ferry across the harbor to Kowloon, standing on the open deck in bright, warm sunshine, the wind in their faces, as the ferry surged bluntly through busy harbor traffic. They looked down into junks, sampans, motor launches, sailed under the prows of anchored cargo ships.

On the other side Powers phoned Sir David, who had nothing to report. Powers said he would phone in every hour.

With Carol he entered the Ocean Terminal, a vast, two-storied indoor shopping mall. Smart shops. Hundreds of them. Jade, ivory, carpets, porcelains, antiques. Although it was Sunday all were open, and they joined the crowds of people who moved along the corridors staring in at treasures displayed.

"The reason I'm not going to sleep with you any-more," said Carol, "is because I might fall back in love with you. You have no idea how much I've suffered over you at times, and I don't want to go through pain like that again."

"Excuse me a minute."

Spying a public telephone, Powers again dialed Sir David. "What's Koy doing now?"

"What are you doing?"

"Shopping."

"That's what he's doing too. Got his wife with him. Seems to be buying her everything she wants. One thing does seem out of the ordinary. He's making a lot of tele-phone calls. At every shop he asks to use the telephone. They let him, of course. They give him access to a phone we haven't tampered with. He's communicating with some-one. We just don't know who."

"And the other three sergeants."

"Same thing. All three of them are out on the street using the public call boxes."

"Something is about to go down," said Powers.

"Whatever they're setting up, they're doing it very discreetly."

Powers went back to Carol, who took his hand, and they strolled along past jewelry shops, statuary shops, art galleries, shops selling expensive woolens. From time to time, when something particularly beautiful attracted her she gave his hand a squeeze, and pointed like a Chinese woman with her chin. Although she was supposedly no longer in love with him, her attitude today seemed to him no different from what it had ever been, and Powers, as he became more and more confused, found her ever more beautiful, ever more desirable as well, and so became less and less sure of what his own attitude should be.

A Chinese screen inlaid with jade, coral and other semi-precious stones caught Carol's eye. Like any wife, she dragged him into the shop to study it more closely. Four panels. A royal family, or perhaps only a wealthy family, seated in a garden, being ministered to by servants while musicians played. The background was black. Most of the figures were carved out of ivory. Carol asked the price, which was $4,000—a shocking sum to Powers, and he said so. But she pretended to be much taken by this screen. She pretended to consider buying it.

"It's really quite cheap," she told Powers.

"To you, maybe."

"I think I'll buy it." The dealer assured her he could ship it to her house in the States at virtually no extra cost. Where did she live?

Powers could scarcely believe his eyes. She was really going to buy it, and he could not decide why. Because she really wanted it? Because she had that much money to squander? Or was her chief desire to impress him?

As he pondered this last possibility he felt ashamed. What devious motives we sometimes ascribe to others, he chided himself. This came from age. After a certain age it was difficult to trust anyone very much. Nothing was ever precisely what it seemed to be. Human beings saw life in a straightforward manner only up through childhood and adolescence—sometimes even until well into their twenties. But then everything changed, and life was not nearly as pretty anymore, and hardly anything after that remained predictable.

Carol had her checkbook out. He watched her write out the big check. When they left the shop she was hugging his arm.

"Isn't that a super screen?" she demanded. "I mean, isn't it gorgeous?"

What was he supposed to say to this? "Where are you going to put it?"

"In my living room. It will look lovely."

"You mean between the barber chairs, or what?"

She studied him briefly. "I may have to do a little rearranging. Would you like a cup of tea? Let's find a tea shop and get a cup of tea."

They sat down on the terrace of a kind of outdoor café in the center of the indoor mall and watched the crowds stroll by. As soon as they had ordered, Powers excused himself.

"Do you have to call in again?" She had asked no other question about these calls.

"Yes, I better call."

The pay phone was beside a jewelry shop, in whose window lay a gold chain necklace, such as Eleanor liked, bearing a $125 price tag. While waiting for Sir David to come on the line, Powers studied it through the glass.

Sir David had gone to lunch leaving a message: nothing new. Hanging up, Powers entered the shop and bought the necklace. He asked the dealer to gift-wrap it for him, then carried the package back to the table where Carol still sipped her tea, where his own tea was cooling. He handed it over, saying, "I bought you a present."

It was money he could not afford and he felt he was cheating Eleanor, but he had never given this woman anything and he wanted her to have it, whatever might become of their relationship afterwards. Call it only a sentimental gesture, but he didn't see where sentimentality was as monstrous as all that. I want to give her something to remember me by, he thought.

Her reaction surprised him. She was as delighted as a child. She turned the unopened package in her hands, and cried, "I wonder what it could be." She leaned over and kissed him. "Thank you. Do you want me to open it now?"

"Open it," said Powers. "Maybe you won't like it." He had never had much success giving Eleanor presents. Why should he hope for better from this woman here? "Take me out of my misery."

Having exposed the necklace, Carol clasped it to her neck. Her eyes were very bright. She was beaming and she thanked him profusely, turning her back to him so he could fit the chain around her neck. The necklace was beautiful, she told him, and gave him a whole series of kisses to prove it.

He was very pleased with himself, absurdly pleased.

"What do you want to do next?" he asked her.

FEW OF Hong Kong's smart shops faced onto sidewalks. Hong Kong was so crowded, its streets and sidewalks so congested with cars and people that it was difficult, if not impossible, for shoppers to stroll browsing past shop windows. Railings even were necessary along the curbs to keep the pedestrians from spilling out into the street and choking off the cars. People couldn't walk around other people. There wasn't room. The flow had to keep flowing. In many cases it was impossible even to cross streets except by underpasses or by bridges that linked major buildings in the central district. As a result the best shops were not at street level at all, but facing onto mezzanine corridors in office buildings, and it was possible to walk from building to building, to walk a mile or more, along corridors lined with shops on both sides.

In one such shop, in a skyscraper known as Prince's Building, Koy sat on a straight chair in the manner of husbands the world over, while Orchid tried on expensive dresses. She would disappear into the changing booth for a moment, then reappear wearing still another unique creation.

"Which do you like better?"

"The first one." But Koy was preoccupied and glanced again at his watch.

"I think I like this one."

Koy gave her an indulgent smile. "Take them both. Excuse me, I have an appointment. Try on a few more. I'll be back in a few minutes."

Moving out into the corridor, he strolled briskly along toward the elevators. A man and a woman, who had been gazing into the antique-shop opposite, turned and followed him. All three waited for the elevator together. No one spoke. When the doors had opened, all three boarded. Koy punched the button for the seventh floor, and the other man reached over and punched eight. As the elevator climbed, all three stared straight ahead.

Koy got off at seven, and the couple one floor higher. Quickly they found the fire stairs, and descended one flight, opening the door carefully and listening for footsteps. It was

Sunday. There were not likely to be many people on this floor, and they were being very, very careful. After waiting about five minutes and hearing nothing, the woman withdrew sunglasses from her handbag, and a white silk scarf which she tied around her neck. She had been carrying a handbag and a package, and she handed both to the man. Her appearance was now sufficiently altered, she judged, that Koy, if she met him, would not notice her. In any case, it was the best she could do. She was an agent of the Corruption Commission, and she stepped out into the corridor and walked along trying to decide which office Koy might have entered.

AT DUSK Powers and Carol sat on the patio of a restaurant on top of Victoria Peak watching the sun go down over islands set like jewels into the silver surface of the South China Sea. Presently the sea turned black. They watched the lights come on all over Hong Kong.

It had been for Powers a splendid, lazy Sunday spent following Carol around just as, at home, he might have followed Eleanor around. He found he was as totally comfortable in Carol's presence as in Eleanor's, as if he had been married to her twenty-three years too. There was no tension between them, sexual or otherwise. In fact, there were moments—even hours at a time—when he accepted her as his wife, in the deepest, most spiritual sense, because there was no other role into which, in his experience, she seemed to fit. He forgot that he had not known her very long, forgot that he exerted no ownership over her, nor she over him, forgot that in truth their relationship was a tenuous one, and as brittle as an icicle or a crystal glass. And he sensed all through the long afternoon that she felt the same as he, as if it was absolutely right that they be together, as if they had always been together, and would always remain together. They did not speak of Carol's story or Powers' case and this was not because the subject was a dangerous one, but rather because they were concentrated on each other and on discovering all the wonders that this day might have to offer them.

From the peak they watched the night deepen. As individual points of light began to glow like stars on the ships and boats in the harbor, it was impossible for Powers to believe Carol's declaration that she was not in love with him anymore. It was equally impossible for him to believe that he was not in love with her either. Nor could he imagine a time when she would not be part of his life.

When it was completely dark they ordered dinner. A famous American actor and his wife had sat down at the next table. The actor, recognizing Carol, nodded to her, and she nodded back. He played a New York cop every week on television and Carol suddenly whispered in Powers' ear that she intended to introduce the fraud to a real cop, himself. They deserved each other, she said, and giggled.

And so a conversation sprang up between the two tables. The actor began to talk to Powers cop to cop, talking tough, describing his experiences in New York station houses, larding his anecdotes with police jargon. Powers kept nodding politely. The man sounded exactly like a cop, which he was not.

This guy is ludicrous, Powers thought. But also fascinating.

He became conscious of Carol hanging around his neck, and when he turned toward her she kissed him wetly, thoroughly, on the mouth.

"Hey, your date's getting jealous," she murmured. "How about paying some attention to your date?"

She resumed kissing him, hanging on, a kiss that lasted a minute or more, her tongue in his mouth in the middle of this crowded restaurant. They were making public spectacles of themselves, and Powers did not like it. He felt as uncomfortable as a soaking-wet dog, and wanted to shrug her off.

"Relax," Carol murmured. "No one knows you here. You don't have to be embarrassed. You can do whatever you like, and your date wants to be kissed."

He gave her an uncomfortable grin, disentangled her arms from around his neck, and held both her hands on the table so she could not start again.

A little later she told him, "I think I'm falling in love with you all over again."

"I certainly am glad to hear that," he said. Either he had won her back again or never lost her, and the way was clear now to take her back to the hotel and to bed, which was all he had ever hoped for since early in the day.

But first it was necessary to conclude their dinner and pay for it, and catch a taxi outside that wound slowly down the twisting roads of the Colony. This took time. Time enough for the mood to cool. Powers sensed this. He couldn't tell if Carol did or not.

When he asked for their keys at the desk, he was handed a message to call Sir David.

They went up to Carol's suite where, as soon as the door had closed behind them, Powers took her in his arms, and the kiss this time was a real one, that went on and on, the deepest and most satisfying kiss of his entire life, he thought, for it seemed to him that he had never before known an emotion this strong, a love this intense. The miracle had indeed recurred. Love must be similar to drunkenness, another miracle. If you have been drinking all day, if the residual level of the alcohol is high enough, then all it takes is another swallow and you are floating once more. You are giddy, uncautious, happy. Bizarre behavior becomes automatic.

"Oh, Carol," he said, "I love you so much."

She went and sat down on the bed, took her shoes off, and began massaging her toes. Powers, meanwhile had plucked Sir David's message out of his pocket. He went to the phone and dialed the number.

"We have a man in custody," said Sir David. "Two of my people picked him up this afternoon, shortly after he sold Koy a forged United States residence card—what your Immigration fellows call a green card, I believe. It's in the name of Orchid Koy—Koy's wife. Koy paid for it with cash money out of an attaché case."

"He must be taking her to America," said Powers. He was thinking it out. Koy had had to buy a forged green card because he couldn't bring Orchid to America as his legal wife. His legal wife was the one in New York. To Sir David, Powers said, "Are you obliged to tell our Immigration Department about this?"

"We usually do."

"Can I ask you not to tell them? Can I ask you to let me handle our end of this?"

When he had hung up and turned from the phone Carol, on the bed, said, "What was that?"

"Nothing important."

Carol was still rubbing her toes. "Tell me what it was."

"No, really. It wasn't important. It has nothing whatever to do with your story, and I can't see where it has anything to do with my case."

"Please tell me what it was."

Instead of answering, Powers lifted her upright, embraced her, and began another long kiss. He was conscious of how much shorter she had become, standing now in her stockinged feet. He also realized that she was not responding.

Carol broke the kiss off. "Are you going to tell me?"

Powers became annoyed. "Why don't we just say I'm not at liberty to tell you. That it isn't my information to give away."

They stood appraising each other.

"It's late, and I'm exhausted," said Carol. "I think we both ought to get a good night's sleep tonight, don't you? I'll see you in the morning."

She had turned away from him and begun undoing her dress. Powers thought: I'm certainly not going to beg you to go to bed with me. Not tonight. Not any night. If you want to, okay. If you don't want to, that's okay too.

"When you wake up," he told her, "if you feel like having breakfast, give me a call."

He strode to the door.

"In any case, we'll have dinner together tomorrow night," said Carol quickly.

"Sure."

Slamming the door behind him, Powers walked slowly toward the elevator banks, his mind crowded with musings and emotions, none of which were very clear to him.

32

THE LIMOUSINE waited out front. Koy, who had come
out of his mansion, was about to get into it when he
noticed a car parked up the street. Not a truck today. A car.
But always something. Below him in the sunshine sparkled
the South China Sea. From its surface protruded lumpy
islets that were as irregular, as angular as the carcasses of
wrecked ships. They looked like pieces of cliff that, having
broken off from the mainland, had floated out that far and
then sunk. The view from Koy's gateposts, and from the
limousine that he now stepped into, was spectacular, but he
did not notice it. Watching out the back window, he soon
perceived the probable tail car. It followed him down the
hill. Not the first car, but another. Two cars then—someone
was going to great expense. He watched it carefully. It contained only its driver, a woman, which was unusual, even
imaginative. Or perhaps the only imagination at work here
was his own. Leaning forward he ordered the chauffeur in
Cantonese to make a series of abrupt turns. That the tail car
made no attempt to follow even the first of these turns, was
possibly good news. Possibly bad news, too. Either Koy was
not being tailed at all or more than two cars were involved
—the expense would be astronomical. Which meant that
interest in him originated at the highest level.

Was he being paranoiac or merely shrewd? Koy shook

his head at himself. Sitting back in his seat, he began to scan that day's *South China Morning Post*, one of Hong Kong's English-language newspapers, which the chauffeur had laid out on the seat beside him.

But he could not concentrate on headlines. He was interested neither in world events nor in sordid domestic violence, and this newspaper, like all newspapers, contained very little in between. He was too uneasy to concentrate on printed words, which seemed to him small and exacting, like the claws of birds—too small to grip him. They did not pertain to the profound uneasiness that expanded as inexorably inside his skull as ice. The ice had begun to stiffen not only his thoughts but even his movements. The chill factor no longer produced mere discomfort: it was becoming real pain.

Koy kept glancing out the rear window, but there were many cars behind him now, too many to tell if some other tail car had picked him up. As his car moved over the spine of the island and down the other side, he blamed Orchid—he had allowed himself to be distracted by his wife. She had caused him to ignore signals. His perceptions had not been acute enough. As soon as they entered city traffic, he ordered the driver to pull up beside a sidewalk call box. The driver had to park half on the curb to let the traffic behind them get by. Koy didn't care—that was the driver's problem. He jumped out and dialed a number at Police Headquarters. As he listened to it ring he concluded that he should not have lingered in Hong Kong. He might have done his business and been gone in a matter of hours. He should have insisted on it. It would have been wiser, and safer as well.

"Go out to a secure line, and call me back," said Koy, as soon as his party came on the line. He read his own number off the dial and broke the connection.

Above five minutes passed before the incoming call made Koy jump. He was already nervous, and inside the call box the bell had gone off like a fire alarm. Speaking in Hakka in measured, deliberate tones, Koy gave certain instructions

—he wanted to know who was interested in him and why—and then hung up and got back in his car.

A short time later the limousine drove up in front of the Hilton Hotel on Garden Road opposite the Peak Tram Building. Koy walked inside and straight to the reception desk, where he engaged a sitting room for the day, paying in advance. Koy almost always paid cash money in advance, ending the transaction then and there, leaving little record, or none. Cash, however heavy the sum, left no finger- or footprints, it had no memory, no voice. It could not give evidence in court. Taking his key, he turned away from the desk and carefully eyeballed the lobby, but picked up nothing. This was only to be expected. There was no way law enforcement—whichever agency it might be—could have known about today's meeting in advance, or planned for it. Yet why, as he entered the elevator was his discomfort so acute? What was he reacting to? What had set him off? He did not know, and wanted to believe he was imagining things, but instinct told him his anxiety was real. There was somebody moving around the outer rooms of his life, bumping into furniture and walls, somebody carrying heavy square objects, bags of cumbersome tools. Inevitably, this person or persons had made nicks in the wood, in the plaster. Koy wanted proof. He was like a man down on his hands and knees searching for these nicks.

Upstairs he waited at the window staring down at the harbor. He watched a Star Ferry boat start out toward Kowloon. Green. Two decks. There were two more coming the other way. A Boeing jetfoil crossed toward the harbor exit en route to Macau, the Portuguese enclave forty miles down the coast. The jetfoil, a kind of railroad car on the hull of a boat, and powered by jet aircraft engines, was still riding low, leaving a heavy wake. But even as Koy watched, its jets came on hard, and it began to lift out of the water. In a moment it was skimming along high on its ailerons, its speed building up to sixty miles an hour.

There came a knock on the door, and Koy crossed to open it. Two of the three former station sergeants entered the room.

"Our other brother is not here yet?" one asked in Hakka.

"We'll wait for him," answered Koy.

DOWNSTAIRS POWERS and Sir David, both looking agitated, came into the hotel and moved directly toward the elevators.

"We have the phones covered, of course," Sir David said over his shoulder. "But we have no bug inside the room. We had no idea this meeting had been set up, so how could we?"

"Sooner or later they'll call down for food." Powers said. "Can we send a bug in on the tray?"

"Indeed we can."

BY THEN the conference upstairs had been underway more than thirty minutes. The three executive vice presidents were reporting to the chairman of the board. The first of them, Sergeant Woo, whose home base now was San Francisco, had made arrangements for moving the oversized mail bags on and off post office trucks operating between Hong Kong central and Kai Tak airport. The false mailbags themselves had been manufactured and stenciled. The first shipment of cash to Bangkok had been sewn into certain of them, and would go out later today; the rest of the money would follow over the next three days. The return shipments of raw morphine bricks should begin reaching Hong Kong a day or two after that, assuming that no hitch developed in the Thailand end of the operation.

"How many Hong Kong postal employees are involved?" asked Koy.

"The minimum," said Sergeant Woo. "The superintendent with jurisdiction over the trucks, and one truck driver."

"And how many members of our organization here are involved?"

"Again only two. One underboss—you know him, it's Chang Man Bun—and one soldier."

The second ex-sergeant, whose name was Li, had made arrangements for secreting the merchandise as it arrived inside the Crown Colony. "I decided to break it down into five loads," he said. "Each load goes to a different underboss. Each one knows only where his own load is hidden. That way, no single leak can result in our losing all of it. Each of them has been ordered to bring his own load forward in a specified order."

"Where will they hide it?" asked Koy.

"That's up to them, just as long as it's dispersed." This was acceptable to Koy. There were many places. Part would be stashed on outlying islands, he supposed. Part would be hidden in junks in the harbor. Part would be kept in safe houses here and up in the New Territories. He nodded his approval. Sergeant Li had recently established himself in Vancouver, and a good deal of the merchandise would enter the New World there. Vancouver had a large Chinese community, and was isolated enough so that pressure from law enforcement was less onerous there than in, say, New York or San Francisco.

About then Koy passed around menus, and the conference halted while all four men studied them. They decided on only four dishes—this was lunch, not a banquet—plus two pots of tea, and Koy phoned down their order.

The third ex-sergeant, whose name was Lao, and who now operated out of Boston, had been charged with setting up laboratories in Hong Kong to refine the Thai morphine into No. 4 heroin. There were many mountainous, isolated corners of the New Territories where danger of interruption was slight, and where a laboratory might be established in any shed or out-building. However, such laboratories sometimes drew attention to themselves. Heroin, being the chemically bonded synthesis of acetic anhydride and morphine, was difficult to work with. In the hands of unskilled chemists the stew had been known to explode. In addition, once it started to bubble it became putrid, it stank. It smelled like a corpse that had been exhumed for its bones too soon. If the wind was right, the ghastly odor could drift considerable distances. Therefore it made more business sense, Lao had decided, to set up his labs on junks, and to synthesize the heroin offshore. At sea, odor ceased to be a problem, coastal patrols could be observed approaching from a great distance, and chemists, with a hundred fathoms of water under them, would be inclined to work with utmost care. Also the heroin, once refined, could be off-loaded directly onto the anchored cargo ships that would carry it to its destination—about a third of it to Vancouver, the rest to Amsterdam for transshipment. Amsterdam had no drug problem of its own, and its customs authorities, therefore, were easier to circumvent. In any case, Amsterdam was Sergeant Hung's problem. To minimize risks further, Sergeant Lao concluded, he had engaged three separate junk captains, none of whom knew of the existence of the other two.

There came a knock at the door, and Lao, who was closest, opened it to admit a waiter pushing a rolling luncheon table whose tablecloth reached almost to the floor. The four ex-sergeants stood close to the table as the waiter raised its sides, removed the covers from the tureens it bore, and presented the bill to Koy, who again paid cash. Chairs were brought forward, and as soon as the waiter had left the room the four men sat down to eat.

SIR DAVID had set up his command post in a room three doors down the hall on the same floor, the closest unoccupied room available. Powers, Sir David and a number of other men stood around a Chinese technician in headphones, who sat monitoring a console.

"All right, the bug is in there," said Sir David. "It's merely stuck to the bottom of the table. It's the best we could do. We didn't have time for anything else."

The technician at the console said, "The bug is working. I can hear the sound of the chopsticks."

"But no conversation," said Powers.

"The Chinese rarely converse when eating," said Sir David. "I've told you that before."

Powers was pacing. "New York cops are always talk-ing with their mouths full."

The technician held up the earphones. "Would you like to listen, sir?"

Sir David pressed one earphone to his head. "He's right. You can hear the chopsticks. When their conference resumes, assuming they are indeed plotting something ne-farious, we should be able to hear every word."

Powers became as hopeful as a fan whose team had reached the one-yard line. There was not much further to go. The touchdown was tantalizingly close. All he needed was mention of a single specific drug shipment that could be intercepted entering the United States. His own testimony would put Koy in the room down the hall, Koy's voice on this tape would tie him in with the shipment, even if he never came close to it personally, and American conspiracy laws would put him away for twenty-five years—and if the voices of the other two American-based ex-sergeants ap-peared on the tape, they would go with him. Powers believed himself on the brink of proving his theory, of decapitating the Chinese Mafia in America with a single stroke. He would have amply justified his trip to Hong Kong, and no one, after that, would be able to stop his advancement to the top of the NYPD.

It all depended on the next few minutes.

Suddenly from the speaker attached to the console, came a hollow banging. Inside the earphone the sound must have reverberated, stinging Sir David's eardrum, for he held the earphone away from himself and stared at it distaste-fully.

"What was that?" asked Powers.

The technician said, "It sounded like someone knock-ing on the door. The waiter, maybe?"

Koy had stepped out into the hall. Standing there were two plainclothes police constables known to him.

"You were right," reported the older of the two, and he told what he had learned. An investigation of Koy was in progress, and the police force had known nothing about it until last Friday when an American television woman had appeared at headquarters. After she left the building the police commissioner had caused inquiries to be made, and the investigation had been traced to the Corruption Commission, which appeared to have committed itself to a major effort. A Captain Powers from New York was in Hong Kong, and was behind it.

"Captain Powers," murmured Koy, and a Chinese proverb came to mind: He who stands on tiptoe does not stand on firm ground. Which seemed to describe Powers' situation in Hong Kong exactly.

Koy now asked a number of brief questions. Where was Powers staying? Where was the woman staying? What was her name? What was the relationship between them? When Carol's name was given him, Koy recognized it, and was both surprised and impressed. The relationship between them, he was told, was exactly what one would expect. Good, thought Koy, that could be useful. But he had been surprised a second time.

Having stepped back into the room, he found his briefcase, and withdrew a sheaf of bills. Returning to the door, he handed the money to the older constable. He was again paying in advance. "Stand by the phone number we gave you," he said. "You will receive your instructions." After dismissing them, he advanced on the luncheon table.

"What was that?" asked former Sergeant Li.

But Koy did not answer. He thought he saw what must be done, but it was best to think it out a short time longer, because the cautious, as Confucius had taught, seldom err. Meanwhile Koy had begun stirring through the tureens with his chopsticks, through the bowls of rice, and he knew what he was looking for. It was also Confucius who had described the most admirable man as the one fond of adjusting his plans. Koy would have to adjust his own. By now he was down on his knees peering under the table. After a moment he reached in underneath it, and his hand came out holding Sir David's bug. He held it gingerly between thumb and forefinger as if it was something foul, something contaminated. The other three men stared from the bug to Koy, who wore an expression of extreme disgust, and who dropped the bug like a dead frog into the tureen of sweet and sour pork, allowing it to sink amid the mushrooms and water chestnuts that floated in the sauce. Death would be from drowning, but it would take too long. Impatient, Koy took up a bowl of rice, and upended it on top of the bug, mashing it down, and the bug died, killed in the landslide.

The other ex-sergeants had risen to their feet. In silence all four men put their suit coats back on, clipped their briefcases shut, and trooped out of the room. Koy closed the outer door as soundlessly as possible, and they virtually tiptoed down the hall to the elevator.

IN SIR DAVID's command post three doors away, there was consternation. Powers, Sir David and all the listening detectives had crowded around the console.

The technician took his earphones off and looked up. "The bug has gone dead."

"Did they find it, or what?" asked Sir David.

"I don't know, sir," said the technician. "We may have lost power for a moment. I suppose there's a chance it may come back on."

Across the room the phone rang. Sir David went to it. As he listened, his face darkened. "I see," he said, and replaced the instrument in its cradle. Turning to the other men, he said: "All four of our Dragons have just left the hotel. They went across the street to the Peak Tram. They're now on their way up the mountain. I guess we can pack it in here."

"This proves it, doesn't it?" cried the anguished Powers. "This was the important meeting. This is what all of them came to Hong Kong for. We had our chance to find out what was going on, and we blew it."

DURING THE first part of the ride up the mountain, Koy was silent, and the other three ex-sergeants did not disturb him. The car rose up above the great white palace that was the governor's mansion, and entered the steeply pitched forest that covered the mountain like a fur coat. The terminal building, with its tiers of restaurants, stuck out at the top like a bald head. The heavy grinding noise of the climbing tram seemed to submerge not only conversation, but also thought, but presently Koy turned to the other three men. It seemed obvious to him, he said, that the investigation was focused on him personally. It was certainly not any concerted action by several branches of law enforcement grouped together. The Royal Hong Kong Police Force had known nothing about it. Customs did not appear to be involved. There was no sign of the American drug agency. It would appear to be the work of only one man, and on a kind of free-lance basis. It would appear that this Captain Powers had managed to interest the Corruption Commission in Koy's activities, but no one else. And the commission did not even have jurisdiction over Koy here in Hong Kong, much less any chance of pursuing the case abroad. This being the case, they should proceed with their plans, and as the tram continued to mount they discussed the allocation of capital expenses, the division of profits, and ironed out other final business details.

At the Peak they disembarked. A series of trails led out along the ridge line, from which splendid views spilled downhill in all directions. The four men walked along one of these trails and conversed in Hakka in low voices, the Chinese tones rising and falling. Powers, on the other hand, seemed a serious problem, Koy said. If allowed to return to Chinatown, might he not continue the investigation that had brought him this far? If so, perhaps it was best if he did not leave Hong Kong. Perhaps his investigation should be brought to an end here and now, and Captain Powers with it. The television woman should perhaps accompany him on his brief final journey, suggested Koy, as otherwise she might raise too strident an alarm. If both vanished there might be no alarm at all for some time. Even then nobody could be sure what had happened to them. It would seem to many that perhaps the lovers had run off together to Tibet or the French Riviera.

This last was no facetious remark. Koy was not trying to be funny, and no one laughed. The others were in agreement with his reasoning and they began to consider how to implement it.

"It must be done quietly and efficiently," said Koy. "There must be no struggle, nothing to attract the eye of witnesses. We are not trying to start an investigation, but to end one. Do I make myself clear?"

"Very," said Sergeant Lao, and the other men also nodded.

Discussion lasted some time longer. There were a number of possible roads to the same goal.

"I wish Hung were here," said Sergeant Woo, and he sighed almost wistfully. "Hung had a real gift for this type of thing."

"I regret having to do this," said Koy.

All four sergeants would fly out of Hong Kong that afternoon, Koy decided, and the job would be done that night, after they had gone. He charged Sergeant Lao with transmitting the orders. The two police constables who had brought news of Powers to the hotel room were standing by, and could be relied upon. He suggested using the sampan of a man named Hsiang Yu, who had done such work before, and was reliable also.

The trail they were walking on ended in forest. They had come to the end of it, and as they turned and started back Koy commented thoughtfully that one other change in plans seemed mandated. The first shipment of merchandise had best be expedited. Fifty kilos of bricks should come into Hong Kong in tomorrow's mail bags. It should be converted immediately in an improvised laboratory set up somewhere in the New Territories, and the merchandise should go out by air to Sergeant Hung in Amsterdam as soon as possible after that, mixed into whatever innocuous cargo came to hand.

Koy paused, thinking it out. Hung would keep some for distribution in Europe. He would split the rest into packages and forward them separately to each of the others. Koy's own portion, being much the biggest, would have to travel by ship the rest of the way—four or five days. He wanted it in New York within ten days at the most.

Former Sergeant Li was shaking his head negatively —there was no mailbag scam set up to protect the merchandise after Hong Kong, he said. To move it to Amsterdam by air was far more risky than by sea.

Koy overruled him. Their various investors were getting impatient, he said. His own were. He assumed theirs were too. And now the imminent disappearance of Captain Powers would present new problems. It would cause a commotion. It would probably be necessary to suspend all operations for as long as this commotion lasted; if they did not want trouble from their investors, they had best distribute some profits before the commotion started.

Koy glanced around, meeting the eyes of each of them. No one spoke. There were no dissenting votes. The motion had carried unanimously.

"Good," said Koy.

The four men returned to the cable car and started down the mountain.

33

POWERS SAT with Carol at a window table in the restaurant on the roof of the Mandarin Hotel. The view, like most Hong Kong views, was lovely—the blaze of lights in Kowloon across the harbor—but Powers had his back to it, and his gaze was turned inward anyway. He saw very little except himself at the moment.

Carol put her hand over his. "Do you want to tell me about it?"

After hesitating, Powers said, "Koy flew out of here this afternoon." The other three sergeants had flown out also, according to Sir David. The summit conference was over. Since Carol knew nothing about any summit conference, he kept these details to himself.

"What does that mean to you?" she asked. Studying his face, she answered her own question. "Not good, eh?"

Powers, who had scarcely eaten, stared into his plate. "No, not good."

"You come all this way, and you've got nothing to show for it. Nothing to take back with you."

"That's right."

"I at least go back with some film."

Powers did not respond. He had only a few items of information that he saw no way to use, and that would not impress Duncan or the PC at all.

"You ought to quit that police department," said Carol after a moment. "You're not appreciated there."

"Quit? And do what?"

"You're a lawyer. With twenty-three years police experience. There's a law firm somewhere that would love to have you. Probably more than one. And they'd pay you two or three times what the police department pays you. You could get six figures easy."

Instead of considering this idea, Powers decided to try a joke. "When I report back to headquarters, they'll ask me what I accomplished in Hong Kong, and I'll say: 'I certainly learned to use chopsticks better.'" Forcing a smile, he waved the chopsticks in his hand. "I've become a real artist with chopsticks, don't you think?"

"I really could go for you," Carol said, and he looked across into her fond and loving smile.

He did not respond to this remark either, but stirred his food around, at last lifting a shrimp to his mouth, and chewing it silently.

"When will you go home?" Carol asked.

"Tomorrow, I guess. There's no point staying around here. Time to go back and take my medicine."

Carol said tentatively, "Why don't we stop in Hawaii? We could spend a couple of days on Maui. Have you ever been to Maui? Maui is beautiful."

They gazed at each other.

"Come to Maui with me," said Carol. She put her hand over his again. "I'll sleep with you there."

Powers removed his hand and took a sip of tea. "Well, that certainly is a very tempting offer."

"How about it?"

He avoided having to answer by signaling the waiter for the check. "I'm so totally depressed at the moment—"

He led her out through the restaurant, past the bar, and into the corridor outside, and there a man waited for them—he approached with deference and flashed his credentials: Detective somebody. A Chinese name that meant nothing to Powers. He wanted to take Powers somewhere.

He looked like what he claimed to be, a used-up, middle-aged detective, a messenger. A Chinese version of Detective Kelly. The New York Police Department was full of detectives just like him. That is, his type rang true to Powers, even though his message did not—or at least not entirely. But Powers was no longer on his guard, no longer alert, only tired, frustrated and depressed.

The middle-aged detective spoke English, sort of. It was possible to make out his meaning, more or less. Police Commissioner Worthington was meeting with Sir David at this very moment, and wished Powers to attend. They had sent the detective to fetch him. The detective had also been asked to invite Mrs. Cone to this same meeting, if he could find her. He was told at the hotel desk he might find her in the company of Captain Powers. Was this lady here by any chance Mrs. Cone, and did she wish to attend the meeting?

The detective didn't seem to care whether Carol accepted the invitation or not, and this rang true to Powers also, putting him further off guard. The detective's job was only to deliver the message.

"Do you mind?" asked Carol. For the sake of her story she was eager to attend this meeting, to learn something more. Powers saw this, though he could not imagine what more there was to learn. At the same time she was pretending to be nice to him. She was pretending that if he wished to go alone she would accept his decision.

"All right," Powers said. "Let's go."

The detective led them downstairs and out through the hotel. In front waited a car with a chauffeur behind the wheel. The car looked like a possible police vehicle to Powers. That is, it looked like a cheap car. It was without ornamentation. He did not really know what Hong Kong police vehicles looked like. In New York he would have been able to read this vehicle—and this detective as well—much more accurately.

He did not like the idea of stepping into a car at night in Hong Kong with two men he did not know. On the other hand, the danger was over, was it not? Koy was gone. The other three sergeants were gone. And he had learned nothing with which he could hurt any of them. If he was not a threat to them, then how could they be a threat to him?

He and Carol slid into the back seat. The detective sat beside the chauffeur up front, and began to converse with him in Chinese in a low voice. There was no sign of tension demonstrated by either. Powers sat back in his corner. Carol took his hand and held it, and he let her. They drove through streets less crowded now than in daytime, though not much. They were driving along the rim of Hong Kong island, with the lights of Kowloon across the harbor, and were proceeding, Powers knew, in the opposite direction from police headquarters. But this did not alarm him either for it was a one-way street. The driver had no choice. Doubtless he was looking for a place to turn and start back.

But instead the car veered inland, and began to climb up over the top of the island toward the opposite side, and Powers felt the first faint twinges of fear, as faint as music from across a lake, as vague as guilt. He tapped the detective on the shoulder and stated firmly, "This is not the way to police headquarters."

The detective, having turned, flashed him a mouthful of grinning teeth. "Not police headquarters," he said. "House. Commissioner Worthington house."

"I see," said Powers, and he sank back into his place, apparently mollified, and hoped he looked relaxed, but his whole body had stiffened, and he watched carefully for whatever would happen next.

When they were quite high, the lights of Aberdeen appeared below. The car began to descend in spirals like an airplane.

"This is the town where the floating restaurants are," said Powers to Carol. His voice sounded normal, he believed. Since no alarm had been given to him, he wished to give none to them. "This is where the boat people live also. Look."

He leaned across her, pointing down on acres and acres of rotting junks moored hull to hull. There was enough light from the sky, enough points of light burning on decks, to show that nearly all were crowded with life. The junks to Powers were the equivalent of Harlem or the South Bronx. They constituted Hong Kong's principal slum. There would be big crime problems in there.

The car had slowed, causing Powers to glance forward—he found himself looking into the same mouthful of teeth as before, except that, even as he watched, the middle-aged detective lifted a steel cigar to his lips. Except it wasn't a cigar, but the barrel of what appeared to be a Webley revolver.

Powers' heart began to pound. Extricating his hand from Carol's he began to flex and unflex his fingers. Her attention was still fixed on the passing junks out the window, and Powers hoped it would remain so a moment longer, giving him time to think out what this meant, or even to form, perhaps, a plan.

They had passed through Aberdeen, and out the other side, and were nearing the end of the acres of boat people as well. The car was slowing. It turned into a lot where a building or buildings had been razed, and it was hidden from the town behind them by a mound of rubble. Powers' options, and there weren't many, flipped through his brain like file cards. Could he push open the door, push Carol out, jump, run? He could, but . . . He scanned each card, and flipped on. After the first few cards, all the rest were blank. It immobilized him. He was as fixed in space as the gun in front of his nose, and likely to remain so. His own guns were thirteen thousand miles away. He was the sheriff, but would not beat anyone to the draw tonight. He felt as dull as a caveman, as unsophisticated. In the face of thousands of years of civilization he had only his hands and feet as tools, but civilization's bullets moved faster and their work was irreversible. He thought of what bullets looked like nose-up in a box, or upended on a table, as rounded, as smooth, as women's breasts though harder of course, faintly oily, objects of terrible potency and therefore masculine in nature, not feminine, more potent than any woman, more deadly than an epidemic. He thought of what bullets looked like when they had been dug out of somebody—out of the two men he had killed. He had seen his own bullets, what was left of them, shaken out of small brown envelopes in the ballistics lab, their heads flattened, still with bits of meat and blood attached. The human body was solid and ruined bullets—it was mutual. Would his body ruin the bullets in that gun? Would Carol's? But the gun he was looking into had a higher muzzle velocity than either of his police .38s, he believed. And the range was shorter—would be shorter. Presumably its bullets would go right through him, never to be seen again. They would not nail him to the seat. An arrow would nail him to the seat. Arrows had more penetration power than bullets, a detail that had always surprised him. Arrows, after all, could be seen in flight, whereas bullets could not. He had seen corpses killed with arrows. In New York City, of all places. He had seen all kinds of corpses, and might see Carol's next. Or she, his. Arrows went right through you and came out the other side, which bullets rarely did. Unless fired at ranges as point-blank as now.

"You get out, pliz."

Powers heard Carol gasp, meaning she had turned and sighted the gun. She knew they were in trouble. Did she realize how much?

She said: "What's the—" her voice broke"—matter?"

The middle-aged detective waved the barrel of the gun slightly. "Out."

Powers reached across Carol and threw open the door. "Get out, Carol."

She did so. He followed and stood beside her in the moonlight. She had begun to tremble. When he put his arm around her, she buried her face in his shoulder and began to sob. Bright girl. She understood the joke. She would not need the punch line explained.

The driver had brought out his own piece, an automatic of some kind. So now there were two guns trained on them. The middle-aged detective said, "You walk, pliz."

Powers walked with his arm around Carol, who still

sobbed against his chest. It was as if they were walking in a funeral. It was as if they were married, and this was the funeral of, say, their oldest son, dead in his youth. The grieving mother had broken down. It was up to the grieving father to guide her to the edge of the grave.

The grave was a big one, the biggest. They crossed the lot to the edge of it. Powers could hear water lapping against hulls, could smell the odor not of the sea but of sewage and rot and mud. A staircase down onto a rickety dock. They descended and walked out along the dock. There were junks nosed up on both sides, with lights shining through a few portholes. But there was no one in sight. Perhaps most of the squatters here had been relocated. Far out on the water the floating restaurants, three of them end to end, were lit up like ferris wheels, like a veritable amusement park. They must be doing good business tonight, Powers thought. Across the water came the noise of voices, the muffled music—a less immediate sound to Powers than his own footsteps ringing like bells on the dock. The two police detectives, if that's what they were, walked about four feet behind, the correct distance for work like this, the perfect distance; they must have learned that at their police academy, as Powers had learned it at his. There was no way to turn and attempt to disarm either of them, much less both at the same time. The hand was indeed quicker than the eye, and a savage punch so fast as to be almost invisible. But bullets were faster. At the end of this dock waited the mass burial ground, the world's true bottomless pit, every corpse in it the victim of an atrocity. There waited also, he imagined, a motor launch of some kind to take them farther out to sea. The deed would be delayed, if possible, until then. An attempt was being made to kill them quietly, without attracting undue attention. That much seemed clear. Otherwise they would be dead already.

Therefore he had to make his move now, or not at all, within the next eight to ten steps at the most. The farther out on the dock they got, the less reluctant the two torpedoes would be to pull their triggers, and the end of the dock was approaching fast. Powers could dimly make it out. And he could hear, approaching across the water, the noise of an outboard motor.

From the floating restaurants searchlight beams probed the darkness. They splashed the harbor with excitement, with fun. The restaurants were big business, they advertised their presence with vivid bursts of light. They illuminated for a moment the oncoming motor launch. A sampan. One man steering from the rear. On the front platform Powers discerned what he took to be a pile of cinder blocks wired together.

Are those cinder blocks for me? he asked himself.

He was as terrified as he had ever been, but it was an intellectual kind of terror and did not incapacitate him. He was still flexing and unflexing his fingers. He was still able to think. He had known terror before. The sensation was not new to him. Keep calm, he told himself. Think it out. If you panic you are lost.

And he began to flip a new set of filing cards through his head.

If he turned and rushed them they would fire. Rushing them was out. They would have no choice. From their point of view, this thing had gone too far to turn back now. He had to confuse them. He had to give them an option of some kind. Make them stop to think before firing.

What about Carol? If he could save himself, did he care what happened to Carol? Whose fault was this anyhow? He felt an overpowering hatred for her, and yet they had shared so much together in so short a time—and were sharing this experience now—that even as he hated her he loved her more than ever, for her flaws as much as her virtues, the way one loves a wife grown old, grown heavy, grown no longer beautiful but part of one's life since forever. It was Carol's fault they were here, but his fault too. They were here together. She was the one who had steered Koy toward him, but that was his fault as much as hers because he was the one who had steered her toward Koy in the first place. Was there not some way he could save her, even at the cost

of his own life? But he was not married to her. Did he have
to die for her anyway?

The sampan had slowed, and was drifting in toward
the pilings. Four pairs of feet clapped rhythmically down on
the boards, making a sound as hollow as walnuts. The end
of the dock—the end of life itself—that sampan—came
nearer. He knew that if this was Eleanor he would gladly
give his life for her, and then it seemed to him that Eleanor
and Carol were the same, his one and only wife, and that he
would give his life for Carol too if necessary. He did not fully
understand it, or see it clearly. It was muddled by terror,
and by the need to improvise some action fast. It was all very
mystical, but in loving the second woman he loved the first
one more, and from now on, somehow, he must take care
of both of them. He looked across at Carol and saw that she
was stumbling along, sobbing. She hardly knew where she
was, only that her life, her beloved life, was behind her. She
would disappear tonight and no one would ever know what
happened to her.

Powers had come to the end of the file cards. There
was not an idea written out on any of them, nothing. His
mind had become a void, and as a result fear at last took
control of him. Love turned back into hate again—the impotent man blamed the woman. He did not have two wives,
only one, whom he would never see again—and the void
was filled with rage.

"Are you happy now?" he shouted at Carol. "I told
you you were going to wind up in the South China Sea. I
warned you."

And then an idea came to Powers, and he thought he
saw a way to save both of them—perhaps to save Carol
anyway. He would give the torpedoes their option and himself a slim chance to survive.

"Look ahead of you," he shouted at Carol. "That's
the South China Sea. Are you happy now?"

It stopped Carol in her tracks. She gazed at him with
stricken eyes, below which tears and makeup coursed down
her face. Behind them the two detectives had stopped also.

She reacted even better than he hoped. She swung her handbag at him. It struck him in the side of the face, and he felt its clasp rip open his cheek. He had not put up his hands to defend himself. Instead he had lunged into Carol, and sent her flying off the dock. He had picked his spot carefully, and had driven her off the dock into the well between the prows of two junks. He saw her fall straight down into darkness, and even as he crouched and lunged again, he heard the splash. The surprised detectives had not had time to sort out what was happening, and he drove his shoulder into the middle-aged one, and sent him off the dock also, crashing down on his back onto the forecastle of the nearest junk. The other man fired even as Powers turned and ran. Crouched and running hard, Powers raced zigzagging up the dock toward shore. He was praying as he ran. He had never prayed so hard before. There were still more shots, and he prayed the detective would not think to chase him, and that the bullets would miss. He was praying that Carol had sense enough to swim between two junks, to stay hidden under the curve of two hulls. If she did, she would be safe. They could not linger long looking for her.

When he had covered about fifty yards, Powers rose upright and sprinted for the staircase. To hit anyone with a handgun at the range this had become would take an extremely lucky shot, and the detective behind him must be out of his mind with distraction. Should he help his colleague? Should he go after Carol? Should he go after Powers? What should he do? Shooting was an athletic event. It required absolute concentration, which the shooter was totally without; his problems had become too complicated to solve, and the target was diminishing all the time.

People had come out onto the decks of the junks. Powers had reached the staircase and had run up onto the embankment. He was ready to sprint into downtown Aberdeen if necessary, but when he looked back he saw he was not being pursued. Instead he discerned the shapes of the two detectives, who seemed to be grappling with each other at the outer end of the dock. They looked like men dancing, or perhaps kissing; and then Powers realized it was merely the second man hauling the first one from the junk back onto the dock again. A moment later he saw them run to the edge and jump down onto the sampan, and seconds after that the sampan, heading outwards, crossed the same searchlight beam as before, all three men staring back toward shore, toward Powers up on the embankment—to them an increasingly remote figure, safe, untouched, as invulnerable as a hero, as a god.

As for the hero himself, he stood now hacking and coughing, trying desperately to catch his breath. As the reaction set in fear overtook him. It was as if he had swallowed poison. He not only couldn't breathe, his knees had turned to soup, and he could barely stand.

But when he had lost sight of the sampan in the darkness, he ran back down the stairs and out to the end of the dock. He could not be sure exactly where he had knocked Carol into the water, he could see nothing down any of those wells, and he began to call her name, but she did not answer. Was she still alive? Perhaps the detective had killed her, one shot into the top of her head. Perhaps he had killed her himself in driving her off the dock. Perhaps she had become mired in mud. Perhaps she had drowned. "Carol," he called, and was amazed to hear his voice come out in a series of sobs. "Carol, oh Carol, Carol."

He heard a groan, and the word "Artie," half choked off. He ran in the direction of her voice, and leaped down onto the deck of a junk, where he hung over the railing, reaching for her face, for her slimy upraised hand. He locked his grip around her wrist, and in a single violent jerk extracted her from the water. He had heard stories in the past about mothers who could lift automobiles off kids they had accidentally run over. Such stories, he realized, must be true, for Carol weighed at least 120 pounds, yet he had yanked her out of the water and six feet into the air with one hand. They stood on the deck of the junk embracing. She was again sobbing against his chest. Her hair was plastered to her head, and from it hung seaweed and bits of garbage.

416

Her dress sucked at her body, and her shoes were gone. But she still had her handbag. What does it take to make a woman let go of her handbag, Powers asked himself, even as he began studying the outer darkness. Could the sampan come back? Could bullets come at them over the water? Holding Carol's hand, he ran her up the dock toward the staircase, up onto the embankment and across it. The car they had arrived in was still there, and he looked for keys in the ignition, but found none. He made a mental note of the license plate—that was his training and it could be important—and then they were in the street beyond, and running toward the lights of the town: some closed gas stations, a seedy hotel, an open pharmacy. They came to a taxi stand. Three taxis in a row. Powers yanked open the door of the first cab in line, and pushed Carol into it. He jumped in beside her and slammed the door.

During most of the ride Carol lay in his arms sobbing. But when the cab drew up in front of the hotel, where elegant doormen helped elegantly dressed people into and out of cabs, she tried to gather control of herself. "I'm a mess."

"It's all right, Carol."

"I can't go in there looking like this."

As he led her across the lobby, heads turned. Carol herself stared only at the floor. Powers had never before seen her so embarrassed. They rode the elevator up. But once in her suite her momentary self-control vanished once more and she began violently to tremble.

Powers held her. "You're safe now, Puss," he said to her. It had slipped out—his pet name for Eleanor; he did not know why.

"Stay with me tonight, Artie. Oh, please stay with me."

But Powers had work to do, and could not stay.

He took her into the bathroom and undressed her. The muddy dress, the muddy underwear, fell to the tile. Her body was muddy too, her hands, her hair. He stood her under the shower. The hot water streamed down.

"You can't leave me alone, Artie."

"You'll be all right, Carol." He had to phone Sir David, report this, get the investigation started.

"Stay with me."

If it were Eleanor as hysterical as this would he stay? Probably. But he was married to Eleanor. He was not married to Carol, and duty came first.

She began to cry. "Stay with me," she sobbed. "Don't leave me alone. Oh, please stay with me."

"I can't," Powers said.

She stood under the spray with her eyes closed, her arms hanging limply at her sides, sobbing. He pulled the shower curtain shut on her, hurried out to the sitting room and made his call. Sir David said he would get to his office as quickly as he could; Powers should wait for him there. It would take him a few minutes.

Powers went back into the bathroom, and peered around the shower curtain. Carol was quietly crying. Her eyes, when they met his, seemed to plead with him to stay, but she said nothing. Reaching into the spray of water, he took her hand, drew her out of the tub and led her naked and dripping across the rug toward the door.

"When I go out, lock the door, and put the chain on. Don't open for anybody but me. You'll be all right." He was trying to think of a way to reassure her and so decided to translate his thoughts into the idiom she best understood. "Nobody will be interested in you anymore tonight. You see, you're not the star here, I am."

But as he reached for the doorknob she clung to him, her arms around his neck, and only by disengaging her hands was he able to step back. "You'll be all right," he said again.

Then he was in the hall waiting for the elevator and looking down at the sopping wet front of his suit. His fear had entirely passed, and had been replaced by an emotion that was far stronger, that was perhaps the headiest emotion ever given man to enjoy. He had saved Carol, and saved himself, considerable trophies both, but the emotion was not pride. He felt like a man who could turn over cars with his bare hands, or drive his fist through stone, but the emotion was not related to virility. It was one he had experienced twice before, both times after surviving shootouts. After killing the stick-up man in the store, and the sniper in Central Park, he had known exactly this same exultation, this desire to shout at the top of his lungs: hey, I'm not dead. I didn't get killed. Look at me, look. I'M STILL ALIVE.

34

"THEY WERE cops," said Powers.

He sat with other men around Sir David's desk: Police Commissioner Worthington was there, together with two deputy commissioners; Sir David had been joined by his chief of operations. It was nearly two in the morning. Everyone in the room looked somewhat discomforted, somewhat disheveled. Most had been awakened out of sound sleep, and their clothes looked as if they had come out of a bin that had been rummaged through.

"The credentials could have been forged," said Commissioner Worthington. "How can you be sure?"

Powers stared him down. The man was angry, for his men were being accused without proof, but Powers was angry too. "Their credentials had nothing to do with it. They looked like cops. They behaved like cops. Chinese cops, but cops. It's something a cop can feel."

"Rubbish," said Worthington. "The accusation is unfounded."

"You're a cop," said Powers. "You know very well what I'm talking about. They were cops."

A half-smile came onto Sir David's face. Sitting behind his desk, he suddenly leaned forward and knocked the dottle of his pipe into an antelope's hoof. "Well, it takes one to know one," he said. But when Commissioner Worthington glared at him, the half-smile disappeared. "You brought us a real headache," he said to Powers. "A real headache."

"How many cops in the Hong Kong police department?" demanded Powers.

Commissioner Worthington muttered, "About twenty-two thousand."

"And photos of all of them on file."

"Right," said Worthington.

Sir David said, "Twenty-two thousand photos."

"I feel sorry for me," said Powers. "But they tried to kill me, and this case has become entirely personal. Where are the photos? How soon can I start?"

He was brought down to an office opposite the personnel section and two of Sir David's officers were assigned to cart stacks of dossiers in and out of the room. Powers sat in shirtsleeves, his tie loose, opening each dossier, glancing at the photo stapled to the inside cover, then closing it and going on to the next.

The trouble with Orientals was that they did all look alike—at least in photos. There were no redheads or blonds, no one with wavy or curly or kinky hair, or with blue eyes or freckles, or with nordic as opposed to Mediterranean complexions. There were no aquiline or hooked noses—all noses were more or less flat. Powers wished Carol were there to help him. Women had a better eye for faces than men did, usually. In the morning she would be in good enough shape to work beside him, he believed. It would cut the workload in two, and she could confirm or reject any choices he made in the meantime.

When he had been working an hour, Sir David came into the room. "How's it coming?"

"Nothing yet."

"I've asked them to bring you the Wanchai dossiers first—that's Koy's old district. Trouble is, a district that size has close to a thousand constables assigned. How many have you looked through so far?"

"About two hundred." He studied a dossier a moment, then closed it and moved it onto a separate pile. "That could be one of them. The driver."

"Are you sure?"

"No."

"You don't have to identify anyone absolutely. If you can collect half a dozen or ten possibles, we can have a lineup."

Powers sighed. "I know that." He kept glancing through the dossiers even as the conversation continued. "How does your extradition treaty with the United States read?"

"It depends on the charge. If we charge Koy with attempted murder, we could extradite him."

"Then bring me some more dossiers," said Powers.

"I'm going home to bed," said Sir David. "If you should find our man, don't hesitate to ring me up. It doesn't matter what time it is."

"Thank you, Sir David," said Powers. And he added, "However this comes out, I want you to know how grateful I am to you."

Sir David gave him an embarrassed smile and a pat on the shoulder, and strode out of the room. But a moment later he poked his head back in. "By the way, we picked up the car. Stolen, of course. My technicians are working on it. Fingerprints, that sort of thing. Maybe some evidence will turn up."

About an hour later Powers was summoned to the reception room. Grateful for a break, he walked out there rubbing his eyes, and was handed a letter by a man who introduced himself as Austin Chan. The letter, Chan explained, was from Carol Cone. He had been lucky enough to get her a seat aboard Pan Am's 1:00 A.M. flight to Tokyo and Honolulu, and had driven her to the airport. She was already in the air. She had sounded almost hysterical when she telephoned Chan. He had gone straight to the hotel, and had stayed with her all the way to the gangway to the plane. He had never known anyone so frightened. All she wanted was to get out of Hong Kong. Had there been no space aboard the Pan Am flight, she was willing to take any other flight going almost anywhere.

When Chan was gone, Powers tore open the envelope. The note was short. A footstool of a note when he might have hoped for a ladder—something to help him see into high hidden places. Carol apologized—she was less of a trouper, she wrote, than she had thought. But she could not bear Hong Kong one second longer, she was too afraid. She would wait for Powers in Hawaii at the Hana Maui Hotel. Come quickly, she wrote.

After a moment Powers folded the letter, shoved it into his pocket, and went back to his dossiers. There was no hurry now. It was as if Hong Kong had just emptied out, as if outside this room, there were no people left alive in the town.

BY LATE the next afternoon Powers had rubbed his eyes so much they were red and swollen. He looked like a mourner who had been weeping inconsolably for days. He felt like a jeweler who had remained bent over his table for hours chipping away at the mass so as to make a small perfect stone. His eyes ached, his back ached, his entire head ached, but on the desk now stood the work he had created: a small mound of dossiers. Not a mountain, nor even a hill, but only a mound. It was so featureless and indistinct as to seem insignificant. It was like one of those ancient burial mounds that sometimes attracted archeologists: it might—just might —contain the tomb they all were seeking. During the last fifteen hours he had dozed for two hours on a leather couch. He had consumed three pots of strong tea. He had examined about 5,000 dossiers. He had been through the dossiers of all constables assigned to the five districts once ruled by Koy and the other four Dragons. Five thousand Chinese constables had trekked across his optic tract numbing its sensors, packing them down. He remembered them like a desert army seen through the heat haze crossing the horizon.

His gaze now felt fixed forever on the middle distance, fixed on nothing. Scooping up the selected dossiers, he walked across into Sir David's office, into sunlight that streamed cheerfully in the window.

"I've got seven possibilities," he said. "Let's have a look at them. Maybe I won't have to go through the rest."

Sir David, who was again dressed in bush jacket, knee

socks and short pants, had been standing at the window peering down on the harbor. Crossing to his desk, he pushed the intercom button, and gave instructions for the seven constables to be picked up and a lineup arranged. He also asked for his car to be brought around in front. "One of my men just called in," he explained. He stroked both his muttonchops. "They found a sampan that seems to match your description. Let's go out and take a look at it, shall we?"

The expanse of permanently moored junks seemed both more vast and more squalid than it had last night. Weathered, rotting wood. Decks and superstructures as patched as sails. Limp, frayed mooring lines. Hulls, after decades of floating on filthy harbor tides, that were as black and scum-covered as the engine compartments of trucks. Powers sniffed the fetid air. At the moment the tide must be out—the odor of sewage and of stinking mud assaulted his nose. Following Sir David and a constable, he started out across acres of decks.

The sampan had been nosed in under the sterns of two junks, where it rode like a suckling calf nursing in a herd of elephantine cows. Powers looked down at it and, whether from fatigue or residual fear, felt himself begin to tremble. The sampan was of course empty, but on the platform in the prow still rested the wired-together cinder blocks.

Sir David eyed Powers. "From the look of you, we have the correct sampan. Do you feel certain enough to identify it in a courtroom?"

Powers shook his head. "No. What I'm mainly reacting to are those goddamn cinder blocks. My toes are curled up tight. The hair is sticking up on the nape of my neck."

He turned away and gazed off toward the town. The onrush of violent emotion surprised him. He found he had to swallow hard. But when he turned back to Sir David, he had himself under control. "You'd think they'd be smart enough to get rid of the cinder blocks," he said. "All they had to do was drop them over the side somewhere." He was again considering the sampan from the point of view of a policeman. He shook his head in disgust. "Criminals are idiots, aren't they?" To the police mind getting rid of the evidence would have been paramount. To leave the cinder blocks to be found was inconceivable. Yet to the criminal mind, other imperatives took precedence, apparently. They left evidence around all the time. Powers said, "Tell your men to check the sampan out. Who owns it? Where was he last night? Where did the cinder blocks come from?"

"Calm down," said Sir David. "We've taken care of all that. Would you recognize the sampan driver if we did find him?"

Powers found himself unable to stare very long at the cinder blocks. By now they might be wired to his ankles, or his neck. Carol's neck or ankles, too.

"I never saw the guy's face," he said. "It was too dark."

"What about Mrs. Cone?"

"I don't know. We could ask her."

"Do you think she'd be willing to return here to give evidence?"

"I don't know," said Powers. "I don't feel sure of very much right now, if you want to know the truth. Do you mind if we leave?"

THE LINEUP took place immediately after dinner. Powers, Commissioner Worthington, Sir David, and an assistant Crown Counsel named Downes stood in a darkened office peering through a one-way window into a second room that was brightly lighted, and in which ten men sat on a bench opposite them—the seven constables whose dossiers Powers had selected, plus three of Sir David's officers. Around their necks, the men wore placards numbered from one to ten.

"We'll have them walk up to the window one at a time," said the Crown Counsel.

"You don't have to," said Powers, turning away from the glass. "Numbers six and seven." This is chilling business, he thought, and imagined he felt no emotion whatever. His mind felt absolutely cold.

"Are you certain?" asked Crown Counsel Downes.

The question enraged Powers. Residual terror surfaced—those two Chinese thugs in there had tried to kill him—and turned itself into fury, all of it directed toward the young Crown Counsel. "Yes, I'm certain," he snarled, and stared at him, breathing hard.

"Okay, okay," said Downes. "Calm down. Nobody doubts your word." Stepping to the door, he ordered someone in the hall to clear the lineup room except for numbers six and seven.

As he watched this happening through the one-way window, Powers' mood changed again, and he tried to explain to himself his physical aversion to these men. It was like looking at cobras behind glass in a zoo. Take the glass away and they'd be in the same room with you. Their bite would be fatal.

He watched eight men troop out of the room. The two left behind attempted to gaze steadfastly at the floor, but were too agitated. Their collars suddenly seemed too tight. They squirmed. Beads of sweat appeared on their foreheads.

All this Powers observed. "Any further doubts, Sir David?" he asked.

"We mustn't count on them giving up Koy," said Sir David. "They are surely Triads, with a code of silence thousands of years older than the Mafia code of *omerta*. I doubt they'll give up anybody. Too worried about death by a myriad of swords, what?"

"Perhaps after they're convicted," said Powers.

"Perhaps. I don't think so. One can always hope so."

It was up to Downes to prepare the strongest possible case against them, and Powers spent the next several days with the expatriate young Englishman. Downes had never prosecuted a case of this importance before, but he was filled with enthusiasm. He wanted to trace the route of the suspects' car from the Mandarin to Aberdeen, and Powers rode beside him in a government car while, with yellow legal pad on his knee and stop watch in his left hand, he noted down the mileage and probable elapsed time of each portion of the ride. He wanted to know exactly how the car had entered the lot at Aberdeen and in which direction it was pointed. He got a tape measure out and measured not only distances, but even the height of the staircase, and the depth of the water beside the dock, and he noted all such details on his legal pad while Powers stood beside him in the bright warm sunshine and shivered as if from chills.

Powers was astonished that such violent physical reactions continued so long after the event. He thought it must be age. Life got more precious every year—and fear penetrated deeper—and this young legal genius kept making him relive the fear over and over again.

"You were standing here," said Downes pacing it off. "And Chin, the older of the two defendants, was on your left side. The other man was slightly in front of him, about there."

Powers shook his head. "No, you have it reversed. Look, if you don't mind, I've had enough of this for the moment." He walked up the dock to the staircase and up to the car, hugging himself for warmth, and the young prosecutor came up behind him looking solicitous, remarking, "I say, you must have caught a virus, a bug of some kind. You don't look at all well."

THE MORPHINE bricks, sewn into the bottom of the bogus mailbags, had reached Hong Kong from Bangkok, had been offloaded from the airliner and then from the postal truck without incident. In a shed on the outskirts of Kwu Tung, a village in the New Territories up near the Chinese frontier, chemical conversion had taken place. The resulting No. 4 heroin was sealed into flat plastic pouches, and delivered by car at night to a textile factory in the city of Tsuen Wan, where two men inserted the pouches into a shipment of children's dresses at the rate of one pouch per box. These boxes were then sealed and loaded in an airline container addressed to the Hong Kong and Formosa Trading Corporation of the Netherlands, a company controlled by former Sergeant Hung.

The container reached Kai Tak airport on a truck, part of a load of similar containers, none of which were examined closely by customs officials. It went out on a KLM flight to Amsterdam the next day.

AT DOWNES'S request, Powers phoned Carol on Maui. The connection with the hotel was made quickly enough, but there was a considerable wait as she was located—apparently at the swimming pool—and brought to the phone.

"Oh, Artie, I was so scared."

"You were no more scared than I was."

"I'm so glad to hear your voice. When are you coming here? It's so lovely. A hot trade wind blows all day long, we can walk on the beach, or hike up to the volcano. It's so gorgeous. I can't wait to see you. When will I see you?"

"I have the Crown Counsel here with me," answered Powers. "Those two men are in custody, and we're trying to put together our case against them. The Crown Counsel wants to know if you would agree to testify at the trial."

At the other end of the line, some eight thousand miles away, there was silence. "Do I have to?" asked Carol.

"It would strengthen our case. But I don't suppose they can make you come back to Hong Kong if you don't want to."

"I'd rather not then. Tell them I won't come. That's all right isn't it? I've been having nightmares. I wake up sweating. I don't want to have to see those men again."

"They'd certainly like you to testify, though. It wouldn't be for about six months, as I understand it."

"It's all so sordid—which wouldn't do my image any good, would it? If there's no other way to put them in jail, I'll come. Otherwise I'd rather not. Now tell me how soon you can get here."

"Carol, I wish you would realize that I don't have your kind of money and I do have other obligations. I've got to get back to New York."

Her voice became low and hurt. "When will you leave Hong Kong?"

"The day after tomorrow."

"Are you mad at me because I don't want to testify? Is that why you won't come to Maui?"

"Not at all, Carol. It's just that I have to get home."

"To your wife?"

"To my wife," he answered firmly. To soften the blow, he added: "And to my job. I do have a job you know." He half expected her to berate him.

But Carol said only, "I'll wait for you. I hope you'll change your mind. Promise me you'll think about it."

"I'll think about it." Rejection was not easy. Neither to give nor receive.

"Will you call me again before you leave there?"

"If you like."

"Promise?"

"I promise."

"I love you," she said.

Powers looked across the desk at Downes. "The Crown Counsel is waiting for me," he said.

When he had hung up, he said to Downes, "She doesn't want to testify."

"Shit," said Downes.

"Listen," said Powers. "I wonder if you'd do me a favor. I wonder if I could use your phone to call up my wife? Can we take a break for a few minutes?"

"Call her later," said Downes. He was flipping through his notes, thinking out how to get by in court without Carol.

Powers shook his head. "I want to call her right now." When Downes hesitated, Powers added, "Just give me a couple of minutes to talk to my wife, and I'll be at your disposal the rest of the day."

When Downes had gone out of the office, Powers dialed his home number. The phone rang five times before Eleanor, sounding groggy, came on the line.

"Oh, it's you." It was the middle of the night there. She was in bed and still half asleep but sounded glad to hear his voice. "When are you coming home?"

"The day after tomorrow." He had worked out his

flight number and arrival time in New York, and he gave these details to her. He said he was finishing up the final details of his work in Hong Kong, and when she asked how it had gone, he dodged the question. He wasn't sure yet. He would tell her all about that when he landed. She gave him news of their sons, both of whom had come home from college in the last two days. Summer vacation had started. She had forgotten how much food grown boys could eat. "Artie," she said, "I've missed you such a lot."

"I've missed you too," he said, and although he had made this same remark to her many times over the years, he thought he had never meant it as much as now.

"Tell me how you feel."

"You mean my strongest feeling at the moment?"

"Yes."

"I feel sex-starved," he said. "Sex-starved for you."

Eleanor laughed. "It's nice when a man can say that to a woman he's been married to for twenty-three years."

"Twenty-four next month," said Powers. "We should really celebrate it. We should give a party."

"We can talk about it when you get home." She sounded very pleased.

When he had rung off, Downes came back into the room, accompanied by Sir David.

"There has been another development," said Sir David. "Koy's wife has booked passage out of Hong Kong this afternoon."

"Destination?" asked Powers.

"Vancouver. Holders of Hong Kong passports need no visa to enter Canada."

"And from Canada, she can walk across. If she's stopped, she can show that phony green card. It's a pity it's not her I'm after."

"Fellow has two wives," Sir David said, almost to himself. "What's more, he appears to love them both."

"When I get back to New York, they're going to crucify me."

"Situation's not so unusual," said Sir David, still musing. "It does happen. Not just to Chinamen either, don't you know? Could happen to an Englishman, Captain. Could happen even to a New York police officer, what? Ask Mrs. Cone."

"I don't happen to have two wives," Powers snapped.

"Sorry. Dirty habit of mine. Thinking out loud, what? You're not going home entirely empty-handed, you know. You did put two corrupt Hong Kong constables in jail."

Powers snorted. "The PC is not going to be impressed." Then he added, "I suppose I can hope that my presence has disrupted the flow of drugs."

"Negative, I'm afraid. I was talking to your colleague, Gaffney, at Drug Enforcement only this morning. He seems to have purchased information to the effect that the drugs have already come and gone. Nothing more specific than that, unfortunately. The first shipment may reach New York before you do."

"That makes me more or less a total flop, doesn't it?"

Sir David shook his head impatiently. "I say, my dear chap, have you learned nothing about the Chinese yet? You're in a position to cause our Mr. Koy a great deal of embarrassment."

"I've thought of that. Why do you suppose I asked you to go on tailing Orchid? It just doesn't seem very satisfactory at the moment."

"You underestimate this thing, I think. What, to a Chinese, is the world's most precious commodity? Is it gold? Is it jade?

"Face," said Powers.

"Precisely. Without face a Chinese can't operate. A Chinese who has lost face sometimes chooses not to go on living. Take away Koy's face and you neutralize him. If Wife Number One turns up in New York, you have the means to do that."

Sir David stroked his muttonchops. His fingers made love to them, both at the same time. He caressed them. "A man with two wives has problems," he murmured.

"Koy is a murderer, an extortionist, a drug dealer. I

was hoping for something better than catching him with his pants down. I don't want to embarrass him, I want to destroy him."

But the idea was perhaps worth pursuing. It perhaps constituted a fall-back position. Powers said, "Sir David, when I leave the Colony I would like to take with me copies of a number of documents, and I wonder if you could get them ready for me."

"Certainly. Which documents did you have in mind?"

"I'll make you a list."

At the airport two days later Powers thought briefly of Carol. He could still join her on Maui for a day or two. It was not too late to change his mind. His confrontations with the PC, and with Koy, would wait that long. He was booked by Pan Am through Tokyo and over the Pole to New York, but in Tokyo could easily change planes for Honolulu. There would be no additional fare. It did not even add greatly to the length of the flight, except for whatever time he might spend on the ground in Hawaii. But as he waited in the departure lounge, he began to examine again his own concept of adultery, and many of his newly discovered insights into life and love as well. To go on vacation with another woman while one's wife remained at home coping with everyday chores seemed to him the ultimate betrayal. There could be nothing left in a marriage if a man would do that. It was a line that he had not crossed, and had no desire to cross. Nor did he desire to tell Carol so by telephone. Stepping to the telegraph desk, he wrote out two brief telegrams. The first, to his wife, confirmed his flight number and arrival time. The second went to Carol on Maui, words that he wrote out in block letters: MUST RETURN NEW YORK DIRECTLY. REGRETS.

And signed his name.

He was hardly thinking about Carol. He was thinking about heroin and how to find it. A few minutes later his flight was announced and he boarded it. He had been halfway around the world, and now was on his way back.

35

KOY, home several days, resolved to telephone Hong Kong, for he had had no signal. However, he was a careful man, and wary of tapped phones; therefore he assigned the job to the embalmer, Chang, and stood by his side while the call was made.

In Hong Kong a telephone rang, but no one answered.

This did not quite alarm Koy. It was an irritation, like tea that has overflowed into a saucer. It could not be overlooked. It could make a mess out of all proportion to itself. He liked things to be exact. In an uncertain world exactness was to be valued above all things.

Outside he went down the front steps and strolled up Mott Street. His bodyguards, seated beside the door, had followed him out. He walked in crowds in the hot noonday sun. It did not seem to him likely that the two constables had failed in their assignment. They were experienced men.

But Koy's uneasiness persisted. Having reached busy Canal Street, he stared across through many lanes of traffic. Canal was like a thunderous river filled with rapids, and not easy for the Chinese to cross. To him, as to many generations of Chinese, the other side, the Italian side, resembled a distant shore. The topography was different over there, language and customs too. For more than a century the Chinese had remained on this side, crammed into their ghetto, afraid to venture out. Only in the last few years had a few adventurous ones pushed out into the current. Some had made it across, and had established a Chinese beachhead over there. Almost half the storefronts, it seemed to him, were now Chinese.

On the corner of Canal and Mott, about five feet from Koy's elbow, stood a pagoda-shaped telephone booth. Stepping into it he dialed the Fifth Precinct.

Captain Powers was out of town, he was told. No one had heard from him or knew when he would be back. Any message? Who's calling please?

Koy hung up, dialed a second number and asked to be put through to Mrs. Cone. A secretary answered, and gave him much the same information. They believed Mrs. Cone might have gone on a brief vacation. In any case, they did not know where she was. Who was calling please?

Again Koy hung up. But as he backed out of the telephone booth, he was smiling. It was faint, but definitely a smile. He had been ready to halt the flow of merchandise to New York, but no news was good news, and he decided to let it come in on schedule. Feeling more cheerful, he walked back to his office, where he canceled his remaining appointments, and had himself driven home toward an unpleasant job that had best be got out of the way today.

THE CONTAINER of dresses had reached Amsterdam, where it was held up by Dutch customs officers until a broker representing Hung arrived to sign the forms and pay the duty. The container was then released. The Dutch officers did not examine it because there had been no request from any agency to do so, no tip from any informant. It was impossible to examine every container of goods that entered the country.

At the Hong Kong and Formosa Trading Corporation the pouches were removed from the dresses and packed into a number of watertight suitcases.

Former Sergeant Hung did not go near the merchandise, neither then nor later. He was merely advised of its arrival, and he ordered it safeguarded pending further instructions.

Hung had already heard from the three other ex-sergeants. They wanted their own portions held back until they saw what happened to Koy's in New York. Koy's insistence on haste seemed to them contrary to Chinese tradition, as it did to Hung. All had been taught to revere patience. Haste, they had found, most times proved unproductive or dangerous or both.

Hung had expected similar instructions from Koy, who in the past had sometimes seemed too patient, more patient than any of them. But these instructions did not come. At length Hung had Koy's suitcases carried on board the S.S. *Rotterdam*, a luxury liner, by a Hakka Chinese stoker who stowed them in the crew's luggage compartment. The *Rotterdam*, carrying eleven hundred passengers, sailed for New York that night.

Just prior to landing the stoker, if he obeyed his orders, would empty the suitcases and disperse their contents under the steel floor plates in various corners of the bilge, in case of any "serious" U.S. Customs inspection.

He had been equipped with a recognition signal. He would be contacted in New York and the merchandise taken from him—he was not told how—for transfer ashore.

THAT AFTERNOON Koy took his wife and children out for a stroll through Central Park, and this time he had the bodyguard follow at a discreet distance. Once under the trees he left Betty pushing the carriage and allowed the older little girls, each clutching one of his hands, to run him along the path until they were giggling and he was out of breath. After that the girls wanted to swing.

They had come to the playground area. Koy lifted their little bottoms onto the seats, pulled the bars down over their laps, and decorously arranged their short skirts. He got them started swinging, running from one swing to the other,

435

pushing them high. Betty, meanwhile, had taken a bench. The carriage was at her side, and when he looked back she was gently rocking it, while at the same time leafing through a magazine on her lap.

Koy went over and sat down beside her. He heard her take a deep breath. She seemed to know what was coming.

"You said there were difficulties in Hong Kong," she said. She wants to get it over with, Koy thought. How American!

Betty Koy was thirty-five years old. She had been, when he met her, a director of an import-export firm that did business principally with Taiwan. She had an American accent both in English and Chinese. She had been something new in his experience—not only a female in business, but also a woman who was not a whore who had had other men. She had seemed to him very exciting.

"Inevitably there are business difficulties," said Koy. "These I took care of, and they don't concern you in any case." He paused and looked across at the two little girls; the swings were slowing. He got up, walked over, and got them started again, running from swing to swing, pushing the girls high, making them laugh. When he came back to the bench, there was sweat on his brow.

"The personal difficulties were not so easy to solve," he said, sitting down again. "I've been obliged to bring my son to New York. In the fall I intend to enroll him in Yale. Yale ought to be possible. We endow a chair there, you know."

This was not the problem, but when they gazed at each other, Koy noted that his wife's face already looked stricken. She knows what's coming, he thought again.

"When does he arrive? When he arrives, of course he'll stay with us." But her voice broke. "There's plenty of room," she said, "for your son."

"It's better if he stays with his mother," said Koy, and paused. "I've been obliged to bring his mother to New York also."

"I knew I should never have let you go to Hong Kong," burst out Betty Koy.

She perceives all, as a Chinese woman would, thought Koy—but reacts emotionally with typical American self-indulgence. The Chinese side of Betty Koy was forever at war with the American side, thought Koy. It was part of what made her dear to him.

"When are they coming?" she asked. Her voice sounded almost normal to him. She has recovered quickly, he thought, as a Chinese woman should, and he was proud of her.

"In a few days. I'll put them in a flat in Chinatown. They'll be more comfortable there."

He studied her downcast profile. The unpleasant job was over and he had handled it well. "I'll have to spend some time with them," he said. "You must understand that. I care for you too much to be other than perfectly honest with you." In her ways Betty was American, but in her soul she was Chinese. She would bow to the inevitable.

"I see," said Betty Koy.

POWERS CAME out through the customs barrier and found his wife there, and they embraced. It was an ordinary embrace on her part, for he had not been gone that long, but an intense and passionate one on his. For the last ten hours she had scarcely been out of his mind. The plane had seemed to be butting against a wall. It was too slow, it would never get him to her door. He had been intoxicated with the idea of seeing her—had felt the same excitement and expectation as when they were courting. The long flight home had brought his life to a pinpoint focus. All he wanted, as he stared out the porthole, was to see her again, to hold her close again. He had felt as eager and consequently as frustrated as a boy, and he found so narrow a focus extraordinary in a man of forty-six.

Now, his arm around her, they went out to their car in the parking lot, Powers carrying his suitcase in his other hand. You're the one I want to grow old with, he thought. There was no one else he could say that to. Twenty-three years of your past belong to me, he thought. Your future belongs to me too, all of it, and I want it. His feeling toward her was akin to the way he felt about his sons. He wanted to know what their lives would become and he wanted to know what Eleanor's life would become also. I want to know what you'll look like when you are an old lady, he told himself. I want to be with you when you are an old lady. But he sensed already that this was not going to happen. He felt like a criminal about to be indicted, as if there was too much wrongdoing in his past and investigators were sure to find it.

By the time he had steered out onto the Van Wyck Expressway and was driving home, he had fallen completely silent. His liaison with Carol would come out during the trial of the two constables, if not before. World headlines would play it like an operatic love duet—passion plus thwarted assassination. The song would carry all the way to New York. At most he had a few more months. The headlines could start at any time, and perhaps he should confess now.

His wife watched him, waiting for him to speak.

"Both boys have summer jobs," she said.

Powers, driving, flashed his teeth, as if for a dentist: "Great. And how were their grades?"

"Jimmy has a B average. Phil had some Cs." Still studying him, she said "So what did you come home with?"

Powers tried the same smile again. "Oh, I have a little something in a box for you." He had bought her jade earrings—he had had no money left for anything better. I gave the gold necklace to the wrong woman, he thought. The necklace was the most devastating detail of all, though one he could probably keep from her. Instead he would offer her international humiliation.

"That's not what I mean," said Eleanor. "What else did you come home with?"

Powers frowned. "I'm more convinced than ever of the existence of a Chinese Mafia. But I still can't prove it. There are drugs coming in here that I may not be able to find." He certainly wasn't going to tell her how close he came to being killed, and Carol with him.

"As bad as that?" said Eleanor.

Even worse, he thought. Some enterprising reporter in Hong Kong could be nosing through court papers even now. And what about Carol's special on television? One look was all Eleanor would need.

To be in love with two women at once was the biggest feeling Powers had ever known. It had seemed to him an emotion of incredible power and allure. It set him apart from other men. But at the same time he saw it as a perversion, because it was totally destructive—destructive of both women, and of himself as well. Its allure had masked its destructiveness for a time, but the destructiveness had always been there and he had seen it as such from the first.

He steered onto the Harlem River Drive. They would soon be home. He would go to bed with Eleanor as he had done now on many thousands of nights. That was something. He would clutch her tight in the dark, and try to hold off the rest until tomorrow.

He entered his precinct at 7 A.M. the next day and went out onto the street at once so as to visit all sectors and foot posts before the midnight-to-eight tour went off duty. He was like a gardener after a long absence, rushing into the greenhouse to discover the condition of his plants. By 8 A.M. he was back in the station house—in time to turn out the next tour personally, after which he entered his office. His executive officer and the administrative lieutenant followed him in and stood beside his desk. Both men carried clipboards thick with the accumulated TOPS, sixty-ones and other memos relative to running the precinct. All this paper, they were about to tell him, demanded his immediate attention. But when he spied Luang through the doorway he sent both of them out. He would meet with them later, he promised. They were perplexed, annoyed, perhaps even hurt to be dismissed—he saw their emotions pass across their faces—and in favor of a Chinese patrolman they hadn't known existed. But their injured feelings were the least of his problems at the moment. He sent his voice like a forward pass between their departing shoulders and out the door.

"I'll see you now, Officer Luang."

Luang, who wore a new seersucker suit, his shield pinned to the lapel, entered beaming. He looked glad to see his commander back, and pleased to be summoned so quickly to report. It was as if this confirmed all of Luang's hopes—that he was trusted and valued by Captain Powers, and was working on his most important case. An ordinary New York cop, Powers realized, would have displayed arrogance under the same circumstances, would have come in here looking cocky. Not Luang, whose manner was entirely deferential.

"Welcome back, Captain," said Luang. He did not offer to shake hands, and it seemed to Powers that he almost bowed.

"Thank you, Luang." The proper greeting, neither more nor less. Although Powers was just as glad to see Luang, who was, in effect, the only other player on his team, nonetheless he thought it best to let no emotion show. Leadership, like most other revered qualities, was mostly the performance of certain specified tricks. The captain of the ship ate alone. He did not fraternize with members of the crew.

Doubtless Luang wanted to hear about Hong Kong, but Powers offered no information, and so Luang, after hesitating a moment, began to report on the wiretap. During Powers' absence there had been no calls at all between Hong Kong and the funeral parlor.

"Any calls to Canada since Koy's been back?"

"No sir."

"Or from Koy to a strange woman?"

"No. There have been no more calls in Hakka, either."

In fact, a day or two after Koy's departure for Hong Kong, realizing that no one in Koy's New York entourage spoke Hakka, Luang had sent the two nuns back to the convent, and he had not seen them since. "But we can get them back any time we want," said Luang.

This meant, Powers realized, that during the entire time of his absence Luang had monitored the wiretap all by himself. But why am I surprised, he thought. These racial stereotypes one hears so much about are, for the most part, valid. The Chinese *are* more diligent than other races. They are extremely hard workers. They put their nose to the grindstone and do not look up. No American cop would have accepted such a burden, especially in the absence of his commanding officer. But the Chinese cop had done so, and Powers felt a rush of admiration for him and fondness as well.

"I owe you an enormous amount of time off," Powers noted, and immediately wondered if he would be in any position to accord it. How much longer would he command the precinct? How soon would headquarters discover he was back? The answer was a few days at most. And then? And then, unless he could find the heroin and arrest Koy, most likely his successor would be in here—who would be under no obligation to pay Luang what was owed. Indeed, he would probably be afraid to do so, lest he seem to associate himself with Powers' profligate expenditure of police man-hours.

All of this had to be concealed from Luang, of course. It meant that from now on Powers was, in effect, lying to him, which he did not deserve, and which Powers hated to do.

Luang had the wiretap log under his arm. Setting it down on the desk, he pushed it across, but Powers only placed it to one side.

"When this case ends," said Powers, "whether in a day or a week or a month—" he gave a wave of the hand as if no fixed limit existed, "then your temporary assignment here will be finished. Have you thought about where you would like to be assigned next? I don't know how much pull I have in the department, but perhaps I can help you."

After a silence, Luang said, "I'd like to stay with you, Captain."

"Yes, well—" Powers was moved. "I may not be staying in Chinatown," he said.

Luang smiled. "Brooklyn, the Bronx—wherever. The shield says City of New York, Captain."

Powers was so affected that he felt like telling the

truth: I don't see how I'm going to find a single specific shipment of drugs, and if I don't, there is a good chance I'll be forced out of the department entirely. He had committed no crime and couldn't be fired, but his superiors could make life so unpleasant he would not be able to stay.

He said, "I may get a headquarters assignment, Luang. Suppose I can't take you with me? Where else would you like to go? If you want to stay in Chinatown, that could probably be arranged. Or perhaps you'd prefer one of the Queens precincts, near where you live. Save you a lot of travel time each day."

Luang said nothing.

"I know the commanders of the one-eleven and one-fourteen pretty well. Those station houses are near you." He owed it to Luang to pay his debt while he still could.

But Luang only smiled. He refused to accept it. "Why don't we wait and see what happens?"

Powers stared for a moment at the top of the desk. The wiretap expired that day, and in the absence of additional hard evidence he doubted any judge would renew it. His voice and manner became crisp and commanding. "I've decided to let the wiretap expire," Powers said. No one was going to discuss drugs on the telephone anyway. "I've got a more important job for you—probably the last you shall have on this case. I want you to resume tailing Koy." He did not expect Koy to lead Luang to the drugs. Koy wouldn't go near the drugs. Nikki Han or Go Low might, and he wished he could tail them too, but this was too risky for Luang to do alone, and he had no one to pair him with. "I want to know who he meets, where he goes. I'm hoping he leads you back into Little Italy."

"You want me to tail Koy," said Luang. But a note of panic had come into his voice and Powers detected it at once.

Why is he frightened, Powers asked himself. What happened to him during the last tail that he didn't tell me about?

"Koy is dangerous," Powers conceded. "We both know that. I wish I could give you a backup, but I can't."

Powers got up and began to pace behind his desk. He remembered Orchid Koy, and to calm Luang down, to make the assignment sound less dangerous, he said, "He's got another woman here somewhere, or soon will have. See if you can find out where."

Again their eyes met. Luang's fear still showed, Powers believed, but it seemed more under control.

"Well, Captain, I certainly would like to have a backup," said Luang.

"Nobody's asking you to take crazy risks, Luang," said Powers coldly.

Luang was unsmiling. "It shall be done as you ask, Captain," he said, and he bowed and left the office.

Powers turned to the log, and began to thumb through it. But nothing of importance caught his eye.

When he glanced up his executive officer and administrative lieutenant were still standing just outside his door peering in. They waited their turn with clipboards clasped like shields to their lower bodies, as if to protect that place where, since the beginning of time, man—even bureaucrats—had always felt most vulnerable. But Powers marched out past them and crossed to the switchboard, where he asked if he had received any calls of a suspicious nature during the last several days.

"Suspicious? No sir," said the switchboard cop. "What's suspicious?"

"People asking for me who gave phony names or no names."

"Just some English guy who called a couple of times."

"Thank you," said Powers. Was it Koy calling? "What did you tell him?"

"That we hadn't had no word from you."

"Any word," corrected Powers. "If he calls again, tell him the same thing." It must be Koy, trying to find out if he was still alive. Who else in Chinatown had an English accent? I've got him worried, Powers thought. "If headquarters calls I'm not in either. I've taken some personals." In addition to vacation time, cops could take off three days a year on personal business, and he was taking them now.

36

AND HE left the station house. If he was to put together a major case there was much work to do and very little time left. A major case meant finding a drug shipment and tying Koy in with the Italians. Or else it meant arresting the others and forcing one or more to give Koy up in exchange for leniency. Powers' emotions, like his ideas, had hardened. He had begun to be driven almost entirely by hatred. If all else failed, he felt capable of killing Koy himself.

In an espresso bar across in Little Italy he met with Detective Kelly, who believed he had an informant willing to testify against Nikki Han and Go Low as extortionists. Also, the word on the street was that a new drug pipeline had opened up. Marco was supposed to be involved. Leaving Kelly, Powers strode across Federal Plaza, and took the elevator up to Immigration. An agent named Baumgartner met him at the reception desk, led him inside, and briefed him on immigration law. An hour later he crossed back over Centre Street to the district attorney's office, where he spoke of the probable new pipeline, and described the case he thought he could bring in against Marco, Casagrande, Han and Low. This evidence was at the moment interesting but probably insufficient, he was told. It would be best to keep the investigations open and wait for something solid to develop. And he had nothing hard against Koy at all.

He went back down to the street, found his car, and

drove to Drug Enforcement where he met with Wilcoxon and with the chief of the New York office, a deputy director named O'Reilly. They had heard about the new pipeline too and were very worried about it, they said. The original word had come from Gaffney in Hong Kong, who had got it from a paid informant. Other informants in New York had been contacted, and had provided confirmation.

"The word on the street," said O'Reilly, "is that the stuff is already here and is being distributed."

"Word on the street?" said Powers. "What word on the street? It's impossible." He was counting backwards to the day of the summit meeting Sir David had almost bugged. If the drugs had already been in the pipeline there would have been no such meeting. "The stuff can't be here yet."

"How do you know?" said O'Reilly.

Powers didn't know how he knew. Was it instinct, and therefore reliable, he asked himself, or only wishful thinking? Because if the stuff was already here then the case was closed, as far as he was concerned, and he had lost it.

"It's not here yet," said Powers doggedly. "You can't move a large quantity of drugs halfway around the world that quickly."

O'Reilly sat behind a big desk. It was bigger than Gaffney's in Hong Kong. The same two flags stood to either side of his ears. He said, "I wish I knew as much about heroin as you do, Captain. I'm only a deputy director."

Powers let this pass. "What about Marco and Casagrande?"

Wilcoxon said, "We've been watching them."

"And?"

"Nothing."

Powers said, "Let's assume for sake of argument that the stuff is not here yet. What can we do to find it when it comes in?"

"You could talk to Customs," said O'Reilly. He was studying his appointments calendar. To him the meeting was over.

"Good idea," said Powers. "Why don't we meet here

tomorrow morning, we three and some of the brass from Customs. Maybe we can figure out how the stuff might come in. Maybe we can even figure out how to find it. Will you call Customs, or should I?"

Unwilling to be upstaged by a police captain, O'Reilly said he would do it, and Powers waited beside his desk until he did. The meeting was arranged for ten o'clock the following morning.

But as soon as Powers had left his office, O'Reilly decided he should clear this with the police commissioner, and he asked his secretary to put in the call.

Powers, meanwhile, drove home, where he loaded Eleanor and a picnic basket into the car and drove out to Jones Beach. He would spend the rest of the day hiding from headquarters, brooding about hard evidence, about Koy.

Where the pathway met the beach they stooped to remove shoes and they crossed the hot sand barefoot, scampering a bit on scalded soles. Powers carried a blanket in one hand and the basket in the other, his gun and shield in there under the sandwiches. Eleanor, who wore a transparent blouse over her bikini, stripped it off. Like a gigantic butterfly it fluttered to the blanket Powers was trying to spread, and she headed for the water. Once he had the corners weighted down he followed, wading in, diving into the next wave but surfacing quickly, and looking back, careful to keep the lethal picnic basket always in view.

Eleanor slogged toward him through water that sometimes surged over her knees. She had been self-conscious about her body when younger, and would never have worn a bikini. Now she did not care. He studied her as she came closer. Not much cellulite for her age, not much flab. A narrow waist still. A nice body, but a number of scars. Some stretch marks from the pregnancies. An irregular dimple near her navel from the gall bladder operation just after Phil was born—do you remember, he thought, she was convinced it was cancer.

"The water's nice," said Eleanor. Her hair hung like snakes.

"Yes." But he watched a teenage boy who seemed to be edging very close to the backet.

"Will you please forget about your gun for a change?"

He stood with his arm around her. The sea surged at them from behind, slapping now their calves, now their thighs.

There was a four-inch scar down the lower part of her spine—his hand slid down over it—from a disc operation about ten years earlier, after she had lain most of a month in pain in traction. Powers had sat beside her day after day wondering if she would ever walk again. It would be wrong to say he loved these scars, but they were part of his life. They represented pain and trauma, comfort given and received, a life lived together. She would carry them to her grave, and so would he. He could not bear the idea of parting with them.

He slid his hand down further, down inside her bikini. It was like putting his hand in her back pocket. He cupped a cold wet buttock.

"Artie," cried Eleanor, squirming away from him, glancing around in embarrassment.

She almost blushed, but he could tell she was pleased. She was forty-six years old and her husband still liked to grab her bottom. She kicked water in his face and ran off through the shallows, and Powers sprinted after her like a schoolboy, then stopped, as if attached to the picnic basket by a rope.

Carol's body bore scars too—he had wondered about some of them but never asked. They were not his business. It would have been like asking her to produce college grades, or her job resume: technical information. Scars represented emotions, not facts, and there was no way to transmit this emotion to one who had not been there.

Eleanor seemed happy. She had two days off and was spending today, at least, with her husband, and at the beach too—a treat. On the blanket later she fed slices of tomato into his mouth, segments of egg, and all the while Powers was sick with the fear that his life was about to change—

home life and professional life both. His possessions would be stripped from him like chevrons. A single brusque rip to remove years. His sword would be broken. He would be forced naked out into the cold, where he would perish. The world was too frigid a place; a man flayed could not survive, except the way Bowery winos survived, propped briefly against walls. Defeat was not noble. It was anguish, frustration and despair. Not just for him—for Eleanor too. And all due to Koy. He stared out to sea and was entirely coldly conscious of the corrosive nature of his emotions. He blamed nothing on Carol. He did not hate Carol. He blamed Koy, hated Koy, and was focused on his need to destroy Koy. He wanted to settle the score—his personal score. He wanted to find the drugs even now en route to New York, but not because of the drowsy misery that came with them. The extorted shopkeepers of Chinatown no longer moved him. He did not mourn the victims of the restaurant massacre; he had forgotten the murdered Chinese boys. But Koy had murdered the old Arthur Powers too, and must pay. It was not justice Powers wanted, only vengeance.

THE NEXT morning in O'Reilly's office Powers was introduced to two senior customs officers, to whom he outlined the situation as he saw it.

"So I'm asking you for help," he concluded, and glanced around him. Wilcoxon was studying the blank yellow pad in his lap. O'Reilly arranged and rearranged a row of ball points on his blotter. Only the two customs men would meet his eyes, and they looked puzzled.

"That's all you've got?" inquired the older of the two, whose name was Glickman.

When Powers nodded, the two customs men turned to gaze at each other.

After a moment Glickman said, "I guess we came up here thinking you had something hard. The description of a specific courier. Or a flight number. Or even the name of a specific ship." He shook his head. "You don't really have much at all."

"I can't hand you the case on a silver platter," said Powers, pretending to a patience he did not feel. "Nonetheless, we do have some specific facts to consider. Why don't we go through them one by one?" He saw that they were unwilling, but was determined to force them to do it. "For instance, the shipment we're talking about has made a lot of noise. We've heard about it in Hong Kong, and also in New York. That means a big shipment, twenty-five kilos or more. Maybe much more."

"Very few big shipments come in by air," admitted Glickman. "I'll grant you that much. The passengers can't carry big loads off and it's hard to stash them in the planes themselves because airliners depart again too quickly. That leaves the cargo, which we watch rather closely."

"Good," said Powers. "Then it's coming in by ship. But from where?"

"You tell me, pal," said Glickman. "You tell me."

The second customs officer, Byrne, said, "Do you realize how many hundreds and hundreds of ships enter and leave the Port of New York every year?"

"If it's coming in this fast," said Powers, ignoring Byrne's pessimism, "then it must have come partway by air, probably via Europe. It would get put on a ship there. But where in Europe? Marseille? Genoa? North Africa maybe? Southampton? Make some guesses."

Wilcoxon looked up from his yellow pad. "Holland," he said. "Koy is a Hakka. The Hakkas have Amsterdam sewed up tight. It's their city."

Glickman said, "I have a list of ships arriving over the next two weeks." He opened the briefcase between his feet. After fishing out the list, he searched his pockets for his glasses and put them on. "Well, the *Rotterdam* arrives day after tomorrow," he said, and glanced up from the list.

"Any other Dutch ships?" asked Powers.

Byrne said, "A hell of a lot of ships touch Holland that aren't Dutch, my friend."

Glickman laid the list down on O'Reilly's desk, and all crowded around. They studied it.

Byrne said, "I see two ships out of Rotterdam already

—bound for Boston. Maybe your shipment isn't even coming here directly? Did you ever think of that? They can easily offload it in some other port and bring it in by truck. We've had shipments come in via South Carolina, via Baltimore, you name it."

"We really should have more to go on," said Glickman.

There had been a few moments of excitement, Powers realized. The men had seemed almost enthusiastic. But this was already gone. There were too many ships on Glickman's list, too many possibilities.

"I say it's the S.S. *Rotterdam*," said Powers. Did he really believe this, or was he merely trying to rekindle their hope, and therefore their willingness to work? He was like a man with a communicable disease scratching at them, breathing on them, trying to infect them out of his own virulent dose.

He said, "It's the only ship with the approximately correct dates, and the only one coming directly here. I'm getting to know this man. The *Rotterdam* is his style. It's first class, and it's fast. Those freighters are filthy, and they take ten days or more. Koy is suddenly in a hurry, don't ask me why." Powers believed he knew why. He had somehow broken through the calm tenor of Koy's life. For five years Koy had displayed the patience of a grazing cow, but Powers had stampeded him. He was beginning to act shaken, to act out of panic.

"Koy's style?" inquired O'Reilly. "Are you really asking us to tear a ship apart because you think the ship matches Koy's style?"

"Do you know how big a ship is?" said Byrne.

"He's right, you know," said Glickman. "Usually if we find something on a ship it's because some informant told us where to look. We could never find it otherwise. Ships are huge. There are too many hiding places. We can't go ripping up floor plates and cutting boilers open on your hunch. We can't just destroy this ship. The *Rotterdam* will only be in port a short time." Glickman studied his list. "From here it goes on a Caribbean cruise, I see. Lot of money involved.

Look, Captain, I'd like to help, but it's the flagship of a foreign government, and there are eleven hundred people waiting to board it. Rich people, I might add. If you get people like that mad they can cause a lot of trouble."

The bane of all law enforcement officers, Powers reflected: the screams of the indignant rich.

Glickman said, "We'll check the incoming passengers closely. We'll go through the cargo with care. We'll send a team through the crew's quarters. Unless you can come up with something more specific, there's not much more we can do. If we find something, that will be great. But don't count on it."

"How about informants?" said Powers.

"We'll keep after our informants," conceded Glickman. "Maybe somebody will come up with something."

"I doubt it's even that ship," said Byrne.

"A wiretap, maybe," said Powers.

"On who?" inquired Glickman. When Powers did not answer, he said, "You cops put rather too much dependence on wiretaps, I've always thought."

Powers dropped his gaze.

The meeting ended on that note. Powers trailed Wilcoxon back to his office, and when both had entered he closed the door.

"I want to arrest Marco and Casagrande," he said. "I want to shake up the whole crowd. I want to make something happen. But I don't have enough on either of them. Your guys have been watching them. What do you have?"

"Not much," responded Wilcoxon. "I told you that already. You're welcome to it. We made some observations of Marco meeting with known criminals. Since he's on parole, you can lock him up for that, but it probably won't stick."

"Why not?"

"Because the known criminals are relatives."

"What about Casagrande?"

Wilcoxon withdrew a file from his desk drawer. "I'll make copies of this. You can take it with you."

At the other end of the hall O'Reilly, having walked

the two customs officers to the elevator, had returned to his own office. As he passed her, his secretary said: "The police commissioner's returning your call, sir."

O'Reilly stepped to his desk and took up the phone.

EACH NIGHT Powers received Luang's report at home by phone: Koy did not enter Little Italy, his routine seemed unchanged since last time, and there was no sign of any "other woman." There were reports also from Kelly, but these were no more promising. Although he and every detective in the squad were out pounding on informants, there were as yet no leads.

Each night Eleanor phoned the precinct for him for messages. There was only one significant one the first night: report to the chief of patrol forthwith. On the second night the same message was repeated, but on the third there was a difference: Report to the police commissioner forthwith.

This order he thought he had best obey. He had run out of personals. His time was up. He was obliged like any factory worker to go to work, to punch in, step behind the big desk at the Fifth Precinct station house and sign the blotter, thereby resuming his command and exposing the nape of his neck to his superiors. His job after that was to phone the PC's office to say he was on his way down there. Police Plaza lay about six blocks south. Powers walked it, dragging his feet. He knew he would be kept waiting in an anteroom, perhaps for hours.

He had left word that if Kelly or Luang called in, they were to phone Powers there.

Police Headquarters. A fourteen-story brick cube. Its walls, as he approached, looked three feet thick. Into them small windows had been set like nearsighted police eyes, like embrasures in medieval castles. The building looked like what it was, thought Powers, crossing Police Plaza: a fortress. It was such a heavy, monolithic building as to strike fear into the hearts of most men who entered it, including now himself. In a corner office on the fourteenth floor in a few minutes the future of his career and life would probably be determined. The decision would be made by certain of the men who inhabited this castle. In the police world the laws of feudalism still applied. From that decision Powers would have no more right of appeal than any of those men who, for thousands of years, had lived like him in the shadow of the castle walls.

When he entered the PC's anteroom, the deputy inspector who was chief secretary ordered him curtly to take a seat.

"Chief Duncan is in with him now," he snapped.

"That's nice," said Powers. The man's bad manners brought a grim smile to Powers' face. There, he had his answer already. One entered the anterooms of great men and read the verdict instantly in the deportment of their secretaries. Was the secretary cordial? Charming? No? Too bad. In a sense secretaries usurped the roles of their masters, and ought to be disciplined for it. They warned the victim quite thoroughly in advance. He knew about the waiting axe before he ever got through the throne-room door. After that, actually dropping it on him could not be nearly as much fun.

The deputy inspector had buried his head in some papers. When he glanced up Powers beamed him a big smile. False, but big.

The phone rang.

"That may be for me," said Powers, to bedevil him. After three days he had as little hope left in Kelly and the detectives as in Luang. They could not even find Orchid Koy, who perhaps had not come to New York yet. If she delayed much longer she would be too late to figure in even the most desperate of Powers' fallback plans.

"For you," said the deputy inspector. "Make it short."

Powers, giving the man another smile, took the phone. "Yes, Luang?"

Luang was at the airport. Koy had gone inside and the limousine had pulled into the service lane to wait for him. Maybe Koy was meeting the anticipated female.

Anticipated female? More and more Luang talked like a typical New York cop. It just didn't go with the way he looked and with how hard he worked.

"What terminal are you at?"

Several airlines used the terminal, it seemed. British Airways, Air Jamaica, Air Canada—

Powers interrupted him. "Air Canada sounds right. Call me back as soon as you have more news—either here or back in the precinct."

Powers went back and sat down. He had the feeling that something at last was happening, and this time the smile he sent across the room was real—so real that the deputy inspector, intercepting it, dropped his eyes in annoyance: the condemned man refused to act condemned.

When the traffic lights changed color over the PC's door, the deputy inspector said curtly, "The PC will see you now."

Powers went in. The PC in shirtsleeves sat behind his desk. To his right in uniform, as upright as a judge, as unsmiling and as unfriendly as Powers had ever seen him, stood Chief of Patrol Duncan. Powers wore his summer street uniform: blue shirt and black tie, his gold captain's shield pinned over his left breast, his service revolver riding over his right hip, and he carried his cap, which bore less gold braid than Duncan's, under his arm.

The questioning, if that's what it could be called, was begun by Duncan. "A junket to Hong Kong, that's what you went on. Did you take your wife?"

"No, I did not take my wife," said Powers, speaking slowly, carefully. He had resolved not to be provoked. He believed he had little enough chance to survive this hearing. He was in no position to buy himself luxuries. Anger, to Powers, was like a mink coat. It would warm him up, but its cost was prohibitive.

"How about side trips?" demanded Duncan. "Did you take an excursion into Red China?"

"No, I did not."

"Did you take a girl friend? I've been hearing stories about you. Did you take a girl friend?"

"What the hell are you talking about? Stories? What stories? Explain yourself."

"You know what I'm talking about."

The PC intervened. "Easy, Don." He stood up and came out from behind his desk. He began circling like a prosecutor, like a shark. Powers had to shift position in order to track him. He said, "The only justification for your trip would be results. And you have no results. Or do you? Let's talk about results."

"No immediate results, no," said Captain Powers. "But—"

"But what?" demanded Duncan.

"I don't consider the trip a total waste. I put two corrupt Hong Kong cops in jail and—"

"That is of no conceivable interest to us."

"Well it should be. We're cops. Our job is to protect the good people and to put the bad ones in jail—whatever their nationality."

Momentarily at least, this silenced Duncan. "All right," said the PC, "I'll grant you that much. What else?"

Powers said: "There is a chance—I have a plan, an idea that—"

The PC stopped circling. "Chance? Plan?"

"Commissioner, I went to Hong Kong to gather evidence against the mayor of Chinatown, Mr. Koy. I was hoping for something that would prove him part of an international conspiracy. I intend to continue my investigation. I did pick up a lot of information in Hong Kong that could be exactly what we need to bring the investigation to a successful conclusion." A long, dull speech even to Powers himself. After the barest possible hesitation he added: "Sir."

"What are you talking about, man?" said Duncan.

The PC and Duncan waited for further details but Powers' mouth became set in a thin hard line, and he refused to give any.

"Do you realize how much money your junket cost the City?" said Duncan. "The City is broke. The police department is broke. And you squander money on a useless junket. If the press gets wind of this, there's no way it can be defended."

He had a point there, and Powers knew it, but this was no time to concede ground. "The press is not going to get wind of it," he said.

"Oh no? That ain't the way I heard it, buddy boy."

Powers shouted, "If you've got something to say, say it. And if you don't, shut up."

"Gentlemen, gentlemen," said the PC. He turned to Powers. "I want to hear about your plan."

Powers said, "And so you shall, just as soon as I have it worked out, sir."

"I'm afraid you misunderstood me." The PC's voice had become icy. "I said I want to hear about it right now."

When Powers did not answer, the PC said, "What kind of idiots do you take us for? Do you think I don't know what you're up to? The *Rotterdam* docked at eight A.M. The passengers and their luggage are already off. Nothing. Your plan isn't a plan at all, it's a pipedream. O'Reilly says you have no evidence whatsoever that the heroin is on that particular ship. Even if it is, according to Glickman, Customs probably won't be able to find it."

Powers stared at him. The only thing that made the moment bearable at all was that Duncan was staring too. The chief of patrol was as surprised as he was.

The PC said, "Who gave you the authority to go to Drug Enforcement, to call in Customs?"

Duncan had recovered from his surprise. "Going to outside agencies is not your job, it's the chief of detectives' job."

"I wasn't aware that going to other agencies for information or help was a crime," said Powers to the PC. Again he added carefully: "sir."

"Don't you speak to me in that tone of voice."

Powers said nothing.

"Is that all?" demanded the PC. When he got no reply from Powers, he turned to the chief of patrol: "Don?"

"It will take me twenty-four hours to get a new man

in your precinct," said Duncan. "You are relieved of command as of this time tomorrow."

The sentence had been imposed. It was only what Powers had expected, and there could be no appeal. The most he could ask for was a stay of execution. Turning to the PC, Powers said, "Sir, if I may respectfully point out something that the chief of patrol has overlooked—"

He again fell silent. He had just been fired, and it was only what he deserved—impossible at the moment to convince himself otherwise. Not his fault? Of course it was his fault. These men were correct to dismiss him. The trip to Hong Kong was wasted, the heroin was not on the *Rotterdam*, he was inadequate as a precinct commander, and most likely a failure as a man as well.

"Overlooked?" demanded the PC. "Go on, man."

Powers saw he had created the effect he had hoped for. The PC had read a threat in there, and Powers struggled to put it to use. A single word might give him back life—or the illusion of life.

"Sir, if I could have another week or two, I think I can bring this investigation to a head. Even if we come up empty as far as the *Rotterdam* is concerned, I think I can promise you some important arrests—" Wrong start.

"No," said Duncan.

Powers, trying to ignore him, hoping the PC would do the same, said, "If I am removed from the Fifth Precinct tomorrow, the investigation on which we have expended so much money, so many man-hours, will result in no arrests at all." Too wordy. Last chance coming up. "As Chief Duncan pointed out a moment ago, the police department would not look very good in the newspapers."

Duncan and the PC were both staring at him. Powers could meet only one pair of eyes at a time; he chose the PC's —and stared him down.

An empty victory, or a real one? Which was it? The PC walked over to the window and peered out.

At last he turned. "Arrests? Significant arrests? How much chance there? Don't lie to me."

"I've spoken to them at the DA's office. I'm going over and pick up the warrants when I leave here," said Powers.

"Warrants?" said Duncan. "Warrants on who?"

Tell him nothing, Powers thought. But he did not dare do it. "I'm hoping to arrest a part of the conspiracy, at least," he said.

"Koy? Have you got Koy?"

The only question that counted. "At the moment, no," said Powers. "But I'm hoping—"

"You can't have a week," said the PC, still staring out the window. "A week is too long." He turned abruptly. "Shall we give him two days? Is that all right, Don?"

"That's not even time enough to execute my warrants," said Powers.

"If you get any warrants," said Duncan.

"Very well," the PC continued. "Nail Koy, or find the shipment of heroin. You can have until the *Rotterdam* leaves here."

Powers turned to stare at Duncan—who was smiling. No one showed him out. As he left the room, his shirt was soaked. A rivulet of sweat slid like a downhill skier down the groove of his back.

An hour later Powers stood before the district attorney's desk. "I want as many warrants as you'll give me." He pushed a list across, and for a moment the district attorney studied it: Marco, Casagrande, Han, Low, and Koy.

But the DA began shaking his head almost at once. "I told you this the other day. A warrant on Koy is out of the question. Legally speaking you have no more on him now than you had six months ago. I would need something hard. I was hoping you'd bring hard evidence back from Hong Kong, but you didn't, sorry to say. On the surface at least, Koy is a pillar of the Chinese community. He's a heavy contributor to the Democratic Party. The answer on Koy is no."

Powers said stubbornly, "What about the others?"

The DA sighed. "You don't have much on them

either. Even youth gang leaders and Mafia drug dealers have civil rights, you know. I don't want to be criticized by the press." He stood up and came around in front of his desk. "I'll put you together with some of my people," he said. "It's up to you to convince them of the legal merits in each case. I won't interfere. You'll be here the rest of the day, I expect." He clapped Powers on the shoulder. "I wish I had better news for you."

By the time he got back to the station house it was late afternoon. In his office he hung his cap and gunbelt behind the door, loosened his tie, and from behind his desk phoned Customs. The *Rotterdam*'s cargo had come off and had been fairly carefully inspected, Glickman told him. There were crates and crates of Edam cheeses. You couldn't cut open every cheese. There were crates and crates of Heineken's beer. You couldn't open every bottle. Barring a specific tip you couldn't drill into the shipment of Danish furniture or cut into the tires of about fifty German-built cars. So far, nothing had been found, which wasn't surprising. Inspection teams had gone aboard and had scoured about a third of the ship. They would finish tomorrow.

Powers hung up. After a moment he lifted his briefcase onto the desk top. Opening it, he stared in at the thin packet of warrants; a hand of very low cards in a high-stakes game.

When he glanced up, Luang stood in the doorway.

He thought Luang must have lost Koy and returned for instructions. What else could it be? That meant another day gone with no results—and so few remaining.

"Koy's at the funeral parlor, Captain. I figured I could leave him there awhile." Luang, as he extracted a notebook from the pocket of his seersucker suit, was behaving with unaccustomed confidence. He was almost strutting. "I thought you might want to hear what I've got."

Why is he being so theatrical, Powers asked himself. His mind felt weighted down with the heavy furniture of depression. The process of thinking was as slow as the moving around of sofas.

Luang said, "At the airport this morning he picked up a Chinese female about his own age—about your age, Captain. She had four pieces of luggage. Going to stay awhile, right? If she came in by Air Canada, it was probably flight three twenty-one from Toronto. We could check the airline's manifest, if you think it worthwhile."

Powers was still studying the contents of his briefcase.

"The limo took them to Ten Confucius Plaza. The bodyguards carried the bags inside, and then drove away, and Koy did not come down again for two and a half hours."

"Luang," said Powers, and looked up at him.

"I watched all sorts of things get delivered, Captain: flowers, some rugs, a king-sized bed. It wasn't hard to find out what apartment the stuff was going to—32–N. It was on all the delivery tickets, along with the name Orchid Koy."

The Chinese police officer, having brought home the information he believed his commander wanted, looked extremely pleased with himself.

"The apartment is rented to Jimmy and Orchid Koy, joint tenants. I checked it out."

"Luang," said Powers, thinking: he expects to be congratulated and I can't bring myself to do it.

"Something the matter, Captain?"

Powers flashed a smile. "No, nothing's the matter."

"What next?" asked Luang, beaming with pleasure. "Do I go back to the funeral parlor and sit on him, or what?"

"Yes," said Powers. He stood up and came out from behind the desk. It took effort, but he forced the words out: "You've done a great job," Voice and step became brisk, and that took effort too. "But with a difference. Put a uniform on. Stand on his doorstep. I want him to know who's been tracking him all these weeks. I want him to see you and start worrying. Let's make the bastard sweat."

Powers had resolved that he would wait no longer. He would go with what he had. He would shake the tree and see what fell out. Criminals of this type were not statues. They were men who lived on the edge, and knew it. Often it was far easier to scare them, to push them toward panic, than you might imagine. While Luang changed, Powers began to make calls: to Baumgartner of Immigration, to Wilcoxon of Drug Enforcement, to the DA, to Eleanor—he would be home late tonight. But he told no one exactly what he was planning.

"How do I look, Captain?" It was Luang in uniform in the doorway.

"It's the first time I ever wore it."

"Tomorrow," said Powers, "I'll let you make your first arrest."

"Who?"

"How would you like to lock up Nikki Han?"

"Captain, I'd like that very much."

"You can count on it," said Powers, and waved him out.

After some thought, he picked up the phone again and dialed Carol at home.

"I wasn't sure you were back," he said when she came on the line.

"Today. How are you? I'm so glad to hear your voice."

He had neither time nor inclination for small talk. "I want to ask a favor, Carol. I want you in Chinatown tomorrow with a film crew. I want you to go into the funeral parlor and attempt to interview Koy."

Carol was silent. This was not what she had expected to hear.

"How does that help you?"

"You need footage of him for your piece, don't you?"

"Yes, but how does that help you?"

"I want to put him in a state of psychological shock and keep him there. He probably thinks you're dead. If you've come back to haunt him, then I can't be far behind." First Koy would see Luang, then Carol. And then?

"I don't want to face him just yet, Artie. I'm not ready."

He spoke to her almost brusquely. "If you don't get him tomorrow, you might not get him."

"I'm—I'm too afraid."

"I'll send fifteen uniformed cops in there with you. You'll be perfectly safe. Fifteen." The idea pleased him. Fifteen uniforms. The shock on Koy would be tremendous.

Her inflection changed, became personal. She wanted to talk not about Koy but about Powers. "Will you be there," she asked, "tomorrow?"

Tomorrow? She meant much more than tomorrow, they both knew it, and he hesitated.

"No Carol, I won't be there."

Her voice became wistful. "You won't be there?"

"I'm sorry, Carol."

"I'll always be your friend, Artie."

"I'll always be yours, too," he said. "Hey, who else have I ever been almost murdered with twice?"

There followed a long silence. "Can I count on you, Carol?"

"What time?" she said.

37

T HE NEXT morning, Powers distributed to the pairs of arresting officers his scant supply of warrants. Arrest warrants were like airline tickets. Detectives were like travel agents assigned to deliver each one in person. The passengers were out in the city waiting for them, but did not know it. They held reservations to the end of the line, but would try to disembark along the way, and most would succeed. It was impossible to tell in advance who would land where. The tickets were expensive, and perhaps not worth what they cost.

The New York Police Department made more than 100,000 felony arrests a year, rarely two alike. There were rules—those imposed by the courts to protect suspects' rights, and those imposed by the Department to protect cops' lives. The arresting officers obeyed most of them most of the time if they could. The job called for brutality and delicacy at the same time, like the setting of broken bones, and although correct procedures had been exhaustively worked out, it was no exact science. One arrested killers, if possible, in their beds at five A.M. Squads of cops burst in through every window and door. One caught them napping. One caught them with their pants down as well. It was really quite safe. Naked men—even killers—are not brave, and dreams are more immobilizing than handcuffs; they encapsulate people and render them benign.

On the other hand one arrested corrupt cops at home at dinner time, if possible, snatching them from the bosoms of wives and children, uprooting them from their own dining room tables, because that way they would confess quickest; often they began babbling before they reached the car.

And there was every gradation of arrest in between. There was one common theme—at the moment of arrest an attempt was almost always made to achieve psychic domination of the prisoner. Emotionally, no one ever really wanted to leave home. The start of every journey, even pleasurable ones, tipped every passenger, even vacationers, into a state of emotional imbalance. It was this imbalance that enabled common carriers to control passengers so easily from journey's start to journey's end. If psychic domination was important to airlines and shipping companies, it was vital to the police.

Powers had given his men explicit instructions. The drug dealer, Marco, was arrested by Kelly and a second detective in the social club at 167 Mulberry Street in Little Italy just before noon. They had been sitting outside in their parked car almost four hours waiting for him. When they went in to take him, Marco was seated at a corner table with his hat on, sipping cappuccino with two other men, also Italians, also wearing hats. Powers wanted the most blatant arrest possible. He wanted the news to spread from there throughout the narcotics trade—it might queer either this transaction or another—and throughout the community too. He wanted Marco disgraced, if that was possible.

Kelly and his partner approached the table. "Marco? I have a warrant for your arrest."

There was no violence except by them. The two detectives grabbed Marco under the arms and lifted him kicking into the air. Hands manacled behind his back, they dragged him out to the street, where they threw him as roughly as possible into the back of their car. The second detective leaned over the seat and read him his rights, while Kelly drove. All this time Marco spoke not one word.

Casagrande was arrested at his house in Queens an

hour later. His bell was out of order and the knocking at his front door came as he was eating lunch. He answered wearing a napkin tied around his neck. There were tomato smears on the napkin where he must have wiped his mouth several times.

Facing him were two detectives he had never seen before. One said in a flat monotonous voice, "Mr. Casagrande, I have a warrant for your arrest. You have a right to remain silent, you have a right—"

"Let me see the fucking thing," said Casagrande.

He read it.

"Do I call my lawyer now, or at the station house?"

He was pretending that no psychic domination had occurred, but the arresting detectives knew otherwise, because his pinky ring was twitching.

"At the station house," said the detective, and handcuffed him, squeezing the cuffs tight enough to hurt, giving him a shove so that he fell slightly off balance going out the door, letting him learn at once that walking a straight line with his hands manacled behind him was less easy than it looked. They marched him out to their car still wearing the stupid napkin around his neck—since he couldn't reach it he couldn't remove it. He cut a ridiculous figure, which was what they wanted. He knew this—in the street several neighbors who happened to be outdoors stood gawking at his passage—and it added to his anger and humiliation.

Nikki Han and Go Low came out of Koy's gambling parlor about two o'clock in the afternoon. These arrests too had been orchestrated by Powers for maximum community impact. The arresting officers were to be Luang and his partner for the day, Lawrence Lom, the middle-aged community relations patrolman who had not made an arrest in over twenty years. The pair had been loitering up and down Mott Street for almost six hours, waiting. They did not even know for certain the two gang members were inside the den, and had no search warrant with which to go in looking. Detectives—good ones—were like hunters. They didn't stalk their game, they put themselves in its path and waited for it to walk by. For six hours Lom had been bored stiff, had complained constantly. But Luang, having tuned him out, had remained alert and excited the entire time. The case on which he had worked so hard and taken such risks was about to break, and he was exactly where he wanted to be—in at the climax. He was eager to make his first arrest, to lock up Nikki Han.

When he saw Han and Low come up the steps from the gambling den he dug his elbow into Lom's ribs.

"Let's go get them," said Lom nervously.

"Let them get into their car first," ordered Luang. "Then we have the right to search the car."

Nikki Han had unlocked the door on the driver's side. He got in. They saw him lean across to open the far door. Go Low still stood on the curb, peering around.

"Now," said Lom nervously.

"Wait till the other guy gets in the car too," said Luang.

Luang, gun in his hand, rushed the car even as the second door slammed shut. He rammed the barrel in through the window into Nikki Han's ear. He speared him in the ear with it. The gang leader squawked and ducked away, clapping his hand to the pain, peering up at Luang in surprise.

"What's this?" he cried, first in English, then in Cantonese. His head darted about, because by now Lom's gun showed in the opposite window.

"Get out," ordered Lom, who was beginning to enjoy himself. There was no further risk, and he was remembering emotions as distant as courtship but no less pleasurable now as then. He was acting like a cop again, and it felt good to him.

"Out," shouted Luang in English. Throwing the door open, he grabbed Nikki Han by the collar of his shirt, and heard it rip and was pleased. He dragged him half out of the seat and, once he was suspended over the street, let go. Nikki fell out the rest of the way, crashing to the pavement.

A crowd had begun to gather. Luang's shield was

cupped in his free hand and he was flashing it all around. Lom's shield was pinned to his shirt.

"Up against the wall," shouted Luang, waving his gun. "Give them a toss, Lom."

Lom frisked both prisoners, and he remembered to be rough about it, as in the old days. His hands, snaking up their legs from their shoe tops, turned into karate chops at the crotch. He doubled both men over.

"They're clean," he said to Luang, grinning. They were doubled over and gagging.

"Cuff them," Luang said.

Lom did it, squeezing the cuffs down to the last notch on slim Chinese wrists. He had never arrested a Chinese before. It was like cuffing a child.

"Search the car," said Luang.

Behind him he heard Lom rummaging through the glovebox, under the seats, opening the trunk. He heard Lom's voice say, "Well, well, well, what have we here?"

Without taking his eyes off the prisoners, Luang began to laugh. "What did you find, Lom?"

"I found a piece," said Lom, and he went on searching.

"See," said Luang. "I told you to wait till the other guy got in the car. Now we can charge both of them with possession."

"This car is a veritable arsenal," said Lom. "I got a thirty-eight behind the spare wheel to go with the Browning nine-millimeter under the seat."

Luang stopped laughing. "One of those brothers was killed with a Browning," he said. "Is this the gun, Nikki?"

When Han gave no answer, Luang said, "We'll soon know, won't we, Nikki?"

At gunpoint, they marched the two handcuffed gang members down Mott Street to Bayard Street, across Bayard to Elizabeth, and up Elizabeth into the station house. An enormous, murmuring crowd followed most of the way. Chinese merchants came out of their shops to watch. It was as great a spectacle as the parade of dragons on Chinese

New Year's Day, and this too was according to Powers' instructions. Luang, like any ham actor, played the scene to the hilt, barking the Miranda warning in stentorian tones as he walked, reciting it over and over both in English and in Cantonese: "You have a right to remain silent. You have a right to demand counsel. You have a right to—"

Powers watched as the prisoners were brought up the steps and into the station house. All were docile and none spoke. They were manhandled past him anyway. He stood in the doorway to his office just inside the entrance while the arresting officers pushed and shoved and dragged them across the board floors toward the staircase to the squad rooms above. They were like men whose arms had been cut off, and once again Powers was struck by an old notion— that to a large extent a man's dignity resided in his hands. Take his hands away and he looked incompetent and therefore foolish. Without hands the illusion of dignity could not be sustained.

Upstairs the prisoners were thrown into a cage, like gloves into a bin. They were later extracted, one pair at a time, to be fingerprinted. Dignity, and with it psychic balance, continued to be broken down. Each prisoner was forced to answer questions, to sign forms, to stand here, sit there. They were made subject to ritual. They were forced to kneel at mass. The police department was like the Catholic Church, employing ceremony to prove its absolute dominion over souls.

The interrogations started. Could one of the prisoners be made to talk about the narcotics shipment, or to turn against Koy, thus saving his own skin, and Powers' as well? Marco the hardened Italian mobster, was brought into an empty office off the squad room.

"You're on parole, Marco," said Powers. "We got you consorting with known criminals and we got you tied in with the Chinese. You go back into the can to finish your sentence. Is that what you want?"

Marco, rubbing sore wrists, only glared at him.

"How much time you got left on that parole, Marco? I can look it up, but why don't you tell me?"

Marco examined the ceiling.

Powers walked to the desk and thumbed through Marco's file. "It says here seven years, Marco. Is that what you want to do?"

"When do I get my phone call?" said Marco.

Casagrande was brought into a second office by Detective Kelly, who pushed him roughly into a chair. Powers came in. He was like a dentist who kept chairs going in adjacent rooms. He was running back and forth from patient to patient, drilling hard, no Novocain. If he struck a nerve, the object was to lean on it.

Casagrande, still manacled, was sitting on his hands.

"Who's got a handcuff key?" said Powers. "Take the cuffs off him."

Casagrande flexed his wrists, his fingers. He stared at his hands as if he had forgotten what they looked like.

"As I see it," Powers began, "you're the little guy in this conspiracy. Your brother-in-law and Koy are the big shots. They're the ones who should do time, not you. But the jury probably won't see it that way. The jury will probably decide you're equally guilty. There's a mandatory twenty-five-year sentence for the type of business you've been doing. Do you want to go away for twenty-five?"

Casagrande said, "You got nothing on me. I didn't do nothing. I want to see a lawyer."

"Why should you protect Koy?" said Powers. "What's a Chinaman to you?"

"Who's Koy?" said Casagrande. "I don't know that name."

Powers drummed a pencil on the desk. "I'll make a deal with you, Casagrande. Never mind your brother-in-law. Just give us the Chinaman, and you walk."

He was talking to the man's left profile only. Casagrande rubbed his wrists, gazed into the middle distance, and gave no sign that he heard a word.

Powers met with Kelly outside. When Marco and Casagrande were arraigned later, it was possible the judge would release them. He might not even set high bail. The purpose of these arrests was to elicit information about the narcotics and about Koy, and most judges considered such arrests as affronts against civil liberties.

"So the questioning gets rougher," said Kelly. "Come on."

Casagrande first. Kelly stood two feet from his chair, slowly slapping his sap into his open palm. Casagrande watched the sap as he might have watched the head of a cobra.

"You ever been hit with one of these things?" asked Kelly conversationally. "Turn your brain to jelly and never leave a mark. When I was a young cop, all the fellas carried one. You don't see them much anymore." The sap kept slapping down. Sweat had popped out on Casagrande's brow —whether from concentration or fear was impossible to determine. "If we killed one of you pricks by mistake nobody cared." This was true. Powers had been there. He had seen such things happen, and had turned away, and had kept his mouth shut afterwards.

"Nowadays we gotta be more careful," said Kelly. He dropped the sap into his coat pocket, and continued the intimidation by other means.

"What we do nowadays," said Kelly, "is, we let you go. Then we put word out on the street that you gave up a made guy, a man of respect such as your brother-in-law. Then two or three days after that we find your body in the trunk of a car. And you want to know something, pal? When one of you ginnys turns up in the trunk of a car, nobody cares. Now what I suggest to you is, you give us Koy like we asked you. Otherwise, I figure you got about two days to live."

Kelly was nodding his head up and down. "You think about it a minute, while I go next door and tell your brother-in-law all you've been saying about him."

Kelly, as he entered the adjoining office, was shaking his head sadly. "Marco, you got problems. Your brother-in-law is blabbing his head off. You know that meeting with Koy you had at 167 Mulberry Street? He was just telling us how he got sent out into the street. Koy didn't want to talk in front of him, it seems. He was insulted. I guess that's why he's talking so much. Unfortunately, he's telling us a lot about your operation, too. Which don't interest us, by the way. Now if you want to shut him up, why don't you give us Koy? Otherwise, the ways things are going, he'll cause you so much loss of respect you'll have to put out a contract on him. I know you don't want to do that. Your sister's husband and all."

For two hours the interrogation continued, but both subjects remained obdurate. It was like bombarding boulders with eggs. It was like beating on drums in an attempt to weaken the fabric of the drum. Although one used words instead of drumsticks, the decibel level was the same. But these drums seemed truly inanimate, impervious to noise, impervious to the passage of time. Whereas the effort expended by the drummers was prodigious. The useless, monotonous, echoing reverberation wore out the drummers.

Again Kelly and Powers consulted in the hallway.

"What do you think, Captain?"

"Let's try the Chinese guys," said Powers. He had a screaming headache, brought on by his own screaming voice, which he was losing. He was already hoarse, and getting hoarser.

They talked in whispers, because across the squad room Nikki Han sat on the floor of the cage watching them with small ferret eyes. Since the arrests he had been kept apart from Go Low, who waited his turn in still another empty office guarded by Luang.

"Go Low is our best chance," whispered Powers.

Kelly walked over to the cage. Han only stared at him.

"You pulled the trigger on one of the brothers," Kelly snarled. "We got a witness. We got you for extortion, for possession of weapons today, and for murder. Ironclad evidence. You want a break, Nikki, you give us Koy. We know he was at the warehouse the night you killed that guy. We got a witness to that too. You want a break, you call me."

That would give Han something to think about—

maybe—while Powers and Kelly went into the office and worked over Go Low.

Kelly slammed the office door. Go Low, after hours of immobility, jumped to his feet. "Report just came back from the lab," said Kelly, a lie. No report was expected before tomorrow. "That Browning matches the bullet out of the Hsu boy's skull." Kelly was chortling, rubbing his hands. He's a fine actor, thought Powers.

Kelly said, "We got you for possession of guns, kiddo. And now we got you as an accessory to murder also. You want a break, you tell us about the narcotics shipment that's coming in. You give us Koy."

The Chinese youth stared at Kelly.

Kelly said, "Nikki Han pulled the trigger, but you were there. We got it all on tape. Ironclad evidence. You go away for life. We also know that Koy was there. Koy gave the orders. You agree to give us Koy, you get a break. You give something, you get something."

Low was a dapper youth. His movements were lithe like a cat's. There was a feline expression to his face as well.

The questioning turned vicious.

"You're a pretty sharp dresser, Low." Kelly said. "Think a lot of your appearance, don't you? Nice fingernails, I see. I wonder how you'll like it in the slammer. You've never done any time, have you? You little Chinese guys are very popular in the slammer. They turn you into girls right away. Have you ever been fucked up the ass, Low? Tonight on Riker's Island you can try it out. They'll be glad to see you on Riker's. At the end of an hour, two hours, your asshole won't be virgin no more, Low."

They were interrupted by Casagrande's voice through the wall. "So take me to court," he shouted.

Powers said, "Or we could hold you here. Think about it, Low."

As the afternoon passed, Casagrande kept demanding to be booked and arraigned. He seemed to become more and more agitated, and Powers noted this.

"I got my rights," Casagrande shouted from next door.

"Take me to court and I'll post bail," Casagrande shouted.

His lawyer had charged into the station house and was making the same demands downstairs. He made them over and over again. Powers, locked in the office with Low, could hear both voices through the walls. After delaying as long as he could, he at last ordered Marco and Casagrande booked and taken to arraignment court. But he drew the arresting detectives aside and instructed them, if Casagrande should make bail, to follow him away from the courthouse.

"I want to know where he goes," said Powers, and he watched the two handcuffed prisoners, the two detectives and the lawyer leave the station house. Then he sighed and went back upstairs to resume questioning Go Low.

FROM POWERS' point of view, the most important of his four prisoners, though he did not know it, was Casagrande. Since the man had had no previous police record, his associates had assumed, wrongly, that no police agency was interested in him. He had therefore been assigned the job of getting the narcotics off the *Rotterdam*—which would sail that evening.

Arraignment court was crowded, and two more hours passed before the case was called. The judge ordered Marco remanded, and set ten thousand dollars bail on Casagrande. A bondsman, already on hand, posted it at once and Casagrande rushed out onto the street where he hailed a taxi and jumped into it. The two detectives were close behind him. The *Rotterdam* sailed at 6 P.M., and it was nearly that now.

Ownership of the narcotics aboard the *Rotterdam* had passed to the Italians the night before. Money had changed hands, a down payment that had already reached Koy. The Hakka stoker had been notified. Casagrande had been equipped with the recognition signal. He was prepared to put Marco's plan into operation. The narcotics were to be brought off in the final load of garbage before the ship sailed.

Two longshoremen had been alerted, but for reasons of security had been given no details. The details were the job of Casagrande, now leaning tensely forward in his cab, peering under the disused West Side Highway, toward the pier. Where there should have been a ship he could see open water. He could see clear across to New Jersey. The *Rotterdam* was half a mile out and a mile downstream—Casagrande did not care how far. He could not see it. It was gone. He was too late. He told the driver not to stop, to turn north on West Street and to keep going. He got out on Fifty-seventh Street and walked idly along, looking in the windows in the gathering twilight. The detectives parked. One got out and tailed him on foot from a discreet distance.

On board the *Rotterdam* eleven hundred cruise passengers sat down to a gala champagne dinner. In the engine room the stoker worked stripped to the waist, handkerchief tied around his neck, the sweat rolling down his back anyway. He was worried about the one-hundred-dollar courier fee he had not been paid, and about the plastic pouches still stashed under the floor plates in the bilge.

OUTSIDE THE station house window the afternoon faded into dusk.

Glickman phoned. "The ship has sailed, Captain. We made a good try, what can I tell you? Either they got the stuff off, or it was never on there."

"Maybe it's still on there," said Powers.

Glickman laughed. "You don't give up easily, do you?" But the laugh ended. "I guess this hunch of yours cost me about a hundred hours in overtime. That's a lot when you come up empty. I don't begrudge it to you. Given the facts, it was the logical ship. I thought it was worth a try, or I wouldn't have ordered it. But I hope you don't think we're going to search that ship again when it comes back."

"No, of course not," said Powers. "Listen, I really appreciate all you've done. Thank you very much. I mean it. I just wish I'd been right."

"Oh hell," said Glickman, embarrassed. "Maybe you were. Who knows?"

There was a long silence.

"One other thing," said Glickman. "The PC asked me to call him once the ship sailed. I'm afraid I'm going to have to do that."

"Sure," said Powers. "I understand. Don't think twice about it. And again—thanks for the good try."

He hung up and turned away from the phone.

"You look exhausted, Captain," said Kelly.

Powers had stepped out into the squad room to take the call. He looked around at the rows of empty desks. It looked like a newspaper office. At two of them squad detectives spoke into telephones. There were only three other persons present, Nikki Han pretending to be asleep on the floor of the cage, and a uniformed cop fingerprinting his prisoner at the fingerprint desk. The prisoner appeared to be an addict. The cop was working hard, carefully rolling each lax, uncoordinated finger on to the pad.

"I'm exhausted, all right," said Powers, "aren't you?"

Kelly laughed. "Relax, Captain. You can't expect to crack these pricks wide open the first night. It's a long process. We keep hammering on them the next six months, and maybe finally one of them cracks and gives up the others. Shall we go back to Go Low?"

Powers said, "I don't have six months."

The immigration officer, Baumgartner, having come up the stairs, walked out into the squad room. "Can I see you a minute, Captain?"

Powers went over to him.

"I stopped her on the street earlier today," said Baumgartner in a low voice. "We have that right by law. I asked to see her green card. From her attitude, I'd say she doesn't know it's phony. It's a very good job. I can pick her up and hold her for deportation. You tell me what you want me to do."

"How soon can you get a warrant, or whatever you guys use?"

"I took care of that already." said Baumgartner. From his breast pocket he withdrew the document and waved it at Powers. "But we have to make the arrest. You cops don't have jurisdiction in immigration matters."

"Just let me have the warrant," said Powers reaching for it. "Just let me have that paper in my hands for an hour."

Baumgartner handed it over. "What have you got in mind?"

"An idea that might work." said Powers. "I don't know. It's my only chance." Kelly was right. None of the prisoners would crack tonight, and he could wait no longer. He would have to move in the only other direction open to him. And he peered around for Luang. He found him in one of the offices, feet up on the desk, half asleep.

"Reach out for Koy," said Powers. "Phone the new apartment first. If it's an unlisted number, call telephone company security and get it."

Luang gave a grin. "It is unlisted, Captain, and I got it already."

Luang reached for the phone and dialed the number. While it rang Powers began to pace the room. But he could not keep his eyes off Luang, off the phone itself. He heard Luang say:

"Captain Powers calling from the Fifth Precinct. One moment, please."

Taking the receiver, Powers held his hand over the mouthpiece, and took a deep breath. When he began to speak, he made his voice sound carefree, jovial.

"Hello there, Mr. Koy. How are you? How was Hong Kong? Did you have a good trip?"

No answer came to any of these questions, nor had Powers waited for one. So far Koy had said nothing except hello.

"Yes," continued Powers, "I was away myself for a while. Yes, I went to Hong Kong too. I'm surprised we didn't run into each other there."

There was no answer from Koy, although Powers believed he could hear him breathing. Did this betray shock, fear, panic? It was ridiculous to imagine it betrayed anything except that the man was alive and had to breathe.

"Listen, Mr. Koy, I've got to see you right away. I have some information you might be interested in hearing."

"My office sometime tomorrow," Koy suggested after a moment.

Powers, who could detect no urgency in his voice, realized Koy was playing a game with him. The urgency, if any, would have to be displayed by himself, and then Koy would know more than he knew right now.

"No, your office wouldn't be a good place," said Powers, "and the precinct wouldn't be a good place either."

There was a clock on the wall across the squad room, and he watched the second hand sweep around twice. It became the heaviest silence he had ever endured.

Koy said, "Where do you suggest, then?"

"We need privacy," said Powers. He felt he had won a great victory, but was not sure why. He had forced Koy to speak, to request, in effect, that the meeting take place. And this time Powers believed he had heard a barely perceptible choke in Koy's voice. The man was not made of stone after all, and was worried.

"You and I ought to be able to settle this between us, if you get my meaning," said Powers. "We ought to be able to reach an accommodation, don't you think? The way this thing is going brings no profit to anyone, don't you agree?"

Koy said nothing.

Powers pursued him. "Let me give you an address. It's the perfect place to conduct our business without anybody bothering us. Let me suggest you meet me there in thirty minutes. Got a pencil?"

AT THE other end of the connection Koy took down the address given him and recognized it. Then he hung up the phone. Obviously shaken, he stared across at Orchid.

"You said the phone was put in only this morning,"

he remarked in Hakka. "You said the number was unlisted? You're certain?"

Orchid said: "Yes, I'm certain. What's the matter? All of a sudden you look awful."

Koy's attaché case lay on the table beside the phone. He snapped it open. Inside were stacks of bank notes with bands around them, and a .38-caliber short-barreled revolver for which he had a permit. The contents of the case renewed his confidence, and he snapped it shut.

"I've got to go out for a short time," he said. Without even glancing at his perplexed wife, he grabbed up the attaché case and left the apartment.

38

POWERS STOOD stripped to the waist. His belt buckle was undone and his trousers hung at half-mast. He held the transmitter and its batteries against his abdomen—a package about the size of a Zippo lighter—his forefinger poking it in, while Kelly wound surgical tape around it, and around his body. The Zippo was being embedded in flesh that hadn't been there, Powers reflected, when he was a young cop. Kelly was being careful, patting the tape smooth, so that no bulge showed. Koy would not make him on sight as wearing a wire. Kelly was unconcerned about peeling the tape off later. That was Powers' worry. It was going to hurt, Powers knew.

He held the antenna wires to his collarbone like suspenders and Kelly taped them down. He lifted the microphone to his sternum and Kelly taped it in place. A button about the size of a female nipple at a spot where no nipple, male or female, ever grew. Modern technology could not change the construction of the human body, nor the nature of evil, and perhaps its principal effect was always psychological. Its effect was perhaps less significant than men supposed. And what would be the effect of this gear tonight?

When finished, Kelly stepped back to admire his handiwork. Powers pulled his T-shirt on, buttoned his uniform shirt up the front, then knotted and drew up his tie.

"Pretty good, if I do say so myself," said Kelly, circling him. "Nothing shows."

"Good," said Powers.

Kelly looked at his watch. "We'd better hurry."

"Wait for me outside, Kelly."

Kelly said, "You told him half an hour, and it's past that now."

"He'll be there early, and he'll wait. The longer he waits, the more nervous he'll get. Please close the door on the way out."

As the door shut behind Kelly, Powers sat down at his desk, where he found an envelope and on it wrote his wife's name. Then he took a sheet of paper, and studied it. In a moment his pen began to move.

I am about to meet Koy, he began. I have taken every precaution. I'm not trying to get killed, but it could happen. If so, you should know the following.

He paused. He had been in many dangerous situations in twenty-three years. Why did tonight feel so much more dangerous than all the others? But he knew the answer. Because I'm going to make it more dangerous, he told himself. I'm going to force Koy into a corner from which there is no way out. I'm going to force him to kill himself or to kill me. Either way, the case ends tonight.

What does one write at such a time to a beloved wife of so many years?

The insurance policies are in the safe deposit box, he wrote. Its key is in the top drawer of my dresser. We have two savings accounts, whose passbooks are in the same drawer. Taped to the underside of the drawer is $100 in cash, an emergency fund. It has been there many years. Also in the safe deposit box are the wills we made right after Phil was born, our marriage certificate and other papers you may need.

He stopped writing and brooded. Now he had to be personal, and that was harder. What should he write?

His glance was caught by the television set fixed to the wall beside the door to his office. When he got up and switched it on, he saw that he had come in, as expected, at the tail end of Carol's Seven O'clock News.

This afternoon, according to one of the cops he had talked to, she had managed to photograph Koy entering and leaving his funeral parlor and getting into and out of his car. On the sidewalk she had thrust her microphone into his face and fired off questions that he had not answered. Useful footage, Powers supposed, to go with the film she had shot in Hong Kong. None of which would alter in any way his confrontation with Koy a few minutes from now.

On the screen Carol was talking about strikes in Poland, and she was wearing a summer print dress he had not seen before. He studied her face and listened to her voice, the timbre rather than the words—what did he care about strikes in Poland? But he found it impossible to believe in the intimacy that had once existed between them, the various forms of sustenance they had shared: the intimate dinners, the hours glued together in the dark.

He wished her luck putting her piece together. He wished her luck with her entire life. "Goodbye, Carol," he murmured, and realized he was saying goodbye not so much to a memory, as to an ideal, and ideals had no more reality than that image on the screen up there. Saying goodbye to images on TV screens was not even hard to do, and he switched the set off.

Back behind his desk, he resumed his letter to his wife: If tonight ends badly, he wrote, the police department will want to throw me a spectacular funeral. You don't have to let them do it. That is up to you. You can cry for me a little. Don't cry too much. Most people have only a few good years, or none. We had much, much more, and I never wanted to be married to anyone else the whole time. Love.

And he signed his name. The sealed envelope he tucked into his desk blotter, with Eleanor's name showing. He wondered if some cop would hand it to her, and when.

Looking and feeling extremely sobered, he started to leave the office. He had reached the door, had actually grasped the knob, before he realized he could not say goodbye to Eleanor only by letter. He could not bear to leave her without hearing her voice one last time, and so he stepped back to the desk and phoned home.

"I have nothing special to say," he told her. He kept his words casual. She must suspect nothing. "I'm going out to meet someone. I don't expect any trouble."

"What about dinner?" asked Eleanor.

"I'll call you as soon as I get back to the office."

"Okay."

"Talk to you later."

"Okay." She sounded as if this was the most casual conversation of their twenty-three years together, and he wanted to hold on to her voice as if it were a lifeline, the world's flimsiest. Instead he hung up the phone and strode out through the muster room and down the front stoop toward Kelly, who waited in an unmarked car at the curb.

As he slid into the passenger seat, Kelly said, "Your transmitter works, Captain. I heard you talking to your wife." It was almost an apology.

Powers gave him a brittle smile. "All right, let's go."

Kelly said hesitantly, "Shouldn't we have a few more people with us?"

"No," said Powers. "Like I told my wife, nothing is going to happen."

"How can you be sure?" asked Kelly.

Kelly had been a cop longer than Powers. He had the splayed feet, the paunch, the red nose, the tired manner to prove it. He probably had the wisdom to prove it too. You should listen to him, Powers told himself.

"Drive, Kelly," he said.

KOY GOT out of the taxicab on a lighted street and walked in. He could have kept the taxi with him, motor running. He could have come in his limousine and left it parked outside. He could have brought men with him. He had decided otherwise. He had convinced himself that Powers only wanted money. Powers was a blackmailer, neither more nor less. He was not afraid of Powers and needed no help to take care of him.

To see, yesterday, the Chinese cop in uniform on his doorstep, this man who had been tailing him for weeks, had shocked Koy. But behind it he had seen Powers, then as now an unthreatening figure, though tenacious, and obviously the tail had produced no results; if it had they would show. Results meant hard evidence, and in the realm of evidence, as all cops knew, hard did not mean hard at all. Evidence was a volatile substance. It bubbled and frothed. It called attention to itself. Evidence, if left alone, bubbled over or exploded—it could not be left alone.

No, Koy saw nothing to worry about in that Chinese patrolman. So he told himself.

The television woman earlier today had produced a second shock—proof that the plan in Hong Kong had misfired. He did not know how or, now, care. Fact was fact, and this particular fact could neither be changed nor linked to him. He had felt disappointment to see her still breathing, and in a matter of seconds had got over it. So he told himself.

But the moment he saw her he knew that Powers must have escaped also and was still after him, and the man's tenacity was puzzling because it was unreasonable. Powers seemed to have a fixation on him, and this could not be explained. Except as a prologue to attempted blackmail. He had been expecting the call from Powers for several hours, and then it had come. The only surprise was to hear the new phone ring—the new, unlisted number. How had Powers found out about that? But he was not afraid of Powers. So he told himself.

There had been, also, today's arrests to consider. They meant—what? He was certain the *Rotterdam*'s narcotics had not been intercepted. If it had he would know about it. It was the Italians' responsibility now anyway—no concern of his.

So many shocks inside a period of about twenty-four hours—they were like tremors in an earthquake zone.

Tremors in such places were not significant, he told himself, for the terrain was prone to them. The quake itself might start at any moment, or never. Earthquakes were unreliable, and could not be factored in. One could only ignore the possibility. Philosophically speaking, man was condemned by his nature to overlook earthquakes entirely.

No, Koy saw Powers as a business crisis only, neither more nor less. There had been others in his past of different types, each one recognized and surmounted. Business crises were inevitable, given a career as high-powered and exhilarating as his own. If you do not wish to risk spilling the wine, he had been taught as a child, do not fill the cup to the brim. He had not at the time understood the meaning of this proverb. But from the age of perhaps twenty-one, his cup had always been filled all the way up.

Attaché case in hand, he moved through a neighborhood as desolate and foreboding as any in New York. Tenements in rows, some of them boarded up. Smashed street lights. A burnt-out car. Addicts or winos skulking in the doorways. He did not expect to be accosted, and was not. He knew what every cop knew. Predators could smell fear —it was what set them off. They could also smell the absence of fear which identified their prey as something else, either a fellow predator or a cop—who was only a predator under another name; in any case not prey at all, but something best left alone. In the absence of visible fear they became afraid in their turn, and drew back into the darkness.

Powers had promised to come alone, and Koy believed him. Otherwise Koy would walk out, there would be no meeting, and no shakedown would take place. And what else could Powers want? Powers could have, as Koy saw it, only two possible purposes. The first was that he wished to scold Koy, to threaten him, to heap abuse. Obviously Powers had tried and failed to put a case together against him, and perhaps his instinct now was to act out his own frustration and rage in person. But the expenditure of energy would be great, and the results zero. Answer number one was not the answer. It did not fit what he knew of Powers, who must be, at the least, an escape artist to rival Houdini, and therefore no fool.

The second answer, blackmail, was the obvious one. It was impossible for Koy to conceive of a cop Powers' age who still took evil personally. He had not been such a man himself and had never known one. Evil—crime—flowed forward like the clouds, or tides. One could stand in its way forever without affecting it in the slightest. It just kept coming. Most cops at the start of their careers tried to stop it, or at least slow it down, but instead began passing through various stages of disillusionment. In Koy's experience they all reached the same place at the end—the place he imagined Powers had reached now. They saw people who were so rich as to seem aloof from evil altogether—it simply never touched them—and they wished to join such people on the high ground. Searching for a way to do this without becoming disgusted with themselves completely, many fixed on a method that ran like a dirt road through the brains of all cops, a road every cop seemed to think he had discovered for the first time. Koy was convinced that, five minutes from now, or an hour, or whenever Powers turned up, he would offer to drop his case—a broken case anyway—in exchange for payment of a certain sum of money. And if this sum was reasonable, Koy would pay it. It was part of the cost of doing business. It was perfectly normal. It happened all the time. It was nothing to be alarmed at. So he told himself.

If Powers wanted too much, then perhaps Koy would simply shoot him and leave him there.

He had come to the dark street that ran behind the waterfront warehouses. Widely spaced traffic lights. One or two parked cars. An occasional taxi that flashed by. It was not easy for him to find the warehouse he was looking for— he had only been there once. He peered into alleys until he found the one with the piled doors.

Someone had cleaned it up, or cleaned it out. The bedsprings, the disused furniture were gone. The doors were stacked neatly against the wall in a pile higher than his head. He shined his flashlight on them. Crossing them had been difficult the last time. The doors had rolled around on their doorknobs. It was like crossing an undulating sea. Now their doorknobs had been removed; the sea they represented was forever calm. He walked past them to the end of the alley, from time to time pausing to listen. The only risk was to come upon some derelict unexpectedly and get hit on the head before he could react. But there was no sound.

At the end of the alley the steel entrance door had been nailed shut with a single plank. He yanked the plank off, and the door sagged out so violently it almost knocked him down. He went inside, following his flashlight. Its beam led him forward like a dog on a leash. At the top of the stairs he shined the light all around, remembering the place only vaguely, for it occupied a spot of no significance in his life. His beam picked out light bulbs dangling from long wires, which posited the existence of switches, and he began to probe for them. Instead he found a fuse box half hidden behind a trestle table piled with empty crates. After studying it a moment he threw the lever and a single dim bulb came on out in the middle of the loft. He dragged the table under it and arranged the crates to serve as chairs. He set his attaché case upon the table and, after sitting down, practiced flipping open the single catch with an almost imperceptible flick of his forefinger. The case had a spring inside; once the catch was released its lid sprang up. Koy briefly studied its contents: the tools of his trade. His trade required that he dominate other men. To do this, he had learned long ago, it was best to appeal to one or both of mankind's two most primitive emotions: greed and fear. He closed the case. His tools were out of sight, and he was ready to meet Powers. His hands were motionless on the table. He was a tall Chinese wearing dark glasses and a tan silk suit. He took the glasses off and laid them beside the briefcase. As unmoving as stone, he waited.

39

OUTSIDE, Kelly's car came to a stop at the curb. From the doorway across the street, Luang ran toward them, yanked open the back door and jumped in.

"He came on foot about twenty minutes ago, Captain. He's in there now."

According to Luang, who peered across at the condemned warehouse, there was no one with him, and no backup car circling either.

Powers turned to Kelly. "You'll be monitoring my transmissions. You'll know what's happening."

He took out his service revolver and flipped the cylinder open, counting bullets.

"I'd like to know why we're here, Captain," said Kelly. But Powers did not answer. "Do you expect him to make damaging admissions? Or what?"

Or offer me a bribe, maybe, Powers thought. He had by now thought up several alternative endings more pleasing to him than his own death. Six bullets—he counted their flat brass heads. It was like counting blond children: yes, they were all there. Or take a shot at me, he thought, so I can kill him. But the case, one way or another, still ended tonight. Is that why I'm going up there, he thought—to murder Koy? Do I hate him that much? Closing the cylinder, he rammed the gun back where it came from.

A hundred years ago confrontations between sheriff

and outlaw took place in the middle of Main Street in broad daylight. They drew simultaneously. The game was the same today as it had always been, except that the rules had been changed to favor the outlaw, who was now allowed to fire first. The sheriff was obliged to wait for him to do it.

But Koy was as trained in the use of firearms as he was, and if he fired first would not miss.

Powers lifted his briefcase off the floor. From the glovebox he withdrew a flashlight.

Kelly said, "We should have apprehended him at his residence or place of business."

The stilted police phrasing warmed Powers even now. He was one with Kelly, with all cops. Cops partook of a community nourishment that made them different from other men.

"We should have more men," said Kelly. "We should all go in there together."

"I don't like this very much, Captain," said Luang.

Powers, already on edge, snapped, "Nobody asked you what you like." Immediately he wanted to apologize, but did not do so. Instead he stared at the building, at the dark alley beside it. "Turn the tape recorder on," he ordered Kelly.

The machine lay on the seat between them. Kelly placed earphones on his head. The spools started turning. They held forty-five minutes of tape, more than enough. The confrontation, one way or another, would be over well before that. Powers recited his name, rank and tax number, and the microphone fixed to his chest sent this information into the machine. He added the date and hour, the address. He identified Police Officer Luang and Detective Kelly as witnesses, and concluded: "I am going into the building now to arrest the suspect, Mr. Koy, according to the warrant I have with me."

But it was not the strong warrant he had once hoped for. It did not satisfy Powers and would not impress Duncan or the PC either—unless he could force it to perform a job it had never been designed for, and this he meant to do if he could. He had set the scene properly. He believed he had a good chance. The risk, though enormous, was worth taking.

The tape recorder was still running, the visible link between this minute and whatever was about to happen. Powers, having got out of the car, leaned back in the window. "If I call," he said to Kelly, "come in. If you hear shots fired, come in. Otherwise stay here and wait for me. Is that clear?"

He walked into the alley. He too was surprised by the neatly piled doors. He wondered who had stacked them up, and why. He wondered if he would ever walk back past them, and he wondered what his true motives were. But his thoughts were so dark and disorderly that he could not read them, or perhaps he was afraid to. He detected in himself only righteousness, hatred and lust. The lust was for justice, but it was lust nonetheless, as if justice were a woman he intended to rape. You are not God, he told himself. Nor are righteousness and goodness the same. Righteousness was another of life's seductive perversions, and perhaps the most truly wicked, because it posed as something it was not. Almost any crime could be committed in its name.

Having come to the entrance door, he shined his flashlight in on the broken stairs and began to climb them. No one followed him in, not God, if there was a God, nor even another cop. He was like a swimmer heading out too far. If the unforeseen occurred it would all be over before help could reach his side.

He came out into the loft proper. The dim hanging lightbulb was still another surprise. He snapped his flashlight off, thrust it down into the leg pocket of his trousers, and strode toward the trestle table. Koy watched him approach, but only his eyes moved. The rest of him was motionless. It was almost symbolic. The American rushed towards his destiny. The Oriental waited for it.

"Good evening, Captain. Won't you have a seat?"

Placing his briefcase opposite Koy's, Powers sat down and the two men scrutinized each other. Powers was searching for some sign of weakness, a clue as to how to proceed. But Koy's face showed nothing.

Out of nervousness Powers began glancing around. "Know this place, do you?" he asked. "Been here before, have you? I guess you never expected to see me here tonight? I guess you never expected to see me anywhere."

Koy said, "Get on with it, please. What do you want with me here?"

Powers said, "I thought you ought to return to the scene of the crime. As children we all learned that the murderer was supposed to return to the scene of his crime. Not entirely true in real life, I found. So I decided to make it come true this time."

"You are beating air with air, Captain."

Somewhere over the middle of the table their wills were locked in an intense and furious embrace. They were struggling like wrestlers, and Powers realized it.

Opening his briefcase, he withdrew a pile of papers, after which he set the briefcase aside. "I have some things I'd like you to look at," he said. He squared the corners with his cupped hands. "Those two thugs you sent after me in Hong Kong—"

"I, Captain?"

Powers put his half-glasses on and read from the top sheet. "Their names were Chin Hung Po and Lum Su Ma. Both police constables. They're in custody. Here are copies of the indictments." He waved them. "The prisoners have been doing a little talking. They will probably do more as the trial date nears. We expect they will name their employer, and then a warrant for his extradition will be prepared. Do you know who their employer might be, Mr. Koy?"

The expression on Koy's face did not change. "The gentlemen you name are unknown to me. The name on any warrant of extradition, if such a warrant ever comes to exist, would be unknown to me also."

Powers offered him the indictments. "Take a look at these in any case."

"No," said Koy.

Powers thrust them back into his briefcase. The pile on the table would continue to diminish. When he reached the bottom he would have no more cards to play.

He picked up the next papers in the pile. "I have other things here. These are warrants for a couple of youth-gang thugs who work for you, Nikki Han and Go Low. Some of my men yanked them out of a car this afternoon and then guns were found in the car. The gun charge against them is solid. The warrants speak also of murder. Mr. Han will go for life unless he speaks. Do you think he'll speak, Mr. Koy?"

Koy said nothing.

Powers said, "Mr. Low is more likely, I suppose. He's only eighteen. At that age a ten-to-fifteen-year sentence seems a long time. I expect he'll speak, don't you?"

"Let him speak. Let them both speak. Neither has anything to say."

"You were present here on the night the Hsu brothers were executed, Koy." Powers was finding it increasingly difficult to control his emotion. "You left a few minutes before the execution itself. We have found witnesses who can identify your car. We have the statement of one of the participants in the execution." Yes, Powers thought, Quong, who is dead.

Powers glared at him, but Koy's face remained expressionless.

Powers snatched up more documents. "Here I have warrants for the arrests of Mr. Marco and Mr. Casagrande, your partners in the narcotics importing scheme you put together a few weeks ago. Mr. Marco may or may not make admissions eventually. Mr. Casagrande, as you are no doubt aware, is a weaker type of individual. As a matter of fact, he is given to blabbing. We know, for example, the date, and the address on Mulberry Street where your meeting with these individuals took place. Mr. Casagrande has told us he was not present for the major part of the transaction."

It was the second time today that Powers would try to braid this fact into a usable lie. It hadn't worked the first time, and he saw no reason to suppose it would work now.

Nonetheless he continued: "However, I am informed that whatever testimony he now decides to give will be sufficient to send you to Attica or Green Haven, or one of those places for a considerable amount of time."

Koy's wrist watch flashed in the dim light. He studied its face, while Powers studied its quality. It was gold and as thin as a subway token. "Captain Powers, it is now past dinner time, I'm hungry, and this exercise in experimental theater which you appear to have so carefully orchestrated has begun to bore me. Good night." And he pushed back from the table.

"Sit down," Powers shouted. "I'm not finished yet." He watched Koy sit back down. "In your position I would be most anxious to know what the police had on me, or thought they had on me." For the first time an expression of uncertainty seemed to flit across Koy's eyes. "You see my point?" said Powers.

But Koy recovered quickly. "What is your point, Captain? Having served many years as a policeman, I have sat often enough in your chair to understand your strategy, your tactics, and even your mind, which I find transparent. Am I supposed to break down in tears and admit to these preposterous allegations? While you record them? Are you wired, Captain? Is that the point?"

Powers could visualize the spools turning downstairs in the car. He could imagine Kelly and Luang listening tensely, ready to spring, their guns in their laps.

"You are silent, Captain."

He could feel the adhesive tape constricting his middle, and the microphone button that pressed into the middle of his sternum, at the same level as the religious medals he used to wear around his neck as a boy. Like them, the microphone was a talisman. It was also the modern equivalent of an iron breastplate. It was the best protection a cop could wear. He was safe as long as he wore it, because it connected him not only to those two cops in the car, but also to the legions of cops behind them. He stood behind a shield of twenty-five thousand cops, and could imagine himself invulnerable.

But for as long as he wore it Koy was safe too, for he would make no move. Unbuttoning his shirt, Powers reached in, found the microphone, and ripped it out. He laid it down on the table between them: a dead tadpole. There would be no metamorphosis. It would not transform itself into anything.

The loft was vast. Powers could not see the end of it. Beyond the dim aura of light was outer darkness. "I am seeking to understand evil," he said. "Those two young men were kneeling—" he pointed "—just over there. You sent bullets into the napes of their necks. Did you—did you sleep well afterwards?"

Koy impatiently said, "You have not learned much about the Chinese, have you? The Chinese is moved by self-interest, not brutality. He is calculating, not cruel. The answer to your question is that one must sometimes sacrifice a finger to save an arm."

"That fifteen-year-old boy, Quong. You turned his head to mush. Can you justify that?"

"As a Chinese proverb has it," murmured Koy, "it is sometimes necessary to kill the chicken to show the monkey."

"Have you no concept of evil?" cried Powers.

Koy shook his head sadly. "Heaven does not speak, Captain. It has no fixed will. There is no god in the sky who hands out fantastic rewards or lamentable punishments. The Chinese do not fear future damnation, Captain. Only discord on earth."

It made Powers furious. "Do you have some Chinese proverb to justify trying to kill me?"

Koy shrugged, "You angered the tiger by thwarting it, as the Chinese say. You put meat in the path of the tiger."

Powers waved another paper. "This is a copy of a telex message that the Drug Enforcement Agency sent out to its bureaus in Boston, Vancouver and San Francisco, requesting them to put your three colleagues, the other three sergeants, under twenty-four-hour surveillance. Let's see them get something going under that kind of attention." He thrust the telex into his briefcase and grabbed up the next document in the pile. "And this is the result of another surveillance. We were on you in Hong Kong the moment you stepped off the plane there. One morning you took your wife shopping—her name is Orchid, isn't it? You left her and rode up to the seventh floor where you entered a certain office and purchased a forged green card in Orchid's name. Five minutes after you left that office we took the forger into custody. Here's the warrant on that." Powers thrust it out.

Koy's hands did not move, but his eyes, as if he could not stop them, scanned the paper.

Powers said, "You are sweating, Mr. Koy. You can control your voice and your mind, but not your glands. In that respect the Chinese are no different from anyone else, are they?" He thrust that document into the briefcase. Until yesterday he had had no others. Now, thanks to Luang, he did. He waved the next one. "We're getting near the end now," he said. "I have here an order of deportation for Orchid Koy, your first wife, who arrived in New York yesterday from Toronto and Hong Kong."

"At last the clouds part to show the true sky."

"Note the address of her apartment on Confucius Plaza in Chinatown. It is correct, I believe."

Koy accepted the document Powers held out to him.

"Officer Luang trailed the two of you there from the airport on my orders, after which I personally took the information to Immigration. An immigration officer stopped your wife earlier today and asked to see her green card. Perhaps she spoke of it."

"No," said Koy.

Powers took the document back, pulling it out of his hands. "You betrayed her, Mr. Koy. You betrayed her twice, once in Hong Kong, once here. You led us right to her."

IN THE CAR in the street the tape recorder spools were still turning, but the voices had stopped coming in.

"What's happened?" demanded Luang.

"I don't know," said Kelly. He was fiddling with the dials. "I don't even know if it's him or us. It was working perfectly."

Luang had his gun in his hand. "Let's go in there," he said.

"I don't know," said Kelly. "He told us to stay here." They gazed at each other indecisively. Neither knew what to do.

"I'm going," said Luang, and he sprang from the car and ran into the alley. But at the door he stopped. Powers had ordered him not to come in and he hesitated to disobey.

KOY'S FOREHEAD glistened in the light. "I too have a brief-case to open," he said. "If you will allow me." When Powers nodded, Koy released the catch on his attaché case and allowed the lid slowly to rise. He then turned the case around, so that Powers could note its contents: more money than he had ever seen before.

There was a gun in there too. "Do you have a permit for that?" said Powers.

Koy said, "In China, if an official is honest, we say he has clean wind in his sleeves. Let me see your sleeves, Captain."

Powers ignored Koy's gun. He stared only at the money. Guns to him were normal. But money in amounts such as this was not. He saw Koy's hand reach into his field of vision. He watched it shuffle the stacks of bills around.

"With money," said Koy, "a man is a dragon. Without it he is a worm."

"Close the briefcase," Powers said. He had been momentarily dazzled by what looked like hundreds of thousands of dollars. He had been blinded as if by automobile headlights. It had taken time to refocus his eyes.

"Dollars are like small fish," Koy said, stirring the pond, "—difficult to catch, and not to be thrown back except as bait for something bigger."

Was this a way of saying there was more? How much more? "Stop talking like a fortune cookie," cried Powers, alarmed by Koy's gun. It seemed to be swimming through the money, now on the surface, now in the depths.

"Close the briefcase," he ordered, and to prove he meant it, took his own gun out, and clapped it down wobbling on the table.

Koy misunderstood, perhaps deliberately. "Your thoughts lack subtlety, Captain. One cannot master temptation with a revolver. One cannot conquer greed with bullets. Please study my briefcase a moment longer."

Powers could feel that his face had become flushed. I could arrest him for attempted bribery, he thought, but it wouldn't stand up. It isn't on tape, and he never actually offered me anything, my word against his, and he's mayor of Chinatown.

Koy said: "I ask you to question your standards as you have forced me to question mine."

He saw that Koy was offering him a new life, as Carol had offered him a new life, the one great dream, he supposed, of every man his age: to start over. The end of struggle. Life as excitement and pleasure. Life as a perpetual party. This time there would be enough money and knowledge to gratify every whim. But life was not a party, and whims were insubstantial, impractical, unreal. Whims could not accord pleasure, did not exist on the same plane as pleasure.

"My sleeves," Powers said, "are clean. Now close that goddamn briefcase,"

He reached over and closed it himself. I don't want his money, he thought, I want to kill him. Is that clean?

"Your rice bowl is broken, Koy." He leaned across the table. "You're out of business. Tell yourself that those two thugs in Hong Kong won't testify against you. That Nikki Han and Go Low won't testify. That Marco and Casagrande won't testify. Tell yourself there is still time to make any other witnesses change their testimony or disappear. Your wife still gets deported, Koy. You have committed, as

I understand it, the one unforgivable Chinese sin. You have betrayed your family, betrayed all your ancestors. You could live here and your wife there for years, as long as you continued to send back money and honor. She gets no more honor from you, Koy. She goes back under a deportation order, and you lose face. You're a speculator, Koy. Face is your collateral. Without it you have no credit. I've deprived you of your most precious possession. That's what I've done, Koy. I've cut your balls off. I've cut off your face."

A bead of sweat began its slow trickle down Koy's forehead. Look at him suffer, Powers thought. It was the sweat of a man being tortured, and he felt an emotion akin to joy. He was inflicting mammoth amounts of pain, and reveling in it.

"She gets arrested tonight, Koy. She spends the night in the can." What suffering, thought Powers. It was always so much easier to hurt someone through a loved one. "Tomorrow she goes before a judge for a deportation hearing."

However, Koy's hand began to toy with his briefcase.

"She gets escorted to the airport by armed guards."

Koy frowned.

"Perhaps I can arrange for her to be taken out in handcuffs." Keep pushing him, Powers thought. Make him take action. Make him lose control. "I have one last document," he said and pushed it across. "This is a warrant for your arrest, Koy. The charge is not murder or extortion or narcotics. The charge is one people find funny, Koy, bigamy."

Koy's forefinger tripped the catch of his briefcase. As the lid sprang open his hand dived into it, scattering money, grabbing up his gun and pointing it across the table. From one second to the next Powers found himself staring down a gun barrel. Instantly his body felt frozen. Sweat began to drip down his back like ice cubes defrosting. But isn't this exactly what you wanted, he asked himself. This is assault with a deadly weapon. Now you can kill him. You're within your rights.

But he was in no position to kill anyone. His own

revolver was on the table, and as his eyes fixed on it the hands in his lap began to twitch. I've made a mistake, he thought. A bad one. The worst. It was only slightly out of reach. It was as out of reach as yesterday, as last week. If he went for it, how many bullets would strike him before he could grab it up? It was about two feet away, the same distance as Koy's, identical, you could measure it out mathematically. But the one gun was too distant, the other much too close, proof that nothing is absolute, not even numbers, much less life and death.

This has worked out perfectly, he told himself. You've got a major case against him now. If he kills you, Kelly and Luang arrest him for murder. If not, you have him for assault.

Both faces glistened in the dim light.

"Though a man dies, Captain, he is still part of the cosmos," said Koy in the voice of a priest murmuring a prayer over Powers' corpse. "He is one with the universe. He is not lost."

Out of terror, Powers found, came additional hatred. He was not going to listen while Koy read him the last rites, he was going to cause more pain first. Hatred: the inexhaustible emotion, the true bottomless pit. It dominated even fear. "Bigamy, Koy, you've got both wives right here. It will be very easy to prove. Everyone always laughs except the husband serving the sentence."

Behind the gun, Koy said, "I seem to detect moral indignation, Captain." Powers waited for him to study the warrant, but he did not do so. Instead he asked in a soft voice, "Do you find bigamy such a terrible crime?"

"The usual sentence is two to six."

"You have never loved two women at once, have you, Captain?"

"It's a Class D felony."

"It can happen," said Koy. "It's rather an exalting experience. It does not prove a man depraved. But you would never permit yourself the experience, would you?"

Powers said nothing.

"A pity, Captain. A pity." Koy studied him. "You must admit it's a poor reason to put a man in jail."

Keep hitting him, Powers thought. Hit him again. If you want to live it's your only chance.

"You were granted citizenship as the spouse of an American citizen—which legally you never were. So when you get out of the can, you get deported too, Koy, right behind Orchid, right back to Hong Kong, with no face left."

"One must allow oneself to be swept along by the current of universal change," Koy commented. "Death is not to be feared."

Whose death?

"Your partners and associates will be waiting for you. They'll want explanations."

"The universe is a delicately balanced, infinitely complex mechanism."

"You've cost them money. They'll whack you out, Koy."

"Man must submit to the universe—"

Powers, sweating, eyes fixed on the single eye said, "My men have this place surrounded."

"—the way water submits to the terrain on which it lies."

"If you're going to do it, Koy, make the first one count, because that's all you're going to get."

"Let me give you a piece of Chinese wisdom, Captain. Do not fight unless sure of winning, the Chinese say. Do not shout unless sure of being heard. Do not strive unless you can change something. And there is nothing you can change at this moment." With his free hand he wiped the sweat from his forehead, a concession to the strain he was under, his first real sign of weakness, so that Powers thought: you have a chance to get out of this, you're on the right track, keep up the pressure.

The gun, which had been pointed at the middle of Powers' chest, swung up to eye level. Very slowly Koy's thumb pulled the hammer back. The cocking mechanism clicked, and the thumb was removed. Hair trigger or not, any pressure at all now would set it off. For a moment there was total silence.

"Courage is like jade," Koy said. "It can be broken, not bent."

"You're under arrest, Koy."

The trigger knuckle, Powers saw, did not whiten.

"The three magic words," murmured Koy. His voice had become increasingly soft. "You're under arrest. The supreme celebration of a policeman's life. The biggest words in the language. The supreme domination of one man over another, the power to close a door on him. How many times have you pronounced them, I wonder? How many times have I?"

Powers made the move he hoped would save his life. He pushed back from the table. "That gun is not for me, is it Koy?"

"How well do you really understand the Chinese, Captain?"

Powers rose slowly to his feet.

"We both know who it's for, don't we, Koy? You have no choice. There's no other way out for you."

Powers was sure, but not sure. Though erect, he was immobilized, as if awaiting permission before moving in any direction at all.

"Do it," said Powers, "and Betty Koy won't be stigmatized by a bigamy trial. Orchid will simply be allowed to leave. I'll see to it she won't be deported. That's all I can offer you. Make up your mind."

"To kill you," said Koy, "would make you a hero. Perhaps the worst I can do to you is to let you live."

Make him do it, Powers thought. "Otherwise you'll be marched through crowds up Mott Street with your hands cuffed behind you like a common thug, like Nikki Han. I've alerted the TV crews." He's ready to do it, Powers thought. "You've been had, Koy. Kill yourself or kill me. You have no other choice."

Koy again wiped his forehead. "A question, Captain. Why? What is in this for you? A medal? They don't give medals for serving a bigamy warrant on the mayor of Chinatown, and an order of deportation on a middle-aged Chinese lady. And you had no other evidence against me." He glanced down at the gun in his hand. He had been a cop. He knew the charge as well as Powers. "—until now. Perhaps, having disposed of me, you imagine you will gain much face in Chinatown. However, no police commissioner could afford to let you go back there after tonight, if—if I do what you want. You'll be accused of killing me, you see. There will be a grand jury investigation, headlines. Your superiors will convict you even if the courts do not. I'm afraid you'll never make it to deputy inspector. So why have you done this to yourself and to me? What do you gain?"

Powers clung to a single dogged thought: somebody has to do God's work, even if there is no God; otherwise this planet becomes uninhabitable.

But what he said was: "You're a scumbag, Koy." The ugliest word one cop could call another was used to cover a thought that could not be articulated without sounding ridiculous, even to himself. "There'll be one less scumbag in the world. That's enough for me."

"You cannot bear ambiguity, can you, Captain? You would have gone further in your profession if you could." But his voice cracked and he was obliged to stop. He wagged his gun in the direction of Powers' briefcase. "I wish to study the warrants and your—other papers. Do not think that I flinch from what must be done. I am a gambler, as you noted. I always knew that one day my run would end. I merely wish to be sure. You will walk across this room and out that door, please." The gun wagged again. "Walk."

Koy's brow was a sheen of moisture, but his voice was back under control, and Powers almost admired him. He means to defeat me to the end, Powers thought. He means to do this thing on his own terms only, without any interference from me.

Powers gazed down at his gun on the table. He could not walk out and leave it there. At best, he would face departmental charges for allowing himself to be disarmed. At worst, if his gun was used instead of Koy's, this became prima facie evidence that Powers had done the shooting himself.

"Walk," Koy said again.

Powers said, "I don't leave without that," and pointed his chin at it.

"A policeman has many wives, hasn't he? And his gun is one of them. Take it. Put it back where it belongs—slowly."

Grasping the .38 around the cylinder, Powers thrust it down into its holster. "I'll give you thirty minutes," he said, and turned and started for the door.

Marching away he feared he had guessed wrong, that Koy would shoot him in the back. His shoulder muscles were tensed up against the impact of bullets no muscles could stop. What does one man ever know with certainty about another? His scalp crawled, as if trying to clench muscles under his hair that did not exist. He wanted to run but did not do so. He felt Koy's gun track him all the way across the loft to the door.

No bullets came.

As he reached the alcove and stepped out of dim light into total darkness, he believed he had won, and he yanked his gun out and stood for a moment feeling silent triumph and the aftermath of terror at the same time. I couldn't get him for crimes against humanity, he told himself, so I got him for crimes against love. Then he started down the staircase. At the bottom he bumped into Luang. Their guns collided, then their bodies, and both nearly went down. It was a miracle they hadn't shot each other.

"What—" said Luang.

But Powers was glancing around. He would need witnesses—he was trying to think it out as clearly as possible—and he stepped clear of the pile of doors and signaled out toward the street with his flashlight.

Kelly came running up, gun out and ready, a new problem.

Cops were always eager to start shooting and this was

partly fear, partly a desire to prove themselves to other cops. Powers had been on a stakeout once where one cop, over-wrought, had opened fire at the wall of a building. In an instant every other cop in the squad was firing too, and it did not stop until most of them had emptied their guns. He had heard of similar cases, and he could not afford that here, because when this was over there was going to be a stink and, in addition to witnesses it was absolutely essential to turn in three unfired police guns.

"Put those guns away."

"What's happening?" said Kelly.

"We wait."

"Wait for what?"

Powers tilted his watch until the dial gleamed. Up-stairs Koy must be leafing through the warrants, making certain. I gave him thirty minutes, Powers thought. Why thirty minutes? A number plucked out of the air. Too much time? Too little?

Koy was right in one respect. If he pulled that trigger on himself there would be a hundred detectives here inves-tigating this thing. Powers wished he had brought more wit-nesses. I've handled this all wrong, he told himself. The orthodox way is always best because if it fails you cannot be criticized. Always follow correct procedure, he had been taught at the Police Academy, but his whole career had been marked by a desire to shake up this department he loved so much, to make it start thinking again, the last word in ego-mania no doubt, which explained why he was still a captain after eleven years, and would remain one after tonight prob-ably, regardless of what occurred here next. Would they even let him keep Chinatown? He did not really think so. He agreed with Koy. Tonight was the end of the road for himself and Koy both.

"We both know who it's for, don't we Koy?"

He had destroyed himself and another, and for what? To clean up, temporarily, one corner of a dirty room that would soon be dirty again.

"Make up your mind."

He had usurped the role of the God in whom he did not believe, had passed sentence, and had signed a man's death warrant, something no federal judge had done this year.

"You're under arrest, Koy."

The explosion seemed the loudest Powers had ever heard, though he was expecting it. With Kelly and Luang behind him he rushed up the stairs, but as he came through the door into the loft he lunged sideways and dropped to one knee, fearing at the last moment an ambush, gun clenched in both hands and pointing.

"Get down," he shouted to the men behind him, though an ambush was not really among Koy's options, he believed.

For a few seconds all three knelt in silence. But there would be no ambush tonight, and Powers stood up and walked slowly forward, his gun now hanging beside his leg. Although an American would have preferred to go out in a holocaust, probably, Koy had not done so. An American's culture taught him that to fight was proper, that a man must fight every day of his life, must never give up, that otherwise there is no point to life at all.

But Koy had come from a different place, and had chosen a different way. We are all prisoners of what formed us, Powers thought, and he stood over the body.

Koy, having turned his gun on himself, had blown off the top of his head. He had crashed over backwards to the floor.

Both briefcases were open. The warrants were spread out on the table.

Powers was aware that Kelly and Luang now flanked him. All three stared down at Koy, with Luang and Kelly shifting their attention from time to time to the briefcase full of money on the table, and then to the face of their shaken commander.

"He was nothing but a scumbag," Powers said, and he gazed down not on evil, as he had thought and hoped, but on a man who had died.

40

NOON. The Chinatown pagoda of the Nam Soong Tong.

One by one the old men took their places in the boardroom. Joss sticks, upright in sand in their urns, already smoldered, having been lit previously by servants. Tendrils of incense drifted upwards past the porcelain face of Tien Hau, queen of heaven and goddess of the sea, on her throne on the dais, and the air the old men breathed was heavy and sweet with the pungent smoke.

The last to arrive was the elder Mr. Hong, who tottered in on the arm of his man. Mr. Ting, at the head of the table, waited. When the valet had arranged his employer in the chair and gone out, Ting called the meeting to order.

This was the second meeting at which he had presided since the lamentable events of the previous week. At the first he had agreed to resume his post as mayor of Chinatown, and also to conduct inquiries of great moment to all of them, and his purpose now was to report back.

The departure from this world of the esteemed Mr. Koy, Ting began, although in harmony with honorable tradition that extended far back into antiquity, had nonetheless occurred at a most unfortunate time for all of them, leaving as it did most of their investments unprotected. These investments fell generally into two categories, those within Chinatown, and those in distant corners of the world.

He had thought it best, Ting said, to safeguard their Chinatown interests first, insofar as he could. The circumstances of Mr. Koy's demise being still unclear, he had conducted certain interviews, most importantly with the police.

Preceded by a discreet knock, a waiter entered and poured tea into the lacquered bowls.

The police, Ting said when the waiter had gone out, assured him that present policies would be maintained, unless events of an extraordinary nature—an upsurge in youth violence, for instance—forced headquarters to make a change.

Thus their gambling dens seemed, for the time being, safe. However, the police seemed to be demanding in exchange that normal Chinatown violence and extortions be kept within certain bounds.

Old Mr. Lau, raising his cup to his lips in trembling brown hands, asked where Ting's information had come from. Was it trustworthy?

He had had two long meetings, Ting said, with the precinct commander, who had always proved reliable in the past. "He was commander here before," Ting reminded them, "Captain Gibson, the officer on the horse."

Mr. Lau nodded in satisfaction, and Ting went on to their overseas investments. These had seemed in real jeopardy. The Italians, claiming they had never taken delivery, were refusing to pay in full for the first shipment of merchandise. It apparently had never been offloaded and was still at sea somewhere in the Caribbean. And there had been no other shipments since. But Ting had now managed to contact former Sergeant Hung in Amsterdam. Hung had offered not only to act in their interests in this and related matters, but also to move his base of operations to New York, and Ting recommended to the board that both offers be accepted. Obviously, to invite Hung to New York would mean increased profits for Hung; but it would guarantee increased profits for themselves too. The gangs were useful, but must be controlled, and only a man of Hung's relative youth and vigor could manage this. The esteemed Mr. Koy, though he had disappointed them in the end, had been correct on that score. Hung, Ting said, seemed a more austere man than Koy, and thus would succeed where Koy had failed.

About a week later Hung arrived at JFK International Airport via KLM. He was met by Ting and a small delegation from the tong, and led out to a long black limousine for the ride into the city.

Some months then passed before the ceremony of the red envelopes was again observed, and former Sergeant Hung became mayor of Chinatown.